GUARDING THE PAST

D.L. Crager

ISBN 978-1-0980-4125-0 (paperback)
ISBN 978-1-0980-4126-7 (hardcover)
ISBN 978-1-0980-4127-4 (digital)

Christian Faith Publishing, Inc.
832 Park Avenue
Meadville, PA 16335
www.christianfaithpublishing.com

Printed in the United States of America

Chapter 1

Sitting at his desk in the archeology department, Ben was working on his doctorate at Stanford University. As a research adjunct professor for the department, he has great ambitions to continue in his field of study after he graduates.

There was a knock at the door of his small office. "Come in."

A longtime friend and coworker walked in. "Here's todays mail, Ben."

"Thanks, Nathen. You saved me again from getting out of the office to stretch my legs," Ben jokingly replied.

Nathen ribbed him back, "I know how much you like being cramped up in here burying your nose in the books. Thought I would help out."

"I appreciate it. I owe you big time for always getting my mail. I'm starting to feel guilty," Ben said as he looked at the handful of normal-sized mail handed to him and one legal-size envelope that came by certified mail.

"No problem. It's always perfect timing when I get here for my afternoon class and when the mail arrives in our school mailboxes.

"You know, for not actually being a full-fledged professor, you get more mail than most in the building."

Ben looked up and smartly answered, "I think I do more research and corresponding than all professors put together, but don't tell them I said that." Changing his tone and getting serious, he added, "I've been applying for grants all over the place to get me going once I graduate next month. Hopefully one of these has some good news for me."

"You'll get one. Just keep applying. You're really good at what you do. See you tomorrow."

"Later, Nathen," he said, looking back down at the large envelope as the door closed.

I wonder what this is, he thought, flipping it over and looking for a return address, but there was nothing written. "That's odd, especially being certified mail."

He took out his letter opener from the drawer of his desk. It was a jade-colored stone in the shape of a knife with the handle carved in the image of a dragon. Ben bought it in a small mountain village in China just south of Mongolia over a year ago when he was on a minor expedition at a dig site where fossils of plants and animals were found by local miners.

These past six months, Ben was getting more and more discouraged, because no one to this point had replied to his requests for a grant as anxiety was beginning to show its face.

Slowly, he sliced the end open and looked inside. Pulling out a single unfolded firm piece of paper, a normal-sized envelope fell out onto the desk, having the name of a major airline on it. Looking at the paper, he quickly understood it was an official letter. The parchment was very different—thicker and off white, almost tan as fibers weaved themselves through it, giving it an exotic and an aged appeal. But what caught his eyes was how it was written. It was handwritten but not with a modern pen. From experience in historical studies, he recognized the words were scribed with an old-style pen that was dipped in ink. There was a slight unevenness with the thickness and the darkness of the lines with each stroke of the pen.

Finally, at the bottom of the letter where the signature was supposed to be, a reddish splotch of flattened melted wax a little larger than the size of a quarter took its place. It reminded him of medieval times when kings would put their signature mark on letters, stating it came with his authority and power.

The signature imprint was a male lion roaring as a human eye appeared to be clutched in its jaws.

He looked in the large envelope to see if there was anything else, but it was empty. Ben started to get the feeling someone was playing a joke, then he turned on the reading lamp on his desk to brighten the letter as he read:

Mr. Benjamin Maschel,

With precision you have been selected from others around the world to be part of what we have and who we are.

We are presenting you with an invitation to visit our remote facility in order to spark your interest in continuing your studies and research here with us after you receive your doctorate at the end of the month.

Our invitation comes with an offer of a size-able lifetime grant that has no equal which will be discussed during your visit. Along with this letter we have sent prearranged transportation for you dated one week after your graduation. Also in appreciation for you following through with this invitation we have set up a separate bank account in your name at your present financial institution with a balance of one hundred thou-sand dollars. This will immediately be available to you upon your return from your initial visit as good faith and to demonstrate how we value you working with us. If you choose to work with us or not, the deposit will still be yours.

What we ask of you is simple. In no way form or fashion mention or show this letter to anyone. We are extremely protective of our iden-tity, location and what we have, which is for your eyes only. We are supremely confident who we are and what we offer will be of great value and create a lifelong passionate interest for you.

If you do research or discuss the contents of this letter with anyone, we will immediately be informed through our sources and your invitation and transportation tickets will be terminated. Along with the bank account and the funds within it. Though, you may confirm the account is valid and the deposit within it.

I cannot caution you enough to secure this letter. For you will not be permitted to continue with your travels to us unless the letter is with you starting with your first connection in London, England. The seal below is your only key and pass.

Thank you for your consideration. We look forward to your visit and I guarantee you Mr. Maschel, you will not be disappointed! Again security and confidentiality is of up most importance. Until we meet, Isaiah 55:8–9.

Sincerely
(Wax seal placed here)

Ben dropped the letter flat onto the desk and leaned back in his chair. He was speechless and didn't know where to start. His thoughts were going in different directions at a hundred miles an hour; who are these people, what were they doing, and what do they have to be so paranoid? Then he said aloud, "A hundred thousand dollars just to go visit these guys? No way!" He leaned forward in his chair, taking out his wallet and pulling out his bank card. Picking up his cell phone, he flipped the card to its back and dialed the customer service number.

A woman answered and he said, "Hi, my name is Benjamin Maschel, and I have a checking account with your bank." Hesitating and trying to figure out what to say next, he found the words. "Actually, I have two, but I forgot one of the account numbers and I'm needing to know the balances."

"I can help you. What are the last four digits of your Social Security number and date of birth?"

Ben gave her the information she asked for, and after a couple of other security questions to confirm who he was, the bank personnel said, "Okay, Mr. Maschel, you have two accounts with us. Which one were you needing information on?"

"Ah, the newest one."

"Okay, I see it here. You opened it…this morning?" Her voice questioned, wondering how he could have forgotten the large deposit from just hours ago and then asked, "You want to know the balance?"

He thought to himself, *This morning, but how did they know when to… Oh yeah, the certified letter and its time of arrival. But how do they have all my private information?* He was starting to get concerned.

"Hello, Mr. Maschel? Are you still there?"

"Oh, yes. Um, how much was deposited? I forgot."

"Well, the deposit shows 100,000 dollars, but let me look here…" She paused for a moment and then finished. "But the funds will not be available until after the sixth of June because you're locked into a money market account until that date."

June 6. That's five weeks away, he thought.

"Is there anything else I can assist you with, Mr. Maschel?"

"No, thank you for your help." Hanging up, the date she gave him kept going over in his head, and then his eyes caught the airline envelope. He opened it and looked at the departure date and said aloud, "June sixth."

Leaning back in his chair and staring across the room out the window to the campus, he thought again, *Who are these people?*

His cell phone rang, still in his hand, jolting him a little out of his deep thoughts. He answered, "Hello."

In a loud, happy-go-lucky tone the voice said, "Hi, Ben. It's Mom." She rarely called while he was at school, usually calling him only on the weekends. "Is this a bad time?"

"No, it's fine. Is everything okay?" Ben asked, trying to clear his head.

"Oh yes, sweetheart. Sorry to bother when you're at school, but I have a question…" She paused, a little apprehensive. "I called because your dad was wondering if you would go on the annual father-and-son retreat with the men of our church at the end of June. I know its short notice and you'll probably be busy after graduation and all, but I just thought we would ask."

"Mom, you know how I feel about the church and God thing. I don't believe the way you two do anymore. I'm a realistic evolutionist. The facts of life are the way you see it, not a God-creating believer walking blindly by faith."

"I know, Ben, but it would really make your father happy if you would go with him. It's been a long time since you two did anything together as father and son."

"I'll think about it and let you know. I've got a lot of work to finish up before I graduate, and something else has come up"—Ben reached over, picking up the letter—"that I probably need to do after graduation." His eyes scanned the whole letter, and when it got to the end where Isaiah 55 verses 8 through 9 was written, he asked reluctantly, knowing his mom might get the wrong idea. "Hey, Mom, do you have a Bible near you?"

She perked up, glad to hear her son was asking about something her and her husband lived by and felt very strong about. "Why, yes, honey. What do you need?"

"Isaiah is a book in the Old Testament, right?"

"Yes, you know that, silly. It's about in the middle of the whole Bible."

"Can you look up chapter 55, verses 8 through 9?"

"Absolutely. Give me a second." There was a pause as she opened the Bible sitting on the end table next to her chair. Finding what she was looking for, she said, "Okay, I've got it."

"What does it say?"

"It says, 'For my thoughts are not your thoughts, neither are your ways my ways, declares the Lord. As the heavens are higher than the earth, so are my ways higher than your ways and my thoughts than your thoughts.'"

They both paused as Ben was waiting for more. He asked, "That's it?"

"That's what it says. Why, what are you looking for?"

"Oh nothing. I saw it written on something and wanted to know what it was."

"Well, those are powerful and deep words if you really think about it, son."

He replied, not taking any of her religious stuff seriously anymore, "Uh-huh."

Keeping to her upbeat personality, she asked, "So you'll get back to us on going with Dad on the trip?"

"Tell him I'll think about it." His tone indicated he really wouldn't.

"His heart would jump for joy if you would do this with him. We want you to know that even though you don't believe the way we do anymore, you're always in our prayers, and we will always love you, Ben."

"I know, Mom. I love you too. Talk to you later, okay?" he said, trying to elude the uneasy topic the family had wrestled with for eight years.

"Sounds good. Bye, son."

Hanging up and setting the cell phone on the desk, Ben picked up the smaller envelope again with the name of the airline on it and then remarked, "London, huh."

He looked at the first boarding pass outlined with the date and time stating the departure from San Francisco, California, and arriving in London, England, as the next boarding pass didn't have the name of an airline, destination, departure time, or date. It only said, "Private air service." Ben looked through the rest on the paperwork, thinking something was misplaced within it and then realized, thinking back to what the letter said. "They really don't want me to know where I'm going."

***

Weeks passed, and Ben graduated with his doctorate in archeology. Now he was in Nathen's car, being given a ride to the San Francisco airport.

"So what are you doing in England? I really don't understand what this trip is about," Nathen asked.

"It has something to do with a grant and the research I've been doing. I could get into it, but it would bore you."

"Bore me? Are you kidding?" Nathen laughed. "It's just strange. You've been very quiet about this trip. Usually you won't shut up about your work—digging up old cities, civilizations, and dinosaurs while finding new life from millions of years ago. So when are you coming back?"

"Not sure. The people gave me an open-ended ticket."

"You did your research on them, right? They're a legit company? Not taking you on a wild goose chase?"

Hesitant to answer and not wanting to give anything away, he said, "Oh yeah, they're legit, all right. I can't believe you'd ask that."

"Well, this trip seems to be so hush hush. One would think you're working for another country or something? You're acting like an Indiana Jones going rogue. It's just not your nature."

"Oh please, Nathen." Benjamin laughed at the thought and then said, "As soon as I know anything about this grant, you'll be the first to know."

After Nathen dropped Ben off at the airport, he waited in the long line to get to the ticket counter and check in his extra-large heavy-duty duffle bag. Not knowing how long he was going to stay or what climate he was going to be in—high altitude cold mountains, dry hot deserts, or humid wet jungles—he brought clothes for each scenario. Also, he had a medium-sized, carry-on day pack filled with his laptop and other items he thought he might need to keep him busy during the flights and for possible research and study when he got to wherever he was going along with toiletries and a change of clothes just in case his duffle bag got lost and, of course, his key for the trip—the invitation letter with the red wax signature stamp.

Getting to the counter, the ticket agent smiled, saying, "Next time, Mr. Maschel, please don't wait in the regular line when you fly first class. Use our priority and first class passenger line. It will be a lot quicker."

"Oh yeah, sorry. I forgot," Ben replied in a way so as not to let the lady know he hadn't noticed the ticket was first class. Suddenly, the eleven-hour flight didn't seem so bad. "Thanks!" he said with a smile, taking back his ticket and ID from the agent.

He left San Francisco late in the evening, landing in London mid-morning the next day. Walking down the concourse and passing through customs, Ben got his answer before he fully formed the question, "Now what..."

In front of the crowd of people exiting the concourse, there was a person holding up a sign with the name Benjamin Maschel written on it.

"I'm Ben Maschel," he said to the clean-cut gentleman in his mid-thirties with a tannish complexion almost exactly like his own. But this man had a short-cut solid black beard and mustache, and perfectly combed black hair. He wore a sleek black suit and tie with a snow white shirt.

"Good morning, Dr. Maschel. Welcome to London," the man said in English with a middle eastern accent while giving him a slight bow. "I assume your flight was restful?"

"Yes, it was. Thank you."

"Wonderful. Please come with us. We will take you to your connecting flight."

Ben felt the weight of his backpack being lifted up. He quickly turned around grasping it tight only to see another gentleman mirroring the appearance of the other man smiling as he started giving a slight bow. "Please allow me. It will be in very safe hands, Dr. Maschel." Instantly, Ben was overwhelmed. He was being given the first-class treatment through the whole trip. Being a poor college student his young adult life and with the university always having budget cuts or limits, he lived life as though leftovers were the prized meals.

"Sure. It's got my laptop and other sensitive equipment and valuables in it, so please don't drop it or let it leave your sight."

"Very well, sir," the gentleman kindly replied.

Ben followed the first man through the main part of the airport, with the other man walking in stride right behind him. An awkward feeling was washing through him as though these men knew every-thing about him.

Soon, Ben found himself passing an airport security guard and walking through a door that opened to the tarmac of the airport where the planes were parked at their gates. A full-size black SUV was just outside, with the driver waiting to open the back passenger door. He had the same appearance as the other two men but older, in his mid-fifties, with a much stronger, taller, intimidating build and a full-sized, neatly groomed beard and mustache.

As they walked up to the driver, the man in front introduced Ben to him. "This is Benjamin Maschel."

"Good day, Dr. Maschel," the driver said in a deep accented voice, giving him a much lower bow than the others.

"Hello," Ben said, not sure if he should bow in response. He thought to himself that he faintly recognized the man from somewhere.

"Before I permit you into the car, I must see your key, please."

Ben now understood that what was written in the letter was true and everything suddenly became serious. The three men around him were not smiling but firmly waiting for him to show them what they needed to see.

He turned to the gentlemen that took his backpack as the man held it out for him to open. Ben had secured the letter in its original full-size envelope and then put it inside a hard-sided flat notebook, bracing it up against the back of the backpack so it wouldn't get bent. Taking out the notebook, Ben was stunned at what he saw, and then looked at each man as though he had done something wrong.

"What is it, Dr. Maschel? What is wrong?" the driver asked, narrowing his eyes.

"I...I don't understand..." Ben looked for the envelope the let-ter was in.

"What do you not understand?"

"My bag was with me the whole time. I secured the letter, pro-tecting it just like I was told."

"Do you not have your key, Dr. Maschel?" the original man with the sign asked as he took a step toward Ben.

"It was right here in this notebook, I swear." Ben frantically moved things around in the backpack, trying to find the envelope with the letter in it.

The men looked back and forth at each other and then back to Ben. His appearance was one of bewilderment turning into fear. He suddenly felt he was way over his head in something, and he didn't even know what this something was.

The driver stated, "My apologies, Dr. Maschel, but we do not take our security lightly."

Ben shook his head, knowing he had failed. *But how... Where did the letter go?* He asked himself as he heard the man finish.

"We took the liberty to pre-check for your key. The letter... It is with you." The man still holding the backpack up for him reached inside his suit, pulling the envelope out and handing it to the very distinguished driver.

"How did you... When did you...?"

"Dr. Maschel," the driver spoke up. "Security for this..." the driver pulled the letter out of the envelope and pointed to the wax imprint—"is one that trust has no friend. You must be wise at all times with this." He was still pointing at the symbol. "For that seal must be protected to the point it does not exist."

"Have you spoken to anyone or researched anything about this letter or its contents, Dr. Maschel?" The driver now stepped closer while asking the question.

Ben was beginning to psychologically suffocate as their presence and the pressure they were giving him took effect.

"No, I did exactly as the letter told me. The only thing I looked into was the bank account, that's all. What's going on here? Why are you doing this to me?"

"Dr. Maschel, please remain calm. Everything is being done for the protection of the seal," the driver answered.

"Why? What is so important about it?"

Sliding the letter back into the envelope, he handed it to Ben. Ben put it back into the notebook, securing it back into the pack and taking it from his escort, draping it over his shoulder. The escort replied, "That is not for anyone to know or for us to answer. Our duty is to protect the knowledge of the seal. We know you are telling the truth as we have been closely monitoring you. You have not shared or researched anything in the letter you were not supposed to, and we thank you for your honesty and obedience." The three men dressed in black suits slightly bowed their heads toward Ben as he understood their genuine gratitude.

Then it struck him. "You've been watching me?"

"Yes, for a very long time. For your safety," the driver responded.

"My safety?" he exclaimed with a questioning look at the men, confirming they definitely knew much more about him as he was still at a complete loss.

The driver opened the back passenger door of the limousine. "Please have a seat. We have been out in the open way too long." His eyes began to peer around, looking for something or someone watching them as Ben moved through the open door of the strong black SUV.

Sitting down, the door closed behind him, and immediately, the other doors opened and the three men took their positions quickly.

The escort that had been holding Ben's pack and who had slyly taken the letter out sat in the backseat with him and said, pointing to the pack that Ben rested down between them on the seat, "This must stay with you to the end. You must never let anyone carry it or even get near it." The man put on a sinister smile as though to imitate being a thief.

"I understand. I apologize. I was careless." Ben was uneasy with the chain of events but began to think where he might be going and what these people had waiting for him as a grant. *It must be huge for this tight of security.*

As the vehicle started to pull away, Ben urgently said as he suddenly remembered. "Wait, my duffle bag!"

"We took the privilege to get it off your plane directly. It is in the tail."

He looked over to the guy sitting next to him with a blank look. The man responded to Ben's nonverbal question, pointing backward with his thumb. "It is in the back." He nodded, understanding, and then looked away.

They drove out of the airport into London, getting onto a main thoroughfare. "Where are we going?" Ben asked.

"A ways out of the main city to a remote private airport," the driver responded.

"Where am I headed to next?" Still uneasy, he was starting to feel like he was being kidnapped, but at the same time, the atmosphere was one of which he was on a mission.

"That, we cannot discuss."

"O...kay. Is there anything I can know about?"

The man that held the sign in the concourse sitting in the front passenger seat turned his head back and point blank said, "Nothing."

It went silent as Ben was denied any information and began to look out the window at what England had to visually offer. Soon, it was only the countryside with its green pastures fenced in with old short rock walls as spots of forests dotted the landscape. After a while, they were at their destination, parking outside of a small stone building positioned next to a paved runway surrounded by rows of full trees standing tall. They had the appearance of being sentries guarding the area and hiding the runway which couldn't be seen from any road.

Entering the building, an older, formal-looking woman with similar but lighter complexion as the men and who had long black hair streaked with grayish white hair in a bun walked into the open entry area to greet everyone. Her top was a white blouse with a pink, fluffed-out ruffle draping down her chest. She wore a light pink pleated skirt going down slightly past her knees as white shoes with medium-sized heels adorned her feet. She first asked the driver in a charming county English accent, "All went well?"

"Yes, ma'am."

"Good." She turned, smiling and putting her hand out to Ben as he slung the daypack around his shoulder. "Benjamin Maschel, I presume?"

"Yes, ma'am." He repeated what the driver said, and then she gave him the same slight bow once he answered. He thought to himself, *Why is everyone bowing? It must be a cultural thing.*

"Please make yourself at home." She pointed over to the lounge area that had two plush couches facing each other with end tables and antique lamps on them as a large coffee table separated the couches. The room faced a wall of large windows looking out onto the runway.

They walked into the room and the lady asked, "Would you like some tea?"

Ben looked over to each of the men who had smoothly positioned themselves each at one of the three solid walls of the room. They all gave him a slight nod to accept as he replied, "Yes, that would be nice. Thank you."

"Please have a seat. I will be just a moment."

He walked in and around the room, stopping at the wall of glass and looking out onto the empty runway, and he asked, "There's no plane. When do I leave?"

"Not until the sun sets," the driver answered.

Ben looked back at him. "That's not for, what, six hours or so?"

"Six hours and forty minutes to be precise," the lady said as she walked back into the room holding a tray with an antique tea cup and saucer with a matching teapot.

She sat the tray down on the coffee table in front of a couch and poured the tea cup full, saying, "Your favorite—green tea with ginseng and a pinch of lemon grass and a half teaspoon of honey."

For a moment, Ben was at a loss for words and then said, "Thank you, but how did you know what I like?"

She stood tall, lifting only the empty tray while smiling and said, "If there is anything else you need, please just push one of the white buttons you see placed around the room." She pointed to the ones closest to him on the end tables. "But until your plane arrives, please relax. The billiard room is the next room over." She pointed to an entrance with double doors. "It also has a theater and a library. If you need to stretch your legs and get some fresh air, let these gentlemen know and they will accompany you to the grounds outside." She gave another quaint sweet smile and then asked, "Would there be anything else for now, Dr. Maschel?"

Ben still stood with his pack hanging from his shoulder, and feeling extremely out of place, he only shook his head no.

"Very well. Again, welcome, and please make yourself comfortable." She immediately turned and walked back into where she came.

Again, Ben looked over to the men that were calmly watching on. With his eyes and a nod of his head, the driver of the limousine directed Ben to the couch and tea.

Not knowing what else to do at the moment, he dropped the pack on the couch as he sat down. Picking up the dainty tea cup, he smelled the hot steam floating up. Recognizing the aroma, he slowly took a small sip. He raised his eyebrows and said out loud, "That's really good. I guess the British do know how to make good tea." He smiled around at the guys standing straight almost to attention, with their hands cross in front of their waists. Ben thought to himself as he took several large swallows of tea, *I'm not sure if I'm being protected or if they are protecting something from me?*

After a few moments of enjoying the tea, he sat back on the couch, looking outside. Reaching over to his pack, he brought it close to him, holding it securely. Suddenly, he felt himself quickly becoming drowsy and, unable to stay awake, mumbled out loud, "Why am I so tired?" As his eyes closed, he started leaning sideways. He saw the men quickly come to him, laying his body out flat on the couch as he pushed out the words, "You drugged me."

Chapter 2

Ben moaned, slowly stirring awake. He was in a leaned back position, and his head slowly rocked back and forth on a pillow as though he was on something moving. The thick fog in his head was keeping him from fully waking up as his eyelids felt very heavy. Off and on, a buzz of a fly going by or birds squawking in the distance would come and go.

Beside him, a calm female voice with a foreign accent said in English as he felt something push up against his lips. "Drink, Dr. Maschel."

He tasted cool water slowly fill his mouth and began to anxiously slurp, feeling extremely dehydrated. Water streamed down the side of his mouth as Ben clumsily worked his tongue and lips, drinking and trying to get words out with no success as his muscles were having difficulty working.

The woman said, "You are being taken care of, Dr. Maschel. Go back to sleep. Everything is well." Her words were so inviting, and being very drowsy, he couldn't help himself as his mind went blank, falling back to sleep.

Hours later, he woke up again. This time, his head wasn't cloudy as he rapidly blinked his eyes, attempting to flush away the darkness as he inhaled deeply. The air going through his nose and mouth tasted dirty, with a musty smell to it.

Squinting his eyes while looking around, at first, he thought he couldn't see. Then he sensed he was in a small dark room. Ben couldn't tell if it was the room or the lethargic motion in his head moving as the gentle voice he heard before say, "You are awake, Dr. Maschel. How do you feel?"

Ben went to say something but had to clear his throat first as he wobbly sat up, putting his feet on the floor. They oddly tingled with pain, and he thought to himself, *I must have been laying down for a long time.* Then he asked out loud, "Where am I?"

"We are on a journey."

"What's going on? Why did you guys…drug me?" he said, still working his lips to move properly.

"All will be explained to you in time."

"Who are you?"

She calmly answered, "My name is Mariah. But you may call me Mary."

"Could you please turn on the lights, Mary, so I can see?"

"What I can do is open up a small hole in the roof to let the sunlight in. Please close your eyes. It will be very bright at first."

Ben didn't follow the instructions, afraid he'd miss something. She reached up about a foot above his head and folded over to the outside a small square piece the size of a man's hand of what looked like strips of bamboo covered on the outside with a thick rug. Sunlight blasted in through the small opening, forcing him to drop his head and cover his eyes as though he had been physically hit. "Wow, you're not kidding. It's bright."

His eyes had been closed for a long time, and it was so dark inside it appeared it was nighttime, but now he knew better. As his head was still down, he could see the floor was made of bamboo as well as the framework of the walls that were only about six foot by six foot and five-feet high. With his equilibrium finally coming back, it was confirmed the room was moving, not him.

"Where are we? Why are we moving?"

"Like I said, we are on a journey."

Ben was getting impatient. The feeling of being violated and not getting any answers was beginning to irritate him as he raised his voice while lifting his head, "I want answers! Tell me what's going on. Where am I?"

In front of him, he could finally see the young adult female he'd been talking with. She was dressed in a middle eastern-looking silk top dropping down near her knees where her pants, made of the same material, covered her legs. The clothing was loose fitting and had many designs and colors weaved through it. Her light tan face brightened up with the sunlight as beautiful long black hair flowed down past her shoulders to the middle of her back.

A knock on the bamboo wall came from the outside from behind the woman, "Hello, Dr. Marchel. Are you awake?"

"Yes I am!" He exclaimed irritated recognizing the deep voice.

"Good, I'm coming in." The woman quickly moved to the floor off to the side. A small door flapped open and quickly shut as the stout middle-aged driver of the SUV from London crawled in. It happened so fast that Ben couldn't see anything outside. The man was now wearing outdoor clothing as though he was on an expedition. "How are you feeling? Has your head cleared up?"

"Yes, it has. Now what's going on here? Why did you drug me?"

Confidently stating the driver replied, "I assure you, it is all for your safety."

"My safety or the safety of the seal?"

Keeping to his firm demeanor he answered, "Both. With you sleeping, it was easier to keep you out of sight. The closer we get you to Journey's End, your safety becomes greater and greater."

"You still didn't have to do that. I'm not going to say anything to anyone. I've already proven that. Besides, shouldn't I know where I'm going to be effective as an archeologist?"

"No, not until you are to your destination will you know where you are at. We risk nothing, and we do not want to burden you."

"Burden me?"

"Yes, the less you know, the less knowledge you have to share. And with you out of sight, the less the outside world will know where we are going."

"At least you could have told me you were going to do that to me?"

The large man peered at him raising a questionable eyebrow, "And if we did, would you have drank your tea?"

Ben paused, still trying to figure out if this was real or just a big joke, and then he answered, "No, I wouldn't have."

"Precisely. With you reading the letter with the seal imprinted on it and obeying all the instructions and then flying to London with it, it told us you accepted any and all measures and precautions we would need to take for security and confidentiality purposes."

Ben tilted his head slightly back and forth with a frown, somewhat acknowledging what he said was true. Then he replied, "But isn't this James Bond stuff a bit overboard?"

"Where we are going and what you are about to encounter, James Bond might as well be…what do you Americans call them? Boy Scouts?"

Suddenly, they could feel their transportation had stopped as a man outside spoke up in an unknown choppy language. The driver answered back in the same language and then turned to Ben, reaching under his bamboo seat and getting out a couple of deflated life vests.

"We need to put these on right now, Dr. Maschel."

As Ben reached out for it, he asked, concerned, "Is everything okay?"

"Absolutely. These are only for precautions."

"Precautions for what? Are we on a boat?"

The driver moved his eyes to the woman seated quietly on the floor, understanding that she didn't divulge any information. Then he looked back to Ben, saying, "At the moment, just in case something goes awry, which it rarely does not. But if it does, you would be mentally and physically prepared." He paused, not wanting to give out detailed intelligence, and continued, "We are riding on an elephant and are about to cross a sizeable river."

Ben was stumped, shaking his head and trying to come to the reality of where he might be. "This has to be a dream," he stated under his breath.

"I assure you, this is no dream, Dr. Maschel." Then the man showed a rare smile, holding back for what was to come.

This definitely wasn't anything Ben was expecting. Then, as they could feel the elephant slowly move forward stepping in a downward direction he said, "So how long was I out?"

Knowing what Ben's reaction would be he replied, "Two-and-a-half days."

"No way! Are you serious? Where in the heck are we?"

"That I cannot say. All your questions will be answered at Journey's End."

"And when is that?"

"Our travels with the elephants ends tonight, and then we continue on foot for another two nights."

"Don't you mean days?"

"No, we will only travel by night."

"Let me guess—for the safety and security of the seal and myself."

The driver nodded to affirm Ben's statement then he said, "You are understanding."

***

Ben and a party of about twenty that he could see but was not totally sure had been traveling on foot in the dark with minimal lighting for two nights after leaving the comfortable ride of the elephants. Three men in the party were the ones that met him at the airport in London. A few others dressed as the three were the same nationality, all of whom carried advanced automatic weapons. The rest were obviously native to the area. With black skin, very short black curly hair, and wearing primitive animal skin attire with no shoes. Ben knew a hundred percent what continent he was on but wasn't sure which part.

Some of the natives carried supplies as the others carried primitive weapons, scouting ahead or keeping watch at their backs as the original three men stayed very close to Ben as did Mary. Again, he wasn't sure if they were acting as bodyguards or prison guards restricting him not to veer from the group or run away.

They were in a dense broad leaf forest, but no one would tell him which one. During the daylight hours, he was detained in a tent, which was just fine with him. Traveling all night in the dark, following no trails, and continually going over, under, and around the unforgiving vegetation was very tiring. In turn, he would sleep hard and long, not being used to the extreme physical exertion, heat, and humidity. Mary kept him as comfortable as she could under the conditions with fresh water and cool towels to wipe his face, always giving him the best treatment she could. Even when he took his boots off at dawn to go to sleep, she strangely was always right there to take his socks off to care for his feet, washing them and rubbing a soothing oil on and then putting on a fresh pair of socks telling him, "Your feet are the most important part of your body that needs taking care of when you are in the forest."

Because of the broad canopy of tall trees, he was only able to get brief glimpses of the night sky with stars gleaming brighter than he had ever seen before. This told him he was definitely very far away from any civilization for city lights to flood them out.

Ben's emotions went up and down. The excitement of the unknown and the dreamy adventure of what he was involved in grasped deeply at his male instincts as though a boy playing. But the illusive secrecy and deception of it all tore at his adult control, logic, and understanding, while frustrating him at the same time.

The answers were always the same when he would ask where they were, where they were going, and how much farther. The intimidating driver who Ben found out was the one in charge and his name was Horasha, continually told him, "You must be patient. I cannot explain anything. At Journey's End, I assure you, you will not be disappointed."

It was midafternoon of the third day after the elephants. Ben woke up much earlier than usual. Looking around the tent as he sat up on his cot and pushing the mosquito netting to the side, he was taken back with the absence of the others and their things. Also, the floppy canvas door was tied back, and he could clearly see the outside.

A sudden hollow feeling swept through him, being alone for the first time on the trip in a part of the world he had no idea where. Then, as though right on cue, he heard movement outside the tent. He stood up and said, "Hello, is anyone out there?"

"Ah, yes, Dr. Maschel. You are awake. Please come out. That is, if you had enough rest?" The male voice was very mature, older than what he'd been used to during his travels so far, and the accent was the same middle eastern as the men from the airport and Mary.

Anxious to finally see the forest in its full splendor in the daylight, Ben quickly responded, "I'll be right out!" He only had to put his boots on as they all stayed fully dressed when they slept. Picking up his daypack, which he had been closely protecting and sleeping with, he swung it over his shoulder and then stepped out.

His eyes quickly adjusted to the light while looking around. Everything and everyone was gone except for a skinny, short old man leaning on a cane as a tall, stout, rugged gentleman in his early thirties stood behind him. His legs were about a foot apart as his hands clutched themselves around his back as though he was in a military rest position. It was obvious the big man was a bodyguard or servant to the old man. He was dressed in comfortable but fit attire matching in earth tone colors suited for security purposes including his sleek, lightweight military boots. Side thigh pockets were slightly puffed out with items inside as a strong waist belt hidden under a loose-fitting, thin pullover shirt inconspicuously held concealed compact weapons and restraints.

"Hello… Who are you guys?" Ben said as the hollow and lonely feeling was now in limbo.

"A wonderful day it is, Dr. Maschel!" the old man greeted him in a cheery and uplifting tone as he slightly leaned on the cane decorated with detailed and colorful carvings. He stepped forward to Ben, letting go of his cane, leaning it up against his own body while gently placing his hands on Ben's shoulders, pulling him downward and kissing each of his cheeks, saying, "It is a pleasure to finally have you here!"

Taken by surprise, Ben didn't know how to respond, looking down at the tan, almost olive-skinned man whose complexion was, again, practically the same color as his own skin. He was evenly wrinkled and slightly boney with very long blended silver, gray, and white hair neatly combed back in a ponytail. He was dressed in a loose-fitting bright white pullover long-sleeved shirt made of very thin breathable material with a slight *v* cut down a short way on his bare chest. His full-length pants matched identically as they were being held up with a long, wide scarf-like belt going around his waist several times and then up diagonally across his chest and over his shoulder, tucking into itself in the back waist area. Woven in the material of the belt were different designs full of color like his cane. Finally, on his feet, he wore sandals that were obviously made from local items, allowing his feet to comfortably breathe.

Ben looked at the interesting cane noticing something about the handle, sparking great interest, which gave him goosebumps.

The old man paused, looking through round, thin, wire framed glasses with a confident smile, letting his presence soak in for Ben. Then he stated, "You must have many questions?"

For some reason, Ben couldn't respond immediately. He found himself intimidated, feeling inadequate from this fragile person and unable to put his finger on what it was. He hadn't done anything or said anything to make him feel this way except for him looking similar to Gandhi with a full head of hair and wearing clothes.

As Ben wiped a handful of salty droplets from his brow due to the humid midday heat, he noticed the man didn't have one bead of sweat on him.

The old man gave out a slight chuckle, understanding what Ben must be thinking, and patted him on one shoulder, turning around and saying as he grasped a large, ancient, six-inch fang attached as the handle of the cane, "Come along. We will talk as we walk, filling you in step by step with answers to your questions."

Ben followed as instructed, beginning to relax while meandering around the maze of vines, trees, and other plants as words finally flowed out. "Are you the one that sent me the letter?"

"I am," the refined and polished diamond of a man said as he stopped, turned to Ben slowly, and raised his right hand so he could see what was on it.

Ben slightly flinched back, not sure what he was doing, and then his eyes couldn't help but see a big gold round ring. Raising his hand closer to Ben's eyes and seeing the details, he said, "Oh, now I see it! A lion with its mouth open and a human eye coming out of it. Kind of weird, don't you think?" Ben stated, grasping the man's hand and touching the ring as he recognized it was the same design pressed into the wax of the letter he had received over a month ago.

Instantly, the old man leaned his cane against his leg and raised his other hand high, opening his fingers as though to give out a signal.

Ben let go of his hand, looking up to the other raised one obviously meaning something and asked, "What are you doing?"

Smiling and knowing how naïve Ben was, he calmly said, "Saving your life."

Ben took a step back, surprised at the unexpected statement, and looked around into the thick foliage of the forest, not seeing anything dangerous as the bodyguard held still behind the old man and replied, "From what?"

He hesitated for Ben to think through what he just did as he drew Ben's eyes, with his own eyes to his hand with the ring now grasping the cane.

"Oh, the ring with the signature seal."

"Yes, Benjamin, you have been told about the security and confidentiality of the symbol which comes from this ring…" He held it up again for Ben to look at. "There is no room for error for the protection for the ring. You are new to my guards who are very sensitive to anyone getting close to it let alone touching it, which no one is ever allowed or ever does." He put on a faint smile, telling Ben that what he did was unacceptable.

Ben looked around again at the surroundings as though a bunch of tough guys were at the ready to attack and said, "Sorry I touched it. I didn't know." Looking back to the sophisticated short wrinkled man, he replied jokingly, "We should be perfectly safe. There's no one here but you, your big bodyguard, and myself in the middle of nowhere. How would your guards know anything?"

The old man raised his hand again but gave a different signal. Before Ben took his next breath, there was a native man standing so close behind him he could feel the heat of his body and his breath hitting the back of his neck. Only moving his eyes, Ben saw the forest come alive as over a dozen guards the same ethnicity as the old man and bodyguard appeared out of the shadows and into plain sight. They wore unique camouflage clothes with futuristic gun-like weapons strapped tightly to their chests. Then, just as many native men from the area came into view, holding long spears and pointing them at him as others had bows and arrows at the ready.

"Ben, the world is never safe. Greed, pride, power, pleasure, and money are the poisoned ambitions and motivations of mankind. If the treasure of secrets the symbol on this ring holds is revealed and exposed to the world…" The old man paused, finally putting on a face of concern, which actually disturbed Ben. "May our God please have mercy on us. Especially if it got into the wrong hands."

He paused, collecting his thoughts and changing his facial expression back into the jolly person. He finished with, "So once again, with you being here, it is of the utmost importance that you and this are kept from harm's way."

Not sharing his enthusiasm, Ben shook his head, frantically raising his hands in the air, finally fed up and completely lost at what was going on for the past days. He said, "Could you please tell this guy to stop poking me in the back with his knife!"

The old man waved his hand again, and all the guards and natives, without hesitation, disappeared back into the forest.

Getting angrier, Ben said, "Thank you..." Then he realized he didn't know the old man's name. "What is your name?"

"My name...is Jahar," he answered kindly.

"Mr. Jahar, I don't mean to be rude, but I want explanations, and I want them now!" Ben straightened his posture, putting on an aggressive look as he pointed a finger forcefully to the ground. "I accepted your invitation to come out to see what you have for me as a grant. In the meantime, I did what you asked, not researching anything you said not to. Then I'm drugged for over two days, forced to stumble around in the dark for two nights, and treated as though I'm being held prisoner." The volume of his voice was getting louder the more he talked, and then he pointed between the both of them, aggressively stating more than asking, "Are you going to tell me what the heck is going on?"

Ben paused and huffed out, trying to cool his temper as he wiped away the continuous sweat pouring down his face from the powerful humidity. Mental gears were changing as the old man patiently starred at Ben, absorbing the verbal discipline and telegraphing back that it was all futile. The old man's eyes caught a glimpse of a couple of his guards stealthily coming back into view behind Ben without him knowing it, ready to physically restrain him if needed.

Ben continued, calming down a bit, "Now this secrecy and security thing about a fancy ring or symbol is way overboard. You must be a big fan of *The Lord of the Ring* movies or something because you and your people, whoever you are, are brainwashed by it. And now you're saying I'm in danger being here and you're trying to protect me. I sure hope you have a good explanation, Mr. Jahar!"

He stopped talking, putting his hands on his hips believing he had firmly put his foot down to finally get answers.

The smooth and confident old man with his prominent crown of silver, gray, and white hair full of experience raised his eyebrows with kind eyes. Slowly, he tilted his head down, looking over his small rounded glasses in a manner as to ask Ben without words if he was done.

Understanding the professor-like gaze, Ben responded, "I'm finished!"

Jahar looked past Ben and at his guards, giving them a slight nod of his head to say that everything was fine. Then he looked back, saying, "Good, because I already said you must have many questions. Which means I am willing and am going to give you all the answers in time and in their appropriate order for clear understanding."

Ben relaxed his posture, looking away and instantly feeling like he threw a childish fit not knowing the guards were ever behind him.

"By the way, thank you for reminding me about the letter. Could I have it please?" Jahar stated, holding his hand out.

Completely out of place for the moment, Ben awkwardly unshouldered his backpack, got the envelope out, and handed it to him.

Jahar took the envelope and looked inside. "Wonderful. Thank you for bringing this back to me." He tapped his cane on the ground twice, saying a few words in a foreign language, and his bodyguard reached into a low side pocket of his military pants, bringing out a lighter. Flicking up a flame, Jahar lifted a corner of the envelope with the letter in it, setting it on fire. The paper flared up as Ben began to excitedly babble, "Stop! What are you doing? I need that!"

"Not anymore. I wrote it for you to come to me. You are with me now, so this does not need to exist."

Ben flipped his hands in the air again, shaking his head as a sick feeling washed through him. Helplessly, he watched the only proof of the invitation for being here, understanding it was the only key he had to continue with the trip.

Jahar dropped the letter to the ground, watching it until it was completely engulfed in flames, and then he said, "Let us continue the cordial conversation as we walk, shall we?" He turned and walked away, with his assistant leading them.

Ben was hesitant to respond, slowly following behind him as the old man somehow smoothly weaved his way through the forest as though he was a predator on the prowl. Ben thought to himself,

How is he not fumbling around getting caught up in this thick mess? And he's walking with a cane!

Ben spoke up, "Mr. Jahar…"

"Please, it is only Jahar," the old man kindly corrected him.

"Okay, Jahar. You have a very interesting handle for your cane. It's a smaller Tyrannosaurus Rex tooth, isn't it?"

Jahar didn't stop walking as he lifted the cane up behind his shoulder so Ben could get a closer look. He answered, "Yes, it is."

Ben visually confirmed he was right, giving himself some type of comfort in seeing evidence of why he should be here. Trying to imagine where he got it, he asked, "So where are we?"

"We are in Africa."

"Are we in the Congo?"

"You are very perceptive, Benjamin."

Still following Jahar and trying to step where he did, attempting to mimic his slithering qualities, he asked, "Why am I really here? It's obvious this isn't normal with what's going on."

There was a pause, and then Jahar responded as he continued to walk, "Your invitation to come here has been a long time coming, and we cannot afford to have waited much longer."

"How do you mean?"

"I do not have much time, but before we go into that, let's move forward. First, I need to inform you of who you really are for all this to make sense. What I am going to explain will be very mystifying, to say the least. Can you have an open mind?"

"Sure." He shrugged his shoulders and stated it as though there wasn't anything that would surprise him as he pushed dangling vines out of the way.

"Very well. Hold on tight, Benjamin, because your life as you know it…is about to change." Pausing again as he worked his way around some dense bushes, he said, "Your life's beginning was not as you know it."

"Come again? I don't understand?"

"The parents you know are not your real parents."

Coming out of left field with this information, Ben blurted out, "Say what?"

Jahar calmly continued, "I was with your true parents when they were both born. I knew your grandparents and even your great grandparents when I was younger. I have been watching over you your whole life."

"Hold on. Stop, Jahar. What are you talking about?" He grasped Jahar's arm to stop him and then quickly let go, putting his arms up in the air while innocently looking around for the invisible men watching on from somewhere.

Jahar answered as he continued walking, "Your true parents left here, leaving their obligations behind when they were pregnant with you, wanting to have a different life for themselves, but especially for you. This went against our heritage path and duties as I instructed them not to do, but they did it anyway even though it was an extremely dangerous decision.

"They went to live in New York City, and shortly after getting there and having you, they were involved in a deadly car accident killing them both, which was not an actual accident. They were murdered, but praise God, you survived," he continued without a beat to get all the information out before Ben showered him with questions.

"My guards secretly watching over your family were seconds behind not getting to you before an off-duty fireman got there first, pulling you out of the wreckage. He would not let anyone touch you until the hospital had time to look you over. Then you were given directly to New York foster care, and that is when things really became... difficult, to say the least."

Ben was drowning in the flood of information. It didn't sound real but like things from a movie. Not believing Jahar, he thought of questions to catch him in his fictional story. "How could you be looking out for me my whole life? Do you live in the United States?"

Jahar proudly stated, "No, I live here!"

"Here?" Ben shrugged his shoulders, looking around at the plethora of plants with busy bugs and birds as animal life with all their sounds combined and orchestrated into a healthy forest.

"Yes, here." Jahar spread his arms out, pointing to everything.

"But how could you possibly have been spying on me out here in the sticks?"

"Now, now, Benjamin. I have not been spying but being your guardian. And yes, out here in the...sticks, as you say." He looked back at Ben with a smile. "I have invisible eyes and ears all around the world always focused on what is important for the protection and longevity of my life's work here."

"Now we're getting somewhere. Your life's work. So you're an archeologist or paleontologist?" Ben asked, trying to get relief from this foggy picture of what he was doing in the middle of Africa.

Jahar went along with his inquiry. "Hmm, you can say that."

"What are you working on?" Then he sarcastically asked as if everything so far had been a joke, "Did you find the remains of King Kong and his parents?"

Jahar quickly stopped, surprising Ben as the bodyguard halted as well. And for the first time, he changed his kind expression, wrinkling his forehead and staring at the new young man. Out of character for Jahar, he looked into Ben's eyes again over his glasses and said in a serious tone, "Who said King Kong was a he?"

Ben suddenly captured in his response and gasped out, finally getting somewhere. "No way? You really found prehistoric ancestors of the mountain gorillas? Were they giants like dinosaurs?"

Jahar took a step toward him, hearing murmuring of several men hidden in the vegetation. Ben stepped back, believing he had exposed the deep secret. Jahar couldn't hold it in anymore and joined the other men as he humorously responded, "You are not even close, young man." Then he turned, walking away as the bodyguard hesitated, slowly shaking his head as if Ben was an idiot.

Ben stood there, relieved he wasn't in trouble. But he began to stir with more questions as he shook off the intimidating look from Jahar's assistant. Still intrigued, he attempted again to get the secrets out of the very protected old man.

"So what are you working on, Jahar? It's got to be big, and how does this all fit in with your family heritage, duty story, and why I'm here?"

Jahar kept walking, swaying his head back so Benjamin could hear clearly as he strongly emphasized the first two words, "*Our family*...heritage path. You are my great nephew."

Ben stopped in his tracks again as more preposterous facts were being said. "I'm what? We're related?"

"Come along, Benjamin. Actually... I should be calling you Benaiah. That is your true birth name."

Standing frozen alone in the middle of nowhere, memories of his youth and what he grew up knowing to be true were just thrown up in the air as confetti, dramatically challenging him. He replied to himself, looking at the ground, "My name isn't even Benjamin?"

Looking up and realizing that Jahar wasn't in sight, he quickly caught up with him and asked, "What kind of name is Benaiah?"

"It is a name from the past of a man that was part of a special group of men that has been handed down for many, many generations in your bloodline."

"My bloodline?"

"Yes, your bloodline. Your family has a great heritage going back farther than you could ever imagine."

Stepping over a fallen tree trunk and pushing away more vines dangling from high up, he pressed the conversation envelope for the truth. "This is getting deep. So how far? Wait..." A thought came to him as he said, "Let me guess—Sir Henry Morton Stanley or David Livingston, the first European explores of Africa's interior." He smirked under his breath, wondering when this skinny old man would stop the masquerade.

Jahar raised an eyebrow as he frowned, continuing to walk, he stated more than asked, "Do we look European?" He paused and then said, "We will get to that tomorrow."

"Of course, tomorrow. Come on, Jahar..." He double stepped, trying to keep up, swatting vegetation to his side as bugs flew around his head. "You're just going to leave me hanging? This is sounding more and more farfetched the more you talk. How are you going to prove all this to me? It's beginning to sound very foolish."

"Patience, Benaiah. Patie—" Jahar froze upon seeing his body-guard in front of him quickly swipe out his hand for everyone to stop in place. Ben heard a swift zipping sound from within the thick foliage hit the ground, ending with a thud. Ben looked at the forest floor only a few feet from him, seeing an arrow stuck into the ground still wobbling back and forth at the fletching end. Following the shaft down to the arrowhead, he saw what it was shot into, pinning it to the ground.

Jahar spoke, "Dangers and enemies of all kinds lurk everywhere, Benaiah. Like I said before, there is no room for error for the safety of the seal and you." They both were looking down at an extremely poisonous cobra with the arrow through its head as the eight-foot long body vainly wiggled around.

Ben instantly was overwhelmed with respect for the men he was with and their skills. Never experiencing anything like what he just witnessed in a split second may have just started to pry open some truth to what Jahar and the other men were telling him.

Even though he knew they were mainly talking about being protected from man, this incident was an example of how detailed and thorough the security was.

"Have you ever seen a cobra before?" Jahar asked.

"Only in zoos."

"If that had bit you unattended, you would have less than twenty minutes to give me all the instructions for your funeral and what you would want to say to your adopted parents."

Ben stared at the dying snake as Jahar continued, "That would have been the outcome if the arrow did not hit its mark or if we were not fully prepared with every anti-venom for every venomous snake, spider, or other creatures in the Congo." He looked at Ben again, smiling, and then he nudged him to continue as though what just happened was no big deal.

Ben looked out into the dense forest, trying to see one of the hidden men, and then he said out loud, "Thank you whoever shot the arrow. That was an awesome shot!" There was no response from his complement and then realized something and asked, "Jahar, we didn't bring my duffle bag of clothes and stuff?"

"It is nothing to fret. All will be taken care of before we get to our destination in a couple of hours."

"So we're not going to walk through the night?"

"No, Benaiah. We are almost to Journey's End for you."

Chapter 3

J ahar was right on target with his timing in getting to their stopping point—almost exactly two hours. It snuck up on Ben as a
tent was quietly nestled hidden in a small level opening within
the trees and lush green vegetation. A big awning was stretched out
from the entrance, where two comfortable padded wicker-like chairs
and a small table between them rested under the protective cover.
Tall glasses filled with cool refreshing drinks waited for them in the
shade on the small table.

Two women were standing behind the chairs and holding very
large broad leaves by the stems from a fern, expecting the men's
arrival and ready to fan them. One was Mary, and when Ben saw her,
it put a little energy into his step. The other, a dark-skinned native
woman with very short black curly hair dressed similar to the native
men except she was wearing more clothes and a few pieces of local
jewelry with no weapon.

Surprisingly, but not awkwardly, Ben and Jahar had very little
conversation the past hour. For one, it was hard maintaining a constant conversation, weaving their way as the forest got thicker. The
heat and humidity didn't let up as they zigzagged, walking higher in
elevation, and gradually climbing a mountain.

Also, Jahar didn't want to overflow Benaiah's mind with too
much data at once, but most of all, he was attempting to do his best
physically. Being very old, he also was terminally ill and had a hard
time maintaining his energy level while fighting back internal pain.
This information, he didn't want Benaiah to have quite yet. His doctor was not fond of him doing this introductory hike with Benaiah,
but Jahar was determined to bring him to Journey's End himself to
slowly feed him valuable information before completely exposing
their final destination and to get a clear read of Benaiah's reactions
for this new chapter of purpose in his life.

The sound of a waterfall in the distance slowly got louder as they
rounded the mountain. Benaiah asked what it was as Jahar answered,
short of breath and beginning to show physical signs of weakness. "A

34

large stream comes out high on the mountain, forming a tall waterfall crashing down hundreds of feet." Swaying his cane around, he said, "This whole place is awe inspiring—where the power of God is seen, heard, and felt through his creation. Hidden here deep within the Congo, very few people have ever seen, or for that matter, knows of the existence of where we are at." Now pointing his cane at Benaiah, he stated firmly, "And we will keep it that way!" Benaiah nodded his head, confirming he would follow this sudden direct order or threat and not sure which one it was as their eyes were locked for an uncomfortable moment.

Walking under the awning, Jahar spoke a few foreign words to the women, and the African woman went into the tent, coming back out with a moist towel and handing it to Mary. Then gently, she took Jahar by the arm as to relieve him of his weight and to balance him.

"Please make yourself comfortable and have a seat," Jahar said, moving his eyes to one. "I need a little attention inside the tent." He smiled, trying not to give away his condition. Looking back as he walked through the open flap door, he said, "Enjoy your youth. Getting old is extremely undesirable." Jahar's quiet and strong bodyguard followed Jahar, closing the fabric door behind them as he, again, as many times throughout the day, looked back, giving Benaiah an expressionless stare, every time telling Benaiah silently, *I am watching you.*

Mary bowed as she handed him the towel, speaking English with her accent, "Please wipe your face, neck, and arms clean. Then refresh yourself with the cool drink on the table."

"Thank you, but you don't have to bow to me."

She replied as she straightened up, "In the presence of royalty, we always bow." Her eyes quickly glanced at the closed entrance of the tent, putting on a concerned look that she just said something she was not supposed to reveal.

He sat down, catching her gaze to the tent door, understanding the look, and decided to ignore it as though she never said a word.

Opening the wet towel and lifting it to his face, while wiping away the hot dirty sweat that had been building up, he thought to himself, *Wow, this feels great.*

With his head buried in the towel, he felt one of his feet being lifted up and pulled outward. He slowly peered over the towel to see Mary taking his boot and sock off. With them off, she rolled up his pant leg and then slowly placed his foot in a large wooden bowl of clear refreshing water. He thought he was going to die from something feeling so good and repeating with the other foot. She then lifted the first foot out of the water and applied the special oil she'd put on his feet many times in the past few days and then gently gave him a foot rub.

Benaiah closed his eyes, laying his head back on the tall chair. The sensation of being clean along with his feet in cool water and now being rubbed was overwhelming from all the hiking the last couple of nights and part of today, putting him in a euphoric state of body and mind.

After the massage of both feet, Benaiah felt a comfortable breeze flush over his body from above. He opened his eyes, looking up only to see one of the broad fern leaves slowly waving up and down above his head as Mary was keeping him cool in the hot humid forest.

A good amount of time had passed before Jahar walked out of the tent without assistance, only using his cane. Appearing and sounding much better, he sat in the chair next to Benaiah. He woke up from a shallow nap upon hearing Jahar and couldn't help but roll his head over, openly asking, "Is this how you treat all your guests?"

Slow and careful to answer, he replied, "You have been and will be my only guest of your type, Benaiah. So I must answer yes."

Benaiah tilted his head. "My type? What does that mean?"

Jahar took a drink from his glass and then said, "You are the first to have ever been invited here to Journey's End for the purpose of your heritage path—your bloodline."

"Journey's End is an actual place?" Benaiah said, looking around. "Jahar, I've said this before. We're in the middle of nowhere. Please, would you explain what's going on and what's so secret about all this? And why you're trying to fill my head with a bunch of mumbo jumbo about my parents and name?"

Jahar peered over his eyeglasses, giving the same wise look seen multiple times in the day. Then Benaiah answered back with, "Got it. I'll get the answers tomorrow. Until then, I'm finding myself and trying to understand who I am first, right?"

Raising his gaze through his glasses again, he answered, "In order for you to help me with my life's work, we must have the same beliefs and understanding of the world we live in. Most of all, understanding where we came from and what our life responsibility is. If we do not come to this conclusion during your visit…" Jahar paused, trying to find the right words. "I will have failed as your life guardian. I would have failed at the continuation of what I do and failed to carry out the orders of whom they came from." He looked down and stared at the large gold ring on his hand with the lion head engraved on it.

With a questioning frown, Benaiah replied, "How in the world could you fail with something about me when we have never met? I don't know you from Adam, and the more we talk, the more confused I am and at how crazy this situation is getting."

Jahar tilted his head with a grin, looking back up. "Funny you mention Adam. What do you think about him?"

"Adam who?"

Jahar sat there, not saying a word, letting Benaiah figure out who he was talking about. There was only one Adam everyone in the world knew collectively, so he let him work on it by himself.

It didn't take long, and then Benaiah asked, "Are you asking about Adam-and-Eve Adam?"

"Yes."

"What do you mean what do I think about him?"

"Do you believe he was created by God and the father of all mankind who first lived in the Garden of Eden? Or is he just a good story?"

Benaiah thought, *What kind of question is that? Who cares?* Then he wondered, *Where is he with the Adam-and-Eve, Garden-of-Eden thing? He did mention something about God's creation earlier.* Then he asked out loud, "I'm not sure what answer you're wanting?"

Jahar seriously eyeballed him, leaning over on his elbow on the arm of the chair. "I already know what your answer is, Benaiah. I am wondering if you are going to be honest with me and yourself?"

Starring back and offended at being put on the spot and the questioning of his character, Benaiah stated, "You think I would lie to you after honestly following your strange demands and going through all this garbage?" He grasped his drink on the table between them and then took a quick swig, swishing it in his mouth a second before swallowing.

Jahar ignored Benaiah's question, knowing he was getting emotional. He continued, "You and I know you were guided and taught by your step-parents to believe in God, the omnipotent one who created all things for a purpose by design." Jahar adjusted his position back up straight in the chair, still looking at Benaiah, "The last eight years of your young adult life, you have been dramatically challenged by your secular professors as they taught and guided you to trust and have faith in the things created by God, not in God himself, which is their only teaching foundation used as fact in your worldly education—that all things came to be and suddenly happened without foreknowledge, planning, creativity, and an outside supernatural power. Using only matter, motion, and time as the only factors of our universe's lively existence."

Now looking over the top of his wire-rimmed glasses again, Jahar asked in a matter-of-fact tone, "Please correct me if I am wrong. You now believe our solar system rotating in perfect harmony, balanced in weight and speed, started by itself because of what is called the big bang theory. Then non-organic matter, basically rocks, combined with gas, evolved, and changing over time, created on its own impulse into organic, living things. As the sun, over ninety-two million miles away from earth, centered in our solar system, somehow perfectly, and by coincidence, added itself to the equation to energize and sustain this new fluke organic life?"

He starred waiting for Benaiah to answer, but Benaiah was now wondering if this old man was actually testing him to see if he truly was an honest scientist looking at everything intellectually through clear factual reality, not with empty hope of a fantasy supernatural power that could not be seen or heard and only existing in the minds of weak-minded people looking for false hope to their existence.

Jahar lifted his hands in the air, shrugging his shoulders in a questioning manner, then he leaned over, pointing to Benaiah's heart. "You know deep inside, Benaiah, the only explanation for anything physically, emotionally, psychologically, and spiritually to exist is to first have knowledge of it. Nothing comes to life and continues to live and reproduce without pre-existence and knowledge of what life is in the first place. It is impossible! Any other thinking is absolutely selfish and foolish.

"By the way…" Jahar stated as an afterthought. "Without you knowing, I heavily influenced you into archeology and paleontology in order that, someday, which is today, we would meet, have this conversation, and I would open my life's work to you. With that being said, I know…" He paused, still looking at Benaiah as Benaiah felt Jahar was peering into his soul—at his deepest secrets with his old worn-out eyes. "We both know in society today, especially with advanced first-world countries, it is expected or even forced upon humanity to believe and live an evolutionary life if you want to or not, which is completely a way of life that is a religion in itself.

"But…" He was now pointing his finger in the air. "Evolutionists or scientists of this world do not want to use or be associated with the word religion or faith in their belief or way of life. They have fooled themselves that life is not faith based but scientifically fact based on what you see is what you get. So to them, it is not a religion, but it completely *is*. They worship evolution as the truth, putting faith as only speculation of the world's beginning and history. This is so wrong, worshipping and honoring the created, not the Creator. Would you not agree…great nephew?" His facial expression was firm and very persuasive.

Benaiah was churning inside and becoming overwhelmed with the sudden bombardment of what he called propaganda for the make-believe life he left behind years ago because his eyes had been opened to the truth by those who were highly educated people that know and see the world for what it truly is without the absurdity of the invisible spiritual world that hopelessly reaches for something that doesn't exist. He thought, *No, your God is impossible, old man.*

Looking away from Jahar's intimidating glare, his emotions were flaring, though he was stunned at how precise Jahar was with the battles he himself had at first when he started college. It was as if Jahar could read his mind and heart, making him even more uncomfortable as the day went on.

He seemed to thoroughly know all about him and his chosen line of work. Yet Benaiah still didn't know a thing about this mysterious withering man and his purpose of being here in the Congo. Then adding the comment Jahar said about influencing him to go into the career that he had just got his doctorate in, he wasn't mentally digesting it at all.

A major confrontation was coming as Benaiah had, in fact, chosen evolution as truth and the way of life to live, especially as he had put the historical puzzles together from millions of years with land, plants, and animals. It made more sense with his human understanding. As he let go of the mystical, non-tangible, ghostly soul lifestyle behind, leaving the unfathomable God-faith thing to religious Christian fanatics like his parents, reasoning that it was foolish and a waste of time to have faith in the imaginary spiritual world and living by words in a book called the Bible written by people that had been dead for thousands of years.

But through the lens of science, and combined with math, Dr. Benjamin Maschel believed modern knowledge and technology had flushed out the naïve motives of the plethora of cultures since the beginning of man. All who childishly reached out, making up supernatural godlike figures for the purposes of giving life some type of meaning and hope, especially for an afterlife because of the fear of the unknown and death.

He concluded that there was no better hopeful ending of an imaginary afterlife when death comes than the fossils and ancient cities he digs up repeatedly from their graves of tangible matter.

Wanting the upper hand, Benaiah, with confidence, leaned back in his chair and put his hands behind his head, willing to lay it out there for an honest debate and asked, "The way you're aggressively talking, Jahar, you're a diehard creationist. Believing that a God just happens to exist who no one sees or even knows where this God came from who supposedly made everything…" He spread his arms outward, pointing to the forest. "And did it all in six days."

Jahar sat there for a moment without speaking, and then said a few words in the local African language to the women fanning them. Both quickly put the large leaves down as Mary knelt in front of Benaiah, fitting lightweight sandals on him like Jahar's. Then picking up his boots, socks, the towel, and bowl of water, the women disappeared through the trees.

Jahar looked next to him at his bodyguard, saying in Hebrew, "Jasaph, please give us some room." The tall, strong man moved his eyes firmly to Benaiah, hesitating, and then he looked back to Jahar, saying as he bowed, "Yes, Master."

Benaiah watched the stone figure of a man step away about thirty yards to the edge of the small clearing. He turned, standing at his normal attention and eyed the two of them sitting comfortably under the shade of the awning.

"What was that about?" Benaiah said, looking in the direction the women went and trying to ignore the piercing glare of Jasaph.

"Many topics of conversations you and I will have will *only* be between you and me. And where this one must go, you need to see clearly and have a complete and accurate understanding of who you are and what your responsibility of your life's work truly is, which has been your destiny ever since you were conceived."

Benaiah peered at Jahar, first disturbed that he avoided his question after he was just verbally attacked, intellectually and professionally. And then changing the subject and going back to this secret, seemingly impenetrable truth of why he was here and being fed information that was only confusing him more and more.

Tired of being insulted and wanting immediate and clear answers of what the old man wasn't telling him, Benaiah stood up out of frustration. Stepping closely, facing Jahar, and raising his voice, he asked for the nth time, "What in the world is going on? I've had enough listening to all this garbage. Who are you and why am I really here? You need to give me answers now or whatever this is…"—he lifted his hands up, moving them back and forth between them—"is over.

"I didn't come here to find myself or be preached at. To be told my life has been a lie and that I have some…"—he signaled quotation marks with his fingers—"responsibility of this mandatory work I have to do. I don't have to do anything or believe anything you tell me, Jahar. If that's your real name.

"I came here to start my career and review a grant you offered me for research, so let's get to it…" Grasping Jahar's cane by the prehistoric tooth handle leaning against the small table between the chairs, he finished the sentence, forcefully handing the cane toward Jahar. In a sarcastic tone and poking fun at the way Jahar spoke, he said, "Shall we?" Then he demanded, "Or, you need to get me the heck back to San

Francisco now!" Benaiah pointed the cane over his shoulder in a manner to give direction, but it appeared from afar that he was reaching back to hit Jahar as he continued, "Because I've had enough of this—"

Before he finished his sentence, Jahar caught movement behind Benaiah. Wide eyed and opening his mouth, he tried to get words out as something swiftly flew in the direction of Benaiah's head. But it was too late.

***

"He will be all right. There is no permanent damage. The bleeding has stopped with the seven staples, but we will keep the bandage wrapped around his head for a while as I monitor him very closely for the next few days." The doctor looked up to Jahar, continuing, "The tribesman hit him perfectly and not too hard with the rock from the sling, rendering him unconscious. He could have easily been killed if the stone hit one of his eyes, ears, or had been thrown harder."

Jahar took a big sigh of relief and then said, "I should have been wiser with our first meeting as well as informing the guards to ease up on the strict defense and protection."

"Do not be hard on yourself, Jahar. You need to remain calm and have a clear head in your condition. Mariah and the nurse said you strained yourself too much on your walk and had to give you a couple of shots and an IV. I warned you."

"My condition? I am tired of hearing that from you and your staff. My true condition is old age. This illness is just a byproduct."

The doctor looked around the room at the nurses and, with a nod of his head, told them to leave. Once they finished with what they were doing with Benaiah as he laid on a hospital bed, they left as the doctor quietly continued the conversation. "This illness has an expiration date. You had to get Benaiah here as fast as you could and as naturally as possible. Using the grant invitation was brilliant. It has been a success so far. He is finally here and safe, which is a major blessing.

"Also, all the medical procedures we needed to get done—blood samples, body scans, and immunization shots—they are all completed."

"I know, but I envisioned everything going smoothly and by his choosing. The last thing I want to do is force all this on him. Remember what his parents did and many others over the centuries that ran away because they did not want to be here or have the responsibility of being the next guardian?"

The doctor said, agreeing, "I know."

"They left the safety of Journey's End and then were all hunted down, many tortured for information before they were killed by our enemies. With all the assassinations of my family over the multitude of generations, Benaiah is the only pureblood connection left alive. He is my family's last chance to fulfill the direct orders from our king and for the honor of our family bloodline chosen by him.

"More time, money, and manpower has been put into protecting Benaiah than any other on record. And he has no clue of his historical identity and what Journey's End truly is."

"I know, and I do not have to tell you, Jahar, but I'll remind you again. Satan will not stop lying to discourage you or for you to begin doubting yourself and the steps God has directed you to follow. He is the destroyer; we know that. But we also know…God is in control. We can plan all we want, but the Lord of heaven's armies will always guide our steps around life's obstacles we see or do not see, all for his glory and kingdom and, at the same time, magnificently demonstrating his love for his children.

"So far, it appears he is directing both yours and Benaiah's steps differently than planned. Take heart, my old friend. Everything will work out better than even you, the all-wise Jahar, has planned or understands."

The doctor smiled in a humorous manner and continued, "If God wants the secret hidden in here for over three thousand years to be known to the world, it will be on his timing. In the meantime, you, the guardian of this place, must hold firm in what you are protecting and whom you serve, obediently following his footsteps even when you have no idea where they are leading.

"You have always told us that the ways of God are beyond our understanding. And when we pray about something, we must believe God will answer the way he knows is best. In this way, all things will work out for the good, especially when it concerns his people and his Kingdom." He looked over to Benaiah peacefully resting. "Even with Benaiah, when his time comes, which is very soon, it is going to work out perfectly according to the wisdom of God."

Jahar followed the doctor's eyes, looking at the young man. "I know my friend. But the changing of the guardian has never been done this way or with such urgency for as far back as I can read in the book of time. The world has changed so much and keeps changing faster and faster. I never thought it would have been this difficult or have this feeling of hopelessness when my time came to be relieved as the guardian."

The doctor replied calmly, "I agree, life in this world is getting harder. It is no surprise. It has been prophesied and written in the Bible. But he will always have an answer and find a way, you know that. Stay focused on your responsibility as guardian for the remaining days you have left. And we, your servants, will faithfully, to our dying breath, care for you and Journey's End."

Jahar looked back to the doctor, gently placing his hands on the sixty-six year old man's shoulders and pulling him downward, kissing each of his cheeks. Then he said, "Mitanual, you are a very good friend and doctor. Thank you for the reassurance."

A moan came out of Benaiah, and the doctor replied, looking at him, "I will let you handle this. Let me know when I can help." Then he looked back to Jahar, taking a step back and gently bowing to him, and then he left the room.

Benaiah opened his eyes just in time to see a man in a doctor's gown bowing to Jahar and then leave. He rolled his head over, scanning the room trying to figure out where he was, as a slight stabbing pain on the side of his head came alive as he quickly reached up. Only touching a thick bandage going around his head, he asked, "What happened? Where are we?"

Jahar stepped toward the bed, answering his questions. "You were incapacitated by one of my guards. It appeared to him you were going to harm me. He hit you in the head with a rock from a whirling slingshot, bringing you to unconsciousness. But there is no need for concern. He was very careful not to permanently damage you."

It took a moment for Benaiah to soak the words in his throbbing head, and then he responded. "Well…wasn't that nice of him," he said sarcastically as he sat up, looking around at a fully equipped patient room. Then he asked, "So did you helicopter me out of the Congo to some hospital?"

A humorous grin came to Jahar's face, then he inhaled deeply, leaning on his cane with both hands, saying, "Benaiah, I had planned it differently on how our meeting and your introduction to Journey's End was outlined to work, but…" He swayed his head back and forth. "Human planning and how God directs our steps is like a river. Sometimes we go through calm deep pools with slow-moving clear water, easy to anticipate the next moves. Other times, we are in fast-moving rapids with boiling white water, holding on for dear life. But no matter which stretch of river we go through, God helps us grow in the different situations of our life. What is wonderful about it, is the end result. It is always greater than we planned or envisioned if we selflessly put our faith in God and not in our own understanding.

"With all that said, we have remained at Journey's End."

With another sigh, Benaiah replied, "Great, so it appears no matter what, I'm going to be preached to if I'm standing or confined to a bed." Benaiah rapidly blinked his eyes, trying to fully focus on what was happening, and asked, "Didn't you say we were at Journey's End when we got to the tent?"

"I did. We were and still are. The whole area of the mountain we climbed is Journey's End. We are actually inside it now."

"Inside? You have a building hidden in the middle of the Congo?"

Jahar smartly gave out a quiet laugh and then answered, "No, not built but dug out. We are deep inside the mountain, completely camouflaged from the world with an invisible entrance.

It took a moment for this to compute, and then Benaiah said, "You're pulling my leg, right?"

"I do not pull legs…as you say."

"You're telling me all this is inside the mountain?" He stood up slowly, catching his balance as they walked to the edge of the patient room. They looked out the doorway into a medium-sized circular room—sterile, white, and brightly lit. It was the medical facility which had every kind of equipment one could imagine, with patient rooms connected along the outside curved walls. Nurses and lab workers were busy on things as the doctor walked around looking over their shoulders and double-checking their work as Benaiah continued with questions. "How did you get all this here through the thick trees and ground cover? The same way you brought me?" he said, still not believing Jahar's story of where they were.

Replying in a matter-of-fact tone, he said, "It has taken lifetimes, and we attempt to never come in the same way every time from the outside world. That creates paths, and we do not want any paths leading to Journey's End. We have many ways of coming and going which you will see later."

"So how does my grant in archeology research fit into the picture here?"

Jahar softly chuckled. "I will not wait for tomorrow to tell you. Going down that road once more, I am not sure how my guards will incapacitate you this time if you got upset with me again." He spoke out to the doctor tediously working and waved him to the room. "Let us first get the doctor's approval to leave the medical facility. Then we will make our way to the commons area. It is almost time for our evening meal."

The doctor walked up to the two and bowed to each of them and then asked, "How are you feeling, Benaiah?"

Not hesitating, he answered, "Besides a headache, I'm fine. What's up with the bandage?"

"To cover the staples and help deter infection."

Realizing he didn't have the whole story of the incident, he slightly raised his voice. "Staples, are you serious?"

The doctor eased back a short step, moving his eyes to Jahar with Jahar nodding, and then he looked back to Benaiah. "Yes, you have seven of them right here." He pointed without touching and then continued. "We did not see any other damage with blood tests or from the body scan. You are very healthy, Benaiah. Your bloodline is strong. We also took the privilege to immunize you for the Congo."

"You did what? You guys have that type of equipment here? Right!" he staterd as though they were lying. "I'm going to have to see the facts with my own eyes before I believe a word you two are saying."

"Said like a true evolutionist, would you agree, Dr. Mitanual?" Jahar commented.

"No offense, Benaiah…" The doctor bowed to him. "But absolutely. A much clouded mind means the soul is in turmoil."

Looking back and forth between the men and feeling like he was ganged up on, he stated, "Oh, here we go. I knew we were going to get into this, but I'm not going to let it. No more about me! I want to go to this commons area to see more of this place that's supposedly in the mountain, and you're going to do all the talking, Jahar. Do I make myself clear? Or I'm going to file a lawsuit against you for kidnapping, being assaulted, and causing bodily harm and the doc here for taking my bodily fluids without my permission." Benaiah folded his arms, confirming he meant business.

Both Jahar and Dr. Mitanual peered to each other, grinning as Benaiah was being extremely naive to all that was happening, and then Jahar spoke up, kindly trying not to laugh, "Do we have your permission to leave, Doctor?"

"Yes, Jahar. I am sure he is quite well physically," the doctor stated, looking up and down Benaiah's body, stopping at his eyes and peering closely, looking for anything unusual. Then he turned to a nurse in the central operation area, waving her over. She came to him holding a shiny metal tray with a small medicine cup and a glass of water. Taking the items off the tray, he handed them to Benaiah, saying, "This is for the pain."

Benaiah looked at it and sarcastically said, "For my headache or to drug me to sleep again?"

The older men knew what he was talking about as the doctor answered, "I assure you, this is for your headache only. We want you wide awake for everything Master Jahar needs to show and inform you of Journey's End."

Benaiah took the pain medicine, putting the empty glass back on the tray the nurse was holding out for him. She bowed and then went back to the bright center room.

The doctor bowed to them as well as he walked away, saying, "Have a good evening."

Jahar looked up cheerfully to Benaiah. "All is well! Off to the commons area, and I will do all the talking, as you stated." Pointing a finger in the air, he added, "That is, of course, until you interrupt me with questions I guarantee will come very quickly."

Just as they were beginning to step out of the patient room, Benaiah saw movement come from the back of his patient room. Jasaph, Jahar's bodyguard, had been quietly watching on this whole time. Stepping out of the room, two guards on each side of the doorway were at attention. Benaiah hadn't seen them until they moved, catching him off guard, then they followed behind Jasaph, who followed Benaiah and Jahar.

"Do you always have guards with you at home, work, or wherever you are in this place?"

Jahar leaned over, softly whispering into his ear in a friendly manner, "Everywhere I go except for two special places."

"And where are those?"

Stepping out of the medical facility entrance into a hallway, Jahar turned back and said, "That, I will answer later once we have had our thorough conversation. Then hopefully I will be able to show you, but only if your mind and heart see clearly as I have said before. But as for the guards, you will have to get used to them." Then he tapped his cane on the floor as though putting an exclamation point to his statement and walked away.

Benaiah stepped out, following him and then stopped, reacting to the unexpected hallway that was supposedly in a mountain. It took a moment to fully understand what he was looking at as his brain and the scene his eyes were consuming finally connected.

Peering down a long rock hallway approximately twelve feet wide as it was tall, with an arched ceiling and a flat smooth floor, an extraordinary life-like continuous portrait covered everything. The painting was done in such a way that it gave the illusion of being a live 3D picture of an ancient Roman or Greek marble-covered walkway with strong pillars positioned every twenty feet supporting it.

To the outward sides of the painted pillars, it was an open air scene. Many tones of greens blended with many other colors coming together and forming a picturesque view of a roaming countryside and sky miles wide on both sides. The lighting imitated the later part of a sunny summer day as a comfortable temperature change matched the portrait. Sounds of the outdoors—of a breeze carrying soothing music of birds—flowed down the hallway.

Jahar said, noticing Benaiah was lagging behind, "Come along, my great nephew. There is much to see."

Benaiah followed in awe, looking closely at such a marvelous painting and quickly noticed that between every painted pillar was a perfectly carved-out alcove in the underground rock walls about three feet wide by five feet high and three feet deep. Each one was painted in such a way as to naturally blend in with the scene but had their own soft lighting, illuminating items displayed within them.

Jahar purposely wasn't saying anything as they calmly strolled down the hallway, knowing Benaiah's mind was going a hundred miles an hour and consuming the details as they walked past the alcoves. Not going too far, Benaiah suddenly stopped and gazed into one of them as something very interesting caught his eye. He asked, "What is this?"

Jahar stepped back to look at the description plaque below the items written in a foreign language and answered like it was no big deal, "Oh, that is the battle armor and weapons of Alexander the Great." Then he turned to walk away.

Benaiah couldn't take his eye off the ancient items—a weathered military breastplate, metal helmet, a faded-out sheath with a knife in it as a long sword lay across all of it. Then Jahar's words finally soaked in. "What? Wait a second, are you serious?"

Jahar put on a slight smile, knowing Benaiah was just hooked, and now, he had to gently reel him in to begin the conversation they needed to have.

"There's no way that's Alexander the Great's stuff. He was around—what—about 300 BC? That would make it over 2,300 years old."

"You are very accurate. It is a good thing you studied history. Because here, history is everything for the answers of the future." A few steps down the hallway, Jahar said, "All these items in the walls are only faint paint strokes hidden within the huge portrait I need to inform you of before you start your lifetime work here at Journey's End."

Benaiah mumbled, 'Lifetime work. What is he talking about?' Finally turning from the ancient artifacts, he hurried himself to catch up and then, looking back and forth at each niche in the rock walls filled with something looking important, he asked, "Are all these things old historical items?"

"Yes, most from millennia ago. In this tunnel, we display the military items from important people and battles that changed history to what we know it today."

Benaiah continued to see well-kept but aged uniforms, armor, weapons, rustic maps, even a portrait here and there of the person the items belonged to and asked, "What language is on the plaques below the artifacts?"

"Hebrew." Jahar stopped with an awkward look as though he was stumped and then exclaimed, "I was successful assisting you going into archeology. But... I tried very hard in many ways to get you to learn Hebrew. But you never went that direction. You had an obsession with...French?" Jahar raised his shoulders and shook his head as to rid himself of the absurd thought and then continued walking.

Lightbulbs were coming on for Benaiah of situations in his past—from receiving things in the mail or his church pastor when he was young constantly encouraging him to learn Hebrew to be able to translate for himself. Then he remembered when he was about thirteen and a family moved in next door that was Jewish, only speaking Hebrew all the time and no one knew a word they were saying. Then he blurted out, "Wait a minute, Jahar. Is that why my parents forced me to go to a Jewish middle school?"

Jahar only looked back and smiled.

Putting his hands on his hips, Benaiah said, "Okay, I'm starting to begin to believe you might honestly know something about me, but one thing doesn't make sense"

Jahar stopped and turned around. "And what is that?"

Thinking he finally caught Jahar off guard in this masquerade, he asked, "If you wanted me to learn Hebrew, how come you didn't place me with Jewish parents when I was allegedly adopted?"

Jahar slowly wavered his head, putting on a sorrowful expression, "Like I said earlier today, the death of your parents was abrupt, and my guards were not able to get to you before someone else. We had to act and do everything with precision and promptness to the best of our ability to stay invisible to the world. You were in New York foster care as you were being put into the adoption system. You can check their records now twenty-seven years later, when we get a chance, if you like."

Benaiah interrupted, looking behind him, "My parents had guards like these guys?" He pointed to the men behind Jasaph dressed in strange camouflage military attire as small well-fitting backpacks filled with emergency gear and futuristic weapons like something from *Star Wars* were strapped closely across their chests.

Looking closely back at them, Benaiah popped his head to the side, having a hard time actually seeing the guards clearly. He noticed their camouflage clothing had changed its pattern and color from when he saw them in the medical facility. It was as if it had adjusted to its surroundings, blending with the colors and lighting in the tunnel.

Jahar ignored Benaiah's questions, needing to stay on track with the important information. Though he did look at the guards, nodding his head for them to back away to give them privacy. Taking a deep breath and closing his eyes as though he was fighting back pain, he continued as he slowed his pace so they were side by side and able to look at each other, "Benaiah, I need you to open your mind and take me seriously with everything I have to say. I do not have much time."

Benaiah tried to do just that but wondered where Jahar needed go as he had brought it up a couple of times now.

Jahar's tone was serious, saying, "You are a descendant of the Israel nation. Not just an ordinary Jew, but the Israel nation going back to King David. We all are Israelites here at Journey's End except for the Africans. Our attempts failed to get you placed with a solid

Jewish bloodline family that were Christians as well. Jews believing Jesus Christ has already come and is the world's Lord and Savior prophesied in the Old Testament.

"At that moment in New York, believe it or not, of all places in the United States." Jahar shrugged his shoulders, shaking his head and showing Benaiah he was stumped again. "There was no one on the adoption waiting list fitting that description. Not even a regular Jewish non-Christian couple. But we did find a strong Christian family going back generations in their faith that was already signed up in the adoption process that were of Mediterranean descent.

"Discreetly, we were able to reorganize the state's paperwork, hacking into their computer system so the adoption would go the way we needed it. After the adoption, I secretly met with your new parents and informed them you were a special child. We gave them great encouragement not to ever divulge your adoption until your time came of your true calling. We also blessed them with lifelong protection, physically and financially, until their future passing to the Lord of heaven's armies."

Benaiah was staring at Jahar with a glazed look and then cleared his throat after some brief silence between them. "I could push myself to believe I was adopted because there were some things throughout my life that never made sense, but what kind of bologna are you feeding me that I'm a direct descendant of King David? There is no way you could ever have that technology to look at DNA and trace it back that far to make the connection."

A large grin came across Jahar's face as he tipped his head down while looking over his glasses. "We do not need modern technology to have kept records of our bloodlines going back thousands of years. When I said going back to King David, I was not insinuating a direct descendent of him but from one of his mighty warriors. Therefore, we were chosen..."—he tapped his cane on the floor a couple of times excitedly—"and that is why you are here for your true calling. Come, I am getting hungry. The commons area is just ahead."

Chapter 4

Stopping to the end of the picturesque hallway, a metal door the size of the hallway automatically opened when they approached. They looked out to a huge circular cavern as Benaiah stated, "Holy cow!" The size of it reminded him of the Dallas Cowboys indoor football stadium minus the seating. High up to the natural arched ceiling, there was a large, wide sideways oval opening looking like an eye off to one side with the rays of sunlight shining in sideways reflecting off the opposite wall. It sent soft beams of food down from the sun to all the plant life hidden underground.

Peering around, he noticed it was the only entrance coming in from the outside world confirming they were truly inside the mountain. At each side of the eye-shaped opening, staircases were carved into the rock walls. They gently sloped down, curving themselves around opposite sides until they touched the cavern floor across from where they started.

From the bottom lip of the opening, thick braids of long vines full of leaves and flowers imitated a waterfall that flowed inward halfway to the cavern floor. Benaiah's eyes dropped from the vines to the ground and a large garden, one he'd never seen before, overwhelming his senses. It was perfectly groomed in a natural décor of trees, ferns, and other plants spaced apart, flowing together as a plethora of colors from flowers lightly touching the greenery throughout.

A good-sized stream meandered through it, coming out of the ground and bubbling up near where the staircases touched the ground that then disappeared into a dark hole at the other end of the enormous open area.

He closed his eyes in the breathtaking moment, thinking he was having an out-of-body experience or dream. Inhaling deeply, aromas of many flavors passed through his nose as his lungs didn't want to stop expanding with a freshness he rarely felt.

The sounds of chirping birds fluttering here and there, combined with the whispers of the stream reaching his ears, drowned him deeper in the experience as the perfect Garden of Eden flashed through his mind.

His eyes shot wide open, turning to Jahar and loudly choking out words from the revelation with excitement. "Eden… Jahar, you found the Garden of Eden!" He turned, looking back into the natural hollow part of the mountain; now it had the mental appearance of being holy ground. "That's why you asked me about Adam." Captured in the moment, his hands began to wave around, doing emotional talking as words flooded out. "Did you find any preserved artifacts? Is the tree of knowledge of good and evil petrified in the center?

"This is why no one could find it—because it's underground! You said this was an awe-inspiring place where the power of God is seen, heard, and felt through his creation! You were right! It's incredible!" he screeched out, putting his hands on his head in complete disbelief and eyeing every detail.

Suddenly, it all came together, "Oh wow! I got it! This is what my grant is about and why all the top-secret concern and security! It's sifting through what most people, even myself, think is a fictitious place, but…here it is!"

Still not convinced about all the things that Jahar told him about his parents and the bloodline connection were true, he said, "You have attempted to convince me of who you think I am. Yet knowing I grew up learning in detail about Christianity, combined with my advanced education and what my personal beliefs are now, you're needing my professional opinion on the discoveries made here!"

Like a thundercloud swiftly moving in consuming the clear bright blue sky, quiet chuckling could be heard behind him. The guards couldn't hold it in any longer. Jasaph looked back at them as they stopped and respectfully bowed. The thundercloud brought a heavy shower of embarrassment as it brought a lightning bolt of the same repeating question, *What's going on here…?* loudly echoed in his head, stifling outside sounds of the underground garden.

There was silence as Jahar gave Benaiah time to reclaim his dignity and then stepped up against him, quietly whispering in Benaiah's ear, "No, this is not the Garden of Eden, but…" He raised his finger to his own lips as though telling him a secret. "We are closing in on the time frame of where the true hidden story and our"—pointing a finger back and forth between them—"life work with Journey's Beginning starts."

Confidently smiling with a wink, Jahar gave out a confirming grunt and then again tapped his cane on the smooth rock floor of the tunnel. They stepped forward into the open cavern, which had the same floor as the hallway they came out of for about ten feet, following the caverns wall all the way around for a solid pathway. At the end of the ten-foot wide path, they evenly stepped out onto the gardens soft grassy floor, heading to a specific spot.

Benaiah's head was spinning from all the details of what he'd seen since the medical facility. Then, combined with the endless puzzle pieces of information piling up, he was in great need to have them put together to form this big portrait that Jahar mentioned. He followed Jahar with more excited enthusiasm than self-indulged friction as he thought, *You catch more flies with honey than vinegar.*

They meandered through the pathless garden and over the stream on a small beautiful rock bridge, ending up at the gardens center. During this brief walk, Jahar explained that the commons area was the center point of all Journey's End, with twelve different tunnels going out in different directions and ending up in open caverns of multiple sizes, but nothing like the size of this one. Each tunnel was named after one of the twelve tribes of Israel, with its own specific purpose as the medical facility they came out of. He mentioned the large living quarters for everyone at Journey's End which facilitated all their personal needs—housing, food, clothing, recreation, education, etc. Then he mentioned the research and development laboratory, maintenance and manufacturing plant, and the utilities of operation for power and plumbing, purposely leaving out the other tunnels temporarily for security reasons until Benaiah fully committed to his life's duty.

He explained that all the entrances of each tunnel had electronic wide and thick sliding metal doors just like the one they came through moments ago.

At their destination, Jahar slid off his sandals on the grass and then walked onto a magnificent round marble platform approximately twenty-five feet across level with the grass. Benaiah copied Jahar, taking his sandals off as he looked around intrigued at the obvious lounging area. A low-lying round table was bordered by three large moon-shaped sofas circling the table almost touching each other. They were low to the marble floor as well and lined with many soft pillows along their backs.

Jahar comfortably took a specific seat, leaning on his side and bringing both feet up sideways on the sofa as he leaned his cane up against it. Jasaph took up his protective position, standing an arm's length behind Jahar as Jahar looked over to the couch next to his, pointing as he said, "Please make yourself comfortable."

Not used to low furniture and being much taller, Benaiah awkwardly crouched down and then plopped himself into the most comfortable couch he had ever sat on. Trying to imitate Jahar, he nestled in sideways, bringing his feet up with his head leaning toward Jahar's, less than an arm's reach away.

A funny thought came to mind while looking around at everything and then catching the old man's eyes peering at him, remarked, "This reminds me of the painting up on the ceiling in Rome. Two naked guys lying down and reaching over, touching each other's fingers. You know the one..."

He was cut short as Jahar, knowing what he was talking about, interjected, "Yes, Michelangelo's Creation of Adam. It is on the ceiling of the Sistine Chapel, finished in 1512. Except their fingers are not yet touching, and only one does not have clothes on, who is representing Adam. The other is God who is not lying down but spiritually elevated and pictured breathing life into man with his finger.

"Neither of us are without clothes nor is God or Adam. But you have a good imagination, to say the least, equating it with our situation. Me, attempting to breathe awareness, knowledge, and trust into you in order to bring you to life here in this new secret world."

Without instructions, three women approached the lounge area, two of whom were at the tent earlier. One African woman had a tray with two crystal glasses filled with ice and two bottles of beverages. One was a bottle of expensive sparkling water. She set it on the low table in front of Jahar with a glass of ice. The other was a bottle of a specialty root beer and set in front of Benaiah with his glass of ice. Another younger native woman had a small woven basket with hot cleaning towels, handing them to the two men with tongs. The two women moved to the side as Mary sat a large silver tray down on the table which had their evening meal on it.

Benaiah watched Jahar to see what he was doing with the towel that had a pleasant citrus smell. He quickly understood it was to clean their hands and faces, similar to the towels at the tent, but this one was to prepare to eat.

After the men were done with the towels, the woman with the basket reached over to the men as they dropped the used towels into it. The two African woman bowed to the men and then walked away, disappearing through the garden.

Unexpectedly coming from a different direction and wearing a medical gown, a woman approached the lounging area. Taking her sandals off, she stepped up to Mary, handing her a small medicine cup, saying a few words in Hebrew. Mary turned back and spoke in English, "Benaiah, here are pain pills from the doctor for your head if it starts hurting again while you dine. Is there anything you need to inform the doctor of how you are feeling?" She sat the cup down next to his glass.

He replied, "I'm fine. We just left the medical place a short time ago."

"Good, I am glad you are doing well." She looked back, shaking her head as the nurse immediately left.

Turning back, Mary picked up their covered meals off her large fancy tray. Placing them in front of the men, she lifted the lids off as steam spewed out, exposing the food on elegant china painted in gold around the edges. Next, she set out gold-plated utensils, putting them in their appropriate positions beside the plates and then handed a cloth napkin embroidered with initials written in a foreign language to each man. Finally, she took a bread basket covered by a warming towel and set it between the two place settings.

Mary explained while pointing to the plates, "This evening, obviously you see you will be having a special Italian dish. It is one where the recipe comes from a place you favor, Benaiah."

He tilted his head to her with a questioning expression.

"The spaghetti noodles are topped with a tangy marinara sauce flavored richly with oregano, fennel, and garlic."

Benaiah smiled, loving spaghetti but still trying to understand what she meant.

Mary opened up a medium-sized container on the tray as steam fumed out. She reached in with tongs, grasping a large meatball the size of a baseball, crowning the marinara on each plate.

Raising his eyebrows and realizing what she was talking about, she explained, "These meatballs are stuffed with mozzarella, which are very hot."

"No way! How would you know...?"

Before he could finish, she held up a small dish and a spoon, asking, "Would you like your normal four teaspoons of parmesan flakes spread all over?"

Benaiah instantly was startled, giving her a serious look, and then he turned to Jahar and then back to her as she waited, staring at him.

Slowly coming out of his mouth, and stumped they would know such a personal thing, he said slowly, "Four...would be fine, thank you."

She did just that. Then, after setting the dish and spoon back onto the tray, she lifted the warming towel off the bread basket, exposing the buttered garlic and parmesan rolls shaped like bowties. With the tongs, she picked one up, placing it at the base of his large meatball, which gave it the appearance of a dressed-up Italian dish he had eaten more times than he could count since he was a kid.

He was speechless as she then opened his special bottle of root beer, saying as she poured it into the crystal glass filled with ice, "Your favorite root beer, only found in a dozen places in California, one being the little Italian restaurant in Sausalito north of San Francisco that you cherish dearly."

He had no words. He didn't know if he should be concerned and offended that his privacy was definitely compromised as he thought of many things in his life that these people could knew about him or that if he should be flattered they went to great lengths to make him feel at home.

"Is there anything else you need, gentlemen?"

Benaiah only shook his head, anxious to dig into his wonderful smelling meal as Jahar said in a more questioning manner, "It appears, all is well, Mariah?"

Eyeing Jahar with a smile, she repeated confidently, "All is well," as she pointed open handed around and over the food and beverages, stopping over the medicine cup. There, she slowly brought her fingers together, making a gentle fist, and then she stood tall, inconspicuously giving Jahar a silent message, one that said the meal and drinks brought in were in her sight at all times. From preparation in the kitchen, to setting it on the table before them, clearing it all from being tampered with. The pills on the other hand where she closed her fist, she had no idea of the condition of the pain medicine, if that is what it truly was.

She turned to Benaiah, saying, "We are here for anything you need, Benaiah. At any time, just ask. I will be right behind you next to Jasaph."

When her arm was stretched out over the food, he couldn't help but notice she was wearing something she never had in the past few days during their travels. It was a very wide colorful metallic bracelet going halfway up her forearm and wrapped completely around. It had obvious markings written in a different language, with other details around it except for the top side. In that area was a small flat glass screen approximately four inches long by two inches wide.

Answering her, and still overwhelmed with the food presentation, he fumbled with words. "Thank you, this...this is awesome. It's my favorite." A strange feeling swept through him, thinking, *Are Mary or...Mariah and the others, servants or slaves?* He wasn't used to the extreme treatment of being served like this, so it was confusing to tell the difference.

He looked over to Jahar, who was staring at the pills the nurse brought to Benaiah. Then his eyes slowly moved between their couches, peering up to Jasaph. Jasaph knew exactly what Jahar was thinking without words being said.

Stepping between the men sitting on the couches, he pulled his loose long shirt sleeve up, exposing the same wide armlet as Mariah, catching Benaiah off guard as it was hidden from sight the whole day. Tapping on one side of the top screen a couple of times, he then reached over the pills, underside facing down, as an infrared beam lit up scanning the medicine cup while taking a picture at the same time. Touching the screen again, he stopped the scan and then sent out the information it had gathered. A few seconds went by, and then the screen lit up, giving silent written feedback.

In his quiet firm tone, Jasaph said, "All is well, Master." Then he went back to his resting guard position behind Jahar, next to Mariah, who was standing in the same manner.

As Benaiah quietly watched on, curiosity was captivating him. The armlet suddenly became more than a piece of fancy jewelry. Seeing his expression, Jahar spoke up, knowing what he was thinking, and calmly said, "Here at Journey's End, you will quickly find out we are far, far more advanced in technology than we appear from the outside world and the untrained eye."

"I'm starting to see that. What was all that Jasaph did?" Benaiah asked, moving his hand around in the direction of the pills.

"We must always be cautious, aware, and prepared, never afraid or filled with worry."

The statement came out of left field, not answering his question as Benaiah gave him another questioning frown. Leaning toward Benaiah as though telling a secret, he stated in a low whispering tone only to be heard by him, "Benaiah, trust and faith in man is always a weakness. Check yourself often with whom you trust, looking deep into every situation. You were told over and over on your travels here—confidentiality and security of the symbol on this ring..."—he held it up and then pointed to Benaiah—"and you are of most importance. Am I right?"

Benaiah quietly nodded.

"Every step and breath you take from here on at Journey's End is to be done first and foremost with faith and trust in God alone. Man is man, broken and weak, no matter how dedicated or great they are rewarded. The only other man besides yourself to trust here at Journey's End is me!" Jahar pointed to himself, eyeing Benaiah as seriously as he could.

Keeping the volume of his voice at the same low level as Jahar's, Benaiah responded, leaning in as Jahar did, and asked in an impatient tone, "Would you please be direct and speak in plain English? Again, what was that all about?" He moved his eyes to the pills and then up to Jasaph.

Nodding his head and peering at the pills, Jahar grunted, "Hmm." Then he answered, "I was confirming the pills were not actually poison…to kill you."

"What?" he exclaimed loudly, looking around embarrassed and bringing the volume back down to a strong whisper with wide eyes. "Are you kidding me?"

"This is one area I do not or will not…kid or even pull your leg, as you say."

Looking around the area, Benaiah asked, "But aren't these your servants, employees, or family, relatives, something like that?"

"Yes, in a manner of speaking, all of those, and they are very dedicated. They would die for me. But they are still human, same as you and me. We all are imperfect and broken, slipping up, making mistakes in life here and there."

"But why would anyone want to kill me? I haven't done anything."

Jahar hesitated to answer as he placed a large couch pillow at his feet and then smoothly slid off the couch onto it in a comfortable eating position. He pointed for Benaiah to do the same and watched on as he clumsily tried to imitate him.

Once in position, Jahar said, "Let us give thanks." Jahar bowed without waiting for Benaiah to respond, prayed for the meal, and then asked for different blessings for Benaiah and himself.

Taking up the gold utensils, Jahar calmly worked the food, taking a full bite. Benaiah followed suit and began to relish in the flavor of the spaghetti, making favorable sounds as he chewed. After swallowing, he turned back to Mariah, saying, "Mariah," thinking that this is the name he should be using continued, "this tastes exactly the same as Marino's Italian Table in Sausalito." Then he took a bite of the roll, repeating the same sounds as he said with his mouth full, "How did you do this? It's so good." Gulping the bread down, he took a drink of the root beer. This time, he halfway turned, giving her a thumbs up and then pointed to the bottle, letting her know he appreciated it.

She replied, giving him a slight bow, "You are welcome."

Jahar was relieved that Benaiah was momentarily distracted with the meal, eating a few bites himself. The conversation was not going as he planned again. He knew Benaiah's patience was going to break very soon if he didn't give him direct answers with everything he was talking about. Setting his fork down and whipping his mouth clean with the fancy cloth napkin, he shook his head, deciding to just come out with it.

Reaching over, putting his hand on top of the young man's shoulder, and glancing up to Jasaph and Mariah with a confident grin to let them know he was going to be straightforward with their guest, he said looking back, "To answer your question, Benaiah, why would people want to end your life? The cautious way we brought you here, and the precautions we will continue to take, is not because of anything you have done. It is for the reasons of what I have been trying to tell you. It is all because of who you are and what you are about to become here at Journey's End." He stared back and forth between Benaiah's eyes, wanting everything he was about to say to permanently imprint on his mind and heart.

"The reason you are here is to take my place. I am dying." He paused to let that soak in and then added, "You are the only direct heir left in our family bloodline to be the guardian of Journey's End."

Benaiah's mind began to buzz again with more of this bizarre information. He looked down at the old man's wrinkled, bony hand grasping his shoulder almost in a desperate manner and then looked back up and asked, "How are we related again?"

"You are the grandson of my deceased brother. That makes me your great uncle and you, my great nephew." He pulled his hand away, turning back to his plate of food and took a bite of warm garlic bread.

Benaiah looked out into the garden. It was slowly getting darker as the sun's rays were no longer shining directly into the cavern. He replied, "Do you know how hard it is to take this seriously and believe you? Why didn't you just tell me all this from the start when you sent the letter?"

"You had to be protected. The less that you and anyone out there knew of your true existence or even in here, the safer it would be for you."

The conversation was not being rushed as Benaiah was beginning to show a spark of awareness and interest in what Jahar was talking about. He worked the spaghetti on his plate, wrapping it around his gold fork. Holding his head down as he ate, he peered up with his eyes, looking around as the thought of people trying to kill him was making its impression. Finishing the mouthful, he asked, "So what happened to all our family for it to only be you and me?"

"They are all dead."

"Dead, like everyone just died off?"

Jahar wobbled his head back and forth and answered, "For some…"

A sinking feeling was opening in Benaiah's stomach as he naively asked, "If it's so important for our family or bloodline thing to take care of this place, being the guard or whatever you said, why didn't they just have bigger families?"

"We always have, from the beginning. But over time, they either died of old age or…died protecting Journey's End or were assassinated as with your parents."

Benaiah dropped his fork in his half-eaten meal and then lifted himself up back onto the couch, thinking. The sinking feeling was beginning to feel more like a sick sensation, as though the spaghetti was not settling right.

Mariah noticed Benaiah's awkward body language from behind. She stepped forward, leaning in, and asked, "Are you not feeling well, Benaiah?"

"I'm fine… Dinner is awesome. Thanks again."

She stepped back as he reclined, thinking, and then he asked, "So, Jahar… Our relatives are all dead for the most part because they were murdered…"

"Not all, but a large majority over a great span of time."

"But still… most. Just like my parents from what you've told me."

Jahar gently laid his fork on his plate and then draped his cloth napkin over it being finished. He began not to feel well as his pain was terminal. It took him a moment to slowly sit back up onto the couch, then swatted his hand back to Jasaph to leave him be as he attempted to assist him. Sitting back up on the couch, he tried to hide his pain but still grimaced as he got comfortable and then reluctantly answered, "That is true. More of our family passed on by being killed than of natural causes."

Benaiah sat there, not sure what or how to react, but he was still seeing a distorted picture of what he thought he was here for, which was definitely much different from when he thought he boarded the plane in San Francisco six days ago. It was still very cloudy, what this place was and what was so important about it. And the big questions he was stumped with and that were going around and around in his mind were, *Who are these people killing everyone and for what? What did my family do or have that is so important to continuously be killed over?*

He turned sideways to look at Jahar and the two militaristic people standing behind them, suddenly not trusting anyone. He asked gingerly, "What is special about our family to be in charge here? And what is so important or valuable that needs to be hidden and guarded only to be killed over?"

Jahar inhaled deeply, giving him a confident, encouraging grin. First, to give Benaiah relief that he was safe and secure at the moment, and seeing that he might be getting uncomfortable and on edge with the killing idea. Second, he was enthusiastic that they seemed to be moving forward in a peaceful manner, gradually cresting over this barrier of interest and information flow. Finally, the intelligence he knew Benaiah held, he had asked two of the three important questions for the life of Journey's End.

Benaiah leaned forward, taking another drink of his root beer. Then he settled back, pulling his legs up to the side. He lightly puckered his lips, fully exhaling as his cheeks puffed out knowing that more outrageous information was coming.

Leaning in again to have a more intimate conversation, Jahar gestured around with his hands and stated, "Eyes and ears are everywhere. All meant for my protection and the secrets hidden within Journey's End. Many times, these eyes and ears seemed to lead to another death in my family."

Jahar lifted his hand up with the ring that was resting on the couch arm, waving it in a backward motion. Benaiah noticed, out of the corner of his eye, that Jasaph and Mariah stepped back approximately thirty yards. The same distance away he sent Jasaph out at the tent when he arrived.

Benaiah sensed Jahar was finally going to tell him what he wanted. He leaned in on his armrest, anxiously listening. "Secrets have been hidden in here at Journey's End for a little over three thousand years which all the descendants here know about as well as the immediate African communities. And for most of the first hundred or so years, Journey's End was very safe and secure. But human selfishness and greed naturally flourished as honor, respect, and loyalty weakened. Our first enemy was our first great confidential ally. After their queen and her immediate children passed away, the royalty lineage from then on went into massive ruin, never being great as it once was. This is when they turned on us.

"It took almost two thousand years of fighting to almost eliminate this persistent enemy as they themselves gathered allies of their own from outside African tribes and other southern Middle Eastern nations to get at what we have here. This quiet, almost invisible war was won and has been kept blind from the outside world due in part to the descendants from all bloodlines sent here sacrificing more than one can count. But moreover, from the blessings and answers to prayer from the Lord of heaven's armies, keeping our hidden secrets secure as God and our king instructed us." Jahar lightheartedly wavered his head back and forth and added, "At least the majority of the time."

After making an adjustment to ease the pain, he continued, "Then there are the rogue adventurers and treasure hunters who search out the mysteries and myths of hidden places and treasures deep in the Congo handed down for hundreds and hundreds of years from stories and ancient maps that seem to appear out of nowhere only to find themselves at dead ends or…dead themselves."

He paused, getting serious now and shaking his head with great disappointment. "Our newest enemy as of the past centuries comes from within our own people."

Jahar looked down at his ring, slowly rubbing it as Benaiah spoke up, anxious for an answer to what was said earlier. "Who is this queen and king?"

Jahar looked up, inhaling deeply and building the courage to finally allow hidden secrets within Journey's End to begin to pierce Benaiah's imagination. He peered back down to the ring, whispering, "This ring has been handed down from guardian to guardian of Journey's End ever since…King Solomon gave it to the first guardian when he left Jerusalem to live here deep within the Congo, hiding and securing the greatest worlds treasures from all humanity."

Looking up to Benaiah, he continued, "The Queen of Sheba, whose kingdom was all of Africa south of Egypt, was very close to and had ultimate respect for our King. King Solomon, as you know, had great treasures beyond the imagination. With his mighty wisdom, he knew it had to be taken away far, far from the civilized world, including his people of Israel and especially from his own children.

"King Solomon confidentially asked the Queen of Sheba if there was a place reaching out to the far ends of her reign, in her sparsely inhabited expanse of land, whose existence no one in the world would ever know of. So here we are." Jahar reached out, swaying both arms. "Which is still one of the most remote and unchallenged places on earth."

As Jahar finished, Benaiah had put on a disfigured look on his face, wrinkling his eyebrows together and staring in complete disbelief. He said out loud, "Are you crazy?" Then he straightened up, putting his bare feet on the floor and breaking their confidential bubble, gazing up to the dimly lit ceiling.

"Benaiah," Jahar whispered. "Everything I say to you is the truth. I know this is hard to grasp, and the knowledge of it is a heavy burden to carry. We have fought vigorously over thousands of years to keep the secrets within this place quiet from the world, as I mentioned. With your in-depth studies of history, you had no idea we or this place existed. It proves our continuous battles are being won.

"Therefore, I strongly caution you. The more you know, the greater you will be in danger, especially when I take this ring off and put it on your finger." He paused and then whispered slowly and firmly, "Only trust God, me, and yourself…*only!* Do you understand?"

Sarcastically, and in a normal volume, Benaiah replied, reaching back and putting his hands behind his head, not willing to be fooled,

"And I suppose that symbol on the ring you're protecting is King Solomon's signature mark." Benaiah started laughing as he finished. "Giving you all of his authority and power?"

Jahar jumped up out of his seat spryly for his age, shouting harshly under his breath, "Benaiah, you must have respect and take me seriously! You have no idea of the consequences if all the knowledge and power Journey's End holds is not guarded by a great leader—which your blood is flowing with!"

Before another word was said, Benaiah found himself on his back as the weight of Jasaph kneeled on his chest. He had swiftly reached over with his strong arms, lifting Benaiah over the couch and slamming him down on his back into the grassy area. Grasping Benaiah's mouth closed with one hand, he had a knife in the other pointing at his throat.

"Wait, stop!" Jahar frantically ordered, raising his arms up.

Speaking in broken English so Benaiah could understand, Jasaph growled out, "He needs to learn in another way, Master. A lesson he will not truly forget from dishonoring you and making a mockery of our king and purpose. He will put you and our home in harm's way unless he sees clearly and has a change of heart. So far, this way is not working!"

Jahar lowered his gaze to the floor again, disappointed at how this was going again, and then he solemnly said in Hebrew, "Get Horasha."

He plopped down on his couch, leaning to his side, and wrapped an arm around the middle of his body as his head drooped down so no one could see his pained expression. Jasaph saw it and then spoke loudly in the language Benaiah didn't understand, "Security Alpha, put Master on the IGT. Get him to the doctor immediately!"

Guards swarmed in, perfectly hidden close by within the garden. Jasaph, looking to Mariah who was now at Jahar's side comforting him, said, peering intently into her eyes, "Mariah, go with Master Jahar. Do not leave his side!"

Peering up and around from laying on his back, the lights throughout the cavern evenly and softly came on, and then Benaiah couldn't believe what he saw. Camouflaged guards mystically had moved from everywhere hidden in areas and ways such that no one would ever know they were there until they moved. Throughout the garden, up on the rock staircases, and along the walls leading up to the mouth of the opening as well as dozens peering down over the cavern's opening five stories from above, at the ready for more orders.

Jasaph finished his orders, looking down at Benaiah, "Everyone else, maintain your positions!"

Benaiah suddenly realized this whole time that they'd been surrounded by more guards than he could count as this illusive camouflage kept them secretly unaware to anyone that didn't know of their presence.

As Jasaph's knee was buried in his chest, Benaiah understood he just opened a big can of worms and possibly was the cause for inflicting pain to Jahar. Watching the sudden orchestra of people quickly taking action, he was wishing he hadn't opened his mouth.

Without notice, Benaiah was being lifted to his feet as Jasaph pulled him up by his shirt at the base of his neck, saying, "Benaiah, forgive me. But this must happen to you for you to understand the importance of what is going on here. Later, if you become the guardian, you may do with me as you wish. But right now, I must do what needs to be done so you have a change of heart for the protection of your bloodline and of Journey's End. Prayerfully, you will boldly, and with honor, carry on the orders given by our king who has long past to be with the Lord of heaven's armies. Time is of the essence, Master Jahar does not have much time left." He glanced over, seeing Mariah sitting next to Jahar on the IGT and ready to flying away to the medical facility.

Looking over to Jasaph, Jahar nodded that he was sadly doing the right thing. Then he tilted his head in a manner to bring Benaiah to him. Benaiah couldn't believe what he was looking at while going to Jahar. Him, the guards, and Mariah were sitting on something that didn't have wheels and was hovering off the ground, appearing to be a floating lightweight saucer or craft of some sort.

Benaiah stepped close as Mariah backed away then bent down putting his sandals back on him knowing where he was heading. When Mariah finished, Jahar whispered, "Come closer." Benaiah cautiously leaned in as Jahar softly whispered something so quietly it couldn't be heard.

He moved his ear closer, asking, "What did you say?"

Almost touching Benaiah's ear with his lips, Jahar whispered while groaning in pain, "Your footprint image will give you the key to have the power over Journey's End. If I do not live another day or the ring disappears, one will come to you who understands this and knows the treasure of King Solomon at Journey's End is only an illusion hiding Journey's Beginning, which is the true treasured secret protected even from our descendants." Jahar paused. Benaiah didn't know if it was to hold back pain or if he was thinking of what to say next. "Our worst enemy at hand is ourselves. Free yourself by hiding in the love of God, trusting in him."

One of the tunnel doors opened on the far side of the cavern, and Horasha came flying in on an IGT swiftly through the garden with several men. When he got to the platform, he bowed to Jahar and then knelt at his feet, asking, "How are you, Master?"

"The pain has come back viciously."

Horasha turned to Jasaph for an answer of why he was summoned. He verbally responded, "Benaiah is not cooperating and is compromising our...endeavors." Horasha quickly looked at Benaiah, staring him down with his nostrils flaring. Instantly, Benaiah caved in, inside and out, feeling like worthless mud in Horasha's hands. Horasha slowly got up, stepping toward him and not changing his demeaner. Looking up to the big man with puppy dog eyes, Benaiah hoped the pain he envisioned coming his way was only his imagination.

"Come with me, boy." Horasha slowly stated through his gritted teeth as all the earlier respectful honor was nowhere to be heard or seen. He turned to Mariah, who was quietly comforting Jahar. "Mariah, come with us."

Jasaph quickly responded, "I have her going with our master to be by his side."

Not pleased with him giving her that order, he shrugged it off, and then, in a military fashion, spun around in a different direction than they came into the commons area and started walking automatically, expecting everyone else to follow him.

Feeling a nudge in his back, Benaiah followed. Once they got to an entrance of a specific tunnel, Jasaph quietly spoke to Horasha, pointing to the entrance of another tunnel next to this one. Horasha shook his head, saying, "It would be best to take him here. I know what makes this ignorant young man tick. This will break him more effectively." Then he told the guards that followed, "It will only be Benaiah and himself going in. Stay at attention here until we get back."

Jasaph again wanted to correct Horasha without discrediting him, so he cleared his throat, quietly reminding him that what he was doing is against the rules. Horasha sternly looked at him for continually getting in the way and replied sharply, "Yes, you are right. We are not permitted to go in here alone. I forget these petty things when I have been gone too long. Please join us, Jasaph," he said with a slight devious stare.

Jasaph, pleased that Horasha did not rise to conflict, turned to the other guards that followed, "Everyone else…stay at the ready until we come out."

Turning around and looking up the wall at the side of the large metal door, Horasha nodded at a miniature camera. A red light appeared on a small screen hip high on the same wall. Horasha placed his thumb on the screen, reading his thumbprint. Several seconds later, the screen turned green, beeping as the heavy door automatically opened.

It was dungeon black inside as Benaiah flushed with anxiety, envisioning he was going to be tortured deep inside, never to be seen again. Horasha stepped in as lighting automatically began piercing the gloom. First at the entrance and then systematically working down the long tunnel.

Once the solid door closed behind the three men, Horasha calmed his tone and demeanor, saying, "Come along, I have much to show you, Benaiah."

They began to proceed, following the lights down the hallway, which had a portrait of its own, different than the medical facility tunnel. With each step, it appeared they were walking on clouds on the flat smooth floor as the painting continued a quarter the way up the rock walls as fluffy white clouds billowed outward. Blue sky enriched the upper portion on the walls and ceiling, giving the illusion it went on and on. The temperature was a little cooler as whispering sounds of air movement assisted in the special effects of being where eagles soar.

Shortly, on both sides of the walls, alcoves just like the ones in the medical facility tunnel began to appear, but they were dark and empty. After about fifty yards, Horasha stopped and turned to the first alcove that lit up. It had a portrait inside and a placard with a name on it. Benaiah stepped next to him, looking inside and recognizing the large portrait—it was of Jahar.

"What's this? Benaiah cautiously asked.

"This tunnel holds the history of the guardians and where the book of time is secured."

"The book of time?"

"Yes, it is the continuous diary from each guardian since our inception, keeping records of all events happening here and throughout the world."

Benaiah signed loudly with relief.

Horasha looked back at him, asking, "What is that for?"

Comically speaking and trying to make light of the situation, he answered, "I thought I was in trouble and you were going to torture me or something."

"Who said I am not?" Horasha stepped forward inches from Benaiah's face.

"You can't do that? You wouldn't, would you?" Benaiah pulled his head back as far from Horasha as he could with an uncertain expression.

"That is for you to decide. I am going to show you your family's history from the start until now along with things you would only dream of. If you still think this is a joke, then you will have put me into a position that I will have to…beat the truth into you in the tunnel next door where he wanted to take you." Horasha tilted his head toward Jasaph.

Benaiah's cocky smile disappeared.

"More times than you can imagine, history has shown when royalty had young ones like you, who did not take the responsibility and honor of their parent's crown seriously, they suffered harsh physical punishment to change their minds and correct their hearts.

If that did not work... Well, let me say..." He turned, looking at Jahar's bodyguard with a smile and then firmly back to Benaiah. "Many princes and princesses disappeared, never to be seen again."

Horasha didn't move as he stared Benaiah down, with him looking away almost in a shameful and daunting manner.

"Benaiah, your bloodline is powerful, going back to King David's mighty men. You better start...not only acting as one, but being one. Because here"—he strongly pointed a finger to the ground—"you are royalty." Horasha and the guard knelt before him momentarily to let him know they were not kidding and then got back to their feet.

"That is all the respect and honor you will receive from us until you quickly prove you are more than an ignorant, selfish, worldly idiot. Your great uncle is dying. He has been through more than anyone here being a mighty warrior like his forefathers going back three thousand years. Do not..." Horasha grabbed Benaiah by the chin, forcefully turning his head like a child, making him look him in the eyes. "Do not let this most honorable position as guardian of Journey's End die with you after your family line dedicated their lives serving and carrying out orders from the wisest, wealthiest, and most powerful king of all times."

Horasha let go of his chin, and out of nowhere, an uncontrollable burst of laughter erupted out of Benaiah. He grabbed his mouth to stop it from coming out as his eyes widened from the shock of what he was doing at a serious moment. The more everyone informed him of this place and who he truly was and where he was from, it sounded more and more like a fiction novel, almost comical.

Fire ignited out of Horasha's eyes as he quickly took him by the neck with both hands, walking him back up against the rocky tunnel wall while choking him.

"You pathetic pile of elephant dung! I told Jahar many times you would not work out! I watched over you and protected you your whole life. I know you better than you know yourself. You live a life of no honor and respect, hollow of faith, insulting our God, your Israelite people, even your honorable and gentile step-parents!"

Benaiah couldn't breathe let alone get words out as he started to hit Horasha's arms, trying to get him to let go.

"Enough, Horasha," Jasaph said calmly. Then he had to repeat himself louder, grasping one of his arms. Horasha quickly turned to him as though he was surprised there was someone else in the hallway. Looking back to his prey, he snorted out in disgust and then let go as Benaiah dropped to the floor on his knees, gasping for air.

"This will be your only chance to redeem yourself. Take everything you are about to see and hear to heart. Because if you do not, one of two things will happen to you, or maybe both, from what I mentioned about royal children not obediently following their royal obligations." Then as a warning of the possible pain to come, he grasped the gauze bandage that was still wrapped around Benaiah's head and jerked it off, pulling his head to the side.

Horasha leaned down, snatching Benaiah's chin again for him to look up and asked, "Do you understand?"

Defeated and bewildered with what was going on, he replied, not knowing what else to say. "Yes… I understand."

Just like Jekyll and Hyde, Horasha suddenly acted as though they were best of friends. Pulling him up to his feet and putting his arm around Benaiah's shoulder with a big smile, he said, "Good. Now that we have that straightened out, let us move on."

Chapter 5

They left Jahar's portrait that was lit up in the perfectly chiseled-out niche in the side of the mountain rock wall. Horasha spent time pointing out and explaining to Benaiah many of the guardians of the past as they made their way down the airy and lofty feeling tunnel painted as though one was hundreds of feet in the sky. It seemed to go on forever, as Jahar was the eighty-ninth. They stopped at the last niche at the end of the tunnel, where a very old fashionable wooden door stopped them from going any farther, oddly looking out of place.

"This is the first of all the guardians that started Journey's End," Horasha stated. "He took on the heavy honor from King Solomon directly to secure the treasures brought here."

"How do you pronounce his name? I can't read Hebrew," Benaiah asked.

Horasha sarcastically responded, looking at him disappointedly, "I know. You chose French as a second language." Looking back at the plaque in front of the portrait, he said proudly, "His name was Shuriah. He is named after his warrior father, Uriah."

"Uriah? Isn't that…the name of the guy King David sent to the front of a battle so he would get killed? Because David got his beautiful wife Bathsheba pregnant and tried to hide it or something?"

There was a pause from Horasha because Benaiah soured the conversation and then calmly answered, "Yes, but Uriah was not just…a guy! He was one of King David's mighty men!" Proudly, Horasha beat his chest a couple of times, adding, "And probably the most dependable and honorable of them all."

Now, Benaiah paused, trying to remember this story he learned as a kid, and then he replied, pointing up to the portrait, "So you're telling me this guy here, Shuriah, was in the Bible?"

"No, that is not what I said. He is not mentioned in the Bible but was the student or apprentice of Uriah. Like in the *Star Wars* movies. They called them padawans. Learning and training one on one under a Jedi master for the sole purpose to become one."

Benaiah firmly squeezed his lips shut, trying not to laugh at the statement while looking at the big burly man with the full black beard to see if he was joking or not. Then Horasha answered Benaiah's facial expression, shrugging his shoulders, "What? So I like *Star Wars*. Do you have a problem with that?"

"No, not at all." Giving out a slight chuckle, he was relieved it appeared the tension had weakened. "Just the way you said it and the analogy, you made it sound like it was a real thing and they had superpowers or something."

Horasha's smile suddenly changed as Benaiah saw it coming and took a step back, knowing he went too far too fast. Jasaph saw it too and then quickly stepped in front of Benaiah before Horasha could get his hands on him, shaking his head.

The two strong men had a staredown for a moment, and then Horasha took a deep breath, calming down and relaxing his fists. He commented as he gently moved Jahar's bodyguard to the side, "Everything here was and is real, Benaiah. You need to open your mind and soul to new understanding and directions for your life. You live in a world that only ends up six feet underground exactly like your pathetic dinosaurs bones."

Jasaph spoke up, "If I may, Horasha?"

"Please, be my guest." Horasha stepped to the side, swiping his hand out and pointing to Benaiah as he said, "I have watched over him for most of twenty-seven years, and the majority of his later years, I have wanted to bend him over my knee for being unwise and unworthy to be the next guardian."

Lowering his voice while still facing Horasha, he said, "Watch your words. He *will* be our next master. With this history and knowledge vacant and hidden from him all his life, what other expectations should we have of him?"

Horasha gave a deep grunt from being disgusted and then slightly rolled his eyes to the side.

Jasaph turned to Benaiah, giving him a faint bow and now putting on his formal facial expression of his own with his back to Horasha. "Benaiah, you are to be the next guardian of Journey's End. It has been your destiny since you were conceived. We are asking you to open your mind and heart to a world that only a handful of people know.

"What is here would change the world more than likely in a horrible way if it knew what is hidden inside this mountain. That is why King Solomon secretly transported his treasures, which continually flowed to him in mass quantities. A treasure that grew greater than one could fathom from the known world during his forty years of his reign as king."

Benaiah slowly shook his head, wrinkling his lips to the side and then asked in a screechy tone as things were starting to come together from what Jahar told him. "Wait a second here... You're telling me this treasure, I assume, is all Solomon's gold? And all these guardians starting with this dude—sorry, mighty warriors." Benaiah glanced to Horasha and then pointed his thumb over his shoulder to the alcove. "Have been protecting Solomon's treasure here in the middle of the Congo for three thousand years?"

Jasaph and Horasha nodded their heads.

"Then show me." Anxious for what they were saying to be true, Benaiah got serious.

"We cannot do that," Jahar's bodyguard answered.

"Why?"

"Only the one wearing the ring has access to the treasury."

"Is that what's behind this door?" He pointed to the large antique wooden door.

"No, it is in a different location. This is where the book of time is kept," Horasha answered. He took a step to the door, and like the main entrance to the tunnel, there was a small touch pad hip high which Horasha pressed his thumb on. A moment later, the sound of a large metal security door opening behind the old decorative door was heard.

Horasha explained, "A guardian a couple of centuries ago had this door put in to give it a homey feel because they go through it so often, spending much of their time in here in private." Turning the ornamental handle and then pushing it open, the old hinges squeaked as it slowly opened wide, and all three peered inside the cold dark room.

Horasha continued, "The book of time is the oldest, continuous detailed record kept known to man from the past three thousand years. From all four corners of the world, not just zeroed in on the areas the Bible covers based around Israel. The accurate documentation that is written in this book would change the world as well. Many history books would only be good for keeping fires going because they are missing key facts or are completely wrong. Unworthy man has the tendency to alter truths to fit a world that is only a dream, not reality, in order to make them look and feel better. That is not done here."

"Why would you want to keep historical facts secret?"

"Because our wise king told Shuriah that what enters Journey's End will always be extraordinary, with overwhelming powers that would only be poison for man. So never divulge its contents until God changes his orders for the purpose of the Kingdom of heaven, and so far, over the millennia, a guardian has not been given such instructions from the Lord of heaven's armies."

Benaiah lifted his open hands in a defensive position. "Don't take this wrong, but you're still talking about King Solomon, right?"

They nodded their heads, and then he continued, "He's dead… Wouldn't his orders die with him? Besides, what would he know of future things and events? He wasn't a prophet." He ended his statement not sarcastically but in a way as if he knew what he was talking about in the Bible and folded his arms.

Both the other men smiled at his naivete, and then Jasaph responded first, "Would you agree that King Solomon was the wisest man to have ever lived excluding Jesus Christ?"

"If you believe what the Bible says, sure." He shrugged his shoulders and frowned as though he didn't trust or believe in it himself.

Horasha stepped in. "For a historian and archeologist with a PhD, you are not very intelligent, are you?" The two older men snickered together at him.

Benaiah popped his head back, changing his expression as though insulted.

"Do not play dumb with us, Benaiah. You know there are plenty of other resources and historical facts besides the Bible that proves King Solomon's reign and his extraordinary wealth and life-style," Jasaph stated.

"Yeah, there are, but there's nothing that I'm aware of besides the Bible that states him being the wisest man."

The two men looked at each other and started laughing out loud, and then Horasha explained, "That proves what we are saying about historical facts that are not God breathed. It is continually being twisted or purposely left out to hide or change the impression of the past. The book of time, as we will show you, gives precise and thorough information of the world's history and events step by step as it happened from the past three thousand years. You will be convinced of who you are, where you came from, and how all things came to be as you know it. Or..."—Horasha grinned nodding to the guard beside him—"you could choose to go to the next tunnel he wanted to take you in and beat the truth into you and get all this over with painfully?"

Benaiah began to feel he would have the upper hand in this challenge and said, "Since you guys are so convinced this circus is real, I'll let you two give me the last laugh. Show me this book of time and I'll judge for myself." He pointed into the dark room.

Horasha, many times, had secretly heard this tone from him, knowing where it was going. He pointed to the portrait of Shuriah. "Before we go inside, start your examination with this portrait of the great Shuriah. Jahar quietly guided you into your field of study for a reason. So you would have the skills to be able to identify ancient items you will come into contact with here at your new home. With your knowledge and experience, soon, you will be apologizing to us for your skepticism. A word of advice, though. Your greatest ally to assist you from further embarrassment and physical torture is changing how your heart thinks."

Benaiah wasn't too keen on the statements, glancing uneasily at both robust men with stout postures and chiseled features staring at him, and then he turned his back, peering into the alcove.

His eyes slowly moved around, looking closely at the details of the materials the artwork was on and noticing specific things that got his mind thinking of ancient resources used. Then he refocused to the portrait itself. How the painting was drawn, what clothing the man was wearing, and then his eye noticed what was on the ring finger of Shuriah. It appeared to be the same ring Jahar wore that was to be kept so secret.

"Nice touch adding the ring," he said in a sarcastic manner. "Without my tools and laptop, I can't verify the exact age of this. Besides, there is no way the integrity could withstand the years you guys are insisting this was done in to remain in such good condition."

Horasha hesitantly answered back, knowing he was entering the world Benaiah had the advantage. "There is a special tree here in the Congo that has a sap within it which has been used all these years to preserve delicate items such as this, and nothing within the mountain is exposed to weather, and the atmospheric conditions are perfect in here for slowing down the decaying process."

Benaiah grinned, trying not to aggravate Horasha again as he replied, "You sure like your movies, attempting to pull the mosquito-trapped-in-the-tree-sap idea from *Jurassic Park*."

Horasha slowly shook his head sideways, flinging his hands out and commenting, "We are trying to help you, Benaiah. But you continue digging yourself a deeper grave by not even attempting to believe what is going on in this most special of all places, harming your destiny."

Jasaph was the one now that had lost his patience. Leaning forward, he poked his index finger onto Benaiah's forehead, popping it back and saying, "Your head is filled with so much worldly dung that there obviously is no room for any Godly wisdom to enter your heart." He then poked Benaiah in the chest and then turned back to Horasha, stating, "I told you we needed to go to the rehabilitation facility." Turning back and eyeballing Benaiah sternly, he bellowed, "The dung in him needs to be beat out of him because it is not coming out on its own!"

Taking a casual small step back and to the side directly behind Jasaph as though adjusting his stance, Horasha added, "I am beginning to agree with you, and for that, I must do what must be done."

Swiftly, Horasha reached up with both hands around Jasaph's head and, with lightning speed, twisted it to the side, and over rotated it. A loud gruesome crack was heard, shooting sickening cringes down Benaiah's spine as Jasaph's body dropped to the floor lifeless.

Without changing his demeanor and tone of voice, Horasha continued talking to Benaiah as if nothing happened. "You are welcome for saving your life—again."

Benaiah couldn't move as his mind and body were frozen, his mouth agape in complete disbelief while staring at the dead man. After a few seconds that felt more like minutes, he slowly raised his eyes to the killer, terrified of what was going to happen next.

"I know that was shocking, having never seeing anyone killed in front of you. Remember... I have been your lifelong bodyguard, watching every move you have made since you were born. Many times, I had to eliminate people protecting you without you knowing. Many of those kills were outside enemies of Journey's End attempting to hold you hostage and even kill its next guardian to get to the treasure within."

Horasha looked down at the dead man lying at his feet with no remorse. "His family bloodline is next in line to be the guardians of Journey's End if or when yours dies off. Of course you know that you are the only one left after Jahar has passed on until you have a son of your own. I am guessing he wanted to get you into a position that your death would be an accident, and the rehabilitation facility is a perfect place for that to happen, because it has happened before." He nodded, putting a smile on his face and making light of a past experience.

Finally able to move, Benaiah took a step back, truly horrified and sick to his stomach. Suddenly, he flinched to the side, bent over, and vomited.

"Come on, Benaiah. Warrior up for once. This might be your first kill, but it will definitely not be your last." He smirked out a laugh as though it was nothing.

Clearing his mouth and spitting out the remnants of the nasty taste of digesting spaghetti, Benaiah slurred his first words until his tongue started working again, still focused on the dead man at his feet. "But...but you have been the one threatening me. How do I know you're not the one that wants to kill me?"

"Oh, that is my normal personality, but it was all an act this time. Remember that he would not allow you and I to go inside this tunnel without him?"

Wiping his mouth with his arm, Benaiah tried to inconspicuously keep his distance. He nodded uneasily, lifting his hand and rubbing his neck, thinking Horasha wasn't pretending when he couldn't breathe.

"It is a rule that no one is allowed in the special secured tunnels by themselves." He lifted his hands and shoulders, adding, "I tried, but he caught me, and I believe his stepsister Mariah is in on assassinating you and possibly Jahar as well."

Benaiah thought for a second, moving his eyes back and forth. He asked, "You're talking about Mary? The one I first met on the elephant?"

"Yes, that is the one. Remember in the commons area me saying I wanted her to come with us, but he said he had already given her an order to stay with Jahar?"

"I do." Benaiah opened his eyes wide, seeing Horasha could possibly be going somewhere with this.

"I am suspecting he is keeping her close to Jahar so when the right time presents itself, she can kill him without anyone knowing it was her, which is a great cover-up, because Jahar is very fond of Mariah since she was a baby and treats her like his own daughter.

Benaiah thought back to when him and Jahar were talking about being poisoned with the medicine given to him on the couch. Was Jahar being lied to by Jasaph when he trusted him by saying it was safe to take?

Benaiah stared down at the dead bodyguard as things began to make sense, and finally, trust in someone began to realistically show itself for the first time in days. He said, "I can see what you're talking about. What do we do now?"

"You must be protected..." Horasha paused, knowing what he was going to say next might not go down very well. "And by now, Jahar is probably already dead since you two are now separated but deceptively safe inside the mountain. Besides, Jahar's mind is not what it was. It is my duty to protect you from even him." Horasha gave Benaiah a slight bow.

Benaiah looked up quickly, with wide eyes full of confused questions.

"Jahar is very sick, and at his old age, his mind is not always clear. You probably noticed in your short time together that he sounds paranoid and does not explain things in detail or beats around the bush…as your people say."

Benaiah couldn't deny what he said, but at the same time, he couldn't get out of his mind Jahar telling him in confidence appearing to be in sound mind not to trust anyone except God, Jahar and himself only.

"He probably told you not to trust anyone, right?"

Benaiah mentally stumbled back. Horasha just read his mind, and then he gave his answer away by not responding quickly enough.

Horasha smiled, knowing what was going through the young man's mind, and said, "Anyone in his position needs to be extremely protective, so I do not blame him for telling you that. I would have done the same thing. And he is right. You do not know who to trust here. That is why this…" he pointed between them "is difficult. But if I wanted you dead, I would have easily done it long ago.

"Such as when you were in China over a year ago just south of Mongolia, where you bought that emerald-colored stone letter opener with a dragon carved on the handle. You were in a pit, digging around for ancient relics, and I could have simply caused a rock slide, burying you and the whole team. Everyone would have thought it was an accident."

Benaiah popped his head back, astonished that Horasha would have all that detailed information about him.

"Or when you and your step-parents took you to Maui, Hawaii, when you were in eighth grade. You snorkeled out farther than you should have, and the current was quickly taking you out to open ocean. You panicked as the waves were getting bigger and the people on the shore looked like tiny ants. The ocean and you, no one else, would have been blamed for your death."

Benaiah's mouth dropped open, shocked at that nightmarish feeling embedded in his memory.

Horasha smiled. "You remember. I was the one that took you by the arm swimming you to the shallows."

"No way? That was you? I never even told my parents about that. I would have gotten in trouble. You just disappeared. Why didn't you say anything to me then?"

Still smiling and showing his white teeth through the full black bread, Horasha only shook his head.

"Okay, okay, I know." Benaiah raised his hands in defense as the excitement of these revelations from the past anchored him like a stake firmly being hammered in the ground. Confirming in his soul that this fantasy story he'd been hearing and walking through was real. Suddenly, a kinship feeling came across Benaiah with regards to Horasha knowing the details of his life. Then another thought came to him as words slipped out. "If you knew that one, then you would know all the other things I did...?" He stopped talking as embarrassment flushed through his face.

"Oh, Benaiah, I can get into all the details of the things you did. Where should I start? How about your second girlfriend in high school? Or when the police were running after you and your friends across the football field the night of senior prank day when you all toilet-papered the building, setting off the school alarms?"

Benaiah was in awe that Horasha knew the details of his past and then, embarrassed, he said, waving his hands out, "No you don't have to bring that stuff up. Is there anything you don't know about me?"

"Only what you would dream about at night sleeping." Looking down at the dead descendant, Horasha said, "Enough of this. We need to get going."

Horasha knelt, shutting the man's silent eyes, "I am sorry, my friend, but I could not allow you to kill our next master." Then he stood, turned around, and walked into the dark room of the book of time.

Benaiah took another good look at the lifeless body, sick at the idea of not only watching someone be killed but also that the person was right there in front of him. He hesitantly walked around him and stepped past the old wooden door and steel-framed opening where the security steel door had raised up into the ceiling.

A large crystal chandelier hanging high from the center of the tall curved rock ceiling had automatically illuminated, exposing something very different than he imagined. Horasha commented, "Every new guardian redecorates many of Journey's End rooms and tunnels to fit their personal tastes. Jahar, as you can see, likes the elegant appeal of early European."

Once inside, Benaiah stopped and slowly rotated his head, following a continuous bookcase going around the medium-sized circular room that was approximately fifty feet in diameter. The shelves were twelve high to the ceiling, and the first nine lower shelves tightly filled with thick books, with only a few on the tenth as the other shelves were waiting to be used.

Beneath the chandelier in the center of the wide room looking like an island was a large antique wooden desk. It had thin drawers with fancy handles on each side under the flat desk top, appearing as if it belonged in a historical castle somewhere in Europe. The detailed craftmanship was carved down each corner leg with decorative artwork weaving throughout the whole piece of furniture.

A high-back padded armed chair was tucked in its appropriate seated position at the desk. It matched but was a little more updated as it swiveled and was on wheels.

Benaiah stepped close to the desk, seeing at the top right-hand corner a neat stack of blank paper matching the letter he originally received from Jahar. To the left of the paper was a fancy glass bottle of black ink with a stylish old pen resting flat in its holder. Nodding to himself, it confirmed he was right about what the letter was written with. To the far left upper corner of the desk was an old ceramic dish candleholder with a round finger loop on the side for it to be carried. A lifeless, half burned, maroon-colored candle stood erect in the middle of the dish with drips of wax stringing down the sides. Again, he nodded to himself; it matched the wax used to press Jahar's ring in for King Solomon's signature mark.

Next to the desk on the right was a wood-framed lounging sofa with a curved designer back. A book laid open face down on the sofa as though someone temporarily left it to come back to finish reading.

Benaiah's eyes worked the large library for a moment, expecting to see a large, thick tattered book safely sitting on a pedestal under covered glass spotlighted from above and bringing all the attention of the room to itself. Then he asked, "So where's this book of time?"

"You are looking at it." Horasha slowly pointed around to the organized shelves. "We say the book, but in reality, it is a continuous flow of information from bound pages to bound pages.

"Obviously, over three thousand years of writing, it would be impossible to just have one book." He proudly smiled, admiring the plethora of history, wisdom, and knowledge resting on the shelves.

Slowly, Benaiah strolled along the bookshelves. Each of the bound pages of history had unfamiliar writing on the ends facing out. "Let me guess, these are all written in Hebrew?"

"You guessed correctly. Now do you understand why we tried so hard to get you to learn the language of God's chosen people? You easily grasped hold of history and to get into archeology when we subliminally presented it to you. But to thoroughly learn a different language, especially Hebrew, you did not want to have anything to do with it."

"Why should I? With technology today, our computers are the interpreters. It's faster and more accurate and less apt for misinterpretation."

"That is called laziness and an excuse. You will waste time here learning Hebrew before you can completely move forward with your responsibilities. You must learn to read and write Hebrew accurately to carry on where Jahar has left off." He spoke in a manner as if he was dead already.

"Get use to this room. You will spend much of your time documenting the activities here at Journey's End as well as all major and minor world events."

"That sounds boring, Why not hire a professional journalist?"

"As Jahar told you, you cannot trust anyone. Every guardian of Journey's End being of pure blood of King David's mighty warriors, take the same oath that was decreed in the cave of Adullam, where they hid, taking refuge and growing in a brotherhood—a family never to be equalled. But more than that, they were strengthened physically, mentally, and spiritually as the presence of God blessed them in special ways to become mighty men of faith, integrity, courage, and strength as David had when he killed Goliath as a boy." Horasha stood tall with his chest out, boldly clenching his fists as though he was one of the mighty men himself.

Benaiah gave him a curious look. "What does that have to do with hiring a journalist?"

Unexpectedly, Horasha burst out, "Everything! Are you not hearing me, Benaiah? Secrecy, security, and purity reigns here. You must take the same oath as Jahar, and every guardian before him, that you will fully dedicate your life to faithfully follow the orders given by King Solomon and for all guardians to come until God gives new instructions for this special of all places, serving and protecting it with passion, honesty, accuracy and thoroughness equaling that of God's perfection.

"The weighted responsibility is yours because you are the only blood family Jahar has. Everyone else, such as myself, is a part of your Israelite family. But we are all servants, here to serve and protect the health and welfare of the guardian and to fulfill his orders and desires as well as all of Journey's End.

"Once you see clearly who you are and what your destiny and legacy is for Journey's End as a member of the descendants, you will be the most honored person of this special of all places. Honesty and integrity will assist you in accurately keeping records for the book of time." Horasha crossed his arms to let his body language speak as well, adding, "Not some hired journalist."

Horasha cleared his throat, shaking his head, "It would not have been so difficult for you to understand and naturally take this honored position when your time came if your birth parents were not so selfish by leaving Jahar all by himself."

He looked away, mumbling under his breath while still thinking about the past, "They got what they deserved."

"What?" Benaiah heard what he said. He couldn't believe he said it after preaching to him about family.

"Nothing," Horasha responded, wishing it wouldn't have left his lips as he dropped his arms to his sides. Stepping up to the desk, he pulled the rolling chair out and sat down. Reaching into one of the side drawers, Horasha pulled out a handful of letters, plopping them on the desk.

"What are those?" Benaiah asked.

"These are all the companies and organizations who responded to your request for a grant."

"What? How did you get those?"

Horasha once more looked at him in disbelief.

"How could you do that to me?" He picked up the pile recognizing names and company logos on the letters.

"Why would you..." Suddenly, Benaiah switched gears as an eruption of anger came out. "You screwed with my life! These have a time limit on them for response to accept the grant or not! I'm never going to get in with any of these companies because of you, Jahar, and whatever is going on in this place. I can see why my parents left!"

Ignoring him, Horasha reached in to where the letters came out of the open drawer and pushed a hidden button that was on the underside of the desk top. Hearing movement of mechanical sounds, both the men looked up and around the room, seeing all the bookshelves twisting around on center hinges every ten feet. Once making a hundred-and-eighty degree turn, they stopped and relocked themselves together. Now, high-tech blank screens surrounded them from floor to ceiling.

Horasha opened the drawer on the other side of the desk, placing his hand in the same spot and pushing another button. Before him, instantly hovering inches above the desk, a transparent control panel of lights appeared.

"Wow! That looks like a hologram panel you see in the movies!" Benaiah stated, impressed.

"Oh, now look who watches movies. The difference is that this is real."

Benaiah quickly became interested at what was going on in this instant curious sci-fi room as his stomach returned to normal and the vision of Horasha breaking Jasaph's neck slowly evaporated from his mind. "What is all this?"

Horasha swiped his hand across the panel of lights in different directions then pointed in the air at a light as though he pushed a real physical button.

Both looked up at the screens as life-sized movement caught their eyes, and they saw a different picture on each ten-foot wide panel that had twisted around. Turning around in a circle himself, Benaiah saw on the dozens of screens circling the room a different city was pictured on each panel from around the world.

Leaning back in the big chair with great confidence and pride, Horasha stated, "These are live images from around the world. You name the largest city to the smallest town and location, and we can see and hear what is going on right now. This is how you will gather your intelligence for the book of time."

For a moment, Benaiah pondered what was happening, and then, trying to connect the bounty of wild running questions that needed answers, he asked, "How are you able to do all this—and from here?"

"Has Jahar not discussed with you our advanced technology?"

"No… Well, not in any detail. We did not get that far into the conversation because I was thrown to the ground out in the commons area by Jasaph."

"Again, your fault, Benaiah. No one else's." Then Horasha proudly smiled, saying, "The wealth our king sent here to be hidden safely from the world virtually has no end in the human mind. We have the world's largest safety deposit box." He chuckled at himself at the thought of the analogy. "Your Fort Knox in America is but a bedroom closet compared to the mansion here where his treasures rests.

"With that financial backing over three thousand years you can imagen the power we hold. Anything at any time from anyone can and will be ours." Horasha began to swell not only with pride but with sharp whispers of greed.

Strongly curling an arm up and making a tight fist, he added, "With the continuous pinpoint accuracy of reconnaissance like that of an eagle's eye…"—he looked around, admiring the cities on the screens in front of them—"the guardians from the beginning up to now, along with the ones serving them, gathered the world's knowledge and ideas at their infant stages of development. Then we…" He hesitated as he swayed his head back and forth with a devious smile, knowing truly what they were doing. "Borrow it from them and rocketed forward staying years ahead continuously out of reach of the rest of the world. We also throw in confusion and delete records of what and whom we have taken—I mean borrowed the information from delaying them toward progress."

Benaiah smiled. "I am an eyewitness to that. You are experts in confusing people."

Horasha understood that he was poking fun but ignored the comment. Eyeing him excitedly, almost in an envious manner, he put his hand on Benaiah's shoulder as he was leaning forward on the desk with both hands. "All this, Benaiah, is being handed down to you. You are not only in the wealthiest place on earth, you are also in the most advanced."

Benaiah stood up straight, forcing Horasha's hand to fall to the side. He frowned and said to himself, "Yeah, right." Then using his same joking tone, he said, "Is that why we road in here on elephants?"

Quick to respond, and putting him in his place, he answered, "Elephants and their tracks are hard to follow and easy to lose. Planes, helicopters, and anything running with fuel and electrical equipment can be seen and tracked from any satellite and computer-detecting equipment on the ground. This is one of the many reasons why Journey's End is not on anyone's map from the outside world. Camouflage is one of our greatest weapons."

Instantly, the camouflage the guards were wearing came to mind which had impressed him. "That makes sense but still…" A yawn snuck out of him from being tired from a long day. "It's hard to believe you're farther advanced than anyone else and yet no one knows about this place."

Then he was reminded, thinking back to the commons area, of his last moment with Jahar, and he asked, "What was that thing Jahar got on and you came in on in the garden? They looked like… like flying saucer things?"

"They are not outer space flying saucers but similar. I'll get to those later. I want to show you this while I have it up." He looked back to the screens, pushing a transparent button while saying, "Let us see what the world calls 'the most powerful man on earth' is doing right now."

Instantly, the oval office from within the White House of the United States came on a ten-foot wide screen directly in front of the desk about twenty feet away. The perfect distance to be able to see the full fifteen-foot high screens all the way around the room.

"Nice picture, but it looks like no one's home, Horasha."

"That is not a picture. It is true time." Just then, a woman walked into the room, setting a folder of papers on the president's desk, and then she walked out.

"The president is not in here." Swiping his finger across the hologram control panel, all the screens around the room lit up with other places in the White House. They took a minute, twisting around and peering at the multiple rooms on the screens.

"He is not home. Let us go to other geographical areas the president frequents." Moving his hands again back and forth in the air of lights, different locations came on all the screens. Quickly finding what he was looking for, he said, "Found him. He is at his favorite golf course." Horasha pushed a transparent button, and the one screen in front of them suddenly surrounded them with a panoramic view on all the screens of the front parking lot and clubhouse.

"How do you know?"

"The course is empty except for the six black SUVs in the parking lot and it is..."—he searched for the time and then said—"zero nine fifteen hours there right now. That means it is getting late here."

He looked to Benaiah, who was wide-eyed and trying to absorb everything. He commented, "No wonder you are yawning. You have to be tired." Looking back to the live footage, he said, "That time in the morning, the course should be packed."

"That doesn't prove we see the president."

Horasha gave out a big sigh, attempting to be patient. Moving his hand to other parts of the illuminated images floating above the desk, two light levers appeared in front of him resembling a remote control of a video game. Looking back up to the screens, he began moving the levers, and the broad picture of the front of the golf course began to move.

"Everything you see on these screens come to us by miniature cameras that are very small drones the size of a ladybug and actually are designed like them."

"We're in the Congo—in the middle of Africa, right?"

"Yes."

Benaiah gave him a frown, saying, "You're expecting me to believe all this? There is no way you have cameras like that every place in the world that you can control from here. I'm not stupid."

"Careful, Benaiah, I told you we have the most advanced technology in the world and why. We are, and will always be, decades ahead of what you see or are aware of. Millions of these tiny insect-looking cameras are in every little hidden spot in the world.

"Of course, none of these are here in and around Journey's End." Horasha looked forward at the screen and added, "They have their own self-energizing system by using simple atmospheric pressure. Each one is programmed to work in specific places until it expires, and then they simply disintegrate."

"Why don't they work around this place?"

Horasha slowly moved his eyes back to him, thinking, *Is he really this stupid or just hardheaded?* Then words fell out. "Are you serious?"

Benaiah gently smacked the side of his head with his open hand and responded sarcastically, "Oh, I forgot. For security and confidentiality reasons."

Horasha shook his head, still bewildered as Benaiah continued, "Give me some slack here. I just found out about this place today or yesterday, whenever it is now." He yawned again, saying, "You've known about this your whole life."

"You are aware of it now! Stop being naïve. You are running out of time because Jahar's is—or already has—passed away. You must come full circle with what Journey's End is about, so you may lead with your heart as well as your mind. If you do not..." He shut his mouth and then acted as if he didn't saying anything and then looked back to the screen, moving the miniature drone around the course until he finally found a group of people.

"There he is." He directed the fly-sized drone around the green the people were at until it was hovering over a golf cart, setting it down on the roof and looking in the direction of the men putting.

"They can't see this thing?" Benaiah asked.

"Only if they are looking for small insects. It's almost invisible because of its size, and it doesn't make a sound. Let me zoom in."

They watched the president of the United States miss his putt. "He is not very good," Horasha commented.

"Can we hear what they're saying?" Benaiah asked as Horasha looked down at the controls, moving his hand as though he was turning up the volume. They came into the middle of the conversation as the president said, "Three putting again. I can't believe it!"

"I can. When are you going to take lessons, Mr. President? I'm sure Tiger Woods would be happy to give them to you next time he's in town."

"Watch it, Senator." The president gave a friendly smile. "At my age—"

"Excuse me, Mr. President." A stout-looking gentleman dressed in a black suit and dark sunglasses, almost looking like Horasha, but clean shaven when they first met, approached him on the green, holding out a cell phone while smiling. "It is a phone call from your granddaughter."

Grasping the phone from the secret serviceman, he said, "Sorry, gentleman. This is very important business."

Horasha chimed in, "Now I can show you our true abilities." He pushed more floating buttons on the science-fiction-like keyboard hovering above the desk until a new scene came into view on the screen next to the president. A young girl sitting in the back seat of a car had a phone to her ear and the conversation was heard.

"Hi, Papa."

"Hello, baby girl. How are you today?"

"It was really good until Mom got me out of school to go to the doctor's."

"What are you going there for?"

The girl put on a sad face. "I have to get a checkup and a shot. I'm really scared. Can you do something about this?"

"Like what?"

"Tell mom and the doctor that you overrule everyone and don't let the doctor hurt me."

A laugh came out of him as he covered the phone to whisper to the guys around him. "She wants me to strong-arm her mom and the doctor." The guys chuckled at the innocence.

"Sweetheart, your mom loves you very much, and the doctor has my orders to take very good care of you. We all have to have shots once in the while."

"But they hurt."

"I know, but it will be over sooner than you think, so don't worry about it."

"Will you give me money for taking the shot?"

Another laugh came out as he told the guys, "Now she's trying to blackmail me into giving her welfare."

"She's going to make a fine politician one of these days, Mr. President," one of the other men whispered to him.

He smiled at the comment and then told her, "I'll pay you what I paid you last time as long as you save some and give some to someone that needs help."

"Okay, Papa. I love you."

"Love you too, baby girl. Call me when it's all over, okay?"

She replied, "Okay," and then hung up.

Back in the cavern of the book of time Horasha asked, "So what do you think about our technology now?"

"Impressive." Standing tall, Benaiah folded his arms, giving him a favorable grin.

"Jahar has watched over you your whole life through these screens in this room. I was his hands and feet because he could never leave Journey's End."

Benaiah looked at him stunned, dropping his arms.

"Jahar has not told you?" Horasha could tell this sudden information was fresh news. On the other hand, he knew this would be the last thing Jahar would have told Benaiah. He decided to go over this subject now because Benaiah needed to have this knowledge.

Swiveling the chair to directly face Benaiah, Horasha said, "Once you become guardian, the mountain inside and out is your permanent residence. No more world traveling, no visiting outside relatives. No more visiting dig sites for new fossils and old cities, and on and on. He only left Journey's End once, and that was to meet your new step-parents after they adopted you. I know you know the story."

Benaiah moved his eyes around, thinking out loud and dumbfounded that Jahar had been a prisoner in this place for who knows how many years. Then he said, "Maybe he mentioned something about not being able to leave this place? He's told me so many confusing and unbelievable things, I just might not have heard him. But with that bomb of information, I can understand once again why these people you call my real bloodline parents left Jahar and this place. Who wants to be trapped here for the rest of their lives?"

Watching Benaiah's body language as he listened, Horasha said, "I will give you that. And I do apologize if we have been overbearing with information. But there is so much to cover and to do before you relieve Jahar, if he is still alive. Because if he is not, you are now the guardian of Journey's End, and we need to get the signature ring on your finger as soon as possible."

Benaiah took a slight step back, inhaling any extra boldness he could find and replied, shaking his head, "I'm not taking over for Jahar!"

Chapter 6

Horasha predicted this would be Benaiah's reaction, being his life shadow. Like Jahar, he knew, throughout Benaiah's long college years, that he had taken the poisonous bait from arrogant rogue professors following Satan's lies and deceptions, teaching self-absorbed free will living to do whatever one wants, questioning and defying powers of authority and the natural moral laws of order and responsibilities.

Hearing Benaiah's matter of fact rejection to take over for Jahar confirmed he had swallowed the poison and ignorantly walked through the deadly doors that many young innocent minds and souls are drawn to. He had been living with no Godly boundaries, where responsibility, respect, honor, and strong moral values are viewed as signs of weakness and worthless quicksand. Only to find out later in life that it ultimately leads to a dead-end, unfulfilled life struggling to reach a false illusion that there is a greater climax of happiness and self-fulfillment that they can create themselves.

Horasha reflected on the multiple times he told Jahar they needed to take him away from that world and retrain his mind and soul in preparation for his purposeful and mandatory destiny. But Jahar continuously rejected his recommendations, reminding him, "Mighty men of King David in their younger years, were men in trouble, in debt, and discontented, which included their mind, body, and spirit. It is not until the young with innocent hearts experience purposeless, non-relational achievements do they find themselves in a worthless life. This is when they finally grasp and tightly value the refuge of family, obedience, and responsibility to a higher power. When Benaiah experiences this transformation, his dedication to Journey's End will have a firmer starting platform of a mighty man we need now."

Horasha shook his head to himself, remembering the day when he got the deadly news of Jahar's illness and thinking to himself, *Now what? Jahar's reasoning is void for Benaiah. He has not been able to fully engage his futile worldly endeavors to transform in the way envisioned for a successful heart transformation to be the next guardian. Rebellious he will be in our hands as his unsatisfied mind and disobedient heart topples three thousand years of confident and responsible leadership.*

Taking a deep breath and calming all his thoughts and emotions from Benaiah's statement on not taking over for Jahar, he replied with psychological warfare, "Benaiah, I am not going to argue about this right now or attempt to convince you to change your mind. I was wrong on voicing my thoughts that Jahar might now be dead. It is he who needs to hear from you directly that you will not take over for him as guardian, just like your parents did.

"If he is gone, then you will have to tell the descendants in Journey's End the bloodline of Jahar has ended for being the guardians and present the ring to the next ranking bloodline family to take on the honor and responsibility, following the commands of our king."

Benaiah was a little shocked, even disappointed, with Horasha reaction and asked, "Why are you suddenly not upset?"

"Why should I be?" Shrugging it off like it didn't bother him, he swiveled the chair to its normal direction on the desk knowing he got to him.

Benaiah walked around to the front of the desk to look Horasha in the eyes and then pointed to the door of the room. "Are you kidding me? You just killed Jahar's bodyguard because of me. You said your life's work has been protecting me to be the next guardian." Benaiah stopped talking and then looked down confused. The more he spat out words, the stranger this situation was getting. Then he asked himself, *What is Horasha doing?*

Staring down in thought, some engraved words caught his eye that were artistically written across the front of the desk. It took him a few moments for it to completely compute, but when it finally did, he jumped back away from the desk a couple steps wide eyed and stated loudly, "You have got to be kidding me?"

"I am not kidding. Calm down?" Horasha responded.

"No, no…" Benaiah waved a hand at him. "Not that. This here!" Excitedly, he moved his hand down, pointing to the carved words.

"What are you talking about?"

"I'm not sure what language it's written in, probably Spanish, but I'm pretty sure that says Christopher Columbus?"

"Oh that. I thought it was something important," Horasha said, sitting back in the chair as if it was no big deal.

"Is this really Christopher Columbus's desk?"

"Yes, it is, directly from the Santa Maria. Preserved in the same way as everything else here."

Benaiah was overwhelmed thinking of its adventurous travels and all the extraordinary decisions made behind the desk.

Horasha added, "If you want to hear the whole story of what and where Christopher and this desk ventured, plotting his travels and documenting the details of the voyages, I can get the book of time out and read for you..."—he hesitated, mentally jabbing at Benaiah—"because you cannot read Hebrew."

Suddenly, the historical career doctor had a reminding surge of interest, altering his attitude about Journey's End as his thoughts went back to the tunnel from the medical faciality and all the artifacts he saw there. Then words Jahar said came to him when they were at Alexander the Great's body armor. *All these items in the walls are only faint paint strokes hidden within the huge portrait I need to inform you of before you start your lifetime work here at Journey's End.*

As Benaiah stared down at the words in the front of the desk, Horasha said, "We need to figure out how to get us out of here safely."

Not listening, another thought came to him as the five-hundred-plus-year-old desk spurred questions within the elusive yet stimulating historical information Jahar gave him, and he asked, "Tell me about Journey's Beginning?"

Coming out of nowhere, Horasha responded, "Journey's Beginning? What are you talking about?"

"Jahar started talking about Journey's Beginning?" Benaiah felt a sudden urge to take this seriously and sensed there was more to the story that Jahar started to tell him earlier about the underlining truth of this place when he was whispering something about Journey's Beginning, but his own sarcastic attitude about this fantasy storybook situation had gotten in the way again.

His imagination ran, seeing a huge amount of gold somewhere inside the mountain that belonged to King Solomon, and then he thought to himself, *Why permanently hide it and keep it a secret? Why not use it for good or, for that matter, for Solomon's descendants?* Then World War II came to mind when the Jews were being slaughtered by the Nazis. Shaking the dreadful thought, he looked at Horasha for an answer to his question about Journey's Beginning.

Horasha, stumped, asked curiously, "I do not understand the question about Journey's Beginning? Do you want to know how all this started?"

Benaiah responded as though he knew the secret and it was all right to talk about. "You know, Journey's Beginning, what Journey's End is protecting."

"Protecting? Where did this come from?" Horasha asked, narrowing his eyes with interest.

Instantly, a red flag shot up, seeing Jahar in his mind telling him again, *Trust only God, Jahar, and himself.* He thought, *Why wouldn't he know what Jahar stated was the most important thing about this place?*

Then he quickly came up with a reply, playing dumb and beginning to understand that Jahar might have started to tell him true hidden secrets for his ears only. "Oh, I don't know. Since this place is called Journey's End, there must be a Journey's Beginning, right?" He shrugged his shoulders, tilting his head.

Horasha bit into his response. "You know the beginning of this place. I told you about Shuriah, and Jahar told you about the Queen of Sheba helping our king hide all his treasure from our people and the world."

Benaiah quickly thought to himself, *How does he know Jahar talked about the Queen of Sheba to me? He wasn't around, and we were quietly talking. Jahar was accurate when he said there are eyes and ears everywhere.* Then he decided to go along with the change of conversation, "Yeah, you're right." He shrugged off his question. "So...you mentioned something about getting out of here?"

"Yes, we have a big problem with Jasaph being dead." Horasha tilted his head toward the entrance of the book of time.

Benaiah looked over the desk past Horasha at the body lying on the ground, expecting him to get up any moment, not completely convinced he was dead. He wasn't sure if he didn't believe or didn't want to believe it since this whole adventure seemed to be a dream.

"He was Jahar's number one guard and deeply admired by all guards."

"But what about you, Horasha? I thought you would have more power than him?"

"In age and ranking, yes, but in loyalty, no. I would come back a couple times a year for…what you would call a vacation and did so for your twenty-seven years of your age. Being absent, one becomes out of sight, out of mind per se, losing influence over the years."

"You vacationed here?" Benaiah asked, surprised.

With pride, he answered, "This is my home. Everything about this place is mystical. The outside world is complicated, full of filth, chaos, and selfishness."

"No, it's not! This is the complicated place."

Horasha stood, pushing the chair back with the back of his legs. "Young man, you have not a clue of the real world. When you live in the midst of it, you become it. Just look at you and your attitude."

Benaiah stood his ground, feeling a bit comfortable because the desk was between them, and replied, "At least I know what's going on out there and who my enemies are and who I can trust. Here, I don't have a clue what all this is about, and basically…I don't trust anyone. Isn't that what Jahar and even you told me?"

Pausing for a moment, Horasha stared at the person he had protected for half his own life and then looked down at the holographic control panel, swiping his hand over several lights and then dotted the air to turn the video cave back into the library. As soon as the control panel disappeared, the screens simultaneously shut off and began twisting around. Benaiah looked around as the bookshelves showed themselves again, stopping where he first saw them when they entered the room.

As the bookshelves locked together, Benaiah looked back to Horasha. A shock jolted him back as a lightning bolt of fear went through him. "What the heck?" he said, catching his breath and putting his hands up backing away. "What...what are you doing?"

Horasha had pulled a long shiny knife out of a sheath hidden within his pants around his waist and was non-intentionally pointing it in his direction. His intentions for getting the knife out were completely different from what Benaiah's reaction was, but a thought crossed Horasha's mind upon seeing him in this state of mind, and he decided to play it out and said, "I figured the only explanation why Jasaph is dead is that you killed him attempting to run away because you do not want to be here like your parents. Then you would go out and tell the world all about Journey's End. I had to stop you, defending myself at the same time, which forced me to kill you."

"What? You're crazy!" Benaiah began to panic, looking for another way out besides getting around this powerful trained killer.

With a crafty smirk and slowly shaking his head, Horasha said, "We cannot let you go back to San Francisco or anywhere else outside of this most special of all places. Journey's End will not allow it. You, an outsider, leave with the little knowledge you have of it? Not on your life!

"You should have figured this out by now. I can tell Jahar never mentioned that piece of the deal yet, has he?"

Wide eyed and watching the knife while listening, he only shook his head. Benaiah was freaking out, understanding he had been set up by the fictious story Horasha came up with and tried to defend himself. "I'm innocent. I didn't do anything, Horasha." Quickly, he got emotional, not knowing what to do, and started caving in, knowing he would lose trying to fight this beast of a man as he whimpered his words, "Come on, we're...we're almost like brothers having spent so much time with each other."

Horasha slowly made his way around the desk, dragging he tip of the knife on top of it and said, "Nice idea, but you never knew I existed."

"Please stop, Horasha. Don't do this." Attempting to think of a way to stay alive, he stepped farther back, and then it popped into his head. Excitedly changing his demeanor and putting his hands up, he said, "Wait! We can cover up Jasaph being dead another way. I'll never tell anyone you killed him!"

With his hands up and putting on a giddy expression while taking a cautious step forward, he explained, "If you and Jahar are right about everything you told to me about being the next guardian, I can make you a rich man, right? Wait, what am I saying?" He got more energized as his eyes widened at the smart idea. "I will make you a powerful man! I'll get you the signature ring!"

Horasha stopped stone cold. His hand slowly dropped down, letting go of the knife as it clanked freely onto the wooden desk. His facial expression drooped as a deep sadness within permeated out, filling the space between the men.

Benaiah suddenly realized his words and reaction was completely wrong and Horasha was only joking. He saw in the older man's eyes the few words out of his mouth had sucked the life out of him. Under the slightest pressure or conflict, Benaiah caved in, bringing the horrors Horasha feared would happen.

For the first time, Benaiah saw himself in a completely different light—a selfish, weak coward. He saw the images of those words coming out of Horasha's eyes.

He was right, Benaiah thought to himself. *I'm not worthy to be the next guardian. The first thing I did under pressure and threat was throw away what is considered to be the most precious, almost holy of all things in Journey's End.* Even though he was still clueless of what this place was, he definitely understood this one detail. The signature ring from King Solomon was not to be used in the manner that he just did—as a pathetic bargaining chip.

"Horasha, I'm sorry. I...I thought you were going to really kill me," Benaiah pitifully stated.

"You...you did not even try...to fight...you just gave up. I have spent my life protecting you, killing many of our enemies, even our own descendants, for you. As many of us have died keeping you alive. Even my friend, Jasaph..."—he looked over to his lifeless body in the hallway—"so you my wear the ring to continue your reigning bloodline to be our next master."

Horasha leaned on the desk with both hands, looking down and trying to rid himself of his nightmare becoming reality. Shaking his head hard to reorganize his thinking, he slammed both hands on the desk. "Jasaph was right! We should have taken you in the other tunnel to beat and torture the crap out of you, boy!" Rage exploded from him as splatters of saliva showered the area. "So we could make room for a man, if there is one in you. To show up, ready to prove himself with dignity, honor, and boldness. One that will have the courage to be a mighty warrior! Never backing down from any battle and choosing his steps wisely for victory!"

His body swelled, clenching his fists and inhaling as he stepped up to Benaiah without stopping or saying a word, slammed a fist hard into Benaiah's stomach. Benaiah doubled over, as the air was knocked out of him, and he gasped for air.

Horasha continued, "You are not even close to being worthy to step into our home. When your parents left, it not only broke Jahar's heart but took most of the life out of him. He thought all was lost for his bloodline until you were born. I will not allow his heart to be ripped apart once more if he is still alive. More time, money, and lives have been spent keeping you alive to take over for him. But look at you." Benaiah raised his head, giving Horasha a target for his fist to come around, smashing into Benaiah's jaw and twisting his whole body around, dropping him to his knees. With his head drooped down, blood began to drop from his mouth.

"Stand up!" Horasha screamed. "Come on, Dr. Benjamin Maschel, stand up!"

He paused, strutting around his prey. "That is correct. Your name is truly Benjamin. You have not earned your birth name. You are named after one of the greatest warriors King David ever had, able to kill three hundred enemy soldiers in one battle by himself. But look at you. You are pathetic!"

Horasha lifted his foot up to Benaiah's shoulder, kicking him hard backward onto his back.

Benaiah landed, bouncing is head against the floor. Dazed, he struggled to sit up and then fell back, pulling his hands up to his head as it started pounding in pain. He groaned out, "I'm sorry, Horasha. Stop, please."

He rolled to his side in a fetal position. Horasha stepped up to him as though he was going to kick him and then noticed blood not only coming out of Benaiah's mouth but from the side of his head as well. It was slowly streaming out, saturating his hair and hands.

Bending down, he noticed it was coming out from where the staples were, and he stated roughly, "Now look at what you did! You made me rip your skin around the staples and reopen the wound. You're bleeding all over Jahar's expensive rug!" He pushed on Benaiah's hand that was where his head hit the ground, telling him to put hard pressure directly on it. Turning around, he walked to the emergency closet that was in every cavern. They were filled with all types of first-aid items, food and water, weapons, extra high-tech camouflage clothes, boots, and other survival gear. Being deep inside the mountain with all the tunnels blocked by electronic security doors, they were prepared for; power outages, cave-ins, earthquakes, and bomb explosions.

Ruffling through the boxes of medical supplies, he pulled out several thick gauze squares four inches wide by four inches high and several feet of two-inch wide self-sticking wrap. Then he grabbed antiseptic cleaning wipes and a small bottle of a skin glue.

Sitting Benaiah up, Horasha knelt down, moving Benaiah's hand out of the way. He told him this was going to hurt and that he would give him some pain pills when he was finished. Horasha thought it would be good for him to suffer some more so he could attempt to redeem himself by taking the pain. Wiping the small gash clean, he quickly poured a thin line of skin glue into it and then squeezed his scalp, closing the wound around the staples. Waiting a few moments, the glue held firm, and then he placed the square gauze over it as he wound the wrap tight around his head several times.

Having calmed down, Horasha thought through the countless conversations he'd had with Jahar about Benaiah. Jahar was convinced his great nephew would come full circle in his mind and heart to qualify to be the next guardian. Moreover, he had heard from God multiple times that Benaiah was going through powerful training to perform at a level and in a manner like no other guardian that had reigned before.

As though starting over, Horasha said peacefully, "Like I said earlier before all this. We need to get out of here safely with a good story." Benaiah, on the other hand, wasn't as calm and ready to go as he cringed in pain, rolling his eyes around. The blows his stomach and face received from Horasha's steel fist and being slammed to the ground hitting his head were taking their effects to a physically untrained warrior.

Horasha took a hold of his chin, saying, "Look at me, Benaiah! Do not think about passing out on me, boy!"

"I'm not going to pass out. Leave me alone," Benaiah stated embarrassed as he aggressively jerked his chin away from Horasha's hand.

"I have not left you alone for twenty-seven years, and I will not start now. Besides, we are in this together. Twenty-seven years ago, I dedicated my life to you and will faithfully serve out my loyalty first to Journey's End and then to you and your bloodline. But with the plan I have, we do need to separate for a little while so that Jasaph's family and loyal security comrades will not accuse me of murdering him and, at the same time, keep you out of their hands until the ring is on your finger, taking over for Jahar.

Benaiah replied, holding both hands to his pounding headache, "You did murder him."

"Protecting you is not murder. Murder is what I see he was planning as he was setting you up."

"What are we going to do then?"

"First, you need to beat me up around the face and then knock me out."

Benaiah released his hands from his head, raising it to look at Horasha to see if he was joking, and then he replied, "Say what?"

"I need you to punch me several times in the face and then with the butt of Jasaph's knife like this..." He stood, picking up his heavy knife from the desk. "Hit me in the back of the head, knocking me out."

"You are a crazy man! Why would I do that? Or for that matter, how can I? I'm a boy, remember?" His sarcasm returned, sensing at this moment he was back to being in Horasha's best interest.

Horasha blew off the remark and explained, "It needs to look like there was a fight, with Jasaph beating me to the point I could not save you. Then he started hitting you, but you had grabbed my knife that fell off me during our scuffle and you stabbed him to defend yourself."

Horasha handed the knife to Benaiah and then walked out of the book of time over to Jasaph, lifting his body up as his feet dangled to the floor. "Come over here and stab him."

Benaiah was perplexed and horrified at the same time. "I'm not...stabbing him!"

"You have to. This is a good start in following your bloodline and being a mighty warrior." He encouraged Benaiah as he looked behind himself at the portrait of Shuriah so he would understand where he was going with this.

"Stabbing a dead man?"

"It is not about stabbing a dead man. It is about finding or fighting away through any diversity protecting your lineage. But ultimately here, right now, it is protecting Journey's End, which is your duty. Now, stand up and impale him through the throat!" he ordered loudly, grasping the heavy body tightly.

Benaiah wobbly stood, gritting his teeth at the throbbing pains of his head and mouth and gravitating to the logic Horasha was telling him. He replied, "Why the neck?"

"It will explain or even hide the broken neck."

Benaiah looked down at the knife and then up at the dead man's face. "I can't do this?"

"You have to. Now, come on and do it!"

Benaiah thought he was going to suddenly throw up, swallowing and choking out several times.

With a disgusted reaction, Horasha said, "Could you, for once, be a man instead of a weak, ignorant, and pathetic Dr. Benjamin Maschel."

The words struck a nerve, one he didn't know was buried untouched, deep within his soul. A fire was ignited as he lifted his head up, tired of the degrading accusations, then he whipped away the blood and saliva from around his mouth that had been dripping after Horasha hit him.

"I am a man! I'm respectful, honorable, and a responsible person contrary to what you think or believe, Horasha!"

Believing he was building courage for Benaiah, he blurted out, "Then show me! No... Prove it to everyone and yourself that you are worthy to be the next guardian. Demonstrate to everyone you are not just a worthless, worldly, educated, feeble person who is dead in life but a man that has the legendary courage and strength flowing through his veins, able to take on the most important position on earth and proudly wear the signature ring of King Solomon!"

Benaiah recovered as the reverse psychology gave him momentum. Pulling his shoulders back and stepping in very close, he slowly raised the knife, pointing the razor sharp blade upward near Jasaph's neck. The angle and position he had it could easily go straight up Horasha's throat as well as the limp body he was holding—they were only inches part.

Tilting his head to the side, he suddenly eyed Horasha in a wicked manner. Blood still slowly oozed from his mouth and the side of his neck where Horasha didn't wipe clean. Forming his lips together, he spit blood out close to Horasha's foot as if he was in a duel in a western movie said, "You want me to stab him..." Nudging his chin toward the body then to Horasha, "why not you first?"

Horasha just realized the tables were turned while not showing a reaction as Benaiah added, "My story is..." Pausing to think through what came to mind, he said, "I had to kill both of you because Jahar, my blood relative, told me I can't trust anyone. I was scared not knowing what to do when you two were fighting, but my bloodline..."—he toyed with the last word, wobbling his head—"instincts told me that, at all cost, I had to protect Journey's End."

There was a pause between them, and then Horasha calmly said, "Benaiah, you need to point the knife at..."

"Stop! I'm talking now! I'm tired of all this…this madness. All of you think you know everything—that you're going to control me, but you're not!"

Benaiah took a deep breath, flexing his chest out as his eyes widened, piercing Horasha's. Horasha understood Benaiah had made a decision and gained the courage he needed. Not sure who was going to get stabbed, he mumbled something in Hebrew and then closed his eyes in a peaceful manner.

Swiftly, Benaiah thrusted the knife to the handle as he felt hair raising resistance and crackling vibrations going through the knife handle as the blade slithered piercing the windpipe and spin. He stood back motionless after doing the most gruesome thing he had ever done, unable to believe he actually did what he just did.

Benaiah looked at Horasha, who had held his ground, and asked himself, *Why would he let me kill him? He must be telling the truth—that he's completely devoted to me, and Journey's End.*

"Either kill me or put the knife in his throat," Horasha said with his eyes still closed. "Jasaph was a big man, and he's getting heavy."

Benaiah asked out loud, "Why would you let me stab you?"

Horasha opened his eyes at the question, and seeing Benaiah had stepped back and didn't have the knife in his hands anymore, he understood the job was done and answered, "If that was what it took for you to believe me, then sacrificing my life would have been worth it for you to be the next guardian, bringing complete fulfillment of my lifelong duty."

Laying the body down, Horasha saw the knife through the front of his throat and commented, "That is the closest you came to killing anything except for when your grandfather Paul took you camping."

Benaiah froze, thinking back in time, and then asked, "You… you know about that too?"

Horasha recalled the event. "You were ten, if I am correct."

"Where were we?" Benaiah was still stumped at how much these people know about him.

"You and your grandfather were camping near the Redwoods in northern California. He taught you how to shoot his old twenty-two bolt-action rifle."

Benaiah was mentally surrendering deeper to Horasha the farther this conversation went, and then he asked the final question. "What did I shoot?"

"Are you asking about the first thing you shot or the first and only thing you have killed?"

"I don't know. You tell me?"

"Grandfather Paul told you never to shoot anything you are not going to eat. So you two shot pinecones and pop cans. But during the second day out, he let you go by yourself a little ways from camp. A gray squirrel ran across a downed log in front of you and then stopped to chew on something in its paws. You looked back to make sure your grandfather was not following, and then you shot the squirrel. You were devastated for a week upon seeing the innocent dead animal and knowing you killed something. But what hurt you the most was disobeying your grandfather. You have held on to that ever since. I saw it in your eyes at his funeral four years ago."

"So it is true what you say, Horasha. You have been with me my whole life."

Horasha nodded and said, "Thanks for stabbing Jasaph instead of me."

Benaiah smirked, pulling himself back into this adventurous fantasy of Journey's End. "Me too, but you completely gave it away, changing my mind when you prayed."

"How do you know I was praying? You do not understand Hebrew?"

"I understand that when a person knows they're going to die, they revert to their basic primal instinct of belief or faith for help and comfort."

Horasha thought about the wise words Benaiah said and then asked him, "So what are you going to revert to as the truth? Your science book that teaches evolution or the Bible that teaches love and life?"

Benaiah inhaled deeply, ignoring the irritating challenge, and asked, "Now what? Jasaph has a knife in his throat?" Then the events completely mentally digested as he began to panic, bending over and putting his hands on his knees. "I just put a knife in a man's neck... I just did that. How could I?" He started to gag, trying not to throw up.

Horasha stepped up to Benaiah, patting him on the back, and then he bent down, retrieving Jasaph's big knife and walked back into the book of time, saying, "You will have to get used to it. It is a normal thing, at least for us, the ones that will be protecting you."

Turning around when inside the library said, "All right, I am ready to take the beating from you. Then you need to hit me hard in the back of the head knocking me out as I said before."

Benaiah wiped his mouth again from the drips of blood still slowly oozing as he slowly walked into the book of time and asked, "Then what do I do?"

Horasha set the knife down on the desk and turned to the couch, aggressively tipping it over backward and pushing it to the side as the book resting on it flew to the floor. "The real story goes..." He looked to Benaiah, giving him a stare of admiration for the story he came up with. "The fight went back and forth, moving the couch over and exposing this."

He bent down, grasping a hidden handle in the rug and pulling up a trap door, dropping it backward, and exposed a small tunnel. "After you killed Jasaph, you were afraid to go back to the main door, not knowing what to expect. So you decided to escape through what looked like a hidden emergency tunnel, which it is."

Benaiah knelt, peering down the dark hole as his head was now pounding with a headache as he was getting anxious to get this over with. He pressed Horasha, "And...?"

"And when I wake up, I will go out the main door telling everyone what happened, distracting them. I will be sent to the medical facility, where they will find out I have a slight concussion confirming I was unconscious and that my story is true."

"Won't Jasaph's guys or family do something to you?"

"No, my family is out there as well, and we have procedures in play, as with any society, to deal with any situations as this."

"You said your family?"

Horasha paused, knowing he brought up something confusing with its own details. "Yes, my family. My bloodline."

"Your bloodline?" Benaiah asked, surprised, seeing there was a broader and deeper picture of the history of Journey's End.

"Including Jasaph's, ninety mighty warriors came here at the beginning from Jerusalem to start Journey's End with Shuriah, starting all the bloodlines. Remember me stating earlier that his bloodline is the next chosen one to take over the guardian reign?"

Benaiah hesitated thinking and then nodded.

"Well, Shuriah, who was at the time the general of the Israelite army, structured the order of the bloodlines by the ranking of his officers that he chose to join him in this epic adventure King Solomon created. Now, only forty-two of the original bloodlines are still alive after three thousand years."

Benaiah started to drift into deep thought about this new revelation and then shook it off, adding it to all the other rabbit trials needing clarification. Then he asked, "What am I supposed to do in the tunnel?"

"This emergency tunnel mazes down and around for a while and then eventually comes out on the side of the mountain near the base of the waterfall. Have you seen it yet?"

"No, but I heard it. Jahar said the water comes out of the mountain that flows through the commons area forming the cascading water."

"That is correct."

"When I get outside, then what?"

"You do nothing. Stay put. They will find you, but do everything you can not to get eaten by leopards or bitten by snakes, scorpions or spiders."

"Who's they?"

"The ones that were here before Shuriah. The ones that showed the Queen of Sheba this wonderful hiding place."

"Africans?"

"Not just Africans, but the small people."

"Small people...?" Benaiah thought for a moment and then asked, "Pygmies?"

"Yes, that is what you call them. We call them..." He hesitated, looking for a word in English. "Hmm... invisibles."

"Invisibles? You mean ghosts?"

"Close enough. You will understand, when you think you see them and then you do not."

"You're not talking about the Africans I've seen working with you since the elephants?"

"No, they are the same color but are a different people that live in harmony only with the Africans around Journey's End."

Benaiah, suddenly enthusiastic about the taste of something in his field of study, said, "I definitely want to meet them. Research shows the pygmies of central Africa are the first *Homo sapiens* to have evolved. Evolution's Adam and Eve…" Benaiah gave out a quick laugh of confidence and then asked, "Aren't they almost extinct?"

Horasha rolled his eyes unamused and answered, "No, they are very much alive. Who do you think taught us thousands of years ago how to camouflage so well? Later, in years when technology came around, we invented the state-of-the-art camouflage attire based on their disappearing abilities into the forest vegetation."

"I saw that! The guard's camo is amazing at how it adjusts colors."

"Not just colors but with 3D effects as well, matching the immediate surroundings, but they only work when they are worn and in contact with body heat. When they are off, they are gray like the backup ones in the closet where I got the first-aid items for you. Oh, almost forgot…"

Horasha went to the closet-like storage unit imbedded in the rock wall between two of the large bookshelves as Benaiah watched him get out a flashlight, asking him, "Do you have anything in there for my busting headache?"

"Of course there is." Horasha retrieved a couple of pills and a bottle of water.

As Benaiah swallowed the pain reliever, Horasha looked close and around Benaiah's wrapped head, making sure the bleeding had completely stopped. As Benaiah set the bottle of water down where Horasha put the flashlight on the desk next to the knife, Horasha stated, "We need to get down to business. Everyone will start getting suspicious if we stay in here too long. Now hit me!"

Chapter 7

Both the men were surprised when Benaiah didn't hesitate. Reaching back, he slugged Horasha straight in the nose.

Simultaneously, they flinched back in pain. Horasha shook his head as blood began to flow down into his full black mustache, saying, "Hit me again, but in the mouth and the sides of my face."

Benaiah stood back, holding his hand in pain. "I didn't realize hitting someone was so painful."

Horasha shook his head, drooping it down in disappointment. "I forgot, you never hit anyone or was in a fight."

"Yes, I was!"

"Fighting means both sides are engaging in combat. When those three teenagers attacked you after school when you were a freshman, I thought for sure that would ignite the inner warrior in you, but… we both know the whole story."

"They were three older guys from school. What was I supposed to do?"

"More than just let them hit you and steal the ten dollars out of your wallet."

Remembering the incident more and more, Benaiah started to get angry. "If you were there why didn't you stop them? You were my bodyguard right?"

Horasha paused, bracing himself for Benaiah's reaction and hoping this would ignite him. "Yes, but when I paid them ten dollars each to beat you up…?" He shrugged his shoulders with a grin.

He saw it coming, closing his eyes as Benaiah exploded. "You paid them!" Then he smacked his fist to the side of Horasha's face, sending him stumbling backward. Like a wild animal, Benaiah jumped at him, sending them both to the ground, with Benaiah sitting on top of Horasha's chest as he lashed out with both fists, hitting him repeatedly, yelling out, "I had nightmares about that all through high school!"

After taking many punches, Horasha began to get dazed, lifting his hands to stop the beating and trying to speak between hits. "Stop…That's enough…Benaiah, stop!"

Finally, he had to do a judo move, lifting his legs up and placing his feet over Benaiah's head and pulling him backward, pining him to the ground as he rolled forward with his weight on Benaiah.

Both panted as they eyed each other with blood smeared all over their faces. "Benaiah… The nightmares…" Pausing to show sincere concern. "I saw them in you. So from then on, I understood that was not the right approach. No one ever touched you again, did they?"

Benaiah, still fuming, moved his head to the side, attempting to ignore him, and replied, "No."

Horasha stood back and said, "I am sorry for you and me…" He turned around, taking his shirt off.

Benaiah looked up at Horasha's back, slowly getting up and questioning, "What are those?"

Turning back around and putting his shirt back on, he solemnly answered, "Lashes, for every time I did something to or for you that Jahar did not approve of. In the tunnel next to this one that Jasaph wanted to take you in is where discipline for Journey's End is done."

Just like Jekyll and Hyde, Benaiah did a one-eighty upon seeing the barbaric remnants of being severely whipped across his back as thin long lines of healed lumped skin crisscrossed his body.

Benaiah didn't know what to say; he was stunned.

"Jahar was right again. It was the wrong approach. When I say we live in two different worlds, I mean it."

Benaiah dropped his head almost in shame, thinking to himself he was the cause of this man's extreme agony and permanent scaring.

"Do not go there. We cannot afford this emotional roller coaster right now. These are not your fault, but my…"—He pointed both hands to his chest—"discipline and honor marks."

"Honor marks. What in the heck are you talking about? What is honorable about beating someone?" He was deeply disturbed as a different picture was being painted in his mind of the old, wise, and innocent Jahar."

"Like I said, we live in completely different worlds. It will take time here for you to understand, which we do not have at the moment." He walked to the desk, picking up the hefty knife. "You need to hit me right here." He pointed to a specific spot on the back of his head where he knew he would easily become unconscious without major damage.

Benaiah reluctantly took the knife as it felt exactly as the one he thrusted into Jasaph's neck. He wasn't up to the task anymore after seeing the torture Horasha had already endured, and then adding on the unexpected pounding he just gave him, he said, "I don't think I can do this."

"Do not start down that road. Just hit me hard, to get it over with." He turned around, kneeling to face a flat surface on the lush rug to land.

There was silence for a moment as Horasha knew he was hesitating. Then something else came to mind. "You remember Stacy, your girlfriend in high school, and Melissa in college?"

Benaiah wrinkled his face with a big question mark. This topic was completely unexpected. "Yes?"

"You were getting too close with them, and we could not afford you to get distracted by females, so..." Horasha closed his eyes, clinching his teeth with anticipation of the pain coming. "I made them go away."

With the sudden shock at the thought, Benaiah screamed out, "You did what? I...I loved Melissa. We were engaged to be married! How could you! You...you where the one that ruined my life with her? I have been blaming myself for the last couple of years!" Horasha opened the perfect storm of Benaiah's greatest heartache. Without hesitating, Benaiah stepped forward, raised the butt of the knife, and slammed it down perfectly on the spot Horasha pointed out.

Reaching back to repeat, he stopped as Horasha's body went limp, flopping to the ground unconscious.

Staring down at the man who came between him and the love of his life, anger raged within him, thinking of his own painful emotional scars that were permanently embedded in his heart. Then he wondered how many other major things they did to interfere, shaping his life to fit the way he and Jahar wanted him to go. Then he mumbled under his breath, "You snake. All of you here are slithering untrustworthy people... You had no right! I see clearly again why my parents left this place."

He took a moment to think through what he was going to do and then, looking around the room at all of the books of time lining the shelves and then back to the two bodies lying on the floor, said aloud, "I'm going to make some changes of my own as your plans are going to back fire. Since you believe you guided me to be an archeologist—a job that is all about exposing history—that's exactly what I'm going to do. I'm going to find this treasure of King Solomon's that you said is here. Then I'm going to let the world know all about this place and everything in it!"

He walked over to the closet, finding camouflage uniforms and boots. Taking his clothes off and putting the high-tech military attire on, he added one of the compact backpacks filled with emergency items and strapped on tightly to his chest one of the futuristic weapons, looking exactly like a guard.

Looking down at his waist, he noticed the gray suit began to change colors as the 3D definition was coming alive and starting to warm up from his body heat. He said with a devious smile, "Nice!"

Standing next to the emergency tunnel entrance on the floor, he reached over to the desk, taking the flashlight. Turning it on, he shined the beam down the wide hole and saw a rock staircase going down at an angle about twenty feet or so, ending at what looked like another level tunnel floor. But this one was much smaller than the ones he'd been in.

Taking a deep breath, he boldly stepped down, working the flashlight and wiping away old spiderwebs, focusing on every spot and remembering Horasha's warnings about being bitten by snakes, scorpions, and spiders. After the last step, Benaiah hunched down on the floor almost to his knees and brightened up the short and narrow tunnel ahead of him. The six-foot tall man joked to himself, attempting to evade that he was a bit scared, and said, "Those pygmies had to have made this tunnel."

As soon as he said that, the stream of light down the tunnel appeared to waver and move like heat vapors rising off a hot surface, and he commented, "What the…"

He quickly jerked the flashlight around the claustrophobic underground hole, trying to see what he assumed was movement. Then he rapidly blinked his eyes, making sure they weren't obstructed with cobwebs or dust walking down into the cool dingy place.

With his vision okay he shook it off as being exhausted and still recovering from Horasha's punches. Resting down on one knee, he twisted around, looking back up the rock steps and seeing a part of the chandelier hanging from the ceiling of the book of time. Second thoughts whisked through him to retreat, and then he firmly dismissed it, determined to carry out his own plans to expose this place.

Looking back down the tunnel, he instantly thought, *The light from the flashlight had slightly changed. The batteries must be dying already.* Then, inquisitively, he looked harder and thought, *No… The walls down the tunnel look different. They seemed to have changed.* He squinted to readjust his focus and then slowly put his hand out in front of him for balance as he started leaning forward to walk through the low ceiling tunnel.

Before his arm got fully extended, his hand unexpectedly touched something firm and warm. A spine-shrieking sensation shot through him with ice tingling fear from not knowing what was happening.

The answer explosively came to him. Shuddering, Benaiah backed up against the rock stairs as a pair of eyes sprang wide opened. A naturally camouflaged pygmy had opened his bright white eyes, reflecting the light from the flashlight and exposing his ghostly presence less than an arm's length away from Benaiah's face.

Benaiah's heart pounded, breathing heavily and feeling trapped in the small dungeon. He kept the flashlight up for defense but also to attempted to refocus at the mystical appearance of someone suddenly appearing out of nowhere.

He moved his eyes up and down as the image of a fully grown barefoot man standing fully erect with his head only inches from the top of the low ceiling came into clear view.

Tilting the flashlight back up, he looked toward the eyes, but they had vanished. Benaiah blinked rapidly as they suddenly disappeared in one breath, and he looked around, trying to focus for anything he was just looking at.

A soft sound came to his ears as though someone clicked their tongue in front of him. Instantly, another set of eyes were illuminated by the flashlight a couple feet back from the first original pair. Benaiah flinched his head back at the surprise and said out loud in a frightened tone, "Who are you? What do you want?"

Distinct movement was seen from the second man raising his arms. Benaiah squinted, telescoping his head forward to get closer at what now was pointing at him. He got his answer when he heard a quick blowing sound from the pygmiy's mouth, instantly feeling a stinging sensation hit his neck.

Reaching up and feeling a small object sticking into his skin, the mystery suddenly became real as he said, "You've got to be kidding me... A poisonous dart."

Within seconds, it took effect. Falling forward to unconsciousness, the last thing he saw were several pairs of bare feet moving up to him and feeling many hands grasping his body so he didn't hit the ground.

***

Jahar had been lying motionless on the bed in the patient room with his eyes closed and hands interlocked, resting on his chest for approximately thirty minutes. The doctor walked back into the room accompanied with the African woman of Mariah's age who had been working alongside her and serving Jahar and Benaiah at the tent since midday.

She had stayed behind by Mariah's orders in the commons area, gathering information as she kept an eye on for what was going on after they left with Jahar. She gasped upon seeing Jahar lying on the bed, appearing to be dead. Glancing over with sad eyes to Mariah standing next to him, she smiled, shaking her head and telling her silently, "He is not dead."

A sigh of relief came across her face and then changed, nodding her head to tell Mariah she needed to urgently talk. Mariah reached out, touching Jahar's arm and gently tapping it with a finger several times. She was giving him a silent message if he was awake and then took a step back and bowed. She walked out of the room, passing everyone, including four of Jahar's guards watching every move at the patient room entrance in the medical facility.

The African woman followed her as the doctor watched on, wrinkling his forehead and wondering what they were doing and then walked over to Jahar.

A short distance away from everyone, the women stopped as Mariah whispered, "Where are they?"

"Horasha took him to the book of time."

Concerned, Mariah asked quickly, "Why there? Is my step-brother Jasaph with them?"

"Yes, he is the only one Horasha let in with them."

She peered behind her into the room, watching the doctor, and she quietly spoke, "This is not good, Tahla. Horasha is up to something." She looked back to her. "We need to get more of our people in there."

"We cannot. Horasha's people are at the tunnel door as well as Jasaph's family. And remember, the security door controller is of Horasha's bloodline. He has the authority not to unlock it for anyone."

Mariah thought for a moment and said, "He has to for Jahar. Come with me." She turned as they walked back into the room.

Stopping behind the doctor, Mariah asked, "How long until our master can leave?"

The doctor compassionately said, "Mariah, he is on his final hours. Today drained him too much."

She looked at Jahar with grave concern and then noticed their silent and secret call for her that no one else knew. He slowly moved his right pinky finger up and down and then did the same with his left pinky. She thought to herself, *He is pretending to be asleep.* Needing to respond so he would know she got his signal, Mariah casually stepped around the doctor to the end of his bed and casually placed her hand on his toes that were covered by a thin blanket. Pretending to be saddened about his condition, she gently stroked his feet and then tapped her finger several times.

She was thinking of how she was going to get Jahar to the commons area so he could give orders to have the tunnel door raised to go into the book of time, and then she remembered something. Staying in character, she said, "Doctor, our master has mentioned many times the commons area is where he wants to pass away while smelling the sweet aromas, hearing the birds and stream as he watches the sun's rays shine across the cavern. We need to take him there to rest, not here."

"I agree. Jahar has spoken of that, but here, I can carefully watch him to administrate medical help when he needs. I assure you he will never be in pain again as he slowly passes to be with the Lord of heaven's armies."

Still watching Jahar's hands, she focused on the large signature ring and then turned to the doctor as they locked eyes as if playing mental chess, anticipating the next one's move. At that moment, as though perfectly planned, a nurse walked in with a shiny metal tray in her hands with a full syringe laying in the middle of it. She stopped next to Journey's Ends lead physician, saying, "Here you are, Doctor."

Making the first move, the doctor confidently said, "This is a normal medical procedure. He needs this mild sedative for his body and mind to stay calm, making this honorable process of passing easier on everyone." The doctor adorned a grieving expression.

Calmingly reaching for the syringe, he continued, "Everyone here loves Jahar and wants the best for him." He lowered his head, peering over his glasses, "That includes me, Mariah, one of his oldest and dearest friends."

Eyes still locked, she was uneasy with his response. It gave her a bad feeling even though she was playing him for what she thought was best. Then she boldly said without thinking it through, "Then you would have no problem proving your words by injecting that into your nurse's arm."

Silence momentarily froze the communication within the room from Mariah's conversation, sending unexpected chills through everyone that heard her. All the guards—two at the back of the room and the two at the entrance—made slight movements to position themselves to be at the ready.

Shattering the sudden ice-cold atmosphere by raising his voice so everyone in the medical facility could hear him, he stepped up to her face. "How dare you accuse me of such a thing! I am a doctor! I have dedicated my life to helping others!"

Not flinching at his response, Mariah felt she had the right to mentally put him up against the wall and stated, "If not her, then me. Prove me wrong!" The guards frowned, looking at her as Tahla softly bumped her side, saying under her breath, "No, Mariah."

The doctor was disgusted. "I will not! There is nothing to prove. My proof is decades of service faithfully caring for Jahar and everyone else including you. Besides, why suddenly are you…"—pointing at her—"in charge of what I do and what happens with Jahar?"

He did have a valid point, but she held her ground. "Jasaph told me not leave Jahar's side when they took Benaiah away."

"That does not answer my question, Mariah. What are you trying to do here?" His eyes left her, scanning everyone in the room to join in with his investigation.

Quick to move her mental chess piece, she replied, "Only fulfilling our master's request. Unlike you, telling everyone here that you will not grant Jahar his dying wish to pass away in the commons area. Your motive is a selfish one. You know how Jahar feels about actions like this and what the consequences can be." The guards, nurse, and Tahla physically wanted to move away from the doctor as Mariah had him now rationally chained to the wall.

The doctor was motionless on the outside but enraged on the inside. A female positioning him the way she did, making a blatant wrongful accusation, especially in his domain. She had him in check, so he decided to play her useless game, holding up the syringe. "Fine, you want this injected into you? Nurse, prep her arm."

A loud inhale was expressed from Tahla, and then she stepped in front of Mariah. The only African person in the medical facility wearing her native attire stated, "No! Me."

Doctor Mitanual looked at her, "I do not care who it is."

Mariah, grateful for her courage, whispered in Tahla's ear, "I will be all right."

She whispered back, "I must, even if it is only sleeping medicine…" She shook her head. "You cannot be drugged to sleep. You have to stay aware of all this going on with Jahar and the ring."

She had a point. Mariah didn't think about that, and then she looked into her eyes, grasping her friend's shoulders, "Okay, Tahla. You may do this for me."

Without hesitating, Tahla walked to the back of the room next to the camouflaged guards watching on and sat down next to where they were standing. She looked up to the doctor across the room, raising her arm up, ready for the shot.

The doctor turned to the nurse, giving instructions as she quickly left and came back with a hospital bed on wheels and preparation items. The nurse said, "You will need to lay on this. You will not be able to stay up in a chair as your body will be too relaxed."

Tahla got onto the bed as the nurse prepped her arm. It was very awkward for the nurse, with everyone intensely staring at her and causing her mind to begin playing games and second guessing herself with what was going to happen. Peering over to the doctor when she was ready, he responded confidently, nodding for her to continue.

As the needle went into her arm, Tahla looked down her body at Mariah from the stretcher, slightly scared, but she managed to smile, knowing she was doing her duty. Mariah smiled back to her servant and childhood friend, expressing gratitude for what she was doing for her.

It wasn't long until Tahla was asleep. It seemed everyone was holding their breath and anticipating the worst. Nothing out of the ordinary happened as slow confident exhales were heard, signaling that everything was fine. Then questionable inhales swelled, with thoughts running through everyone's mind on why Mariah had insulted the doctor, insinuating that he could possibly be killing

Jahar, especially when he was already passing away slowly anyway. She was feeling the tension build as eyes from a lynch mob started to peer her direction.

"Doctor?" the nurse apprehensively exclaimed, instantly dissolving aggression between everyone.

All eyes went to Tahla lying lifeless as the nurse checked her pulse and then bent over to listen to her chest. "She is not breathing!"

Stumped, the doctor quickly went to her side, putting his stethoscope on and listening at different areas of her chest. Not hearing anything, he ordered, "Start compressions and move her to the next room to the analyzing scanner. It will ascertain exactly what is wrong with her."

The nurse jumped on the bed, starting CPR as everyone looked on in shock. The doctor saw no other movement from his orders and then yelled out, pointing to the two guards sitting down, "Move her now!" Not being their normal job, they were waiting for other medical workers to respond.

Each went to an end of the rolling bed, quickly guiding it out and into the room next door as everyone else got out of the way and then funneled into the large center room to watch on. Other medical workers swarmed into the scanning room as they positioned Tahla's bed directly under the scanner, attaching different monitoring wires on her body. Once finished prepping, the lead nurse quickly pushed a button on the wall, and a glass cover the shape of the bed dropped down, encapsulating Tahla and her bed on all sides, locking them together and making a tight seal. A metal bar began to move from head to toe and then back on the roof of the glass cover, illuminating a red line crossing Tahla's body.

The main nurse spoke up, "We started the scan, Doctor!" Not hearing a response, she peered around at all the people staring at her and then questioned out loud upon not seeing him, "Doctor?"

Mariah, the guards, and medical staff peered around at each other, looking for him just as the door of Jahar's room slammed shut and locked. Mariah yelled out, "No! He is going to kill Jahar!" The guard closest to the door worked the locked door handle. Not able to open it, he stepped back and started kicking it to no avail.

Another guard stepped in, telling everyone to look away while raising his weapon and began shooting around the handle. After about six shots, he stepped back, and the first guard easily kicked the door in, forcefully stepping in.

The guards swarmed in and then stood motionless, walling everyone else out. They began talking as they moved their heads in all directions as though looking for someone, and then they went silent.

"Is he dead?" Mariah cried out, not hearing anything.

One guard looked back to her, nodding for her to come in. She slowly walked in with her head down and seeing the worst in her mind. Two guards parted, letting her by as she looked up toward Jahar. Her hands went to her face, covering her mouth, and then she said with complete surprise upon seeing an empty bed, "Where is he? Where did they go?"

She looked around the room, but both the doctor and Jahar were not there. She quickly stepped back into the main working area, yelling out to all the medical workers, "Where is the emergency exit tunnel?"

They all pointed to the opposite side of the facility from where she was as she responded, "That is what I thought!" Walking back into the room, the guards had already been searching for a mysterious exit door. Journey's End was littered with them everywhere, dug out over the centuries and surprisingly appearing up here and there. They weren't coming up with anything until they couldn't move a tall linen cabinet next to the bed that was flush to the wall.

One guard searched around inside the cabinet for something out of place and then noticed an extra support bracket slightly slanted under an upper shelf as though it was missing a screw. He straitened it back up and heard a click as though it locked itself. Having a feeling this could be the key to the mystery, he twisted it back as far as it would go, feeling a disengaging jar in the cabinet. He stepped back with everyone watching on and then reached to the side, pulling the cabinet toward him. The whole piece of furniture easily opened as though it was on hinges, exposing the hidden dark tunnel behind it.

Without hesitating, Mariah ordered, pointing, "Save Jahar!"

The guards were already filing in and turning on miniature flashlights attached to their weapons strapped tight up against their chests. When the last guard went in, Mariah grabbed his backpack, holding on and telling him, "You will be my eyes."

They quickly shuffled along, only getting about fifty yards when the first guard stopped, aiming his weapon at something ahead. Giving a signal to the other guards, they immediately got into a protective position. Creeping his way forward, it was very quiet and musty in the confined place. As everyone watched on, he stopped to light up the area looking at the details. Satisfied, he slowly bent down to the ground. Reaching out with the tip of his gun, he poked at the object. Going to a knee, he held the weapon up so the flashlight would brighten up the tunnel further ahead. Not seeing anything, he looked back down, leaning over to get a better look.

Turning to his comrades, he quietly spoke in sign language, asking Mariah to come forward. She didn't hesitate, but halfway to him, she got a glimpse of what he was kneeling at with his flashlight pointed at it. Appearing to be a lifeless body, she went to the ground on her knees as her heart began to pound.

Before she fully released the emotional pain, the guard looked back at her and whispered, motioning with his hand, "No, no, Mariah. Come here."

She slowly got up, easing her way next to him and opening his shoulder to let her have the full view.

Reluctantly, she scanned the body lying on its side and facing away from them and was instantly thrilled with joy, saying softly, "It is not Jahar!"

As soon as the other guards crept to her side, the lead guard went down the tunnel, closely looking at the rocky dirt floor for evidence of what happened to their master.

One of the guards reached out, rolling the body on his back and closely examining the doctor for signs of what caused this. Mariah spoke up in almost a disappointed tone as she touched his wrist, seeing his chest slightly moving up and down. "He is alive."

The lead guard quickly came back, squatting on the other side of the doctor and eyeing everyone with answers. "Jahar went down the tunnel. Invisibles have taken him. Four pairs of smaller bare footprints continue from here."

Mariah looked back down at the doctor, thinking to herself, *Why would they do this and take Jahar?* Examining closer, she was the only one that noticed a tiny red dot had beaded up at the side of his neck from a tranquilizing blow dart. Immediately answering her question, she thought to herself, *They are watching closely over him. Thank you, little ones.* It gave her peace of mind.

The lead guard, not noticing what she saw, said, "We need to go. If Jahar is still alive, he needs us. If he is not, we need to retrieve the ring for the new guardian."

All the guards murmured in agreement, and then Mariah said, "Go find Jahar. I must go back. I have something else I must do."

Confused at her sudden change of direction, he said, "No, you will come with us. It is not safe, Mariah." The lead guard stated.

She gave him a grateful grin for his concern, saying, "Daniel, I will be okay. But I have to check on Tahla."

"You cannot trust anyone. Something is very different here, Mariah, since Horasha has returned."

The other guards blurted out in unison brief words to agree with him. Mariah, nodding her head, said, "I know, I feel it too. The atmosphere had changed, building toxic tension and paranoia more than normal. But no matter, we need to split up to have more eyes and ears. Now go, Daniel, hurry. Jahar needs you."

He looked around to the other guards, giving them a nod and then turned, continuing down the tunnel. Taking a few steps away, he stopped, turning back to Mariah. "You stay alert and put on a cloaking suit with all the equipment to arm yourself."

She smiled, "Do not worry. Remember, I have more extensive training than anyone with the Israeli Defense Force as I still serve undercover with them continually. I will be fine." Then she was the one to turn away, going where they came from without looking back.

She came out of the tunnel to an empty room. Having a hollow feeling about it, Mariah cautiously tiptoed to the entrance around the debris from the door being shot up and kicked in.

Slowly peering around the damaged door frame into the central open working area of the medical facility, the hollow feeling was suddenly filled with echoes of eerie silence. Nothing was moving. She looked at the details of quiet motion, wondering why all the people had disappeared.

Suddenly, a soft muffled sound came from the analyzing scanner room next door. She slithered out, hugging the wall while staying concealed the best she could, and then she carefully inched her head around, looking in the room. Starting at her feet, Mariah saw Tahla was still lying on the bed, but the scanner cover was lifted back up to the ceiling. Moving her eyes and making her way to Tahla's head, Mariah saw movement. A hand was slowly stroking Tahla's forehead as the muffled sound became clear. She heard a woman softly humming an African grieving song. Recognizing the song, Mariah's heart sank, confirming her servant—her lifelong friend—was dead.

Growing up as little girls, Tahla was trained by her people to take care of and watch over Mariah. Mariah never took advantage of her position, as with many of the descendants from Israel. They appreciated and owed the African people for their help and dedication in keeping Journey's End invisible to the world.

Flashes of cherished moments went through her mind as sorrow bled from her heart. She knew the time for grieving needed to wait as she inhaled deeply, swallowing down all her emotions and clearing her mind for what was urgent and at hand. From the dart mark on the doctor's neck, Jahar was with the invisibles. It gave her comfort but wondered why they were there and they did what they did. Then her thoughts went to Benaiah. She couldn't help but think of the five past days with him and how different and innocent he was. She tried to imagine him taking Jahar's place, squinting her eyes for that vision to appear. But she could not see him or anyone else, for that matter, wearing the honored signature ring. Mariah had never known another guardian. She had only heard stories and seen their portraits down the hallway to the book of time.

Breaking her moment of reflection, she felt a hand on her shoulder. Shocked, Mariah jerked to reality as the nurse walked out of the room upon seeing Mariah with her eyes closed as though emotionally distraught.

The nurse spoke up. "Mariah, I am sorry. I could not save Tahla."

Changing her demeanor to regain emotional control and superiority, she roughly spewed out many questions at once. "Why would anyone want to kill Jahar? Who did this? Where is everyone?"

"Mariah, calm down." The nurse moved her hand down from Mariah's shoulder, taking up her hands. "No one wanted to kill Jahar. I ran the body scanner, and it came back that Tahla had a negative reaction to the shot. There was no poison in it that could have purposely killed her. The sleeping medication somehow slowed down all her organs to the point that her heart and lungs just stopped. It was a complete accident."

"How am I to believe you? You are only covering for the doctor or...even yourself, for that matter!" Mariah jerked her hands away, positioning her body defensively.

Holding her ground peacefully, the nurse responded, "I have told you the truth." Hesitating, questions were now coming to her. "For years, you have seen the medical facility take care of Jahar. Then when he got sick, you were always there when we gave him shots and administered many procedures and medications. How could you begin imagining there would be something in that one syringe now? If I did not know better, we should be looking at you to blame for this, putting the doctor in the position you did." The older lead nurse put her hands on her hips, reversing the table on Mariah.

"Accusing me is preposterous and you know it!" Then she asked herself the same question, and all she could come up with is telling the nurse, "I had a feeling."

"A feeling?" The nurse said in an unbelieving tone, tilting her head. "Tahla died because of you having a feeling?"

Ignoring the accusation, she said, "Yes, a feeling. Everything has been strange the past couple of days."

The nurse dropped her arms to her side, letting her guard down as she agreed, nodding. "I understand that one. I feel it too. It feels... heavy. Dark. I do not know how to completely explain it."

Mariah pondered what she said and replied, "Accurate words, but I will add one more—evil."

Straightening her shoulders, the medical worker raised her head tall, taking a deep breath and peering around at the empty facility. "Yes, that is it—evil. It makes sense. The dark one has come here with a vengeance, and his timing with his demons is perfect."

"What do you mean?"

"With Jahar soon to pass away, it alarms every one of the unknown, because he is one of the last wise men of old. The younger generations are different people. Each generation progresses and changes from the last, but the changes of the recent ones are extremely dramatic—far more than ever. Benaiah taking over as guardian, an unknown to most everyone, is not only alarming but frightening. He might be of Jahar's bloodline, but he is no Jahar! Creating confusion, distrust, and even selfish greed within everyone—all formulas of destruction. Journey's End is silently in peril, and the dangers are coming in strong from within, not from our normal outside enemies. Satan is a brilliant deceiver as he attempts to slither in chaos."

Absorbing the wise observation from the nurse, Mariah thought how Jahar would respond. Reflecting back over her years with him, he would always remind her that "we are only human, with the limited ability of twenty-twenty hindsight—that God is the only one able to know and understand the whole picture of life from yesterday to tomorrow, for he is the only one with twenty-twenty foresight and has the heart and ability to put together the fragmented and broken pieces of life together for the good if we faithfully move forward, letting go of our understanding in all situations, and believe the Creator of the all things wants and knows what is good for us to grow our relationship with him."

Mariah looked around the large center room of the medical facility and asked, "Where did everyone go?"

"After finding out that Jahar and the doctor were gone and telling them that Tahla passed away, they all became very concerned." Shaking her head, she corrected herself, "No, that is not the right word... Very scared is more accurate."

"Scared of what?"

"You, of course…Mariah."

Mariah frowned, "Me?"

The nurse raised a finger and pointed at her. "Yes, you."

"Why?"

"Everyone knows you are Jahar's favorite. You are like his grand-daughter. You two have spent more time together your whole life than anyone else. Then with Tahla being your close friend… Well, what else would you believe they would think your actions would be?"

"My actions? What have I ever done to anyone here besides be friendly and helpful?"

The nurse paused, putting a hand back up to her hip as she said cynically, "Mariah, stop being naïve! You are IDF—a highly trained killer. You have been involved with many deadly situations around the world for years, and not just normal combat. Extensive deep recon and assassinations with the Israeli military. You combine that with having one of the highest scores going through Journey's Ends security defense program while all the time being Jahar's righthand person. You are the deadliest descendant in Journey's End. Everyone knows that… So most everyone fears you."

Mariah never looked at herself from that lens, but as the nurse verbalized it, it made complete sense. She said, "It is true I have been with the Israeli Defense Force covertly for years and continually do intense missions with them but only to stay close to our people abroad and in the world's political realms even though they have no idea of my true identity. But still, that does not mean they all needed to hide."

The nurse shrugged her shoulders. "Like we concluded, darkness is here creating illusions and lying to anyone who will hear and believe him."

Slightly turning her body and facing the main tunnel entrance from across the room leading to the commons area, Mariah pondered through their conversation while envisioning what was going on throughout all of Journey's End. She thought, *The ultimate order from our king is to protect Journey's Beginning, which is here, deep in its permanent hiding place until God orders a guardian otherwise.* Pausing, she mumbled to herself, "I have to find the ring and Benaiah!"

Chapter 8

Mariah quickly went down the hallway to the commons area without an IGT. Once in the grand open cavern, she followed the walkway along the circular wall, passing several tunnel doors until she got to the entrance of the book of time. Eight guards were at attention, securing the door.

Approaching the first guard, her demeanor was straightforward. "I assume by you being here that Horasha, Jasaph, and the new one, Benaiah, are still inside?"

"Yes."

"Good. I need to get a message to them."

"No one is allowed inside. Horasha's orders."

"This pertains to Jahar. I must see them." She moved forward to step between two guards as though they would move out of her way, reaching for the thumb pad.

They didn't budge as she bounced off them firmly stating, "Step aside!"

She caught a glimpse of a guard at the end of the eight who was one of Jasaph's relatives and hers as he ever so slightly moved his head, squinting his eyes and telling her no. She understood he was mentally telling her this was a fight or confrontation that must not happen right now.

"We will not, Mariah. We have our orders," the guard said, holding his ground.

She paused, glaring at all of them equally so as not to give away the silent message she received, and calmly said, "I admire your dedication, but always be aware of the bigger picture that the Lord of heaven's army is painting for Journey's End. I leave you with this question. Will you have the same courage to wisely follow the path God lays down for us to follow when we cannot see the road? Or will you follow man, who feebly makes his own plans which always ends at a dead end or in destruction?"

The guards looked at her somewhat confused and not quite sure how to respond with the creative challenge that sounded as if it came from Master Jahar himself.

Stepping back, she twisted around, military-style, reminding them of her training and abilities, and then she marched her way across the garden to the personnel living quarters entrance.

Pressing her thumb on the identification pad, the solid door quickly raised. A short way down, the only naturally hollowed out tunnel, decoratively painted differently than the others, quickly ended up opening into the second largest natural cavern next to the commons area. It had the immediate appearance of being an outside, hustling and bustling small city.

Walkways crisscrossed like streets separated by walled and open-air buildings that varied in height up to four stories. Extraordinarily controlled lighting illuminated colors onto the round fully enclosed ceiling, mimicking the outdoor sky and making changes from day to night in normal time, giving it a 3D effect.

Even different weather patterns were projected as simulated sounds true to nature could be heard. This, psychologically, was effective for Journey's End personnel filling their senses to balance emotions and moods living inside the mountain.

Each of the miniature city buildings had its own purpose. One was a multi-level restaurant, with each level having a different ethnic food with matching décor. Another building was an extraordinary exercise facility with the building next to it being a complete spa for hair, nails, massages, and relaxation. Even a movie theater with two different screens showing different movies had its own structure.

The library and educational building were the largest buildings, where all the children and adults could achieve any level of knowledge they wanted. Finally, the busiest building, a large super store, had clothing, toiletries, tools, electronics, games, furniture, food, etc., providing daily essentials for the more than five thousand descendants calling Journey's End their home.

At one time, approximately two thousand personnel were at the hidden location in the Congo. Another thousand were out around the world on different continents being outside support. The remaining were at strategic locations echoing out from within Africa and beyond as security, keeping this most special of all places socially camouflaged from existing to the rest of the world.

Walking between the buildings, Mariah took the straightest route to her home as children played and the adults finished up their normal daily activities in the late evening while thinking through her next plans.

The housing for all of Journey's End descendant families were in this cavern except for the rotating guards on duty. The native people lived in their villages outside in the forest, and the guard's sleeping arrangements were down the armory tunnel. Jahar had a private location where his quarters was the most secure, beside the treasury, which was hidden secretly within the mountain somewhere.

The individual housing facilities were like condos, evenly wrapping around the whole outer circular wall going up four levels. Starting with the ground floor, there was a front door to each condo along the wall every twenty-five feet. Six sets of stairs and two elevators went up to each level, with an outside handrail walkway circling around to all the front doors on the three upper levels.

Mariah's home was on the ground level near the emergency escape tunnel at the far end. In all the tunnels leading away from the commons area, each had an emergency exit leading to the outside of the mountain. They were highly secured especially on the outside camouflaged to a point it was hard work to get to these tunnel exits, if one even knew of their existences.

Once in her home, she quickly grabbed her security duffle bag which was always at the ready and filled with her cloaking uniform, support equipment, emergency backpack, and weapon. She changed into everything in the duffle bag and then put on a bulky pair of workout clothes over it all, disguising her intentions. Being late in the evening, Mariah knew she wasn't going to get any sleep tonight, so she went into her kitchen to quickly down a meal.

As she ate, it was quiet and lonely…again. At twenty-seven, Mariah never had a significant other. She was a beautiful but lonely woman with heart's desires of being married and having children. Always following the footsteps God provided, she continually was lead to military training. At the same time, she played an opposite role when at Journey's End, being a friendly, gentle granddaughter-like companion supporting Jahar. But in the back of her mind, she always wanted to know God's true purpose and will for her life.

Jahar always knew what was on her mind and where she was in life as wonderful gentle words of wisdom continually flowed from him, comforting and encouraging her. "God's will for his children is to love him and love others. He knows our heart's desires because he created them within us. And when we persistently and selflessly pray what is in our hearts moving forward in faith, the Holy Spirit will bring peace, helping us to be patient as we live in high expectation of him for what lies ahead. This will always strengthen our relationship with him, filling our hearts with joy."

Finishing the quick meal, Mariah thought through her plans again. First, make a visual diversion of hide and seek when she leaves the condo just in case she's being watched. Second, escape through the caverns emergency door. When out of the living quarters and long emergency tunnel into the forest, confirm Jahar's location with the invisible ones. Next, find the outside entrance to the secret emergency exit tunnel into the book of time, which is on the other side of the mountain. Then do whatever she needed to do to get Benaiah away from Horasha.

Once she safely had the next guardian, take him to Jahar so Jahar could give them their next instructions to weave through the chaos that was infiltrating Journey's End and ultimately crown Benaiah, giving him complete authority before it was too late.

Casually walking out her front door, it appeared she was going to the workout facility. Going to the center of the underground city in the big cavern, she blended in with the few people coming and going, taking a detour into the large department store. Strolling around in the beverage department, she picked out a sports drink.

Being late at night, only one person was in front of her waiting in line to check out. Recognizing who it was, Mariah spoke up. "Hi, Tamera."

They had a brief conversation, and when it was her turn to check out, the counter person chimed in, "Mariah, I do not see you here this late very often. What is the occasion?"

Mariah answered, "I could not sleep, so I decided to get this and go work out." She pressed one hand on the personal account pad identifying her, bringing up the balance available to her, for her monthly withdraw.

The accounting pads track the quantity of items an individual withdraws from the store, regenerating a fresh balance monthly. No monetary exchange is used for transactions as Journey's End has no payroll or taxes. Everything is provided for all the descendants in equal quantity. As for the secluded African tribes deep within the Congo, their services are reimbursed with medical care, food, and the protection of their lifestyle and culture.

Journey's Ends financial resources are practically endless, so monetary gain is not a drive for success or conquering. Instead, honor in fulfillment of duty well done is taught and expected from birth. This rewarding force maintains the focus, not only by being obedient to the orders from their king three thousand years ago but to do it extraordinarily.

An idea came to her to help with the distraction from any eyes outside watching, and she quickly spoke to Tamera, who was stepping out the exit door. "Tamera, wait a second."

She turned back to Mariah, saying, "Okay."

The counter woman looked at her screen and then said, "You may leave with the drink. There is plenty on your account for this month."

While leaving, Mariah replied, "Have a good night, Camelia. Thank you for working late for us."

"You are welcome. See you soon."

Stepping out onto the mini street with Tamera, Mariah walked with her as they headed to a stairway going to her condo, which was in the exact direction Mariah needed to go to secretly exit the living quarters.

They had casual conversation along the way as Mariah unsuspiciously worked her eyes, making sure there was no one purposely watching them. Once at the stairs, Tamera said, "It was good to talk with you, Mariah, I will pray you can get some sleep. I know how stressful it has been with Master Jahar and his condition. You two are very close." She gave Mariah a smile and then walked up the stairs.

Watching her leave, Mariah was grateful for the words and then thought, *I have not even prayed for myself, Jahar, and Benaiah today.* She wanted to ask Tamera to pray for her and what was going on, but knew she could not.

As Tamera made it up two flights to her level where her home was, Mariah leaned up against the wide pillar holding up the second floor stairway. Hidden from eyes looking on from within and across the living quarters, Mariah paused, bowed her head, and prayed.

"Lord of heaven's armies, the God of creation, Father of all. Jesus, thank you for your blessings. Please lead me to Jahar and Benaiah. I pray Jahar is alive so he may put the ring on Benaiah's finger to be the next guardian, but only if that pleases you. May your will be done here as in heaven. Your people at Journey's End are under attack from the evil one more than ever. Please send Gabriel and Michael to battle for us, keeping the demons at bay during these times." She knelt on one knee. "I thank you in advance for I believe you answer prayers in ways to work for the good of our relationship with you. I ask in the name of the Savior of the world, Jesus Christ."

Keeping her head bowed, she opened her eyes, inhaling deeply and building courage for her next move. Carefully taking her loose-fitting workout clothes off, Mariah bundled them up tight and then slowly reached out, tucking it under the bottom step of the stairs.

Looking down at her cloaking uniform, she confirmed it was working as she slowly stood. Before peering around, Mariah reached back to the attached hood and then pulled the face cover down, securing it under her chin. Easy to see through, she looked around, pinpointing everyone moving from the ground up to the top fourth floor of the condos.

Pulling out of her pockets skintight gloves of the same material, Mariah put them on as she looked back down ground level a short ways from her, spotting the emergency exit. Because children freely ran around the living quarters, maintenance made an extended small glass atrium room two-door system. The first door was a safety glass door so the rock wall door inside the room leading into the tunnel couldn't accidentally be opened.

Mariah gradually made her way to the first door. As long as she didn't move too quickly, the camouflage uniform would keep the majority of herself invisible. Once at the door, she double checked around her, making sure she wasn't being watched, and then she slowly made her way through, closing the door behind her.

This second door was more difficult to get through since it was armed with an identifying thumb pad needing to be disarmed. Her heart rate slightly increased since this locking system would not only alarm the living quarters, but immediately go to Journey's End Control Center. They would send a full unit of twenty four guards to assess and neutralize the situation.

Carefully detaching the hand pad from the rock wall, wires were exposed and stretched out. Kneeling down eye level with the wires, she retrieved a miniature tool kit the size of a man's wallet from a side thigh pant pocket. Opening it, she took out a small screwdriver and wire cutters.

A tingling sensation went down her spine as she thought she felt slight air movement behind her. Pausing, Mariah slowly peered around through her masked face to see if someone had opened the first door behind her. Seeing it was closed, her eyes moved side to side, but there was nothing out of place. She shook it off as jitters, never imagining she would have to do this in her own home.

Looking back to the wires, she thought about her next move. As she reached up with tools in hand, she suddenly found herself choking as her body was powerfully jerked back. Someone was cloaked behind her and had their arm around her neck like a giant python. Much bigger and stronger, the attacker firmly held Mariah in place as she struggled, gasping for air and trying to fight the large arm.

A deep voice whispered in her ear, "Your bloodline is weak. We will not allow you to blend blood with Jahar's family through Benaiah. We foresee your plans, and if he does not prove himself worthy to be guardian, Jahar's bloodline stops with him, and my family will take over, not yours!"

The shocking words instantly exploded purpose that she must not be the one to die. Knowing she wasn't going to get anywhere by fighting muscle for muscle, she had to use leverage. Adjusting her feet equally flat to the floor, she fought to lean forward, squatting down and compressing like springs. With the mini screwdriver still in one hand, she stabbed the forearm around her neck inflicting excruciating pain causing an instant reflex to let go as Mariah exploded springing her legs upward flipping backward over the camouflaged man.

Successfully finishing the flip, her mind was in complete combat mode. Swiftly wrapping one arm around the man's tree trunk neck as an anchor, she then used the small screwdriver in her other hand to stab him at his lower back precisely in the kidney. The anticipated reaction from the pain aggressively arched his back, exposing his chest. Mariah then reached over his big shoulders and began rapidly stabbing the man's chest like a sewing machine, making Swiss cheese out of his heart and lungs.

Pain no longer mattered in the attacker's mind, but survival to live became his driving power. With brute strength, he was able to rid himself of his enemy by standing up and slamming his back against the closed inner door as hard as he could, smashing the lightweight female.

Mariah dropped to the ground with the wind knocked out of her as the person reached down and lifted her off her feet, throwing her against the side wall and hitting her head.

Slightly dazed, she looked up through distorted vision, and adding to the fact he was wearing a cloaked uniform from head to toe, she could barely make him out. But with bright red blood oozing from his chest onto the outer part of his clothes, she calculated where his head should be. When he bent down for her again, she powerfully snapped her leg upward, hitting her mark with her boot to his chin, whipping his head back and making him stumble backward. Still standing but wobbly and weaving back and forth, the big man choked out his last words. "You might have killed me...but my family will be the next guardians." Seconds later, he fell forward flat on his face inches from where Mariah sat.

As the dead body lay at her feet, she grasped the weapon strapped tight to her chest and pointed it outward, looking around to see if there was anyone else going to attack her. Breathing heavily, Mariah carefully looked in detail for any faint movement of anything out of place camouflaged within the small glass atrium. Then peering around the outside of the small room, she searched tediously for anyone else invisibly watching or sneaking in on her. The atmosphere inside the residential cavern was now night time. Artificial stars and a partial moon were lit up on the rounded ceiling as sounds of frogs, crickets, and other night creatures were heard.

She thought to herself, *He had to have been following me since I left the commons area.* Looking back at the man she killed, she noticed he didn't have the emergency backpack or weapon strapped to his chest, giving him perfect flexibility and invisibility. Staring out again, she was somewhat confident he was the only one stalking her. *But why?* she thought. *Obviously, he was not trying to stop me from going out the exit. He was on a mission to kill me.*

Reaching out to the man's head next to her, she pulled back the hooded mask and froze. Clenching her teeth, she inhaled, making a sound of dread, and then she dropped her head knowing that the man she killed could explode emotions with the already tense relationships within Journey's End.

It was Horasha's younger brother, Burak. He was ten years older than Mariah and always bullied her when she was young, not only because of their age or that she was a girl but mostly because they were from different family bloodlines. This was one of the greatest silent rivalries within the descendants that had been increasingly getting stronger by the centuries.

She raised her head, changing her attitude, and whispered to the dead man, "If I knew it was you, I would not have killed you so fast but made it more painful, Burak!" Then she kicked his arm out of her way while getting up.

She stood quietly in the small room of death as her heart calmed down. Sadness seeped in even though she despised him more than anyone else. He was still a member of her people, and his interest was to protect Journey's End. Then her thoughts went to Horasha, shaking her head. *He is not going to like this.* Taking a few more moments to collect herself and rethink what she was doing, she decided to continue with her plans. Searching Burak, he didn't have any communication device or his armlet on him along with the pack and weapon. She concluded, *You must not have talked to anyone else of my position and what my plans were, only taking it upon yourself to make the decisions along the way. Your last decision killed you. You knew better. I kicked your butt more than once during trainings.*

She shook off the interruption of her duty of saving Jahar and Benaiah, finishing what she needed to do to get by the identification pad. The door opened successfully, not setting off alarms. She then dragged Burak's body into the pitch black tunnel hiding it and then shut the solid door, pulling out a flashlight from her pack.

Quickly going down the long tunnel, she had to swipe away spiderwebs off and on that strung back and forth in front of her. Far down the tunnel, Mariah noticed the long stringy webs seemed to have disappeared. Looking closer, they had been broken as they draped straight down along the walls. She started making out fresh footprints on the rocky dirt floor. Stopping, she had the sensation of being watched and then thought, *But how? Who would know I am here? There are no cameras in the tunnels that I know of, and I did not pass anyone in this confined worm hole.*

The dark dirty underground hallway appeared to be closing in on her. It had been a long time since she felt claustrophobic and didn't want it to get to her. Working the flashlight back up the tunnel from where she had come, she looked for anything that made her feel this way.

Twisting back to look where she needed to go, a dark face from an invisible was staring up at her only inches away. Mariah's body jolted in shock as she simultaneously felt a sting on her neck. The surprise seemed to have zapped her strength, and after a few seconds, she realized she truly couldn't move a muscle and quickly fell asleep. Before it went black, her mind put the puzzle together, feeling hands holding onto her as she collapsed while saying, "This is what happened to the doctor…"

The next morning, Mariah found herself waking up to forest sounds of bugs, birds chirping, and monkeys in the distance screeching at one other. She blinked rapidly to focus on where she was, seeing a glow of light coming from the side piercing the darkness around her. Taking a moment, she realized she was lying flat on her back and looking up at the ceiling of a small forest hut. Many thin long tree limbs standing vertically were bent over and coming together at the center top, framing a circular dome hut. Large broad leaves were tied by their stems to the long rib-like limbs, with vines on the outside used as shading and waterproofing material. From the outside, it appeared to look like giant green scales of a snake protecting the inside.

There were no windows and only a small open entrance everyone had to duck down to get in or out the home. This is where the light was coming from as Mariah rolled her head in that direction.

A rare African language only spoken by a special people was heard repeating several times as Mariah was waking up. Mariah spoke the language along with all the descendants, so she was not alarmed at where she was at. Intimately knowing these people as close friends, she responded, speaking the language as she rolled her head toward the voice coming from the other direction. "I am feeling fine but weak. Why did your men dart me?"

"Honorable Mariah, we had to save you. Something is wrong in the forest."

"Save me from what?"

"The same thing we saved Jahar and the new man of your people from."

Mariah sat up quickly with the news and then regretted it as her head suddenly pounded with a headache. She reached for her forehead as the older pygmy woman softly said, "Drink this and move slowly for a while. You will feel better soon."

Mariah took the drink from the woman on seeing the familiar face and smiled as she reached out for the cup and drank. Looking around the hut, Mariah asked, "Uba, where are they?"

Uba was an elder female of the pygmy tribe with African dark skin. She squatted next to her while wearing the normal native clothing of her people, male and female alike. It was only a small animal hide wrapped around her waist. Their hairstyle was that of the other Africans of the Congo—very short and showing the curvature of their heads. Though being an elder and a person of honor in her tribe, she wore a white beaded necklace made from items in the forest and anklets made from brightly colored bird feathers.

When Uba smiled back, Mariah saw her ornamental sharpened teeth which her people prized in their women. Many tribes decorated their bodies in different ways that was appealing or showed ranking of honor for them such as tattoos or piercing of the face with items protruding out. Within this special hidden pygmy tribe, Mariah, as with most outside people, were bewildered in understanding this alteration the females do to themselves—sharpening the upper front teeth to fine points, appearing to be a predator's.

Uba answered, "They are in the man hut. Jahar is awake, but he is very weak. We did not dart him. The other man is still sleeping. He is weak, but in a different way." She pointed to her head, meaning his mind, and Mariah quickly giggled to herself at the observation.

She continued, "Is he good for Journey's End or bad? Our people saw him with Jahar outside yesterday, and he acted strangely. He was friendly and then would be mad at Master Jahar. This person talks too fast and cannot make up his mind on how to act as a man or a child. Concerned of his behavior, one of our guards put him down thinking he might hurt Jahar."

Mariah understood her confusion. Outsiders always talked faster and were quick to make decisions, changing their moods every moment as though they were indecisive or running out of time, which was strange to Congo's interior people, because their emotions flowed like the sun and moon, always moving at the same speed, hovering over trees, and never rushing to disappear or reappear.

"He is a blood relative of Jahar and supposed to be taking Jahar's place when he passes on to be with the Lord of heaven's armies."

The woman stopped smiling and put on a concerned look. "We have never seen this man. How can he be of Jahar's blood?"

"His parents left here before I"—Mariah pointed to herself—"was born. We are the same age." She thought for a second and then added, "Both he and I were born outside of Journey's End, and both our parents were killed away from here as well." Mariah never really thought deeply about it until now, thinking how ironic it was. Her parents were on a recon mission in Israel where they had her during their three-year mission and were killed by a bomb, and yet, she survived.

The old woman thought back and then asked, "Ranadi and Antia?"

Mariah nodded, giving Uba a surprised look that she remembered their names all these years.

Uba stated, "Jahar was very sad for a long time when they went away. It was one of the worst times in his life."

Mariah agreed. "That is what everyone has told me."

"But when you were brought home after your parents died, you made him happy again."

"No, he was not happy because of me but the new man, Benaiah. We were born close to the same time."

"Oh, Mariah, do not be fooled. He is always happy when you are with him."

"Maybe so, but when Benaiah was born, Jahar's dream was renewed, for there was another male in his bloodline to carry on to be the guardian."

A thought struck Uba, and smiling, she said, "I see what Jahar is doing. He brought this Benaiah here to make you happy because you have no man at your old age!"

Mariah blushed, saying, "I am not old, Uba."

"I had five children, the youngest being four years old by the time I was your age."

"You need to mate this man for life and have babies. Then you will be happy in here." She pointed to Mariah's heart. "You have been sad and alone too long as a grown woman only getting older."

"I have not, and I am not old," she stated defensively.

The old woman put on her wise expression, peering into Mariah's heart through her eyes, and said, "We watch everything and everyone in the Congo for your protection as you protect us. We know, Mariah… Our close friend is not a happy woman."

Mariah caved in, putting on a smile and appreciating the wisdom and mothering given to her. Uba stood, and Mariah gave her a hug. She was no taller than Mariah was, sitting upright. The average height of a pygmy women was four-and-a-half feet compared to a grown pygmy man just under five feet. Separating, Uba stated, "Let us go to the men."

Coming out of the small round hut, Mariah had to lean way over not to hit her head. She took a moment, once outside, to stretch and inhale deeply as the drink took effect and cleared her head. Looking around, there were a dozen huts hidden in the forest, with several fires going as many pygmies stared at her presence. Even the children stopped their playing to look at Mariah. Then a signal came from Uba, and all at once, they came running, surrounding Mariah with cheers, smiles, and hugs around her knees. She was a good friend of the pygmy people just as she was with the other African tribes, but the pygmy's moved around often, staying to themselves elusively away from others. Even though they were the eyes and ears of the rain forest, no one ever knew of their presence. The other Africans called them chameleons with two legs.

Uba and Mariah walked to the man hut as Uba called out to someone inside. A response was heard, and then Uba told Mariah to go in as she stayed outside. Bending way down, Mariah hesitated, peering in and letting her eyes adjust to the darkness. Once everything came into view, she went straight to Jahar who was lying quietly with his head propped up and eyes closed, asleep. She quickly knelt next to him, taking one of his hands on his chest, and then she leaned over, touching her forehead to his, whispering, "I am here, Master."

Jahar woke up, slowly opening his eyes, and then he smiled upon seeing his favorite person as he weakly squeezed her hand.

In respect of the pygmies showing they had nothing to hide or keep from them, Jahar mandated the descendants always speak the pygmies' language when they were in their homes. Mariah said, "I thought I lost you. I am so sorry I did not protect you from the doctor."

Slowly and in a quiet tone, he replied, "You protected me, Mariah. I heard everything. How is Tahla?"

Mary dropped her head, wanting to cry out and drape herself over him to pour out her aching heart, but she held back, looking up and trying not to cry, with her chin wrinkling up, "She is gone."

Jahar let go of her hand and opened his arms for her to dive into him for comfort. She didn't hesitate, gently resting on him and softly crying as if she was his own child.

Two pygmy men inside the hut and Jahar grieved with her, closing their eyes as Benaiah lay next to him asleep. Overhearing the conversation while sitting outside next to the entrance, women sorrowfully started singing on the outside to support Mariah in her time of pain.

After exhausting the built-up anguish, she propped up, wiping her eyes, and asked, "Why is this all happening? People are dying for no reason."

"People? Who else?"

Mariah hesitated because it was of her doing, and she slowly said while looking away, "Burak."

"Burak?" he questioned, slightly raising his voice, surprised. Being keen on body language, he knew Mariah had a story, but he also understood that she and Burak had been at odds since she was young. Even though he was always the instigator, she never turned down a challenge to put him in his place.

Jahar gently laid his hand on top of hers. "What happened, my forest flower?" This was the nickname that he gave her when she was a baby.

"He attacked me when I was sneaking out the emergency exit of the living quarters."

"Why did you kill him?"

"I did not know it was him when he came behind me fully cloaked and wrapping his arm around my neck, choking me. He said my weak bloodline would not mix with yours after you die. So he was going to kill me."

Jahar wanted to smile big because he had prayed for years that she and Benaiah would marry someday. Containing himself while staying in concerned character, he asked, "You were defending yourself?"

"Yes."

"Why were you sneaking out the emergency exit?"

"To find you and Benaiah."

"Benaiah? He was with Jasaph and the guards who called Horasha to assist in his…"—Jahar sighed out disappointed—"rehabilitation."

"They did not go to the rehabilitation facility. They went into the book of time. Tahla told me it was Horasha's decision to go there and that he would not let anyone else but Jasaph go with them in there."

"The book of time?" Jahar questioned, thinking why he would have taken him in there.

Mariah shrugged her shoulders, bewildered herself.

"Maybe he thought before taking him to the rehabilitation facility, Benaiah would benefit more from seeing what we have and what our abilities are. Seeing the guardian's portraits from the beginning would help with historical sequence in leadership, and the library would overwhelm anyone.

"Horasha knows Benaiah better than anyone else, being his shadow his whole life. Maybe he knew this would be more effective in convincing Benaiah to open his mind and heart to why and what he is here for in there then physically being…treated?" he said to be nice about it.

The two pygmy men had leaned into one another, whispering during their conversation. They calmly looked at Jahar and Mariah, waiting for a moment to talk and not wanting to interrupt Master Jahar's conversation.

Seeing the men wanted to say something, Jahar nodded to the one sitting closest to him who was the chief, his dear friend. The men had not said anything to Jahar about what was going on or that Benaiah was even lying right next to him since they retrieved him. They let him quietly sleep. The chief looked up at Mariah and then back to Jahar, giving him a look that something was wrong, and then he spoke up to the women outside for Uba to come inside. Everyone immediately knew there was something deeply wrong to call a female into the man hut. Uba cautiously walked inside as the chief moved his eyes toward Mariah for her to sit down next to her.

Tension built in the small hut as Jahar stared at the chief trying to get information of what was going on, and then the chief gently said, "We saved the new man for you, Jahar..."—looking over at Benaiah lying on his back next to him—"knowing he was important to you. He was wearing this." The chief reached behind him, picking up a cloaking uniform, "He also had on him all the equipment your guards carry." He pointed farther behind him at a gun, knife, and backpack.

"He was going out the escape tunnel of the book of time when we darted him. My men went up the stairs to look in the room he came from and found two men lying on the floor. One injured unconscious, the other..." the Chief paused and lowered his head, not wanting to share the news, but he had to continue. "Was dead—stabbed in the throat."

Mariah gasped as Jahar's hand tightened his grip over her hands.

Looking up into Mariah's eyes, the chief said as gently as possible, "The dead man is your stepbrother, Jasaph. I am sorry, Mariah. We were not there to save him."

Mariah lifted her head to heaven, screaming out in anguish, "No!"

Chapter 9

Uba stood at eye level, wrapping her arms around the kneeling Mariah as her heart broke open. The villagers outside chanted words of comfort for Mariah as the ones inside, including Jahar, remained silent, letting her pour out the agony of the horrible news of her stepbrother being killed adding to the loss of her friend-servant, Tahla.

Taking a few minutes to calm down, she leaned into Uba for mental and physical support. Uba slowly stroked Mariah's beautiful long black hair for a while, relaxing her as her breathing became choppy, inhaling deeply to refuel her body with oxygen.

Leaning away and looking into her eyes, Uba asked, "Do you want to lie down for a while or go for a walk through the forest to clear your heart and mind?"

Before Mariah answered, everyone heard a moan come from Benaiah, who was lying down on the other side of Jahar. The pygmies had undressed him from the camouflaging clothes, leaving him only with his underwear on and a blanket covering him from his waist down.

Mariah looked to him as he tried to blink away the deep sleep he had been in, moving his hands up to his face. It was as if everyone in the hut except Benaiah stopped breathing to calculate what exactly was going to happen next.

Something within Mariah erupted as an explosion of adrenaline went to every cell in her body, making the first move, answering their question while yelling out in English, "You! You killed my brother!" Faster than a leopard on its prey, Mariah leaped over Jahar, landing her whole body on top of him and wrapping her hands around his neck, choking him. "I am going to kill you!"

At a disadvantage with his mind cloudy and physically weak from the sleeping dart, Benaiah's efforts at removing her grip were useless. Gagging out words and not understanding what was going on, he was quickly succumbing to his demise. The chief yelled orders as they swarmed Mariah, attempting to get her off him. Uba stepped in, trying to help as well, loudly saying over and over, "No, Mariah! Stop!"

Mariah was possessed with revenge as the adrenaline gave her the strength of several strong men. Jahar strained to sit up and then leaned over weakly, dropping his hand down on top of Mariah's at Benaiah's throat, exposing the large gold signature ring. Like a thunderbolt hitting the earth, it got her attention.

As if it was a magical spell, instantly, Mariah released his neck but kept her hands in place. Benaiah gasped for air, choking and coughing as his red face began to clear up from gulping down life-giving substance.

Jahar slowly withdrew his hand, lying back down exhausted as she removed her hands from Benaiah's neck while sitting up on top of him. She moved her eyes up to Benaiah's as he saw rage staring at him. Slowing moving off him while keeping their eyes glued to one another, Mariah waited for Benaiah to make a wrong move to give her reason to end his life.

Jahar pierced the heavy dark moment with a light peaceful voice. Speaking in English, he said, "Mariah, calm yourself. He has the right to explain. Benaiah, tell us what happened in the book of time?"

Benaiah was still coming out of his drowsy state while attempting to understand where he was. Without words, Uba knew what he was physically going through and looked around the hut, finding what was needed for him. Picking up the hollowed gourd filled with water, she poured water into a small wooden cup next to it that was premade with different herbs to help Benaiah come out of his sleep when he woke. It was what Mariah just drank in the other hut and the same drink Mariah gave him when he first woke up riding in on the elephant many days ago.

Benaiah drank with Uba holding it for him knowing that he was weak as he peered up and down the small old female from the interior of Africa. Remembering the flavor, he said, "I've had this before." Then he looked to Mariah and added, "And I'm the same… innocent guy now as I was then." He raised himself up, held his head in his hands for a moment, and then started his story, looking over to Jahar.

"Horasha took me into the book of time, only letting Jasaph in…" He turned to Mariah. "Your brother."

She exploded, getting into his face, "You knew he was my brother?"

"Not until later…" Giving her a defensive frown, he looked back to Jahar. "We were at the last portrait before going into the library and talking about your king's orders and stuff. Horasha told me to examine Shuriah's picture for authenticity. I made a comment about the ring being a nice touch and that there was no way the portrait could have held up so long. He said something about a special tree sap preserving your items you have here. I joked about him believing the *Jurassic Park* movie with the mosquito in the dried sap story. Earlier, we had a confrontation at the entrance of the tunnel near your picture because I wasn't taking things seriously and not believing anything you guys have been telling me." He looked to Mariah, inching himself away from her, "This time, instead of getting mad at me, he stepped behind Jasaph, breaking his neck."

Jumping at him, she shouted, "He was stabbed in the throat!"

Benaiah flinched back raising his hand to defend himself said firmly, "That came later for a cover up." He eyed her, holding his ground, and then he added, "Horasha said he did it to protect me because Jasaph's bloodline is next to take over being the guardians if I was dead. He informed me you were related and that I could not trust you and any of your family because you were planning on killing me." Benaiah massaged his neck still eyeing her. "So far, he's right."

Jahar cleared his throat to let everyone know he was going to speak. "How was he planning a cover up for this murder?"

"It wasn't murder to him but carrying out his duty of protecting your bloodline, Jahar. He even mentioned that since you were dying, you might be mentally losing it. He believed he had to take cautionary measures to make sure I'm the next guardian to wear that monstrous ring."

Mariah butted in harshly. "All lies! Answer the question!"

Benaiah's head was clearing up, and his body was gaining strength as he began to fill with his own anger and frustration. He replied, "Mary or Mariah, I'm sorry your bother is dead. I really am. His death was the first for me, and I will never forget that. He was a great bodyguard for Jahar, a soft-spoken man who came to my defense a couple of times in the tunnel." He changes to a sarcastic tone. "After he tackled me, threatening my life while holding a knife to my throat." He gently rubbed his neck again.

"All of you are crazy and out of your minds! You brought me here by drugging me. After that, you made me walk in the dark through this hot and humid forest while tripping all over the place. Then you knock me out." He reached up to his head, feeling the new bandage. "My life is threatened, and you give the okay to have me beaten like you whipped Horasha!" He stared at Jahar as Jahar's eyebrows slightly rose, surprised he had that information as Benaiah spattered out, "Yeah, he showed me his scarred back from you ordering to have him whipped because you didn't agree with how he did things."

Adjusting how he was sitting, Benaiah continued, somewhat protecting him. "Horasha takes me somewhere different so I'm not harmed, then he kills a man to save me. Then after showing me the things in the book of time, he ends up beating me to a pulp because basically he doesn't like my attitude." Benaiah pointed to the tender areas of his face and the bandage of his head. "Splitting my head open again."

Benaiah slowly shook his head. "Now, here is where it gets crazier. He purposely tells me things he…or I should add, you,"—he pointed to Jahar—"did to my personal female relationships in my life that I didn't know about, ticking me off! He told me this for the sole purpose that I would get mad enough to punch him over and over to make it look like Jasaph and him got into a fight."

Mariah looked down at his hands and saw definite fresh wounds on his soft knuckles that came from hitting someone.

"He wanted me to finish him off by hitting him in the back of the head with the butt of his knife to knock him out. He said, once I was done, to escape through the secret tunnel under the couch because he knew the invisible people or pygmies…"—he looked back to the old African woman ready to wait on him—"would somehow find me and protect me until he was able to safely come and get me.

"Then, again, I'm drugged, but this time by getting shot in the neck with a dart while trying to escape through the secret tunnel, and here I am." He opened his arms to where he was sitting. "I have done nothing to deserve any of this treatment."

Jahar glanced to the chief, whispering in his language and asking if the pygmy men were sent by Horasha. The chief shook his head, telling him they were already there watching over everyone just as they did with him with the doctor.

Jahar thought through the stories, coming up with his conclusions of what happened as Mariah asked, "Why did you not go back to the entrance at the commons area?"

"He said it was dangerous because your family was guarding it."

"So was his!" she said, still upset.

"He mentioned that, but he said it was safer to go the other way."

Jahar took a moment, closing his eyes and taking several deep breaths. The expression on his face was of one trying to suppress pain, and then he opened his eyes back up, asking, "When was Jasaph stabbed?"

"Oh, yeah." Benaiah straightened up again, trying to keep some distance from Mariah. "Before I beat Horasha, he made me..." He paused, knowing the sensitive subject and said as gently as he could. "Stab his lifeless body to make it look like I defended myself after Jasaph knocked him out while he was protecting me in the imaginary fight."

"Why were you wearing guard clothes?" Jahar asked.

"That one was me!" he proudly stated, and then he looked down and realized he wasn't dressed. He grabbed the blanket to cover up. "Why did you take my clothes off?"

"Answer the question." Mariah holding back submerging her emotions momentarily.

"I had enough of this game. I put on clothes from the emergency closet after I knocked out Horasha, thinking somehow that I could make up my own plans of figuring out what is happening and what you're really hiding and expose it to the world using the camouflage clothes." He boldly looked straight at Jahar and said in an accusing tone, "What in the world are you hiding that scares you so much and makes everyone act like lunatics?"

A loud stinging smack was heard. Like a snake striking, Mariah swiftly slapped him across his face. "Never speak to Master Jahar like that again!"

Benaiah had nothing to lose. He was tired of this painful nightmare as an idea struck him like her hand. Responding as he slowly rose to his knees, he leaned over until his face was an inch away from hers and spoke between gritted teeth while narrowing his eyes, "You ever touch me like that again, I will have your hands cut off after that ring is placed on my finger." He pointed to Jahar's hand without looking.

It went silent as the two had an intense staredown. After a few moments of not blinking, something different began to happen between them. The harshness dissolved as hints of attraction were subconsciously cast out to one another. The sudden boldness of Benaiah finally acting like a man of her people and standing up for himself and embracing his position strangely warmed her heart.

Benaiah, on the other hand, was succumbing to her beautiful eyes, soft facial features, and her breath whispering up against his skin, which caught his attention more than once since waking up to her on the elephant.

Out of the corner of Mariah's eyes, she saw Uba kneel behind Benaiah and then slowly bow, facing him. Uba whispered words to the other pygmies in their language with her head down, pointing out the bottom of Benaiah's feet. He was kneeling and sitting upright, with the flat of his feet together, facing them. Mariah understood what Uba had seen and what she was doing as the other pygmies slowly bowed to Benaiah as well after seeing what she was pointing at. Following their lead, Mariah broke the attracting gaze, setting back and bowing to him as well.

When she backed away Benaiah felt he was drawn forward as though they were connected. When he realized what she was doing, he sat back on his heels, inhaling deep and recovering from the breathtaking moment. Changing gears, he was surprised how successful his counterfeit aggressive move was to control her. Then he second guessed himself and thought, *This truly might be real.* With that thought, a feeling of power began to swell up within him.

His gaze went around the darkened hut. Finally becoming aware of the others, he put on a perplexed look and thought to himself, having not formally met them yet, *Who are these small Africans?* Benaiah's eyes reached Jahar's.

With him wisely knowing what the new man to the area was thinking, he gently spoke as he pointed his hand around while speaking English, "These are our oldest and dearest friends—the Congo pygmies."

Benaiah refocused with that eye-opening knowledge and examined the details of the people that looked like children at first glance. He saw facial and chest hair on the men as the old woman behind him next to Jahar, had exposed breasts as they all only wore waist wraps.

Benaiah's science mind started churning and said, "I have never seen a pygmy in real life. Many in-depth studies are showing us they are descendants of the original man that had evolved from primates."

Rising back up, Mariah stated, "Jahar, he needs to know! He continues to be foolish. It is becoming embarrassing."

"Know what? And could everyone stop bowing to me?" Benaiah irritatingly asked.

Jahar coughed, lying back and grasping for energy. Mariah jumped to his side, and asked, "Do you want me to get one of the other doctors besides Mitanual?"

Closing his eyes, he replied, "No. No doctors. They will only try to keep me alive. I am ready to finally go home." He opened his eyes, looking at the two younger adults as he said, "I have dreamed of you two being with me when I take my last breath—the next generation to carry on what has been put in play eons ago."

Benaiah knew Jahar's condition, and making statements like that, the old man who called him his great nephew truly was dying. Suddenly, he heard powerful whispers in his mind say, *Move forward in faith, and I will show you measurably more than you can imagine.*

Benaiah cringed at hearing these words, but more than that, he didn't want to admit who he thought was speaking to him.

Then his thoughts swirled with conversations from yesterday as pictures of the things he had seen flashed through his mind's eye. In a moment's time, he concluded that this whole trip, starting with reading the letter back in his office at the university to now, was not a theatrical event. He now was kneeling beside a dying old man in a pygmy hut somewhere in the Congo with a beautiful woman.

Jahar lifted his wobbly bony hands, one toward Benaiah and the other up to Mariah. The atmosphere within the hut was changing as the two repositioned themselves at Jahar's side, gently taking a hand as the pygmies moved and sat by his feet.

Jahar closed his eyes again and began talking in English, "Mariah, Doctor Mitanual was trying to save me, not harm me. He did not know who to trust exactly as your imagination was running its course.

"Would you please start interpreting for me to our friends what I am going to tell Benaiah? I will continue to only speak English for now on, with no intention of being disrespectful but to help Benaiah clearly understand what I need to say."

He paused to let her inform the invisibles and then continued as he opened his eyes. "You do not know this, Mariah, but besides you and me, the chief also knows of Journey's Beginning." Jahar looked down his feet to his old friend and continued, "The great ancestors of the invisibles are the ones that showed Shuriah the secret hiding place in Journey's End for the treasures of all treasures that you will show the next guardian." Jahar shook Benaiah's hand, indicating directly who he was talking about.

As she interpreted, the chief gave her a big smile, nodding and acknowledging that Jahar was telling the truth.

Jahar looked at Benaiah, saying, "I agree with you, Mariah. Benaiah needs to know and see Journey's Beginning for himself. Remember when I first showed it to you, my forest flower?" He turned his head to her with a smile as he thought back in time when she was a young girl.

Mariah gently lifted his hand to her face, softly kissing the back of his hand and saying, "I have never forgotten that incredible day, Master."

He changed the subject, looking straight up and slightly grimacing to fight off pain as he continued, "I privately asked the chief several days before Benaiah arrived for special help. I sensed many things would possibly get out of control as I passed on the position of guardian.

"The silent dark one has always slithered around Journey's End to influence anyone who would listen." Looking back to Benaiah, he said, "But when you left San Francisco to come here, his intention to confuse, disorient, and lie to everyone has flooded this place like I have never experienced before."

Jahar went silent for a moment, waiting for Mariah as she interrupted and then continued, "I asked the chief to keep a close watch on the descendants and the other African tribes. If it appeared to him things were going to get corrupt, he was to secretly capture you, Mariah, and myself, taking us away from the danger and chaos. First, for our protection, but more to deescalate the tension within our families. That is why we are all here right now in his home. Unfortunately, some have already died fearing what is not to be feared."

Jahar squeezed Mariah's hand, seeing she was trying hard to hold back the tears.

Benaiah nicely but naively questioned, "What are we not to fear?"

Everyone looked at him as Mariah answered for Jahar, "It is best to answer who we are to fear... God and God alone. Not a person or our illusive thoughts, imaginations, and worries as I did." She dropped her head shamefully. "Tahla is dead because I was afraid. My stepbrother and Horasha's brother are dead because of selfishness and paranoia. No one had to die."

With wide eyes and a blank face, Benaiah didn't say a word at the astonishing news of two more people's deaths, thinking to himself, *Jahar was right when he said people continually are being killed because of this place.*

Starting to breath shallower, Jahar said, "My forest flower, you know very well deaths as these are not the first or the last. These situations are our unfortunate burden, and the nemeses we carry from generation to generation. Because..."—he paused as he rolled his eyes, looking up to Benaiah—"of what we have and must protect, all because of Shuriah, who was a mighty warrior, general of Israel's army, our king's personal bodyguard, and Journey's Ends first guardian.

"The other guardians have always called him the world's first archeologist for what he found." Jahar grinned, shaking his head in admiration and continued, "And for the fantasy-like but true knowledge and ancient historical artifacts in it from the beginning of time, such as your dinosaurs, Benaiah, for a start...and more things you will only believe when you see them." Jahar gave out a faint laugh, imagining what Benaiah's face and thoughts would be when he first laid eyes on what he was talking about.

Benaiah perked up at finally hearing what he'd been waiting for—a spark of information on what he thought he was summoned here for and his life's work was all about as Jahar continued, "I do not have enough time to fully explain Journey's Beginning and all it contains. Mariah is going to have to show you personally for you to understand the magnitude of this secret that only the three of us are aware of.

"Our king, being so wise, had to protect and preserve Shuriah's incredible find that I am speaking of. Solomon knew the rulers to come after him, even his own children, would not understand the immense value, influence, and responsibility that Journey's Beginning held. He believed it would only be exploited for themselves and wasted away, lost, or destroyed forever."

Benaiah attempted to paint the picture in his head of what was being said without a brush and paint. Respectfully but confusedly, and doing well not getting frustrated as he had several times before when Jahar was explaining things, he asked, "I'm not clearly understanding what you're talking about, Jahar."

Mariah quickly answered to let Jahar rest but, more importantly, so he knew that she remembered everything about the true secret purpose for Journey's End. She looked up across his chest to Benaiah. "King Solomon understood human behavior more than any man alive. Knowing man's weaknesses which, in his later years, he saw clearly in how he himself became weak, even in his spirit. He could not trust himself. Our king wisely had to do something drastic with what he was now responsible for that God made aware to him through Shuriah. He knew no other man would be able to handle that along with all the personal riches he had acquired during his magnificent forty years of reigning."

Jahar squeezed Benaiah's hand, knowing what he was thinking as he said, "Soon, you will see for yourself what we are talking about. Then…" Jahar smiled again, pushing out another quiet laugh with his heart feeling free. "You will understand what we have been discussing and building up for you to take charge of. Ultimately, you will see how God marvelously works in and through all things for the good of his children who love him and have been called according to his purpose. He is calling you, Benaiah…descendant of King David's mighty warriors." Jahar squeezed both of his own hands with the two young adults' hands, confirming to them his confidence he had in God and the both of them.

While Jahar was talking, Uba had gotten up and poured some water in a cup for him. After his statement, she kneeled by his head, putting the cup to his lips. Taking a couple of swallows, he closed his eyes and whispered to himself, "God give me enough breath to tell Benaiah more of Journey's Beginnings and to pronounce him guardian of Journey's End."

Benaiah wasn't understanding why, but his whole body uncontrollably and visibly shivered as if he was cold. Mariah looked at him, taken aback as the pygmies whispered to one another. Uba got up and wrapped the blanket fully around him. He attempted to defend his uncontrollable actions. "Thank you, but I'm not cold. It's hot in here."

Mariah translated, and then Uba took the blanket away, fully exposing him and his underwear. "Oh no, no, but thank you." He reached over with his free hand, grasping the blanket and draping it over his lap to hide himself.

Jahar wisely spoke, nodding that he knew what was happening to him. "It is all right, Benaiah, I understand the battle within you. It will all come together once God has lifted the veil from your mind's eye when you witness the hidden knowledge in Journey's Beginning, which I fully trust that God will help you transform your mind so your heart will be transformed to rest where it belongs."

Jahar asked Uba for another drink of water and then cleared his throat. Peace filled his small frail body as Benaiah struggled to settle down. Conflict was rampant in him as religious babble continued to come out of the dying man. At the same time, explosive sweet words like dinosaurs and ancient artifacts weaving their way in the conversation kept him interested and on edge.

"Benaiah, the reason I tried very hard to guide you in your younger years to be interested in archeology, paleontology, and history was for what Mariah will show you soon after I make you guardian. Historical facts and findings from the beginning of time and throughout time have always been warped or have had great gaps of unknown. We have recorded precisely every significant event for the past three thousand years since we have been here."

Benaiah shook his head and said, "Horasha showed me the book of time, explaining what and how you do it."

"Good, but did he say anything about any records prior to that?"

Benaiah shook his head.

Jahar nodded in agreement. "No, he did not. What Mariah and I are talking about are recorded, accurate, and detailed events of the first two thousand years of mankind's existence starting with Adam and Eve."

Benaiah straightened his back, almost letting go of Jahar's hand as a shadow of disappointment showed itself in the conversation. Hoping to get an answer better than what he was thinking, he said, "You're not going to preach to me about Genesis, the first book of the Bible written by Moses and supposedly given to him by God during his forty years lost in the desert. I know the story." His expression changed to discontent as he heard himself talk.

Jahar replied, "That is true. But I wonder if you actually had a plethora of extraordinary comprehensive written documentation, giving boundless insight from the time of the Garden of Eden for the next two thousand years that no one knows in detail of all the living things during that time and what truly happened until Noah?"

Not impressed so far, he said, "We already have the story. Adam and Eve were kicked out of the garden because they ate the forbidden fruit. Then the people after them got so bad and evil that God drowned them all, supposedly flooding the whole earth. But before that happened, God picked Noah and his family because they were good people, and he built a big boat, filling it with all the different animals of the world, one male and one female of each kind."

She wasn't sure why, but Mariah laughed and then covered her mouth.

"What?" Benaiah asked aggressively.

"Nothing, sorry."

"No… What is so funny? I'm telling you almost exactly what your Bible says. You know that." Benaiah was digressing rapidly in his enthusiasm of this Bible story stuff.

She shook her head, looking at Jahar, then the pygmies, and then back to Benaiah, saying, "What you have said is true. If you believe the Bible or not. God did flood the whole earth to erase man's extreme evilness. Then he let man have a fresh new start through Noah and his three sons. Just think, Benaiah, if you had all the knowledge of what happened between the time of creation and the mass destruction of the flood?

"Everything you have learned and believed to be true through your worldly science of evolution about the earth—its development, age, and even the monstrous animals of old and animals you think are only myths—would be completely turned upside down.

"You are going to look and feel so foolish from the way you are and have been acting and speaking once you see the truth for yourself."

Just getting his doctorate, he was finally going to be able to snuff out any religious beliefs that science had proven wrong. As he knew this challenge was coming to a head, he confidently said, "I doubt it. You live by invisible faith hiding here in the Congo. I live by visible facts out in the real world where reality truly lives."

She looked at him, bewildered at his persistent mental ignorance and emotional arrogance, and asked, "Really, you are that sure of yourself—or should I say full of yourself?"

"Mariah…" Jahar calmly said to keep her on track.

"Sorry," she said to both men, slightly tilting her head down with a bow, and then she looked back up and continued, "You did not know Journey's End existed until several days ago. You have only seen pieces of its splendor and few artifacts amongst the tens of thousands you still have not seen. Even meeting the pygmies for the first time right now." She pointed around to them in the hut. "And you still want to play...stupid?"

Maintaining his composure, he replied confidently, wanting to continue the conversation to find their weakness and missing link. He said, looking into Mariah's eyes, "Sorry. Please...continue with this entertaining story."

There was a brief moment of silence as Jahar began having a harder time breathing, and then he said with a grimace, "The reason I guided you into archeology and paleontology was to help you grow with the two strong words you brought up, faith and facts. Very soon you will have the grand clear view, of which one is more powerful, and which must come first in life, faith, for the second to ever exist, facts. Life is about living by faith and only through faith the facts of life are truly reveled, not the other way around." He paused to make sure Benaiah absorbed what he was saying and then continued, "What Mariah will be showing you, your science will expose the truth of many things we are talking about, as we live by faith. Even things you thought were...fairy tales.

"But more than anything..." He inhaled as everyone heard raspy sounds coming from his lungs. "To paint a bigger picture of God who orchestrates..." Jahar started to cough and pulled a hand up to his chest to help with the pain. Everyone, even Benaiah froze. The reality of the old man dying right now was staring them in the face.

Able to get air in, Jahar finished his sentence. "God, who orchestrates life as we know it is painting a portrait of faith for all to see his glory."

Strangely, for everyone looking on, they saw that Jahar's eyes seemed to be peering around as if unable to see anything as he spoke out, not looking directly at her, "Mariah, as I said, it is up to you now to show and fully explain Journey's Beginning."

He coughed a few more times, wandering his nearly blind eyes toward his successor. "Benaiah, descendant of King David's mighty men, the last of our bloodline. My dying request is that when you finally see and understand what we are here for, choose wisely... choose wisely what you do with the heavy knowledge. You...you as guardian come with immense power but great responsibility far beyond anything you could imagine."

Moving his head straight forward, he continued, "Take care of him, Mariah. That is what you have been groomed for. Be patient. He will come full circle." He gasped for air as his face and skin appeared to be changing color and then compassionately smiled, going to a different topic. "I know God is answering your prayers, my forest flower. I hear your heart has started to beat a fresh song... I feel it." He weakly lifted his hand. "Put my hand on the side of your face." She gently lifted his hand back up as he slowly stroked her cheek with the backside of his fingers. She swelled with emotion while attempting to hold it in and squeezing her eyes closed.

With all his strength, Jahar let go of Benaiah's hand and lifted the one which had the signature ring on it out toward the pygmy chief at his feet. Mariah opened her eyes on seeing what he was doing and spoke through the quiet tears with choppy words, explaining to the chief in their language what Jahar was asking of him. "Master Jahar wants you to take the ring off his finger."

The chief looked at the three descendants of Israel and then sat up, gently grasping his hand. Gingerly, he twisted and pulled, unable to get the ring off without hurting Jahar. He looked over to Uba, saying a few words, and then she left the hut quickly, coming back and handing him a specific branch of a low-growing plant. He broke the thin branch, pouring the drops of clear liquid on Jahar's finger. Working the liquid around, he began twisting the ring again, and it quickly and painlessly came off as the chief smiled while holding it up like a prize.

For some odd reason, Benaiah mentally took swift protective ownership of the ring, not liking the look on the chief's face. Even though he was acting out in innocence, he sharply asked, "What is he going to do with it?"

Surprised at his quick reaction and hearing some hostility, Mariah replied calmly, "Jahar is having the chief perform the guardian ceremony for you now to receive the ring, crowning you master of Journey's End. Just like the chief's father did with Jahar at his father's death and so on back in time up to Shuriah, who Solomon put the ring on originally."

"Why would the pygmies have anything to do with this?" Benaiah asked, not seeing the significance.

It was a valid question he needed to know the answer of. Running with it and taking her mind off Jahar while still holding his hand, she paused to reflect on the whole story and then began, "The Queen of Sheba had great respect and trust in King Solomon as he did in her. She reigned in the region of what we now call Yemen, south of Saudi Arabia, where the southern tip of the Red Sea and the Sea of Aden come together. Crossing over into Africa where these seas touch, she also reigned what is now Ethiopia and a majority of everything west of there and south of Egypt.

"Her people had heard rumors of a mystical indigenous race deep in a vast rainforest hidden away far from any civilization. When Solomon came to her for help to move the secret items, we have been talking about from the rest of the world, she herself traveled here, approaching the pygmies for help because of how important it was."

Mariah paused, looking over to Jahar with his eyes squinted closed and listening to his forest flower speaking wisdom to the next guardian. Even with the physical pain, his soul was at peace knowing everything was going to be all right.

Turning to the chief smiling back at him, she continued, "Without their forefathers, whom the Queen of Sheba made friends with, and their generations thereafter, we would not have been able to survive the Congo let alone know where to successfully hide the precious treasures through the millennia." She paused as she bowed to the chief, giving him honors and respect even though he couldn't understand what they were talking about. He nodded back, still with a smile on his face.

Looking over to Benaiah, she asked smartly, "Does that answer your question?"

Having heard from Jahar in the commons area pieces of the same story aroused the drive for more. Like an addiction, he needed more information and the proof of what they've been talking about. Benaiah decided to surrender and go down the path they all seemed to have laid out from him, making it easier and hopefully quicker to see these mysterious items of Journey's Beginning.

Fighting from fidgeting around like a child waiting for Christmas morning, he composed himself, responding, "I think I'm beginning to see a picture here."

"Good." She looked to the chief while saying words foreign to Benaiah and responded with excitement. He looked over to the other pygmies who were quickly saying something and pointing to Jahar and then Benaiah. They all agreed with what was said as Uba replied to Mariah, "We will be right back. We need to prepare the chief for the ceremony."

They all stood and swiftly left. Benaiah watched the short people leave, still in awe that he was in a pygmy hut in the middle of the Congo. It strangely gave him a good feeling, as though, for some reason, all his schooling was coming together and making sense of his worldly calling. Jahar jerked his and Mariah's attention as Jahar began gasping for air, telling them, "I...I must...go, children..."

They looked up to one another and then back to Jahar as Mariah said loud enough that even the people outside the hut heard, "Jahar... Please do not go. I am not ready for you to leave."

Jahar was working his mouth, but nothing was coming out as he rapidly blinked his eyes. His body was slowly wrenching as though something in him was fighting to get out.

Then, final words escaped. "I...love you. Abba is with you... always, my children..." He wobbly lifted his hands up as if he was reaching out to someone reaching for him, so the two young adults grasped one hand each. His bony hands gripped them tight and then dropped to his chest, with their hands touching, one on top of the other, as they felt Jahar's last breath leave his body soulless and void of life.

Chapter 10

"I love you too, Jahar," Mariah softly said as she leaned forward, laying her head on his chest as tears slowly flowed from her eyes again.

Benaiah looked on silently, not quite knowing what to do. Two days in a row now, a man had died in front of his eyes. One was gruesome and unexpected, the other peaceful and natural. Watching and hearing the love go between the persons mimicking a father and daughter relationship, he began looking inside himself and searching for relationships in his life where he had anything like that.

Regret began slithering around in his mind at how he ignored his parents after high school being the one creating a gap between them and being on his own as his beliefs of life were going in a completely different direction. Then his ex-fiancée walked into the mental picture, stirring gray emotions, and then he thought to himself, *That honestly worked out for the better. It turned out to be a superficial relationship anyway, and our life goals didn't mesh.*

With his hand still on Jahar's chest and Mariah's head lying next to it, he gently moved his hand out and softly touched her head. He began stroking her hair in a comforting manner as Uba had done, staying quiet and respectfully allowing her to grieve.

Suddenly, Uba stormed into the hut, speaking quickly to Mariah in their language. "Mariah, quickly, you have to leave!" She knelt beside her, holding Mariah's camouflage clothing, the compact weapon, and her backpack from the other hut.

Mariah lifted her head, eyes full of tears, and replied, "Uba, Jahar is gone."

Uba stressfully spouted, "I see, young one, but you two must leave—and now!"

Benaiah asked, "What's wrong?"

There was a moment of silence as Mariah forgot she needed to translate and then asked Uba the same question, sniffling back the pain. Uba responded, "Horasha and many others are searching for

Jahar and him." She looked up at Benaiah. "They are coming this way. You must go now!"

Mariah translated, and then Benaiah responded, "That's good. We can talk this over."

"No, it is not!" Mariah said, clearing her head. "Horasha has a temper. You know that. I killed his brother, and if he knows, he will definitely try his best to kill me. He already believes his imaginary lie that my family is dishonestly after the most honorable position of guardian."

Without thinking it through, and unconvinced of who were the good guys and who were the bad guys or if there truly were bad guys from what Jahar explained earlier, Benaiah asked, "Are they?"

Blindsided by the question, her face went blank and she stared him down with her watery red eyes.

"Sorry, I don't know who to trust. It just came out." Immediately understanding he put his foot in his mouth, he looked to Uba, handing Mariah their clothes and other items and said, "Take the stuff and let's get the heck out of here."

Another pygmy rushed in speaking in their own language, "They are just outside the village. Hurry!"

Benaiah leaned over, grasping his cloaking uniform and putting it on as Mariah did the same, keeping their backs to one another. Yelling erupted from the outside as Mariah recognized Horasha's voice, and she whispered as they turned to one another, "It is him!" She fully pulled the head cover completely over her face.

Rushing to finish getting dressed, they heard shooting ring out in the village as the pygmies began screaming in terror and running in every direction.

Uba broke their silence inside the hut by pointing around to the bottom edges of the hut for them to hide. Mariah picked up the compact weapons, handing one to Benaiah as Uba picked up both the packs, stashing them under the blanket that Benaiah had on him earlier. Then she placed it next to the two as they began disappearing with the clothes warming up to their body temperature.

Mariah understood the screaming and crying words and whispered to Benaiah as they were head to head, pinching in as deep as they could so their body outlines blended in with the structure,

"They shot the chief! He had Jahar's ring in his hand and they accused him of kidnapping and stealing it from him."

Again, Benaiah was caught in a situation he didn't know what to say or do as Mariah calmly flowed with instructions. "Stay very still no matter how close they get to you. They may even touch you, but do not react. Once they leave, we will put on our packs and fade away into the forest. We are on our own, and I will protect you as Jahar said earlier. Do you understand?"

Her breath stroked his face through the face coverings with every word, and he became captivated by her confidence and could only nod.

"Good. Now remain calm, breathe slowly, but be ready to react at a moment's notice. If they do see us, do not worry about me. I will take care of them. You run for your life into the forest and hide. The pygmies will find you. If not, Tahla's tribe will. You must remain safe for you are the key to all of this coming together. I trust what Jahar believes." She smiled with confidence.

Again, he nodded then whispered, "Nothing can happen to you, Mariah. You must show me Journey's Beginning."

Breaking a smile, she said, "You are right. We both must survive, and we will. Abba is with us always. Remember the last words of Jahar?"

Benaiah wavered his head, not necessarily agreeing with the words but acknowledging her faith and what Jahar told them.

She continued in a low whisper, "I am asking you as Jahar did. Be wise with your choices from now on! Follow your heart, not your head. Logic does not work in the Kingdom of God. What we are doing is God's work through one of his anointed kings, even if it has been three thousand years."

A thought came to her of a Bible quote that Jahar would say all the time. "Do you know the Bible verse in Isaiah 55:8–9?"

Benaiah thought quickly, knowing he had heard it recently, and then he remembered his mother reading it to him, being in Jahar's letter over a month ago. He nodded as their eyes moved back and forth and got caught up in an awkward moment of silent attraction. He said, "The letter Jahar sent me ended with it."

"Good, then you know God's ways are not our ways and his thoughts are higher than our thoughts—"

She was cut short as they heard a shout come from outside in Hebrew. "This is the chiefs hut!"

A shadow appeared in the entrance as a weapon pierced the inside of the hut followed by a guard from Journey's End.

Taking a few seconds to clearly see everything inside, he suddenly yelled out, "Jahar is here. Master Jahar is in here!"

The feet of many running to the hut was heard, and then Horasha said, "Step aside." He ducked in, peering around like a lion inhaling through his nose, with nostrils flared out as though he was smelling for his prey, with his head bandaged from being knocked out earlier. His eyes ended on Jahar and then looked up to Uba kneeling on the other side of him, holding Jahar's hands with her back to the hidden young adults.

He said in the pygmy tongue to her, "How is Master Jahar?"

Her body started to tremble as she looked away and tried to settle her eyes on something as she licked her dried lips, fumbling to get words out. With a crinkled facial expression and emotions of sadness combined with fear, tears flowed as she answered out loud in agony, "Master Jahar died a little while ago."

In the hut, around the village, and the vast forest seemed to have stopped all sounds and movement. Everyone in seconds flashed back to memories of the guardian. Even the pygmies stopped their cries for their chief in disbelief, recalling the peaceful and kind man that loved the special people and always trying his best to help them as life got harder and harder for them from the continuous oncoming encroachment of the outside world. But most of all from other African tribes from the outskirts of the Congo capturing them and using them as slaves.

"Your chief killed him for the ring!" Horasha growled out, lowering his head and giving her a death look as he knelt on one knee, keeping his head from hitting the ceiling of the hut.

Uba's demeanor completely changed at the false accusation against her chief, and she slowly stood with anger building. Walking around Jahar's body and looking face to face to Horasha with tears streaming down her cheeks, she reached up and slapped him, saying, "How dare you, boy! You murdered the chief without knowing why he had the ring!" She reached up to his beard, jerking his head down and poking his forehead with a finger from her other hand, saying, "Think! Jahar was passing away from his sickness and old age. Jahar asked our chief, his close lifelong friend, to remove the ring to prepare for the guardian ceremony for that new man you brought here."

Horasha's eyes went wide, asking anxiously and almost shouting, "Where is he?"

Still having a hold of his beard, she jerked it toward her so they were almost touching noses, "Wake up! Your mind is not right, Horasha! Clear your thoughts and calm down!"

She paused, letting go of his facial hair and dropping her hands to her sides as she said, "We do not know. Our men saw him come out of the emergency tunnel from the book of time."

"Where did he go?"

"They shadowed him for a while, seeing he was safely going up the mountain to the grand open eye at the top of the commons area. Then they left him, joining our other men in assisting Jahar out of the secret exit tunnel of the medical facility."

Horasha paused, thinking this was not making sense, and then he asked, "Why would they know to help Jahar?"

"Jahar asked the chief before you arrived back to the great forest to keep a close watch on everyone. If it appeared the transition for the new guardian was going to be in jeopardy or if things became dangerous, we were to protect him."

Horasha looked down in his hand at the large gold signature ring and then back to Jahar's body, saying, "Jahar was always as wise man, and your chief a faithful friend." Then he yelled out to the guards, "Honor our Lord!"

All the men that came with him could be heard kneeling in the village, bowing their heads, and then they simultaneously chanted loudly, "Glory and honor to our risen Lord Jesus! Glory and honor to our risen Lord Jesus! Glory and honor to our risen Lord Jesus!"

When they stopped, the silence echoed from the roar of the deep voices boasting out. After a moment, Horasha prayed out loud, "Lord Jesus, receive our Master Jahar and the chief. If it pleases you, please let them hear the words from your mouth, 'Well done, my fine and faithful servants.' They served you until the end, boldly and with wisdom. Bless Journey's End and the new guardian-to-be as well as this tribe and its new chief-to-be. Until you return to us, Lord Jesus, give us the strength as mighty warriors to serve you as our great ancestors served you and your people. Amen."

All the men concluded together, "Amen!"

Going to both knees close to Jahar, he touched their foreheads together for a moment, closing his eyes, and then he leaned back. Feeling Jahar's skin warmth told him she was telling the truth about his time of death and said, "My old friend, you were an incredible mighty warrior to the end. Thank you for being a wise and loving grandfather to us all. May we make you proud as you watch over us."

Horasha sat back on his feet, thinking things through and then ordered out, "Bring me a machete!"

All the guards looked at one another wide eyed with questions at why he wanted a machete. One of the men reached in, handing the long sharp knife to Horasha. Uba, still standing next to him, backed up as he grasped it from the guard. Benaiah and Mariah both quietly inhaled deep as their muscles tightened, ready to point their weapons in defense.

Holding it firm in hand, Horasha eyed Uba with an intense frown. The tension escalated by the second for everyone as Uba internally began to panic at what he was going to do, and then he said in a gentle tone loud enough for everyone outside the hut to hear, "Uba, I have committed a horrible crime here in my moment of passion to protect our king's signature ring. That is our sworn duty in serving the guardian—to protect it with our lives. Instead, I took an innocent life, the life of your chief, our dear friend.

"There is nothing I can say to justify what I have done or fill the void I have left your people. But…there is something I can do…" He paused, looking down at the machete in his hand as everyone looking on braced themselves.

He lifted the machete to Uba. She stared at it, wondering what he was doing as he said, "Take it."

Uba didn't move.

"Take it!" he demanded this time.

She took it from him as he bowed down in front of her sideways. "Uba, I give my life to you and your people. Cut my head off!"

Silence exploded throughout the village except for the shallow crying at the chief's body splitting everyone's attention. She gripped the machete in two hands, feeling the hard wooden handle and looking at both sides of the shiny blade. Moving her eyes and looking down at the top of his head with his neck completely exposed, she contemplated what to do. Then she raised it until it hit the ceiling of the hut and then swiftly came down, stopping suddenly right at the skin. The guards looking on, shocked at the whole thing and inhaled, making gasping sounds.

Horasha heard them and felt the blade and, at the same time, waiting for the worst. She held the sharp knife there for a moment and then said, "Horasha, you have been gone for so long that your judgement is clouded and your wisdom has become distorted. Your heart, though, has remained strong for the truth as I saw it in you when you were a child.

"Why would I take a valuable life from Journey's End who believed they were protecting it?" She paused for a moment and then told him, speaking louder, "In front of all who hear me, I accept your life as payment for your actions. What we do with it will be up to the new chief, the son of the one you killed."

Murmuring was heard back and forth from her people and the guards as they knelt outside. He remained motionless, waiting for more instructions. She lifted the machete off the back of his neck, telling him as he looked up to her, "Our chiefs must be put to rest. By your people's religious customs, Jahar must be entombed by nightfall. Take him and prepare for his burial ceremony, and we will do the same with our chief. Once all the preparations have been made, we will all meet at the tombs of the dead at sunset, where our chief's body will be entombed next to our chiefs of old forever, across from Jahar's and all the guardians from the past."

Slightly bobbing his head in agreement and pressing his lips together, he inhaled, still looking up, and said, "Thank you for sparing my life, Uba, elder of the pygmies, and for allowing me to honor the life of Master Jahar. After the new guardian is inaugurated, I will present myself here to your new young chief. He may do what he needs to do to with me as payment for killing his father."

He leaned forward, tucking his arms under Jahar's body and easily lifted him up. He made his way out, stopping outside the hut entrance and looking at everyone staring at him. A heaviness swept across the village as the deaths pierced the mood, pouring sorrow and sadness everywhere.

He slowly walked forward, passing everyone, who parted a pathway for him. He stopped at the small body lying on the ground in a pool of blood and surrounded by his people kneeling next to him, quietly mourning.

Horasha thought for a moment and then said with remorse, "I am sorry, Chief. You were a great friend to Jahar and to our people."

Waiting for a moment and staring at his horrifying actions, a young man slowly stood, making his way to Horasha and peering lifelessly up into his eyes. Horasha mentally heard the words the silent man was saying to him and then verbally responded back in pygmy, "You will have my life to do with as you please, young chief." Horasha bowed and then made his way out the village, disappearing into the forest as his men drudgingly followed single file behind him.

Wailing began rolling throughout the indigenous community of the Congo. Uba went to her knees as the adrenalin rush physically crippled her and her spirit was tormented with the two simultaneous deaths.

Mariah slowly, and cat-like, made her way toward the old woman listening to and watching the open entrance for anything representing sounds of her own people. Benaiah followed her lead, pulling up their face masks as he imagined what took place between Horasha and Uba.

Wrapping her arms around Uba, they grasped each other, sharing the pain. Benaiah peeked out the door, looking in the direction of where most of the pygmies gathered around their dead chief. Moving his eyes in all direction and not seeing anyone else, he whispered, "It looks like they're gone with Jahar."

Mariah looked over Uba's shoulder, acknowledging him with a slow nod. Then she began whispering into Uba's ear, "Uba, I need you to listen carefully. I must take Benaiah to a special place that is only known to the guardians and your chiefs. Now that they are both gone, your new chief must know of this most secret of secret places.

"When I was young, Jahar showed this place to me because Benaiah's father, who was to be the next guardian, as you know, left for the outside world. Jahar was heavy with this burden for a long time and strongly felt he needed to show someone else trustworthy and innocent. Again, he was a wise man who followed his heart and showed me. As both leaders of ours now died at the same time, the special place of great knowledge would have died with them."

Uba separated and held her out by the shoulders, putting on a small smile and whispering so low Mariah barely heard her, "Our chief was wise as well. Being the next oldest to him in our village, he told me where to find the entrance of what you speak of. I have never seen what is inside and was ordered to never go there or say anything about it until something like this happened."

Mariah mirrored her shock with a smile as Uba added, "The men only trusted us women."

They held in giggly smirks of sisterhood joy as best as they could, realizing they were both entrusted with the deepest of secrets and all these years were able to keep it from everyone as well as each other.

Benaiah interrupted, anxious to get going to see this place that had been in their topic of conversation. "Mariah, we need to get going, don't you think?"

She looked to him, nodding as she hugged Uba with new confidence and a deeper appreciation for one another. Letting go, she put on her backpack as Benaiah followed her lead, asking Uba, "Could some of your men shadow Benaiah and take him to the pool of the waterfall? I am going to follow way behind to watch for others hiding trying to find us."

Uba said yes and then stepped halfway out of the hut, calling for some men. They came to her, and she explained what they needed to do and then quickly left. The men covered their bodies with multiple colors and designs of natural camouflaging muds and staining plants, returned, and waited.

Mariah knelt next to Benaiah at the doorway and quietly watched all the movement going on outside as she explained, "We are going to leave the village in the opposite direction Horasha left. I need you to go with Uba's men. They will safely lead you to a waterfall."

"The one I heard when I got here?"

"Yes."

"What are you going to do?"

"I will be following way behind, watching for Horasha's men who are hiding and watching the village. We cannot afford to have anyone see us and know where we are going."

"You sound very sure of yourself that there is someone out there. They just left with Jahar's body in mourning."

"If it was me, I would have men looking everywhere for you. You are the most important person alive right now at Journey's End."

She reached behind his head, pulling on the elastic hood and looked for something small as she said, "Good, you smashed the tracking device."

"What?" Benaiah asked.

Mariah looked at Uba as Uba smiled, saying, "Our men broke them when they saved you both."

Benaiah questioned, "What did she say and what did you mean I smashed a device?"

She explained, "The cloaking clothes keep you visually hidden as well as invisible from infrared heat sensing equipment and satellites. It also controls your body scent, grabbing odors from outside and keeping your own odor inside the clothes so animals cannot track you, but there is a tiny tracking device sewn in the fabric so we can keep track of all our guards."

"Are you serious? These do all that?" Benaiah asked surprised, tugging at the suit.

"I am...serious. The technology we have is far beyond the rest of the world."

"Horasha said that in the book of time...library place. But he didn't thoroughly explain all you said." He looked down at the clothes, admiring them.

She shrugged her shoulders, saying smartly, "There are many things Horasha has not told you."

He looked up, staring at her and thinking reluctantly, and then he agreed, telling her, "I painfully found that out."

Keeping them on track, Mariah said, "For the clothes to work optimally, make no sudden moves or sounds. Slowly glide through the forest like a quiet breeze, and do exactly what the invisible men do.

Believing they were on the same page, she looked away to the closest man waiting on the outside of the hut and said in pygmy, "Bring several men in here with you."

Four men walked in, not having to bend over very far through the entrance. She discussed her plans with them to get Benaiah out of the hut without being seen or raising suspicion and then told Uba, "You need to pretend you fainted. Have the men carry you out to the edge of your village in the direction Horasha went. They need to be loud and getting everyone's attention in the village, showing that there is something wrong with you." Looking at all the men again, she said, "When your families come to see her, lay her down inside the forest and slip away unseen to meet up with Benaiah…" She pointed to him and continued, "On the other side of the village in the forest. After you leave the hut with Uba, I will have him invisibly go around the hut in that direction as you distract anyone from the outside watching in on us. He will wait for you there. Then take him to the pool at the base of the waterfall, hiding him, and then leave. I will find him there after taking care of anyone that should not be following you."

All the men nodded, agreeing with the plans.

Confidently, she peered around, thanking them for doing this and that she was very sorry for what happened to their chief. Then she looked to Benaiah, telling him in English the plans she just told the others.

Mariah peered around the hut, and seeing they had everything, asked Uba, "Are you ready?"

"Are you, forest flower?"

Jahar's words for her sparked some extra mental fuel as the two women nodded to one another with smiles.

Uba laid down where Jahar's body was, and then the men gently lifted her up, going out of the hut while talking loudly.

Looking to Benaiah, she said, "Are you ready?"

He looked at her with a goofy frown as a thought crossed his mind from a scene in a movie and then leaned into her, giving her a quick kiss.

They separated, and he responded with, "Now I am."

Taken completely off guard, she froze, staring at him as he added, "Let's do this."

He started to twist around to the entrance, but she grabbed his arm, pulling him back and planted a huge long kiss on him, wrapping her arms around him.

They both indulged in the unexpected physical attraction of their very young relationship. After a few moments, they slowly separated as Mariah brought her hand to her lips to wipe away excess moisture, slightly embarrassed but also amazed at what just took place. They deeply peered into each other's eyes as a brand new adventure was born.

Loud chatter was heard outside, signaling Benaiah's move. He said hesitantly with his head still in a fog from the kiss, "I've got… I've got to go. See you later?"

Inspired with a new emotional sensation, she replied warmly, "Yes, I will not be too far behind."

He turned slowly, looking out at the activity on the far edge of the village. She touched his arm, squeezing it as he looked back, and said, "Be careful."

"You too." Turning around, he lowered the elastic cloaking face mask and then cautiously stepped outside, keeping up against the hut and inching his way around to the backside. As Mariah instructed, he attempted to imitate the breeze in the open, slowly weaving around other huts until he got to the thick forest edge and going in a couple of yards.

He nestled in under a large fern with the leaves hanging over him as he watched the village, waiting for the men to show. After about five minutes, he was getting impatient and started to look around, wondering where they were. Not seeing anyone, he slowly sat up on a knee and turned to look behind him. Almost having a heart attack, his body jerked back from shock, taking his breathe away.

Recovering, he took a second to look at what he was seeing as it fully came to him, peering through the material over his face, that all four men were only a foot away from him and squatted down, watching and waiting on him.

They stared at each other for a moment, and then simultaneously, the pygmies stood and waved Benaiah to follow. Staggering out and putting him in the center of the group, they slowly slithered through the forest with great ease. After a while of watching the men make their way through the vegetation, he recognized a pattern, impressing on him that he had seen it before, and he whispered out loud when it came to him. "Jahar walked that way!"

The pygmies stopped when they heard his quiet voice. Benaiah did the same, realizing he had rattled the smooth flow and silence of their bodies. A loud squawk from a bird high above in the canopy of trees pinpointed the group that was intertwinned amongst the plant life below as Benaiah looked up, searching for the feathered alarm of the rainforest.

Not seeing anything, he looked back down, anticipating the pygmies staring at him upset for giving them away. As his eyes got to the forest floor, his body flushed hollow. The four men had disappeared, and he quickly looked in all directions, trying to see where they went as panic began to swell at being alone and having no idea where he was.

He stopped and listened, only moving his eyes. Finally, he heard what sounded like branches moving off to his left. Twisting his head toward the sound, he saw a tree limb about twenty feet from him sway to a halt. Next to the branch, there was an area that his eyes were having a little trouble focusing on. First, he thought there was something in his eyes, and he squinted hard, but as he did it, it moved toward him.

They're after me, he thought to himself as his heart started to pound in his chest. Not knowing what else to do, he stayed perfectly still, hoping his clothes were keeping him invisible. Then he heard a familiar sound from last night in the exit tunnel of the book of time, and he thought, *That's a blow dart.*

Peering around and only moving his eyes for the pygmies, he heard a collapsing thump go to the ground where the hazy mirage was at.

One by one, the pygmies began to show themselves, slowly standing from kneeling on the forest floor and perfectly blending into the vegetation. Benaiah was in awe at watching the men reappear only a couple of yards away from him. They had never left his presence.

Catching each other's eyes, the indigenous men slowly made their way to the spot of the thumping sound as Benaiah followed. The shooter of the dart bent down, reaching to what seemed just air as Benaiah watched on. He was astounded when a man's head appeared upon removing the face mask. It was a guard in cloaking clothes.

The shooter turned, looking up to Benaiah and putting his finger to his own lips and then pointing to the sleeping man, telling with his hands, "Be quiet or they will know where we are and come after us."

Benaiah nodded he understood. True realization and clarity opened up to Benaiah that he was completely out of his element. Feeling foolish, he thought to himself, *And they want me to take over for Jahar? I can't walk or even talk right.* Looking down at the exposed face and then back to the pygmy gesturing to him, he thought, *How in the world did they know this guy was here, and how can they see him?* It was baffling to him.

Continuing, they slowly made their way to the waterfall, leaving the guard to sleep off the dart. Benaiah could tell they were rounding the mountain just like he did with Jahar but not going upward. When he finally heard the waterfall, he was reminded of what Jahar said. *This whole place is awe-inspiring where the power of God is seen, heard, and felt through his creation. Hidden here, deep within the Congo, very few people have ever seen, or for that matter, knows of the existence of where we are at.*

A short time later, the group of five safely made it to a very large pond of clear water that was about seventy-five yards across. Near the edge, they knelt down cautiously, peering through the brush and tall grass and looking up at the cascading waterfall dropping down hundreds of feet from up the side of the mountain. Billowing clouds of mist echoed out with the roar from the water hitting the pool and drowning out soft to moderate sounds of the forest, forcing everyone to raise their voice to be heard.

All were admiring the grand view and power of nature, when suddenly, the pygmy men dropped low, looking in all directions and spreading out in a protective circle around Benaiah. Benaiah twisted his head back and forth, trying to understand what instantly frightened them.

One of the indigenous men, seemingly the leader, looked back to Benaiah and knew he needed to hide him better. Even though the suit was working, the man in the suit obviously didn't have the skills to survive in the Congo forest. Quickly thinking, he gave Benaiah his hollow blow dart stick that was about the length of his arm and gestured toward the water. Signing as their only form to communicate, he told Benaiah to crawl low and go into the water, pointing to some vegetation growing out of it near the edge. Then he told him to submerge himself and put the stick in his mouth while holding the other end out of the water to breathe, appearing to blend in with the other grass like vegetation in the water.

Benaiah knew exactly what the small, naturally camouflaged man wanted him to do and thought, *I saw this in a movie as well. How did he know how to do this? Did he see it too?* Then, internally, he laughed as he looked at the situation and thought again, *They probably taught this to the movie people.*

Taking the reed-like stick, he did exactly what the small African man signed, crawling and staying lower than the plant life to the water's edge. Before going in, he hesitated, wondering what creatures were in it and swimming around looking for a meal.

About thirty yards from where he just came, yelling broke out amongst the pygmies, using their voices as a diversion. As smooth and quietly as he could, trying not to create movement on the water surface, he slithered in, following the ground as it quickly dropped deeper by the foot. Drifting low along the bottom and holding onto rocks, he put the hollow stick in his mouth like a snorkel, breathing perfectly.

There was something childlike within him that was beginning to enjoy the adventure. Glimpses of friends, even his parents, flared up in his mind as he said to himself, *If they could see me now—a true Indiana Jones.*

The cool water was refreshing and surprisingly clear as he was able to see underwater while inching his way out about ten feet from the shore and blending into the patch of grass and other water plants floating on the surface. The shouting got louder although he could still barely hear the muffled sounds, being less than two feet from the surface. Looking up, the bright sunlight easily shone down, piercing through the shimmering water. The vast canopy of the rainforest had a hole in it as the waterfall was able to keep away the trees and other large plant life from smothering its beautiful grave.

Benaiah patiently inhaled and exhaled the life-giving air through the sturdy stick, grasping it tightly with his lips. For a moment, he forgot why he was doing this as he began admiring a completely different view of life from underwater. Suddenly, a dark shadow appeared from above as the calm water shattered, going in different directions. Someone had just stepped to the water's edge and was looking around.

He almost choked, unable to get the volume of air his mind told him he needed as the surge of fright shot through his body. Intently trying to see the invisible man who was casting the shadow from an angle, he had the great urge to swim away, but something kept him from moving. At first, he thought it was inner strength, and then he realized he physically was restricted. Panic began to take control as he started to internally squirm. He looked up at the dark shadowed figure just in time to see it move away and then felt something squeeze his arm. His mind raced, wondering what was going on as creatures from the deep came to his imagination. Slowly twisting his head to the side to see what had him, he tried to keep the snorkel steady, peering to his arm, but nothing was there. The gripping sensation was still strong. He worked his eyes in all directions, but they were getting blurry as they were getting irritated from the water. The tightness around his arm went away as he blinked, trying to see anything.

Then to his complete amazement, the water gently swirled and then, magically, a beautiful face, like in a dream, slowly appeared out of nowhere. Taking a second to focus and guess what in the world was going on, it instantly came to him.

It was Mariah. She was underwater with him, removing her elastic cloaking face cover so he could see her. She was the one holding him still so the man above looking around at the water wouldn't see him.

Chapter 11

After a few seconds of soaking in the moment, they both looked up toward the surface, watching for more activity. Not seeing anything, Mariah pulled off her camouflaged glove and then held her hand out, motioning for Benaiah to stay and then pointed up, telling Benaiah what she was doing. He nodded as she covered her face back up and ever so slowly floated to the surface, raising her camouflaged head like a crocodile until her nose was out of the water.

Gently exhaling and inhaling deeply fresh air, she had been holding her breath the whole time. Able to see and hear clearer, it was as if all the people around had disappeared, which is what needed to happen. Taking another deep breath, she slowly descended so as not to make a wake in the water. Exposing her face again, she grasped his arm and signed for him to take a deep breath and then follow her underwater, putting back on her face mask and glove.

He nodded, filling his lungs, and then he took the hollow stick out of his mouth, turning with her as they swam out toward the open water, swimming a few feet deeper to not accidently expose them at the surface. She picked up speed, sidestroking her arms and paddling her legs hard, going straight across the deep pool to where the waterfall plunged to its resting place. Benaiah, having some difficulty seeing her blending in with the water, did his best to mimic her stroke for stroke as his imagination rolled on as this storybook scene played out.

His lungs began to ache as the water became extremely turbulent, boiling upside down and letting him know where they were. He pushed on, trying to keep up with her as she disappeared in the white churning water which was juggling him in all directions. Finally, large rocks came into view as the water got calmer and the light from above got dimmer with every stroke. Looking in all directions and not seeing any sign of Mariah, his lungs were on fire and needed to be quenched with air. He struggled for a moment and then thought he saw movement dropping down into the water resembling an arm that was reaching out for him. Gladly, he took it, rising to the surface and hoping the hand was a friendly one.

Coming out of the water, he gasped for air several times until the pain in his lungs was satisfied. Lifting his mask, Benaiah wiped the water from his face as his boots took hold of the rocky shore, and then he sat down, looking in all directions and hoping to only see one person. With relief, it was only Mariah kneeling next to him with her mask flipped back behind her head.

"You did great, Benaiah!" she commented loud enough so he could hear her over the loud waterfall about fifteen feet away crashing into the lake. They were sitting inside a shallow cavern hidden behind the falling water.

He took a moment to get his bearings, looking around and unable to see the forest from any direction as they were completely enclosed by the cavern rock walls and the wall of water. The only light in the cavern was coming through the curtain of water falling.

He asked, "Are we safe?"

"For now."

He leaned forward toward Mariah's face as she flinched back until she was flat up against rocks, putting her hand up to his chest as she asked, "What are you doing?"

Not saying anything, he stared into her eyes for a moment and then pressed forward, gently touching their lips. Her hand soon loosened from his chest, reaching up to the back of his head and caressing his hair. Expressing themselves to one another in the romantic setting, it was difficult to stop. Slowly backing away, Benaiah reached to the side of her face, gently moving her wet hair behind her ear as he said, "Sorry, if I'm being too forward."

Her mind was dizzy with thoughts as she answered, "Oh no… no, you're not."

"Good. I wouldn't want to force you to do something you didn't want to be doing."

She couldn't help herself as she burst out with a laugh, bringing her hand to her mouth to control herself.

"What was that?" He cocked his head back with a questioning frown.

"Benaiah, you could not force me to do anything. I wanted to kiss you as well."

Looking at the backside of the beautiful glimmering water cascading into the large pond, he asked loudly, "Will you say that when I become guardian?" He raised one eyebrow, turning back to her.

Taking a moment, she was at a loss for words, thinking of the possible reality and what her role was going to be professionally when he became the new guardian. The only answer she had still looking forward was, "No, you have... I mean, you will have the power to force me to do anything."

"I understand that. I was asking about the other thing."

She turned to him not knowing what he was talking about, and then it came to her as she looked away almost shocked but more embarrassed than anything.

Seeing her expression, he asked with a smile, finally having the upper hand, "Well, will you still want to kiss me?"

She had little to no experience when it came to personal relationships like this, never having a close male friend. Needing to change the subject, she replied, "We can talk about that later. I need to show you..." By habit, she whispered the next words. "Journey's Beginning."

"What?" He looked at her confused.

She leaned up to his ear, saying, "I need to show you Journey's Beginning."

"No, I asked you a question and I want an answer."

It was like pulling teeth for her for some reason, and then she answered loudly, "It will depend on you."

"Me? Why me?"

"I cannot have a relationship with someone that is unequally yoked with me."

He looked at her a little offended. "You're going to get religious on me now?"

"I must, for my relationship with God will always be first in my life, and if he said that I must choose one that has the same faith as me, then I must obey."

"Really?" Benaiah stood, looking down at her. "If that was true, then you explain why Jahar sent for me to take his place when he knew I was not buying into this creation God thing?"

Mariah slowly stood in a posture of defense and confidently stated, "Jahar was wiser than we will ever be. He knows from the Bible that God has put in all men the awareness of him as well as examples of his creations for all to see, hear, taste, touch, and smell. You know this, but you will not admit it because you want to hide yourself from living by faith under the loving power of God."

Benaiah backed off a step on the rocks, surprised that he was suddenly verbally attacked again.

She continued, "We have explained many things to you which, less than a week ago, you were oblivious to, including your true identity. Jahar knew exactly what he was doing, especially when he allowed you to be immersed in the outside world and have you study what you have been learning, Dr. Benjamin Maschel." She said slightly sarcastically, and then she added kindly with a smile, "I say all this to explain that when you see what I show you here now, you will completely have a transformation of your mind about the world as you know it, which in turn, will transform your heart, convincing you to be a believer in the Creator God by using your own weak factual methods of living.

"You see, Jahar somewhat prophesied that if one of our own was thoroughly drenched in the dark outside world you live in and believed all the lies taught in your secular schools, which you were and do, then, when you see actual physical proof from the Bible of old, it would make that person passionately more of an extraordinary spiritual leader for Journey's End."

She stepped up close to him, placing her hand to his chest above the small weapon strapped to him and looking deep into his eyes said, "I am going to believe Jahar is right, and I will believe God will answer my prayers. My prayers for a strong Godly man to come into my life." She paused, looking away in a shy manner. "When you transform with a new heart, we will be equally yoked." She looked back at him. "Until then...I will want to kiss you, but I must not anymore. Sorry I have misled you."

Benaiah stared expressionless, not sure what to say or do as Mariah kept looking away and then back. After a few moments, she was tired of waiting or scared of the silence—she wasn't sure—and asked, "Say something…please."

"Well, what do you want me to say? From what you just said and adding all the things Horasha told me, my whole life has been a lie and a setup from the beginning."

Not expecting that train of thought, she responded, "No, you have not been set up."

"That's what it sounded like to me, Mariah!" he said, firmly stating her name.

"You are misunderstanding. Jahar always listened closely to God, letting the Holy Spirit guide him on what to do."

"Stop it! Stop playing me for a fool. I'm done with this conversation. If you have something to show me, then show me. If not, then get me the heck out of here!"

He turned around, looking at a small rocky shoreline and stepping away toward the misted cavern wall. He peered back and said, now being the embarrassed one, "If you didn't want to kiss me, that's all you needed to say instead of hiding behind this masquerade."

She dropped her hands to her side in disbelief of at how this definitely wasn't going the way she planned. Just as with Jahar, she thought it would go much easier and with quicker results, but she seemed to continually run into roadblocks. Changing her demeanor, she barked at him, "Are you truly that thick-headed? Fine, you better be rested because you are about to get your butt handed to you with what we have to do next."

She started walking past him to a small opening to the side of the waterfall and said, "Stay right there. I have to…"—she paused—"use the ladies room."

She walked out of sight into the forest and then looked back to make sure he was not following her. When she felt secure, Mariah touched several buttons on the small glass screen on her wide wristband. Then she slowly raised her finger in the air as if she was about to tap a final button to engage something. She tilted her head up to heaven, whispering, "Lord of heaven's armies, Jesus, please forgive me if what I am about to do is against your will. Jahar, if you can hear me, my heart has been telling me…this is my duty. But I do not understand it. It goes against all of who and why we are here."

Keeping a firm military look on her face, a tear slowly streamed down as she hesitated while waiting to hear a response. Moments passed with nothing happening. Dropping her gaze to the screen, her finger pointed to the button and said, "For our king, may your wisdom from three thousand years ago prevail now as God and his Kingdom be gloried."

Tapping the blinking red button on the screen, it turned green and then read out, "Mission executed." With no more hesitation, her intensive military training and work with the IDF, combined with the historical descendant training in Journey's End, she walked back behind the waterfall as though nothing out of the ordinary happened, completely being the Mariah that everyone knew.

Walking up to Benaiah, he asked in his sarcastic attitude, "So where is this mystical stuff you and Jahar have been teasing me about?"

"Mystical? We will see about that." She laughed, taking her backpack off and getting a headlamp, swimming goggles, and miniature underwater airbreather out, telling him to do the same. Then she pointed low, where the falling water was hitting the pool, and said, "We are going to dive to the bottom and find a specific boulder which has King Solomon's symbol engraved on it, exactly like his signature ring. Roll it to the side to expose a tunnel and then go in. This tunnel weaves its way back into the mountain and then angles up above the water level to an open area. We will be hundreds of feet directly below the commons area and Jahar's personal living quarters."

Listening to her, he comically thought, *I have to be on a reality show with hidden cameras. There is no way all this is really happening. Maybe I'm actually on a movie set in Hollywood or at Disney World? And she's an actress. That's why she won't kiss me anymore.'*

Mariah lifted her miniature scuba tank that was four inches wide and an inch in diameter, with the mouthpiece coming out of it in the center, and said, "Put this in your mouth like a snorkel mouthpiece. When you want to breathe, bite down, inhaling very slowly and holding the new air in your mouth, letting it warm up before it goes into your lungs and then exhaling out your nose. Remember, if you inhale too fast directly to the lungs, it could freeze them."

"Nice to know. How long does this last?"

"Approximately fifteen minutes, depending how many times you take a breath."

"Sounds good. Let's get this show on the road," Benaiah willingly replied, clicking his headlamp on and off to make sure it worked. He asked, "Are these waterproof?"

"Of course," she answered with a confident grin.

Being a gentleman and toying with her at the same time, and believing she was leading him on a wild goose chase, he pointed his hand out toward the waterfall and said, tipping his head to the side while giving a half smile, "After you."

She saw his skeptical look, fully understanding what he was thinking, and she turned on the headlamp, positioned her goggles, and then, before putting the breather in her mouth, she stated, "You are going to be apologizing to me over and over very soon." Then she stepped into the water, swimming deep.

He put the breather in his mouth, stepping in right behind her, and whispered under his breath, "We'll see." Then he turned on his headlamp and adjusted his goggles.

***

The autopsy room was kept much cooler than all the other rooms in the medical facility. It also worked as the morgue, with body lockers along the back wall. Three of the six lockers had identification tags on the outside handles with the names Jasaph, Tahla, and Burak.

Horasha was not yet aware his brother was dead as he followed the doctor into the autopsy room with Jahar's limp body in his arms. He laid the old deceased man down respectfully on the stainless steel table in the middle of the room. Looking up at the doctor and trying to make light in a difficult situation, he asked, "The guards told me what happened earlier. Can we trust you not to steal Jahar again?"

Not finding it funny, he glared at him because he had to clear his name, proving he was protecting Jahar and he did not kill Tahla on purpose. But he also had heavy news for Horasha. He attempted to find words knowing he was one to always have an unpredictable temper.

Waiting for a response, Horasha said impatiently, "Okay, I guess I will leave you two alone." A more compassionate thought came to Horasha as he changed his tone. Tapping his finger on the corner of the table, he added, "I know you two were very close. We all lost a great leader and friend." Looking at each other, they nodded in agreement.

The doctor looked at Horasha's beat-up face as gauze was wrapped around his head and asked, "How is your head feeling?"

Reaching up, he replied, "It is fine. Thank you for the bandage."

"Too bad about Jasaph," The doctor said, looking down at Jahar's body, only rising his eyes up to Horasha in a manner of suspicion.

Horasha played it nonchalantly. "It completely took me off guard as well. I had no idea he would go to such extremes attempting to kill Benaiah." Then he laughed. "But what is more surprising is that Benaiah was capable of doing what he did. In all these years, I have never seen a trace of a violent bone in his body."

Keeping to his suspicious tone, the doctor said, "I agree, Horasha."

Horasha wanted to wrap up the conversation, hiding how uncomfortable he was as he said, "Well, please prepare Jahar's body for the ceremony. I will be with the senior rabbi to start the arrangements for the tomb. Sorry again for our loss."

He turned to leave as the doctor said, "Wait." He put on a regretful frown.

Horasha stopped and turned around.

"There was another death today," the doctor said as he swayed his eyes to the side.

"I was made aware of it. Too bad Mariah's servant had a reaction to the shot." Horasha was the one now putting on an expression of suspicion and added, "Mariah is to blame for that, am I right?"

Ignoring the accusation, he replied, "Yes, Tahla died, but there is one more."

"Really, who?"

The doctor hesitated, still trying to find the words, turned to a specific locker, opened the door, and rolled out the covered body.

Horasha understood the doctor wanted to show him instead of telling him. Horasha walked up to the covered body and boldly uncovered the head.

It took a moment for it to fully compute. He did not expect to see who he was looking at. When it did, he shot up a glare to the doctor. "What happened?"

The doctor reached up to the covering and slowly peeled it back, exposing Burak's chest, and then said, "He was stabbed thirteen times with a thin round object like a pen or screwdriver."

"Who did this to him?"

"No one knows. A technician working on a malfunctioning identification door pad at the living quarters emergency door found him."

Astonishingly, at this point, he was emotionless as the doctor waited for his fuse to light up, but it never did as he replied in a monotone voice. "Thank you, Doctor, for showing me Burak's body. He can wait for burial. Please continue with Master Jahar."

Horasha calmly walked out of the room. Several guards were waiting for him just outside as they followed behind him in going out of the medical facility and down the tunnel to the commons area. They didn't say a word as Horasha searched his mind for answers as he internally fought back the pain of his dead brother. Halfway down the hall, he pulled out King Solomon's signature ring from a secure zipped-up shirt pocket. Without warning, he stopped in the middle of the tunnel directly in front of the same alcove Benaiah and Jahar had. Then he turned to the side as the guards almost ran into him. Peering down at the ring for a moment, his mind was churning in thought. He lifted his head up, staring into thin air at first, and then focused on what his eyes were seeing inside the niche. After a few seconds, he said out loud, "You conquered until there were nothing else to conquer. How did that feel, Alexander...the Great? Having the world in the palm of your hands?" Then he lifted his hand up with the ring as though that was exactly what was in his hand—the power of the world.

He stood there relishing in the idea as the guards were slightly miffed at his words while looking at the ring as if it was a trophy as they patiently waited for him.

Shortly, he put the ring back into his pocket, zipping it closed, and turned to one of the guards, saying, "Go to the senior rabbi and tell him Jahar is dead and to prepare for his burial this evening before the sun sets. Then meet back up with me in the living quarters at the emergency exit." Looking to another guard, Horasha said, "You stay with Jahar's body all the way to the tombs of the dead." Pointing to the last guard, he instructed, "You go to the guards control center and tell the commander to locate Mariah and Benaiah. Tell him to keep the intel confidential and not send any messages through our normal communications." He raised his arm with the armlet. "Then come straight to me with the information."

The guards uneasily looked at one another. Seeing their questioning faces, he raised his voice, "Focus! Jahar is gone! At any moment, confusion of leadership could cause a mass panic which we cannot afford. We need to know where everyone is right now, do you understand?" They nodded in agreement with him. "Good, also tell the commander I need two dozen off duty men to complete an interior search of the mountain. That includes every emergency exit tunnel, and by my orders, instruct him not to disturb the normal rotation of the two hundred on duty. They must stay focused on the security of Journey's End.

"Hopefully, the men we left at the invisibles' village to recon or the others we had scour the forest all the way up to the grand opening of the commons area where Uba said their man last saw him go will have news for us soon. It is imperative we find Benaiah quickly! I want to be updated continuously, understand?"

They nodded as he directed, "Good, now go!"

***

Swimming hard downward, Benaiah caught up with Mariah at the bottom of the miniature lake about twenty feet under the waterfall. With the powerful small headlamp moving his head around, he was able to see what she was talking about.

He had taken a scuba class in college because one of the required courses he had for advanced archeology was underwater excavating. Having some skill in what they were doing, he looked around as she was wiping mud and debris off boulders and searching for the one with the symbol carved on it.

Benaiah was the one to find what they were looking for. Rapidly wiping the engraving clean to get a clear view of Solomon's symbol, the water temporarily filled with a muddy cloud.

He reached over to Mariah, tapping on her arm. Looking at what he found, she nodded as she gestured for them to pull at the heavy rock from different corners. Not budging, they realized they needed more strength, so each placed their feet on other boulders next to the rock, sealing the entrance to the tunnel. With their legs, they strained against its weight, pulling with all they had. This time, it jarred, breaking a seal from the other rocks.

Looking toward one another, their eyes said the same thing, *We need a better grip*. Benaiah was doing well with the small breather, but after straining himself the last few moments, he was wishing for more air faster. They regripped, adjusting the positions of their feet, glanced at one another simultaneously, nodding one, two, three, and then pressed hard with their legs. The rock gave way and began to move out of its resting position. As it rolled backward in slow motion, one of Mariah's feet slipped downward, and the big rock rolled on her lower leg, pinning her flat to the lake floor. She screamed out in pain, and the breather fell out of her mouth. A large cloud of dirt billowed up from the floor, rolling through the cool water, and obscuring their vision again.

Not seeing what was happening to Mariah, Benaiah got excited and directed his headlamp into the new tunnel seeing what she said was true. Anxious to go in, he turned to her, expecting her to quickly take the lead. Not seeing Mariah, he swam around the cloud, stumped at where she was and trying to feel outward for her just in case her camouflage uniform was working better than he thought until he felt his pant leg being aggressively jerked down. Looking down, he was shocked seeing her grasping him with one hand and trying to push the boulder off her leg with the other.

Without hesitating, he shot to her side, grasping the rock and planting his feet to the floor. Pulling with all he had, it wasn't working as the rock from this angle was extremely slippery with moss and mud.

Quickly thinking, he went to her head to sign what he was going to do when he saw the breather wasn't in her mouth. Looking through the murky water toward the floor around her, he didn't see it anywhere. Taking a mouthful of air, he then pulled it out and put it into her mouth.

Fighting with every stroke to stay on the floor of the large pond, he searched and found what he needed to save her life—a thick tree branch they moved away earlier. Shoving it under the rock next to her leg, he was able to use it as leverage.

Firmly planting his feet, he squatted down into position. Before lifting, out of nowhere, he consciously thought, *God, give me the strength to save her!*

With everything he had, Benaiah pulled up. At first, there was no movement, and he thought loudly in a controlled panic, *Please, God, lift this rock! Or Mariah will die!*

Gritting his teeth and closing his eyes, Benaiah surged once more as his legs began to shake under the strain. Then, like pressure being relieved from a tight-fitting lid when opening a jar, the rock suddenly began to rise. Before he knew it, she was up next to him and putting his breather in his mouth. He let go of the large stick as it swiftly slammed to the lake floor with the rock on it, shooting dirt up into the water.

Biting down and taking a breath, it took all he had not to instantly let the cold air go into his lungs. Calming down, he was relieved having her next to him as she appreciatively rubbed his back.

She turned to look where she was pinned and bent down, picking something up. Then with a tug, she pulled him toward the hole they uncovered as their headlamps lit it up. Mariah went in first quickly, going down the three-foot wide tunnel and weaseling her way, grasping and pulling on the rock walls, and propelling herself with every surge.

The only thing Benaiah was able to see was the bottom of her boots kicking and pushing off the walls as they slithered their way, seemingly going on forever. Claustrophobia was setting in going deeper as he mentally felt pressure being under the big mountain, and then he thought to himself, taking his third breath, *How in the world is she holding her breath this long?*

Without warning, Mariah's boots disappeared above him, and his chest hit ground as it had quickly angled up and his head poked out of the water. He crawled out, taking a seat next to her on dry ground. Removing his goggles, he looked to Mariah as she took her breather out of her mouth.

Removing his, he said, "I didn't know you found your breather. I was wondering if you were superwoman holding your breath that whole time."

Already have taken her goggles off, she couldn't help herself and leaned over, giving him a hug and saying, "Thank you, Benaiah, descendant of the mighty warriors."

With their heads together, they remained clutched in each other's arms for a while, physically and mentally recovering and thinking of what happened and what might have been.

Benaiah broke the silence, knowing he had something on her from their last conversation, and whispered in her ear, "I prayed for your life."

She lifted her head, looking at him as they blinded each other with their headlamps and said, "I prayed too."

"What did you pray?" he asked.

"That God would give you the strength of Samson, and you instantly lifted the boulder. What did you pray?"

Not wanting to make it a competition or get too religious, he said, "What does it matter? I prayed."

Hearing slight sarcasm, she stood, but her leg faintly gave out at the pain from where the rock landed on her. Working the lower leg back and forth and then rubbing it, she mentally concluded there was no major damage. Taking her pack off, she answered, "I guess it does not." Shaking the remaining water droplets off her goggles and breather, she opened the backpack, storing them in a pouch within it and retrieved a lighter before pulling her hand out.

Benaiah copied her, putting his things away and then shouldering the pack. With his headlamp spotlighting around the small cave, Mariah walked toward something hanging midway on the rock wall next to a dark passage.

Flicking the lighter until a constant small flame appeared, Mariah reached up to what was an old-style torch on the wall. It instantly flared up with a small fire, bouncing a warm glow and brightening up the area.

Lifting the torch out of its rustic metal holder and turning back to Benaiah, she switched her headlamp off. Stepping up to her, he turned his off as well as Mariah looked at him, then into the dark mysterious passage that was going deeper into the mountain, and then back to him, saying, "It has been quite a few years since I have been here. Jahar was truly wise to show me Journey's Beginning as a safety net. What a coincidence that I am actually proving his wisdom."

Remaining sarcastic, Benaiah was starting to get the treasure hunt feeling as he commented, "Only words. Again, just more words. You better have something for me in there."

Fully confident, she maintained her upbeat demeanor, ignoring him as she said, "Through this tunnel and up a rock staircase, we will enter something far beyond your imagination. Then, what is in it will completely revolutionize your knowledge and belief of this world and its history…" With the biggest smile, she finished with, "I guarantee it!"

Her confidence was so strong it energized him. Repeating what he did at the waterfall, he held out his hand, tilting his head toward the dark opening, and said, "After you."

Mariah, giddy with excitement to see the incredible things again, poked the torch into the dark entrance, swiping away and burning up spiderwebs that crisscrossed in front of them and charged forward. Benaiah followed close behind as they went deeper into the mountain. After a short distance, they began stepping up a steep rock staircase. After a dozen or so steps, they came to a large flat landing. Walking to the end of the landing, a huge dark wooden wall stopped them in their tracks.

"A dead end?" Benaiah asked.

"No… It is the door of life."

"What?" He looked at her and then back to the extremely aged large beams of wood symmetrically put together horizontally. She raised the torch close as he stepped up to the door and examined it, rubbing his hand across one of the very old planks. It was blackish in color, and he realized it was a hardened tar-like coating on the planks. Making a fist, he knocked on the massive door, and it felt and sounded like stone. "What is this?"

"Very, very old wood, preserved by a thick layer of a waterproof substance."

Shaking his head in agreement, he looked up about twelve feet to the top and then to each side, which was about the same distance. Not seeing a door handle or hinges, he asked, "How do we open it?"

Mariah turned, looking up on the side rock wall. Moving the torch, she saw what she needed. Hanging up was a long sturdy pole with a wide, thin piece of metal angled and attached to it looking like a long farming hoe. She answered, "With this."

With a little honest curiosity building, he jokingly asked, "Why have a door without a handle? With all your supposable great technology, wouldn't you have built an electric door opener like all the other large doors you have in the commons area?"

"Those doors were built over time by us. This door…"—she patted the solid thick wood—"was built over four thousand years ago, way before Shuriah's and King Solomon's time."

The information was intriguing but didn't make sense, so Benaiah asked, "I thought you said everything your ancestors brought here to be hidden was from King Solomon?"

"They did, all his worldly wealth—gold, silver and jewels— are almost two hundred feet above us in a special vault we call the treasury. It is playing as a smokescreen for what is hidden down here, which is what Jahar and I were telling you Shuriah found. It is secretly hidden here from everyone, including all of the descendants and Africans excluding you and me." She thought for a second and then added, feeling it was important, "As well as Uba."

"Who?"

"The older invisible woman that took care of us."

He worked his eyes back and forth, trying to make sense of Journey's End's secrecy, and he asked, confused, "Why would something be hidden from the other descendants? Didn't your people bring it here to protect it?"

She hesitated, knowing her answer would probably be distasteful to him, and then she replied, "Yes, our ancestors did bring everything here and has been under our protection. But once what I am about to show you was secured and physically hidden from the world, Shuriah ordered everyone to forget and not tell anyone of its existence. If they did share this secret, passing it on to the next generation…" She paused, swaying her head. "They would be put to death as well as the ones they told.

"Unfortunately, hundreds were punished and killed. Even the nations that helped the Israelites get it here until the knowledge of this vanished over time…" She patted the historical wood door again. "Except for the guardians who handed it down from guardian to guardian over the thousands of years."

Still stumped, he said, "Well, let's open it so maybe I can make sense of what you're saying and what you're not telling me."

Smiling and attempting to control herself, Mariah handed the torch to him and then reached up with both hands, sliding the angled metal end into a seam in the wood at the ceiling area coming into focus as Benaiah looked closer. The seam went all the way around the four sides where the wooden door touched the rocky tunnel at the ceiling, walls, and floor.

Prying the top of the large door out, she then strained, pulling it toward her as it slowly creaked open top to bottom toward them like a drawbridge. They stepped back, allowing room for the door to open. As the torch flame flickered off the walls, it had the appearance of a monstrous mouth opening to swallow them up. The wider it opened, faint breaths of air wisped by them as ghostly sounds touched their ears. When the heavy door hit the rock floor, there was a firm vibrating thud that echoed back deep within the darkness, letting everything within know someone was entering its domain.

Benaiah didn't know how to feel hearing such an exceptional deep hollow sound going down the bowels of the darkness. Then his nose flared out as an old odor escaped, recalling similar smells from dig sights and extreme historic things that had crossed his path in the last few years. This suddenly poured out emotion and excitement, causing his heart to pound harder knowing that he was truly and finally going to see what he was here for.

Mariah stepped onto the drawbridge-like door, walking inside a few feet. Waist high in the middle of what looked like a hallway, a rock pillar was holding up a sizable decorative bowl filled with an oily substance. Touching the top of what was in the bowl with her torch, it instantly flared up illuminating the entrance area and back into the tunnel they came from.

Walking inside, Benaiah noticed, stepping off the wood door, that he was stepping onto a wooden floor as well. As his eyes adjusted, Mariah walked a short distance to another stone pillar with a bowl balancing on it. Setting it to flame and chasing more of the darkness away, another hallway going the opposite direction appeared. At an intersection of two hallways, he looked closely, realizing the walls past the entrance on the inside were wood as well. No longer being surrounded by the rocky mountain, he asked, "What is this place, Mariah?"

"It is not a place...but a thing!" she said with excited confidence as though she was presenting the next guardian with the greatest treasure.

Trying to envision something but having nothing come to mind, he asked, "Okay, what is it?"

She paused, pulling the torch close between them so she could clearly see his face, and she said, "You are inside...Noah's Ark!"

Chapter 12

Her words didn't connect in conjunction to where they were—deep under a mountain in the Congo. He asked with a frown, "Excuse me? What did you just say?"

Observing his reaction as the light of the flames from the torch flickered off his stumped expression, she said again, "We are standing inside Noah's Ark."

In bewilderment, Benaiah slowly turned around three hundred and sixty degrees, visually soaking in everything lit up around them. Toward the entrance, he saw the inner side of the outer walls next to the massive folded-out door matching the thick midnight tar appearance of the outside as the planks built on top of each other were solid and airtight. The wide interior hallway walls were a much lighter normal-looking color of wood as was the floor except the floor seemed to have what looked like a stained pathway in the center.

Trying to peer farther down the intersection of hallways clouded in darkness, Benaiah responded as the pendulum continued to sway back and forth, keeping him in a frustrated state of what to believe or not. He smartly questioned, "Now you've gone too far. What kind of joke is this? Do you really think I'm that stupid?"

"This is not a joke, and I know you are not...stupid, even though I called you it earlier. This is the true original reason for Journey's End." She raised her arms out, looking around. She stated, "This...this is Journey's Beginning. Solomon's wealth was an afterthought, per se, and the perfect camouflage to the world." She began to slowly walk deeper down the dark wider hallway leading directly away from the entrance door and holding up her torch as he followed close so as not to miss a word.

"As an archeologist, Benaiah, you have to appreciate this extremely preserved important part of history. Also, the story of how it was found is incredible."

Changing her tone to slightly mock him, she said, "If you read the Bible, as you said you have, you would know in the Old Testament that King Solomon would send a fleet of his ships out with King

Hiram of Tyre's fleet all the time. Hiram's people were expert ship builders and sailors from the area we now know as Lebanon, who helped build Israeli ships and sailed with them. He was originally a friend of Solomon's father, King David, who supplied all the cedar wood for the Temple of God, King David's palace and eventually expanding the palace when Solomon became king of Israel.

"Solomon's fleet explored, gathering items from new places as they ventured out into the unknown world. Every three years, the ships would return filled with gold, silver, spices, weapons, and exotic animals." Mariah stopped, turning to him to make a foundational statement. "Now, this is what you do not know and could not have ever known because it is the secret of all secrets."

She turned back and continued walking. "Shuriah, at that time, was King Solomon's personal bodyguard and general of the Israel army. He went on a special mission for our king that only he could handle, taking a couple of ships and a small regiment. They were caught up in a great storm a short time after setting sail. They wrecked along a rocky shoreline in the northwest corner of the Mediterranean Sea that we now call Turkey. Both ships sank, killing many men on board.

"Shuriah and the remaining men were able to make it to land, finding themselves in a foreign country where many people were very hostile to Israel. Back then, this area was known as Hatti, where the Hittites were from. The most famous Hittite was Uriah, one of the original thirty-seven mighty warriors and Shuriah's mentor. You know who Uriah was—Bathsheba's first husband who King David had set up to be killed in battle because David got her pregnant trying to hide his own shame."

"Yea, I know the story." Benaiah said with a little sarcasm.

Ignoring his interjection Mariah continued, "Anyway, they were hunted for months and chased for a long time to the north, far away, and cut off from the safety of their own country. They ended up scaling a very high and intimidating steep snow- and ice-covered mountain which we know as Mount Ararat.

"A winter storm swept across the fierce mountain, almost freezing our men to death until…" She pointed a finger in the air just like Jahar would always do. "They found an entrance into a cave in the ice and snow for shelter.

"They soon figured out they were not in an ice or rocky cave, but in a giant wooden structure hidden within the snow and ice with multiple levels. On each level, there were hundreds of animal stalls side by side just like King Solomon had for his masses of horses in his stables."

Mariah stopped walking at a second hallway junction, lighting another waist-high torch bowl. Ironically, when she mentioned stalls, he was looking down the new hallway. As far as the light would let him see through the darkness of the ancient ship cocooned underground, rows of stalls went down both sides.

Benaiah was becoming impressed as he looked in each direction and seeing these wooden stalls. Still having reservations, he asked, "So if you're right, and this is Noah's Ark, how in the world did this get here under this mountain…?" He tilted his head, looking at her and believing he had her cornered. He stated confidently, "Three thousand miles south of where you're talking."

Not answering his question directly and wanting to keep to her story, she said, "I will get there. As Shuriah and his men regained their strength, keeping warm in this incredible shelter on the mountain, many things were found in it. But believe it or not, the greatest find was not the ark but what Noah purposely left behind in it."

Wrinkling his forehead, he smirked at Mariah's foolish excitement and commented, "Keep going. This mysterious fairy tale is getting better by the moment."

Understanding his mockery, she only swiveled her head back and forth, putting her free hand on her hip. Then she spoke as though a mother talking to her child. "I have not even begun to scratch the surface. When I finish filling your brain and showing you everything that is here, you will feel as though you finally received an adult PhD compared to the pretend kindergarten certificate you acquired last month."

"Ouch. Nice comeback. So you do have a sense of humor," Benaiah stated as he wandered to the nearest corner stall, turning on his headlamp and peering inside. Looking around at the quaint rustic stall, it felt like he was in a museum. Then he asked like he was cracking a joke while concealing he was faintly beginning to believe the things she was telling him, "So what did Noah leave behind… His diary?"

Giving out a soft laugh, she said with enthusiasm, "Basically, yes! The interior side of the ships outer hull holds the most incredible detailed and complete history book of all time! Excluding the Bible, of course. Everything about the world's beginning two thousand plus years and about two hundred years or so after the flood is completely explained."

Giddy with excitement, she stepped up to him, grasping his arm finally able to share the hidden secrets. Knowing they would burst open his interests, and fulfilling his deepest desires, she slowly said, "Including...dinosaurs..." Pausing and watching his head quickly twist to her as they locked eyes, she then added, "...and dragons. Then where Egyptian and Greek religious mythologies actually came from, including answers to the elusive questions about the wondrous structures from ancient civilizations like with Mesopotamia and the Sumerians. The Minoans on Crete Island in Greece. Even the mystical city of Atlantis, which is not a fairy tale, but one of the many societies of the Nephilim before the flood.

"Noah has the answers to the questions how all these ancient societies were able to build such mind blowing structures and where the ideas came from and why the cultures suddenly disappeared.

"It also plainly explains the earth's growing pains and geography, unlike the puzzles and pathetic theories modern-day experts have come up with. Even when and where the different human races started, with so much more."

The word *dinosaur* alone captivated him down to the cellular level, erupting tingling goosebumps throughout his body and leaving him temporarily speechless as thoughts of the other things Mariah mentioned were exploding like fireworks in his brain.

Finally calming down, he was being torn in two completely different directions as he thought to himself while he looked around again, *Have an open mind. Maybe there is some truth to what she's saying. This place has the right feel, smell, and sounds of being prehistoric.*

The mysterious underground structure she called a ship was still overwhelming to the point it was ridiculous. Then she added what his life interests was about into the mix, so he asked, "He wrote... Noah wrote...about dinosaurs?"

As the flame brightly lit up her big smile, she answered by nodding. His eyes moved back and forth thinking, and then he asked with a questioning frown, "Did you also say…dragons?"

"Oh yes! They are not fairy tale creatures. They actually existed, playing a major role from when Adam and Eve were kicked out of the Garden of Eden to the flood of Noah." She then tilted her head and corrected herself, "Except…for the four eggs Noah reluctantly disobeyed God with by bringing them into the ark with the other animals."

"Come on. Dragons, Mariah? I'm not that gullible."

"Absolutely, they are mentioned in the Bible. God describes in detail a dragon to Job, which he was fully aware of in the forty-first chapter of the book of Job in the Old Testament. But there, he calls them leviathans. And in the previous chapter he describes a Behemoth which we know as a brachiosaurus. So God is talking about dragons and dinosaurs to Job."

He responded, "I've heard the Bible refer to Satan as a dragon."

"Yes, in the book of Revelations as an analogy. But in other areas, they are described for the mighty creatures they were."

Scrunching up his forehead, he commented, "Just when I was beginning to honestly believe all this stuff."

Shaking her head and rolling her eyes, she dropped her hand from his arm and commented, "I am going to rip that bogus title from you, Dr. Benjamin Maschel, right now, so you can at least start thinking and acting like a guardian of Journey's End. Then hopefully, after I thoroughly plunge you into the true real world, you will finally grow up and be…the guardian. Follow me…Doctor." She finished by mocking his naivete, and then she turned and marched off down the new hallway that went the other direction lengthways of the ark, holding the torch out to light her way.

With his headlamp still on, he watched her storm away and then looked back down into the empty ancient animal stall and asked himself, "Could this really be?"

He thought about the old unbelievable artifacts Jahar and him walked by in the cubby holes down the hall from the medical facility and the items from the book of time. Then heard in his mind

Horasha explain how they preserve things with sap from special trees here in the Congo.

Looking back up, Mariah was way down the long hallway with stalls on each side as a dark gap between them grew, and he exclaimed, "Shoot, I better catch up. She's ticked and on a mission."

With the light of his headlamp bouncing around and looking in all directions of the empty animal holding rooms going by in the hollow but solid structure, visions came to life. Images of them filled with different animals making frightened sounds, trying to keep their balance as a raging storm outside beat up against the outside walls and roared its fury of death on earth.

As he quickly got to her side, he spouted out, "Slow down."

She stopped, jerking back to him and putting her hand up to block the light from the lamp on his head. He turned it off as she stated, "I am trying to help you here, and you just want to be a...a..."

"A what?"

"A butt!" she blatantly stated.

Totally out of character for her, he laughed, "A butt? Seriously?"

"How else should I explain your attitude?"

"Attitude? This has nothing to do with attitude. What you are telling me is challenging intelligence."

"Intelligence? Have you not grasped anything from Jahar about wisdom? You can have all the knowledge the world has to offer, but it is completely worthless if you do not take to heart what Jahar was teaching you from Isaiah 55:8–9."

"Are we going there again?" He swung his arms out.

Giving him a stern glare, and thinking how Jahar would handle this, she turned, continuing down the hollow stuffy hallway as Benaiah followed. Being obedient to her duty to help Benaiah, she decided to continue with the story and calmly said, "Back to Shuriah finding the ark. One of the men that survived the shipwreck with him was King Solomon's translator, who Shuriah needed for the mission he was originally on. The man came from a long family bloodline of language learners educated in languages of the past and from nations around the area. This translator was able to interpret the old writings from Noah's time.

"When Shuriah realized what they were in and what Noah's... diary..."—she brought her hands up, giving the quotation sign—"per se, was filled with, he knew this was something only King Solomon, the wisest man, would know what to do with."

"I've got you there..." Benaiah interrupted with a smirk on his face. "The oldest written language is Sumerian, dating back to near thirty five hundred BC. The proof was found in Iraq when the Kish Tablet was found.

"Mariah, you're talking about someone—supposedly Noah—knowing how to write a complete language way before this time period."

She slowly shook her head, saying, "Of course they had a language. They were able to write and articulate more than a couple of thousand years earlier than what you are saying. Knowledge comes from knowledge, which was given to them by God to communicate in the Garden of Eden when he walked and talked with them there. Unlike what you believe, that man's intelligence and skills derived from apes, which we know only have a communication level and ability to only make sounds like 'ooh, ooh, eee, eee,' And still is their language of today thousands of years later saying, ooh, ooh, eee, eee." She was the one now to give a smart look added, "no evolution happening there, is there Dr. Maschel?"

He didn't know if he wanted to get into a heated debate at the moment, because Mariah was actually getting to the core and showing him what was so important. It didn't matter; she continued before he could reply. "An example of man's historic intelligence is written in Genesis 6, with Noah, when God gave him precise measurements to build this huge ship three hundred cubits long, fifty cubits wide, and thirty cubits high, which even proves they had a complete math system in play as well way back then."

With Mariah having a confrontational but simple answer for everything, Benaiah decided to wait to confront her with the truth until they saw everything she wanted him to see. Then he would wrap this fairy tale up in a big intellectual and mental package, proving science is the bible of life, setting fire to what these naïve and lost people at Journey's End believed was the truth and turning it into ashes. "Sorry I interrupted you. Please go on about Noah's diary," he encouraged her, trying not to sound smug.

She paused, reading his eyes and understanding what he was doing, and she decided to start where she left off. "After realizing what they found, Shuriah and his men were able to safely disassemble several smaller planks on the top row with Noah's writing on it to have proof of their find. When the winter storm finally broke, the small group of men left the ark with the evidence and were able to elude their attackers who had given them up for dead. Going a different direction by following the Euphrates River southwest for a while, they then left it, heading directly south. Months after the ark encounter, they finally and secretly made it back to Jerusalem.

"When Shuriah privately informed our king of what they found, he told Shuriah he had uncovered a treasure that was far greater than any worldly wealth. It was a treasure with God's fingerprints all over it. Solomon was very excited but disturbed at the same time. He secluded himself for a while, praying and deeply pondering what to do with Noah's Ark and the knowledge within it.

"He finally concluded that, with the whispers of God, it should not be exposed to the world at that moment in time but preserved for a future day of God's choosing to be revealed for his glory. Not just for the ark itself but, more importantly, the history Noah wrote in it which even Solomon did not understand the complete significance of but which we do now.

"This is when the Queen of Sheba comes into the story we told you about already. King Solomon needed to find another place on earth besides the icy snowcap peak of Ararat to hide the ark. He wanted it in another more hospitable area so that his guards and future generations would be able to live with it, guarding it for all time in a place unknown to the civilized world that was very difficult to get access.

"After secret meetings with the Queen of Sheba about this, her scouts searched out the perfect place to satisfy the most respected man on earth. While this was going on, Shuriah and a large army of thousands of men and ninety mighty warriors took a majority of King Solomon's fleet, along with many of King Hiram's ships and thousands of his ship-building experts and sailors. They sailed to the shores of the people that attacked and chased him and his small group of men to the high snowy mountains, slaughtering every man, woman, and child in their path.

"While the Israelite army was leading the way and eliminating threats along the trek north, King Hiram's men were carrying with them completed pieces of one of their large unassembled ships that was the cargo in their fleet. When they found the ark again on the high icy mountain, they began the long process of chiseling it out and disassembling it. Then they assembled the ship they had brought along with them in place of the ark. Once this was done, they retraced their steps back to their ships with Noah's Ark in pieces and refilling King Hiram's large cargo ships."

Benaiah interrupted, intrigued with the story. "Why did they do that? Sounds like a lot of work for nothing."

"This, again, is one of King Solomon's wise ideas to protect the original ship. They did not know if there was anyone or another nation that had the knowledge of the ark being there, so to cover up that it was gone, they put another ship in its place so they would never go looking for it.

"They logically camouflaged the counterfeit ark by setting one end on fire, as well as small areas inside, and then putting it out. This gave the appearance it had been struck by lightning. Putting the finishing touches for the decoy, they caused a minor avalanche, burying it within the snow and ice, preserving it in the same spot in case someone already knew it was there."

Benaiah grinned while swaying his head and said, "That's pretty smart. Especially now, three thousand years later. There have been several people over the last fifty years that stated they found Noah's Ark or at least pieces of it. One used satellite imaging, looking for shapes of a large ship within the snow and glaciers to locate it, but each one appeared to be a hoax, or it really wasn't what they thought it was."

Grateful for the first complement coming from him, she replied, "Our king, as we have said many times, was very wise." Then Mariah went back to the story. "So when they were finished with one of the most labor intensive feats of all times, never recorded for the general public and taking more than two years, they waited for further instructions on where they were going along the shoreline, with their fleet ready to set sail.

"When the extreme confidential orders finally came, it was accompanied with a sizeable army from the Queen of Sheba, who was to lead them to the hiding place far away, here in the middle of the Congo. They sailed through the Mediterranean Sea around western Africa in the Atlantic Ocean to the Congo River, traveling up a long way. Then they traveled through the dense forest to this most special of all places.

"Calculating travel routes, they decided this was the wisest choice, being quicker and safer, keeping the precious cargo from everyone's eyes on land as they would have had to go through Israel, Egypt, and many other countries with extreme terrain while carrying the immense and curious cargo."

Mariah's torch was beginning to burn low as she changed topics. "We need to go. There are many more torches upstairs."

"Upstairs?"

"Yes, I would think that being a Christian when you were young and reading and hearing the stories and now being an archeologist, you would know historical facts like the details of the ark?"

"I study facts, not storybook legends and myths."

Under the mountain, in the bowels of the large ancient ship, through the dark and cool atmosphere, a calming peace swept through her. Knowing what was happening, she let go of Benaiah's comment and listened as her mind heard comforting wise words, *He is still a child. I will remove the veil from his heart soon, and he will see that I am God, the Creator of all things.*

This picture captured her, giving her courage for a more mature attitude than how she had been responding. She said, "Benaiah, descendant of Shuriah. Refreshing your memory from when your parents read to you about Noah's Ark, there are three levels in the ark, and we are standing in the middle one. Translating cubit into feet, the ship is four hundred and fifty feet long, seventy-five feet wide, and forty-five feet high, all made from gopher wood, which has not existed since the great flood. The outer walls inside and out are covered heavily with pitch—a tar-like substance for waterproofing."

They made their way to the end of the long hallway to a gently sloping wide ramp reaching up to the third floor. At the top of the ramp at the front hull of the ship, she lit up another bowl torch stand in the middle of the hallway which was at the front of the ark. She took another hand torch off a wall close by and replaced it with the dying one. Mariah didn't have to say a word as Benaiah saw what she had been talking about, finally getting to an outer hull wall. On each plank, starting at the top and going across, symbol-like designs were etched deep in the pitch and old wood, resembling ancient markings similar to Egyptian hieroglyphics.

Benaiah's eyes followed each plank, going horizontally and looking at a language he had never seen before. Stepping close, he gently touched the plank at eye level while feeling the carved symbols. A tingling sensation began to run up his spine as the hair on his arms and the back of his neck rose as though he was absorbing electrical energy through the end of his finger from the wall.

Taking him off guard, he dropped his hand to his side, blowing out a loud breath as he asked, "What's that?"

"What is what?" She looked at his face and then at what he touched.

"This wall has electricity running through it or something." She touched where he did. "I do not feel anything?"

He watched her hand and replied, "Don't play games with me?"

Swiping her hand down several planks, he said seriously, "I am not playing... a game."

He reached out, touching it again as though reading braille, and then he looked at her and said, "Sorry, I just had a weird feeling."

Mariah suspected God had something to do with it and turned to continue the tour. Walking into the first stall next to them, she held up the torch to light up the back wall which was the outer wall of the ark said, "Noah continued the year and topic he was writing about on the same plank level all the way down the side of the ship to the back."

Stepping out of the stall, she pointed to the back of the ark, saying, "Then he continued writing on the other side of the ship from back to front, repeating this and going down tier by tier on the planks until he reached the floor. When he was done filling the walls on the upper level, he went down to the middle level, filling it, and then he went to the lower level walls."

Impressed, Benaiah envisioned what a six-hundred-plus year old man looked like as he chiseled away inside the giant ship and smartly said, "That's a lot of carving for a man hundreds of years old, don't you think?"

Her indisputable smile came back as she answered, "He started building this when we was about five hundred years old. What is another few hundred years?" She lifted her hands in the air, shrugging her shoulders in a friendly questioning way.

Continuing, she stated, "He had so many incredible things to write about of his family's history." The tone in her voice matched her smile as she again was finally able to share the secret of secrets she had never been able to tell anyone. "Noah went in chronological order of the different events, starting with Adam and Eve through, I think...five generations after them on this level. Then, on the second level, he continued to his generation, which is the tenth from Adam and Eve until the end of the flood. The lower level walls are filled with information when the ark landed on dry ground until close to his death several hundred years later."

Sparking his interest, Benaiah asked, "So by your calculations, how many years does he have archived in here and what are the dates?"

"We get that from what God told Moses when he gave him the first five books of the Bible..."

Benaiah interrupted, "The Pentateuch."

"So you are going to admit you know things from the Bible?"

Giving her a grin from the side of his face and acting the part, he replied with, "I'm learning to be a team player here."

"Thank you, I appreciate that. Obviously, the creation historical calendar and the evolution calendar are completely different."

"That's for sure." He chuckled.

She lifted a finger in the air again, "I will say though, in your science world there has been a quiet wedge growing toward the creation timing of the worlds geographical and environmental history. Because in every trail of an evolution theory, each one always ends at a dead end with no logical answer except to believe there is a supernatural being that created all things."

Quickly responding, Benaiah said, "Absolutely, there are those goofball scientists in different universities who think they have proof, showing the world is only being approximately six or seven thousand years old, agreeing with your creation story, which is what you're getting at right?"

"Yes, but the proof which we live by is logical evidence that is not only physical, because we do not a have a time machine to go back and see the facts, but faith-based truth, believing what is written in God's Word. Much different than how and what you want to believe. Your proof..."—Mariah slowly shook her head in disagreement—"by science is not proof at all but human selfishness grasping at dreams and things out of thin air with many, many missing links going down rabbit holes everywhere, proving that your claims will only be theories with no guide for why the universe came about to where we are going into the future. Completely leaving out what mankind is eternally about—heart and soul, not flesh and blood." Mariah stood firm, holding her ground and waiting for a confrontation as her smile turned to a firm challenge.

What she said was nothing new as he was almost expecting it. Maintaining an abnormally calm composure, he replied, shrugging his shoulders as though it didn't bother him, "So...are you going to continue your story?"

Still holding her ground commented, "Wow, I was waiting for you to respond again from your backside."

"No, I want to hear what you have to say about this place. This is good stuff for writing a fiction book." He gave her a smart-aleck grin, adding, "Oh, but wait you have one—the Bible."

She paused, looking at his facial expression with the light wavering from the torch and seeing he was sarcastically toying with her. Drawing from inner strength, Mariah completely ignored him and went back to answer his timeline question. "Starting with Adam and Eve when they were out..."—she raised her hand, giving the quotation sign to emphasize the word *out*—"of the Garden of Eden, it begins somewhere around 6,000 BC. Then to Noah, ten generations down is about two thousand years later, so it would be 4,000-ish BC.

"I need to clarify the world's starting time of yearly dating with Adam and Eve..." She hesitated to make sure he heard clearly what she was telling him. "Time and dates as we know it began after... they were kicked out of the Garden of Eden.

"Adam told his descendants that he could not calculate how long they were in the garden from when God created him. It could have been two years or twenty thousand years. Time was of no matter, because death was not comprehensible for it had not happened yet in the garden just like heaven. God is omnipotent, the Alpha and Omega. He has no beginning or no end, and the Garden of Eden was a perfect place God created in which he walked with his children and cared for them. Nothing decayed, died of old age, or had an expiration date. No animal killed another. They were all vegetarians in the garden." Again, she shrugged her shoulders and stated, "Except...for everything on the outside of the garden, where the prince of darkness dwelled, and still does, as he was and still is allowed by God to rule. Everything there, as does now, died of old age or is killed sooner or later as everything physical has a limited lifespan, not the glorious infinite amount of time the garden had or heaven has where our God reigns.

"When they entered into this new changing world of good and evil where death already existed for plants and animals, that is when negative aging, leading to death and decay, began for mankind. This is when..." Again, she gave the quotation sign but this time for the word *when*. "Adam and Eve started keeping track of time and their age, for God told Adam that, now, his days were numbered.

"You see, many people naively start calculating in their minds the calendar years after the six days of creation or when Adam and Eve were in the garden when, truthfully, man has no clue of that time frame or the duration thereof. But through Adam and his wife exiting Eden and entering the world of good and evil, that is when the actual time clock for humanity as we know it started."

Benaiah's head began spinning with this eye-opening information that he never heard before.

"Sorry about the rabbit trail. So...Noah finished writing in the lower level with the approximate year being thirty-eight or thirty-nine hundredish BC, give or take a hundred years. Very simple really."

Believing he was going to easily change the tide of the conversation, he raised his eyebrows and asked, "How are you going to explain the twenty-five-million-year-old dinosaur fossils I dig up all the time?"

Chapter 13

He wasn't expecting her quick response being so matter of fact. "Easy. Your dates are completely wrong. Man dreamed them up, and they do not exist. Your historical dating processes like carbon or radiometric dating, again, are all only theoretical and have no factual evidence. We have the Bible, you have nothing. Dinosaurs were alive while Adam and Eve were in the garden until the world flood killed them off a couple of thousand years later as Noah floated around on the ark, not your mythical man made up millions of years ago."

Your own science proves this by stating the sun is continually getting smaller. If we reverse the aging process by your millions of years and apply that to the sun being larger, the earth's surface temperature would be a thousand degrees. That is lava-flowing hot and nothing could grow, including your ferocious dinosaurs.

She turned quickly in a military fashion and then walked away knowing he would follow. Leaving him stumped, she said, "Let us go down a short way. Jahar showed me, in many of the animal stalls on the dividing side walls, drawings of Noah bringing to life his writings from the back walls as he saw things. He has etchings of many different dinosaurs in scenes with dragons, protecting man from them as well as fighting the Nephilim."

Benaiah stopped and raised his voice. "Wait a second?" The explosion of information she was blurting out completely took him off guard, blowing his mind.

She didn't stop. "Keep up with me. This is going to be great! You will see."

Benaiah was at her side, dodging in and out of stalls and seeing snapshots of different drawings but kept going until she finally found what she knew he needed to see. Finally bobbing into the stall she was looking for, they froze. The back wall was full, top to bottom, with these momentous hieroglyphics as both sides of the partition walls looked like scenes from caves found around the world of stick figures of man and animals. But these were not all normal animals. Included were many drawings of dinosaurs and the like.

"No way…?" Benaiah slowly breathed out the words as his eyes got wide. Stepping forward for a better look, he turned on his head-lamp. Starting at the top, he scrolled his eyes, following an action scene, continuing down until it finished at the floor. He knelt to get a better look but popped back up as his knee was poked by something hard. Looking down, he said with excitement, "Are you kidding me?" Benaiah bent down, picking up a sandy colored object in the shape of a banana about six or seven inches long by two inches wide, with one end coming to a point.

Holding up the incredibly preserved item, Benaiah asked Mariah, "Do you know what this is? It is the same thing Jahar used as a handle on his cane."

She shared his excitement more for him than anything and quickly nodded.

"Nah, it couldn't be. Are you serious? You're not playing a game are you?"

"You are the expert, remember? You tell me."

He looked closely and asked, "Do you have a knife?"

"There is one on your belt."

"Oh yeah." He pulled it out of the sheath and then gently tapped on it to hear how dense it was. Then he began to shave a small piece and stopped, asking permission. "Do you mind?"

"No, there are plenty more all over the place. These are what Noah used as his writing tools."

"More?"

Her face was now glowing, not only from the reflection of the torch but more from seeing Benaiah finally interested in what he needed to see and know about Journey's Beginning. She answered, "Many more, along with skulls that those go into and the extremely large bones they used as tools, furniture, and many other things."

His face went blank. Thinking he was in a dream and trying to reassemble in time the pieces of history he was holding in his hand, he said, "I'm having a hard time with this… I…"

She stepped up next to him. "It is okay. First, finish what you were going to do with the knife."

He looked down and then slowly and gently scraped the rounded edge of the ancient giant tooth.

Mariah informed him, "The first layer you will scrape off is a clear sap preservative. Your second scrape you will be cutting into the tooth of a tyrannosaurus rex or another dinosaur like it. Again, you are the expert. You tell me."

Benaiah closely examined the first shaving, softly rubbing it between his fingers and then took her off guard when he tasted it with the end of his tongue.

He took his time tasting it and then scraped off the second layer which was much harder and grittier. Repeating the same process, he noticed two definite textures and taste, with the second layer having a strong mineral and salty flavor.

Out of nowhere, Mariah had a sudden thought, scaring herself for a moment and gasping out loud, making Benaiah flinch. She pulled up her sleeve and looked down at her wrist at the screen on the armlet.

Touching one of the glowing lights, the time appeared as though it was holographically hovering off the bracelet as she exhaled with relief. "Phew. For a moment there, I forgot about…" she awkwardly hesitated as though she was thinking of something to say. "Jahar's burial this evening at the tombs of the dead. It is hard to keep track of time in here."

"Burial tonight? He just died this morning."

Mariah realized again how naïve he was about everything, not only of Journey's End but of Hebrew traditions as well. "When Israelites of old passed away, we were buried as soon as possible, preferably on that day before nightfall. We continue that tradition here."

He wavered his head a little to acknowledge her as she added, "I have been thinking of how and when we need to present you to everyone safely as the new guardian of Journey's End. We know we cannot trust Horasha and his family. The safest way I have come up with is when the majority of all the influential descendants are together with the invisibles and other African tribal leaders. That would be this evening at sunset when they put Jahar and the small ones' chief to rest."

His face was blank and turning a ghostly white, with his stomach suddenly feeling queasy, "What's wrong? Are you getting sick from licking the stuff you shaved from the tooth?"

He hesitated and then replied in a way not wanting her to know that the rush of a possible alternate reality he never expected was hitting him. "No… I don't think so."

First, everything he believed about the world to be true suddenly was appearing to be false. Second, the idea of him taking on the powerful guardian position was screaming out in his head, *You are not worthy!* Having no experience and thorough knowledge of Journey's End, compared to Jahar, he was nothing without wisdom, leaving him feeling small and inadequate. Lastly, he thought back to yesterday when he told Horasha he was not taking over for Jahar because guardians were prisoners to this place, and he was not willing to sacrifice his life of freedom.

Watching Benaiah's face, Mariah had an idea of what could be going through his mind and decided to do a quick overview of Noah's story from the start to keep him focused on where he was at now and to inspire him. She mentally went through the ark, ending up at the lower level. The special things hidden away down there, she thought to herself, would give him the final knowledge and awareness needed for him to make the complete transformation to be the next guardian.

Looking back up deep into his eyes and seeing the flame from the torch flickering, Mariah let him hear his roots again to refocus him. "Benaiah, descendant of King David's mighty warriors, soon-to-be guardian of Journey's End. You need the knowledge no other descendant has except for me." She gave him a wink as her mind went into the future, thinking of the possibility of sharing everything together in life as well as this.

"Let us go back to the front, and I will highlight things along the way, finishing up with Noah's last words on the lower deck." Her stomach started growling as she added, "We have not eaten anything since yesterday. Are you hungry?"

He nodded, still reveling with the unknowns in his head.

Taking off her pack, she pulled out a couple of energy bars, giving one to him and, slinging the pack back on, she said, "Come on."

When they got back to where they started, she began the story just like Jahar told it to her when she was a girl with Adam and Eve.

"You know the story of the Garden of Eden and them getting kicked out for disobeying God. But what you do not know is, all the animals that were in the Garden Adam had named were the same animal and bird types Noah had saved from extinction, which are the same animals of today.

"At this same time frame, there were other types of animals on the outside of the Garden of Eden, as I mentioned, blocked from going in. What we now call…dinosaurs."

She walked several stalls back down looking for a specific drawing. Finding it, she said before walking in, "Adam lived over nine hundred years, and back in the old days, we know family history and stories were handed down from generation to generation, being repeated over and over in detail. It was part of their social culture. Noah knew the story about the beginning from his grandfather Methuselah and others when he was a child and wrote it down in here."

She stepped into the stall, lighting it up. There, taking up half of one of the side walls, was an intricate drawing of what looked like a beautiful garden. Benaiah thought to himself, *That looks like the garden in the commons area.*

Surrounding the outer edge of the garden, there appeared to be a fence of swords on fire, protecting it except for one small section where the swords were lifted high as an arch.

Benaiah stepped close, examining the artwork. Two human figures, a man and a woman, had walked out of the garden, past the open raised gate of swords, with the animals of Eden following close behind. In front of them and surrounding the garden, covering the rest of the stall's side walls, were drawings of extremely different plants and animals. Unlike the normal-sized plants and animals in the garden which were smaller, more delicate, and more human-sized in stature.

Benaiah didn't say anything as he slowly examined the details of the portrait. He lifted his hand, gently following the carved lines of everything outside the garden and mentally saw them coming to life as he knew what everything was but only in fossilized form.

Soon, his fingers didn't understand what they were feeling as his mind didn't want to admit what he was looking at. He asked, "Is this a...dragon or... What was the other name for them?"

Mariah stood next to him, brightening up the ancient artwork with the torch and answered, "Yes, it is a leviathan." Then she turned to the other walls, pointing out, "So is that, that and that."

Benaiah was struggling, knowing he was between a rock and a hard place, and thinking to himself, *Do I believe this stuff?*

Then he asked out loud, "You said something to the effect that dragons protected man?"

"That is what Noah wrote. He said the grandparents of old explained that Adam and Eve were forced by God to leave the perfect, gentle, and loving world they were created in where God physically walked with them. They entered what appeared, compared to Eden, to be a haunting, imperfect world of isolation, death, and destruction, claimed by darkness and evil, and having no clue what any of these giant and powerful creatures were.

"It was a place where God did not walk with them as he did in the garden. He was there, but only in Spirit, for everything now was different in the world of good and evil. Man was on his own, free to choose to follow the powerful darkness of this world or the mighty Light of the universe.

"In this world, they soon found out they were physically defenseless against most of the giant beasts that could roar like thundering clouds as the ground trembled with every step they took. Some were extremely violent, thirsting for flesh and blood. Others could just crush them to death by stepping on them or getting in the way of their powerful swaying tails. This is where dragons become their protectors.

"As God explained in the book of Job about the leviathan, they were the perfect fighting machines. You know this too, Benaiah, that even in the minds of people today, we think of them as the ultimate beasts but only as mystical fairy-tale creatures.

"Think of what people write about dragons—breathes fire, impenetrable scales of body armor…" She turned, having seen something when they walked in, on the floor, leaning up on one of the corners of the stall, she pointed out, "Like that…and powerful wings, legs with massive claws, and a tail strong enough to break a full-sized tree in half. Then add major attitude, and what do you have? The greatest fighting machines."

Benaiah moved his attention to the object she pointed out, as she added, as if it was nothing important, "It is all true. They could even stay underwater for great periods of time, where they did some of their sleeping. A few drawings in a couple of the stalls somewhere show them underwater fighting giant fish or other water creatures of some kind."

Benaiah knelt down at the object which, at first glance, looked like the head of full-sized spaded shovel coming to a point and slightly curved. He started to reach out to touch it, but Mariah quickly said, "Do not touch! It is fragile!"

He snapped his hand back, asking, "You're saying this is a dragon scale?"

"Yes, it is. There are very, very few remnants of dragons left, because when they die, their bodies and skeletal systems deteriorate at a rapid rate from the inside out because of the potent gasses within their system that enable them to breath out fire. That is why you will never have ever found dragon bones or other parts of their bodies. The few pieces in the ark are from when Noah gathered them quickly after their protectors died of old age. At least that is what Jahar said as he read it in the translated transcripts from King Solomon's interpreter."

Benaiah stood, not totally believing what he was seeing, was truly what she was saying it was. Working his way around the stall and peering at the details, he said, "So you're telling me that dragons were guard dogs for man?"

"Yes, that is a great way to put it."

Being very skeptical, he was needing many gaps filled with information, so he questioned, "Most of the time, cultures around the world have legends of things that happened in the past but then are stretched out of proportion over time. How can you explain this dragon obsession of today thousands of years later?"

Her eyes went big, remembering something she said when they first entered the ark. She excitedly stated, "Dragon eggs! There are broken up dragon eggs in their stall." She grabbed his hand like a little girl and ran him down the hall to the far end of the boat, on the upper deck, to a special fully enclosed stall with a reinforced entrance.

Three strong wide wooden planks of old slid into slots on both sides of the door, one on top of each other. Benaiah and Mariah strained, lifting them up out of their position and moving them to the side. Then, on their knees, they crawled through the small entrance into the fully encased stall, standing up when inside. Mariah lifted the torch as Benaiah's eyes scanned the walls of the room, looking for more drawings but finding none. What he did see was the black pitch coating just like the outer walls of the ship on the floor, ceiling, and side walls. Then, along the lower half of the extremely reinforced room were what appeared to be small claws marks scratching downward on the planks.

He was looking the opposite direction Mariah was as she gently touched his shoulder, turning him around and then kneeling while holding the fire close. Benaiah's jaw dropped open, and for a moment, he couldn't get a word out, and then finally, he forced himself to ask, "Dragon eggs?"

She only nodded with a beautiful bright smile.

He slowly knelt, asking, "Can I touch them?"

She nodded, and then he reached out softly, gliding his fingertips over the broken thick pieces of dark, distorted, colored fossilized egg shells and said, "I have seen remnants of different fossilized dinosaur egg shells. This is…one of them. But I guess from what you're saying, they're actually dragon egg shells"

Benaiah attempted to put the pieces together, visualizing how big they were whole and then estimated out loud, "They are about the size of two basketballs put together?"

He then envisioned the baby dragons in the well-fortified stall, looking around at the small claw marks throughout the lower planks. Seeing the plank walls had the thick blackish coating on the inside just like the outer walls of the ship, he asked, "Why are these walls, floor, and ceiling coated heavily with the dark tar stuff?"

Glad that he was engaging, she answered, "Noah, not knowing how long they were going to be floating around in the ark, reinforced this stall just in case the babies hatched and had time to grow. Jahar explains dragons thoroughly in the detailed manuscripts. It mentions baby dragons do not start breathing fire until they are over two years old."

Benaiah, starting to go along with the story, said more lightheartedly, "I get it. Fireproofing so they wouldn't accidently set the ark on fire. Then this stall was made extra strong to hold these mighty fighting beasts inside."

She said with confidence, "You are correct."

Something wasn't making sense as he thought about what Mariah said earlier. "Wait a second. You said when we were up front that dragons were on the outside of Eden and only the animals inside of Eden were brought into the ark?"

"Yes, that is what God instructed Noah, but fear of the unknown was in him. You see, dragons were heavily depended on for protection against dinosaurs for two thousand years, and when the Nephilim came into the picture about a hundred years after the Garden of Eden, the dragons protected the innocent from these new supernatural people as well. Being a natural human descendant of Adam, Noah was afraid of not having any protection, so he brought on four dragon eggs for after the flood, foolishly wanting to believe eggs were not going against God's instructions because they had not hatched yet."

"Wait, go back. The what? The Nephulm?"

"The Nephilim. You might not remember reading about them in Genesis chapter six or in the New Testament in second Peter chapter two and in Jude being called fallen angels or angels that sinned. They are briefly mentioned, and very few people truly understand who they are—except for us!" she said proudly.

Seeing her boasting, he replied jokingly, "So what does the Bible say they are, oh wise one?"

Trying to remember the correct wording, she paraphrased, "In Genesis, it says something like when humans increased in number on earth and had daughters, the sons of God saw they were beautiful. Then the sons of God went to the daughters of humans and had children with them. They were the heroes of old, men of renown… Something like that."

"That's it?"

"That is it. But did you hear what the words are saying? Sons of God had babies with humans, and they became heroes of old…"

Benaiah thought for a second, putting together what Mariah mentioned earlier and repeated them in his head, *From dinosaurs and dragons to where Egyptian and Greek mythology came from…*

It struck him upon putting the mystery together, and he questioned out loud, "The gods of Greek mythology?"

Quick to respond, she said with excitement, "You are getting it! Noah explains that the Nephilim were like giants of men, physically and mentally. Originally angels from heaven at one time, they were transformed into mortal man permanently."

Benaiah drew a blank face.

Seeing she was about to lose him, she stepped to the torch holder inside the stall, taking out the fresh one and setting it to the side while putting the lit one in its place. The fire light flickered off the dark walls as she sat next to the fossilized eggshells, patting the floor for him to sit facing her. She retrieved a bottle of water from her pack, taking a drink and then handing it to him. Taking a couple of large swallows, he then questioned with that same far-fetched looking frown, "Angels? Come on, Mariah. You can do better than that."

"I am serious. Noah explains that some of the angels in heaven looked upon the beautiful mortal women of earth and became lustful toward them. They asked God to transform them to become mortal man to be with Adam and Eve's daughters and granddaughters, for they were very beautiful and there were so many. God granted the handful of angels what their wrongful hearts desired, reforming them into flesh and blood and calling them Nephilim, which means *lustful heart*, because they wanted mortal lustful sex with the human females of earth. These angels, just as Satan and one third of the angels of heaven who followed him and not God, gave into selfishness. But these angels desired to leave the presence of God, only to end up perishing and going eternally in the same direction as Satan was going.

"To bring you up to speed, Benaiah, just in case you do not know or remember, Satan and one third of the angels thought he should have equally reigned heaven with God because he was the greatest angel with a beautiful crown that God gave him. Because of this sin of pride equal to the lustful hearts of the Nephilim, God cast out Satan and his band of angels like a lightning bolt from heaven before all humanity ever existed. He gave him his destructive wishes of pride to rule his own kingdom but void of the Light of God and his love, roaming supernaturally in the spirit world here on earth hatefully because he is not reigning the ultimate and splendid eternal place of heaven."

Mariah felt she was on a run, guiding Benaiah to transform his mind so his heart would follow. "Here is a little bonus to help you when you become the guardian of Journey's End. God has given us a wonderful gift. It is the ability to choose what we do. We get to choose, just like the angels, to follow the Creator or not. He does not want slaves or robots forced to follow and love him. What kind of a father-and-child relationship is that? If we choose not to follow him, he allows us to follow our selfish ways.

"There is a difference, though, between those fallen angels and true natural mortal man, the descendants of Adam. God gives us unlimited chances to come back to him for salvation through the purifying blood of his son Jesus Christ.

"Unlike all the fallen angels who started their lives in the Light of heaven, worshipping God without darkness. We started here on earth in darkness, surrounded by the enemy of God. He, as you have heard, is the Light of the world." She paused, placing her hand on top of his as they sat facing each other. "Follow the Light by faith and obedience and you will see clearly, Benaiah, as if a veil is raised from your eyes, exposing the fingerprints of God everywhere." Her other hand swayed outward.

She watched his face contort with what she was presenting to him. Then he asked, "Could you finish with the Nephilim story."

"You are right. We will come back to the other stuff later. So these new male humans, Nephilim, appearing on earth were different because they were not descendants of Adam, the original created man. Knowing they were doomed never again to be in the kingdom of God, they decided they would act as gods of their own, just like Satan, for as long as their mortal lives lasted. The difference is that Satan was never flesh and blood, they were.

"Having the astonishing heavenly knowledge different than earthly natural man, the Nephilim took advantage, exploiting the use of extraordinary physical and mental strengths. Jahar said this came about because they understood how to use 100 percent of their brain which you know, from scientific studies, that we only use about 10 percent. He also explained that since these special humans had experienced heaven and God's greatness in the spiritual realm firsthand, that is why their limitation of what they could do was so far beyond what natural humans from Adam could imagine. So doing the things they physically could do, and creating the structures they did, made them appear to be superhuman or godlike to Adam and his descendants, but in an evil way."

Benaiah's mouth was slightly open as he hadn't blinked for a while, being almost in a trance while listening to Mariah speak as though this happened yesterday.

"Are you still with me?"

He shut his mouth, licking his lips and blinking several times. "Keep going."

"This is where the Greeks and Egyptians, along with many others, got their ideas for their religions."

Benaiah questioned, "How could they? Per your creation timeline from Noah, the Egyptians weren't around for about another thousand-plus years and the Greeks another fifteen hundred years after the Egyptians?"

Mariah looked at her large decorative wristband, checking on the time, and seeing they were doing okay, she answered, "Good question. To sum it up, because we still have a lot to see and do…"

Benaiah waited patiently as she thought of how to put the cherry on top of this story. "Noah had three sons, as you know, with each having a wife. I told you before that it was very important, and almost mandatory for past detailed stories, to be handed down from generation to generation. This is one in the multitudes of historical information not excluded.

"These alleged heroes of old calling themselves gods did physical feats that were extraordinary compared to Adam's descendants before the flood. Later, Satan took advantage of the now-dead Nephilim and their reputations after the flood to greatly influence one of the son's wives to admire and remember everything about them. So of course, you know what happened. She secretly shared with her children, and for the next several generations down and going against Noah's instructions, she told stories of these perverted heroes with names you probably recognize from Greek mythology—Zeus, Aries, Apollo, Hades, Poseidon and so on as well as Egyptian mythology— Ra, Amun-Ra, Osiris, Horus, Thoth, Isis, etc.. Satan's demons did an outstanding job in bringing these false gods to life in the minds of these future cultures, distracting them from the one true God.

"Noah thoroughly wrote about them down somewhere I think in the middle level of the ark describing them in detail. Even drawing pictures of their extraordinary feats and wicked ways. They are one of the main causes for the grand evil amongst humanity, similar to the Sodom and Gomorrah images played out with their lustful hearts.

"With the different god societies developing, the Nephilim ended up with power struggles amongst themselves just like humans would do and started warring against each other for power to rule their kingdoms. The two religious groups I mentioned were the mightiest of the multitude that started.

"Oh." Her eyebrows raised up with her eyes getting big. "I just remembered, the Nephilim are also mentioned in the beginning of Genesis when Cain killed Abel. Remember when God punished Cain by ordering him to leave the land of his parents to be a restless wanderer on earth and Cain replied, 'Whoever finds me will kill me?' Who was he talking about?"

Benaiah only frowned, not being ready for her question or having a quick answer.

"You see, Benaiah, Cain and Abel were not the first children of Adam and Eve as everyone thinks, not even close. Why would he make such a statement, 'Whomever finds me will kill me,' if him and his brother were the first two children born to Adam and Eve after Eden?" Mariah did not hesitate to give Benaiah a chance to answer. "He said what he did because many brothers and sisters were born before him and Abel for about a hundred years. A large majority of his beautiful older sisters had already been taken by the Nephilim claiming other lands as their own to start their so-called kingdoms.

"After the Nephilim were formed on earth nearing a hundred years after the Garden of Eden, Adam and Eve already had dozens and dozens of children, and those children had children and so on which, in those days, around the age of thirteen is when they started having children. And yes, obviously back then, brothers and sisters had children together."

Benaiah grimaced, saying, "That's hard to imagine being a normal or healthy thing? But if you think about it, I suppose having perfect genes and DNA with no defects or diseases around yet...or for that matter..."—he gave out a laugh—"having no one else to have children with, so you have them with the only people around to have them with."

Mariah frowned that he was making light of the conversation and then went on as though to ignore it, "Anyway, by the time Cain and Abel came around, Adam was a hundred years or so out of the garden, and over a thousand or so people were on earth, including these new Nephilim having children with many of Adam's daughters.

"There are many reasons God told Moses to write down Cain and Abel's story, but the main one is to demonstrate how seriously God takes being obedient in doing right. It is a must for mankind, in our infant stage, to understand that God and his expectation of us having him be the only God in our lives. Then, in Genesis chapter five, after Cain is sent away, it says Adam was one hundred and thirty years old and had another son. This son was the exact image of Adam, and they named him Seth. With Seth began the second generation, as we know it, leading to the tenth, which is Noah.

"As I said, the Nephilim had taken a large number of Adam and Eve's early-on adult female children, starting their own communities away from where Adam and Eve claimed was their home, because God had given direct orders to the Nephilim not to touch even a hair on Adam and Eve but did not say anything about their children. So when God ordered Cain away from his mother and father's home, the people he mentioned that would kill him were the Nephilim and their families, but God marked Cain somehow so these other people would not kill him."

She smiled knowing this thought would enthuse Benaiah. "If the mark God put on him did not protect him first, then a dragon protecting him would come next..."

Her words suddenly did just that as Benaiah jumped in, almost telling Mariah with excitement, "Let's go find these drawings. I want to see them myself!"

She calmly responded, "We do not have time for a slow formal tour of the whole ark right now. You will have all the time in the world to research your dinosaurs, dragons, and the Nephilim later when you are guardian. Right now, I need to tell you and show you the true important things at hand and then get us to Jahar's burial ceremony."

He looked at her as though she had lost her mind and said sarcastically, "What do you think is more important than dinosaurs, ancient societies, and history to me?"

She collected herself, saying, "Benaiah I... No, Journey's End right now needs you to forget your life as you know it and open your mind to a whole new world. I am not telling you that you cannot have your enjoyment investigating and researching all this. I am asking you, though, to postpone it for a while. Can you do that for us?"

He paused, taking a deep breath, looked at the flames of the torch and then back to her, and he slowly nodded with very little passion.

"Thank you. Let me finish with what I was saying, and then we need to go. These blasphemous characters, the Nephilim, were handed down as wondrous stories being heroes of old because of their great feats of superhuman abilities by one of Noah's daughter in-laws. When the gentile Egyptians and Greeks were grasping for answers of the universe, Satan weaseled in encouraging them to acquire these larger than life mock gods handed down in stories. Perfectly fitting into their narrow minded aspirations to say the least.

"Even today, these bogus gods of old waste our time because schools around the world teach these mythologies, distracting young minds from the one and only God—the God of creation."

Benaiah adorned a grin of agreement swaying his head as he said, "I'll bite on that one. It makes a lot of sense. I could never understand that whole Greek god stuff and why it was so important. We're forced to learn that nonsense in school just like Shakespeare. What a bunch of garbage."

His comment encouraged Mariah to boast some more about Journey's End. "Oh, we have Shakespeare's original manuscripts by the way in the book of time, with all the original fancy attire Shakespeare had in his plays in several alcoves down one of the hallways."

He rolled his eyes, not wanting to hear anything about Shakespeare, and he said, "Keep to the story please."

Smiling with a quick spout of laughter and understanding how he felt about the writer, she continued, "Most people forget that everything died, not just man, plants, and animals that God created on land from Adam and Eve to Noah. But also human-created things as well; cultures, societies, lifestyles, cities, ancient highways and structures, but most of all blasphemous religions. He left behind very few physical remnants of buildings and cities from these ancient societies I mentioned before, that are dotted here and there around the world, or I should say Pangea when all the continents were together before the flood. Then the planet and man got a second chance to completely start over anew with righteous Noah and his wife being the next so-called Adam and Eve, if you will.

"The enormous and bountiful primeval plants and animals created outside the Garden of Eden were purposely killed off by God along with evil man and the Nephilim to rid the world of all things representing selfishness, destruction, death, and darkness. The Garden of Eden's plants and animals were perfectly suitable for man and were the only things God allowed to grow back and live. God, being a loving Father, restarted life in a way so man, through Noah, would have a fresh, fair, and freer chance of living, able to rely on God and protect one's self, and no longer needing the protection of dragons from the huge uncontrollable and fierce dinosaurs and the Nephilim."

Benaiah looked down at the broken dragon eggshells and asked, "So what about these four?"

"God has a great sense of humor," Mariah said with a giggle. "When they hatched, Noah forgot about one thing—just because he had four eggs does not mean there would be males and females. Four males hatched."

Benaiah laughed out, enjoying the story, and he replied, "Oh, that is funny."

"But not for Noah or any other man for the next fifteen hundred-plus years."

"I don't understand?"

"Having four grown male dragons together, you can say, naturally, there is a testosterone issue to say the least."

"I can see that, but you said fifteen hundred years?"

"Yes, that was the average life expectancy for dragons." She shrugged her shoulders, adding, "Man lived up to nine hundred-plus years up to Noah, and dragons lived approximately five hundred years or longer.

"You see, when these four grew up, Noah found out he no longer needed their protection and could no longer control them and ordered them, with the help of God, of course, to leave, sending two to the far east of the rising sun and two to the west of the setting sun to live out the rest of their lives."

Benaiah thought for a second and then added with enthusiasm as historical puzzles pieces were coming together, "So that's why dragons are so ingrained culturally in eastern Asian countries like China, and in western European communities!"

Mariah nodded, saying, "Again, you are getting it. And these four males were violent and killed humans when they got a chance. So you see how we get the stories of them being vicious, uncontrollable beasts."

Benaiah had a thought and blurted out, "Wow, these are great stories, but it sure sounds like your God makes many mistakes and has to keep redoing his work?"

Chapter 14

C oming out of left field and blindsiding her, Mariah took a moment to answer. "God does not make mistakes, he is the great I Am. Only his creations, be it angels or man. Remember the gift of choice? It is with our wrong choices, going against the Alpha and Omega's instructions, surpassing his protective boundaries, and leaving behind his loving will is when there is a mistake. When God originally created everything, he said it was good. To him, that means perfect. Adam and Eve destroyed the perfection for the human race, and from then on, man will always be born broken, needing God to transform us continually."

Mariah adjusted how she was sitting to get comfortable as Benaiah closed his eyes, rubbing his head with both hands and trying to file all this information as she sparked back up with something different. "Here is something else that will interest you. Noah wrote things concerning the world's geography. He said the earth went through enormous and terrifying growing pains he had never felt or seen before after the ark landed on dry ground for the next couple hundred years or so.

"He also explains there was an awful stench that lasted a long time from all the decaying dead plants, animals, dinosaurs and humans bodies; Adams natural descendants and Nephilim alike.

"Jahar explained from the transcripts that Noah documented this information so his descendants would know how the world physically changed after the flood, responsibly passing on information as his forefathers had done for him. Unknown to Noah, he did not know how important this information would be for future generations such as ours thousands of years later. Clarifying the foolish theories, speculations, and dreamed up nonsense man comes up with to explain the beginnings of the world and its aging process without a supernatural influence." She expected a rebuttal, but Benaiah just sat there.

So she continued, "He even drew pictures of powerful explosions of water coming up from underground after he finished building the ark at God's command, rupturing the earth's surface into many pieces. Then Noah had a drawing depicting the first falling rain pouring down and appearing as a continuous thick waterfall.

"God had been holding up the vast layer of water in the stratosphere, causing even and perfect humidity levels around the globe, having no need for clouds to ever form to rain for life to thrive. But with perfection again, God released the water from the stratosphere for man to experience rain for the first time and forevermore so he could leave his fingerprints of clouds and rainbows afterward."

Quietly sitting cross-legged across from Mariah, Benaiah did his best to control himself while absorbing what she was saying as she continued to target his beliefs as she again hardly took a breath between words. "Noah wrote in the lower lever of the ship walls after the flood that the ground was always moving and tearing apart, forming canyons or crashing into itself, creating enormous mountains out of nowhere which we know today.

"The original landscape Noah knew before the flood was more of rolling hills, shallow valleys, and a lot of level ground densely packed with vegetation in one land mass which we all know as Pangea. Most of Pangea was centered at the equator, with the tips of its northern shores going to the Arctic Circle and the southern shores going as far south as the Antarctic circle. That is why the so called prehistoric plants and animals outside the Garden of Eden could grow so monstrous. They had longer growing seasons, perfect humidity, consistent midrange temperature levels, and since the ground was so fresh and new after God created it, it was off-the-charts packed with nutrients never to be seen again.

"A major portion of this grand body of water drowning the globe began the evaporation process after the flood for the first time. Since the protective water barrier in the stratosphere that acted like sunglasses for the planet was gone, it now allowed the sun to fully penetrate its powerful rays onto the earth. This is when man saw clouds for the first time along with rainbows. Another large portion of the floodwaters eventually receded, helping with continental drift, forcing to separate Pangaea like a crowbar into different continents while forming the many oceans at the same time. As these waters soaked back into the ground, they refilled old mega aquifers while filling new giant ones that had opened up during continental drifting. This caused rivers underground to begin to flow between the aquifers, creating powerful swelling pressure on the planet surface, assisting with the new ecosystems as the new continents found themselves in different latitudes and longitudes with new and drastic temperature changes.

"There was so much happening, Benaiah, after the flood dramatically remodeled the earth's surface, and I have not even mentioned the volcanos, earthquakes, and tsunamis going on at the same time. All these things assisted in forming our coastlines, large mountain ranges, vast valleys, canyons, and great plains on the earth's surface and on the ocean floors.

"With evaporation happening for the first time and on a grand scale, the world quickly developed an extraordinary thick cloud layer, blocking a large portion of the sun and its heat again, but in a different way. Then, with the explosions of all the new volcanos, volcanic ash heavily polluted the sky. This combination of water and ash overwhelmingly caused new aggressive weather patterns. You combine that with dense humidity and it easily explains the quick ice age. When all this extra moisture froze, forming the huge thick glaciers covering a third of the planet, the weather patterns finally evened out, eliminating the colossal cloud cover. Now the sun was able to melt most of the ice away, bringing the world's weather into balance as we know it today."

Mariah hesitated, taking a deep breath, mentally exhausted from spewing out so much history. "I know I have given you a lot of information."

Benaiah shook his head, dropping his hands to his lap as though to organize the cluster of mental pictures developing in his brain. "You think?"

"I had to give this crash course now because you need to understand the truth about our world's history. Understand that God is the Creator of all things, knows all things, and is the only One to be worshipped because of who he is and all he has done. Not the false religion you are practicing—godless science spiked with evolution. It is viably blasphemous using it as your god, breaking the First Commandment."

For the first time since he arrived at Journey's End, Benaiah didn't feel the alarming urge to defend himself as he had been. Somehow, this bombardment of history and the goings-on of Journey's End, things were actually becoming more vivid, not just with sights and sounds but of a purposeful and meaningful portrait of real life that Jahar talked about.

Mariah softened her tone. "Benaiah, please listen carefully to what I am going to say next." She paused, reaching her hand out again and grasping his. "November 3, 1864 is the date when the false religion the world and you are worshipping was born. It was not twenty-five million years ago.

"It is, if not, the most powerful dark deception Satan has smoothly weaved into the human mind and, systematically, into all cultures of the world. Without getting into a long, drawn-out history lesson which you might already know. Charles Darwin had just been awarded the highest scientific honor in Europe, 'The Royal Society's Copley Medal,' for his research in the theory of evolution. Shortly after, a colleague of Darwin's, Thomas Huxley, held the first meeting for scientists called the X Club.

"This special group of scientists were devoted to influence the world to follow one standard for science research with eight simple but influential and destructive words, 'Science pure and free, untrammeled by religious dogmas.' By the end of the next decade, most leading scientists around the world agreed that evolution occurred, completely voiding in every experiment, calculation, equation, and formula all spiritual, religious, and supernatural influences which includes God being the creator of all things."

Benaiah, trying to keep up with where she was going, asked, "So what are you saying? Science is evil and a horrible religion?"

"Science without God, yes. Evolutionists suppressing the idea or existence of God, yes. You combined these with the normal broken darkness of the world, man continues to spiral into the sewer of selfish human divinity, atheism, and all the other religions linked to it. This religion completely evades the truth, empty of a higher power;—God, who created and orchestrated life as we know it by design and for a purpose. The first step of understanding the truth of life is to live by faith in the supernatural which, in reality, the supernatural always was and always will be after all this physical matter we know and study so hard to understand is gone and has vanished from the universe."

Benaiah pulled his hand from her grip and imitated Jahar, raising his finger and gave the appearance he was going to speak wisdom. "Then why are we proving more and more that there is no God in the first place?"

She stated confidently, "Are you not listening to what I have been saying? You are not, not at all. You are choosing to blindly believe that! Science is doing just the opposite. I have already mentioned that. I will show you later private recorded footage and journals of Jahar and the guardian before him in the book of time, where they have recorded many, many people in the broad field of science who admitted privately they are wrong or have no other explanations besides God creating everything being the only answer.

"Many of these scientists will not admit this openly unless their minds have transformed their hearts, accepting God is the truth of life because their careers are on the line and they would lose their jobs and credibility in the secular world. It is all about money, pride, and self. All human weaknesses.

"Look at Darwin, who grew up in a Christian home as a child. Later, he wholeheartedly believed he found the answers to the universe but ended up asking Jesus Christ back into his life on his death bed. The illusion Darwin created as truth only ended up being a true dead end, and on anyone's death bed, it is always revealed in their hearts of what they know to be the truth after death, choose everlasting life in heaven or painful separation from God in hell."

Mariah straightened out her legs, taking another drink of water, and then she continued, nodding and saying, "I could imagine right now you are having a very hard time, even with all this evidence." She opened her arms, gesturing as though she was invisibly showing him all the things she and Jahar had exposed to him. "And why is this difficult for you? Because you first have to admit there is something supernaturally stronger and far more intelligent than yourself and all that envelops humanity which you cannot explain.

"Second, your identity. I am not talking about you being an archeologist, but what you spiritually believe and your faith is in. And right now, what you choose to believe is basically false. If I may add, it is very boring. God's ways of doing things are extraordinary and exciting. You yourself said we have great stories. You do not even have that, not one story. Just dreamed up non-relational theories."

Benaiah had enough. He narrowed his eyebrows slightly, raising his voice, "You're sitting there, bashing everything I have learned and believed in for years. Let me ask you this, since you're so sure of yourself. How are we supposed to know there is a God, and where did he come from?" He leaned back confidently, folding his arms in the dimly lit room.

Mariah smiled, knowing these types of questions were going to come. "Simple, the Bible says in Romans 1:19–20, 'God has put the consciousness of him in us, through his creations of the earth and sky.'

"Just think about our senses—taste, touch, sight, sound and smell—and the things in life that give them reason to exist and climax. Beautiful sunsets, brilliant colors of a rainbow, the countless number of stars twinkling every night. Powerful lightning bolts and intimidating booms of thunder shaking the ground. How about the incredible aromas from a field of flowers or the fresh smell of an ocean breeze as it cools the skin on a hot sunny day? Or the sweet taste of honey or a fresh picked ripe peach as sounds of a babbling brook and chirping birds caress our ears? Have you ever touched the soft skin of a newborn baby or had a relaxing massage drift you to sleep without you knowing it?"

She paused and continued, finishing her thought before he interrupted, "So tell me... Why would our senses exist in the first place? Or their counterparts—everything that entertains or engages them to function in a manner so our senses would be aware of their existence?"

Being on a roll, Mariah kept heaping onto the topic, adding, "How about human love? Mind, body, and spirit. We could get into the emotional and sensual part of relationships which the Bible explains in detail but is impossible for evolution to even begin to accurately and appropriately theorize. So let us go directly to reproduction. How would something that just came to be out of nowhere know it needed a male and a female to reproduce itself? It never would, for it would have died before it could reproduce. Because in your evolutionary world, at the beginning, a male or female never evolved yet to reproduce, having the opposite reproductive organs and or egg and sperm for that matter. Even the thought of your evolutionary process in this area is just plain ludicrous.

"Look at the pollination process and the multiple items and their different functions working separately yet in unison to recreate. There is no way the flower knew it needed to produce pollen so bees or wind would transport it to another flower so their specific flower type could reproduce. It would have never gotten to a second generation.

"Or take a seed growing into a tall plant. How would an object like this that cannot think or have knowledge know it would need dirt, minerals, water, precise air temperature, and sunlight for it to grow? Or how would its counterparts that I just mentioned know they needed to function as they do to participate in this incredible creation process? Never…never would this ever happen on its own without purpose and foreknowledge. Yet evolution uses a fallback phrase, 'Life finds a way', as an explanation for things existing. Sorry, life does not find a way, for Jesus alone is the Way, the Truth, and the Life. Without a supernatural God to make life happen, it would not ever happened.

"How about this…" She gestured toward Benaiah. "Humans or all mammals for that matter lactate and nurse. There would not be one human and mammal alive today without the pre-existence of the original female of its kind having lactation abilities prior to having a baby. If the mammal did have abilities to reproduce with or without male or female genders, it still would not have known it needed to feed from itself what it just created in order for its new born to live."

Mariah leaned forward to look deeper into his eyes as the light from the torch bounced off the surrounding four walls. "Why would nonliving gases combined with nonorganic rocks over any period of time develop senses, emotions, physical sensations, reproduction abilities or feelings like pain and suffering or pleasure and happiness?

"It would not have. It would not have known any of these could or needed to exist unless something had knowledge of these things before they existed. Something cannot just form into something when this something has no consciousness of itself, its abilities, or what it could be.

"How come humans and all animals, fish and birds of their kind have the same number and size of eyes, ears, legs, arms, wings, fins and mouths that are proportionally alike, as all living creatures basically having the same internal organs, just different sizes, functioning universally the same way? Because everything was created by one God having knowledge with purpose and perfection in mind. Nothing in the universe is random or self-created.

"Everything I have mentioned and everything we know of today had to have forethought for it to have ever existed and the ability to sustain living on, eventually having the ability to reproduce. Knowledge only comes from knowledge…"

Having enough of a one-sided debate, Benaiah cut her off, harshly stating, "Stop beating around the bush and answer the questions. How are we supposed to know there is a God and where did he come from Mariah!"

Not getting defensive, she only shrugged her shoulders and said, "Only he has the answer. That is why he is God and we live by faith, not by your so-called facts. If we had all the answers to the questions piled up for him, we would be his equal or greater. A very wise woman years ago, I think her name was…Evelyn Underhill, said, 'If God was small enough to understand, he would not be big enough to be worshipped.'"

Mariah paused for a moment, letting the statement soak in, and then she asked, raising an eyebrow, "Do you need me to repeat that?"

He shook his head, wrinkling his mouth to the side, thinking as she added, "When Jahar first contacted you in the letter, he was preparing you for this conversation when he wrote the scripture Isaiah 55:8–9 at the end of the letter, which has been mentioned a couple of times since. Let me remind you what it says. 'For my thoughts are not your thoughts, neither are your ways my ways,' declares the Lord. 'As the heavens are higher than the earth, so are my ways higher than your ways and my thoughts than your thoughts.'

"God is telling us we cannot grasp any comprehension or understanding of him but only from what he purposely tells us in the Bible or shows us through his creations on earth and the sky."

She put her hand back on top of his, "We, the created, can never be equal or greater than the Creator God. You must come to reality of this, Benaiah. If you cannot... Well, you will never be guardian of Journey's End."

"Excuse me?" It took him off guard. "I'm supposed to be the only one left in Jahar's bloodline. Who are you to say if I will or will not be the guardian? Maybe Horasha was right about you and your family or...bloodline planning to takeover!"

She jerked her hand away, and then she stood, looking down on him, now offended. The torch was burning low in the holder on the wall, getting harder to see inside the enclosed stall. She took the fresh unburned one from the floor, lighting it with the other, and then she poured the rest of the water from her bottle on the used one to smother it, hanging it in the holder on the wall.

Without warning, Mariah turned and crawled under the small opening, going into the hallway as she said gruffly, "Are you coming?"

Benaiah followed, staying inside the glow of the new fresh flame. Without saying a word in the musty ancient boat, she walked quickly, appearing to be upset. Benaiah knew he had made her mad—even insulted her. But he was only being open, grasping at anything that would qualify or give him any credibility as she basically destroyed everything of who he was.

When she finally reached the ramp to go back down to the middle level, he grabbed her arm to stop her. "Mariah, let's be realistic about this." She turned purposely, swiping the torch in front of him and keeping it between them.

"About what?"

"Mentally stand back for a moment...please. You're too close to this picture you're explaining, as I think Jahar would have put it."

In a firm tone and with a stale expression, she exclaimed, "What is happening here is you are being foolish and narrow-minded!"

"No… What is happening is you're forcing me to absorb and believe everything you grew up knowing and lived your whole life. Then you expect me, at the snap of your fingers, to completely drop everything that I am. Now you're throwing a fit because I am not fulfilling your expectations as fast as you expect me to."

He paused, seeing if she wanted to add anything, and then he continued as she glared at him, "Doesn't the Bible say something like it's foolish making quick decisions? And that God reveals things to us in his time?"

She changed her body language, giving a faint smirk, being reminded of what the Holy Spirit whispered to her earlier about lifting the veil from Benaiah's eyes. "Yes."

She dropped her head, regrouping, and then she looked up as he continued, "Wisdom is what you and Jahar are wanting and what Journey's End is needing from me, right? Not just knowledge?"

She nodded.

"Wisdom comes from experience, right?"

Again, non-verbally, nodded yes.

"Then let the wisdom come as I experience everything over time. You, Horasha, and everyone else will know if I'm not fit to be guardian, but all I ask is time. In time, I'll know if I'm the right person or if I want to do this."

Mariah sparked up, "Being guardian, there is no trial period. You are or you are not. No maybes."

"You can't hold me to that!" Benaiah straightened his stance in defiance.

"Yes, we all will. Your president or the king or queen of a country does not take on the position just to try it out, do they?"

He was the one shaking his head now.

"No, they do not, why…" She temporarily paused, wanting to answer it herself quickly, and said, "The people of the land must have complete confidence in the leadership of their country or they become very restless and fearful, tearing apart the social structure and economy which, in turn, creates individualism and attempts to lead themselves as wars breakout."

Benaiah quietly thought for a second and then asked, "How much time do I have to decide?"

"By tonight, after the burial."

"Are you kidding me?"

"Sooner the better. This leaves little time for Horasha's family, mine, or even the African tribes to do more damage to one another or to Journey's End, for that matter."

"You're leaving me with no choice, are you?"

She ignored the question as he followed her, stepping onto the ramp and going to the middle level. She turned her head back, saying, "There is one extremely important room on the lower level with things I must show you. They may have the greatest influence in helping you to clearly and quickly make the right decision. They are the only things on the ark that are not from Noah's time but from eras later, wisely acquired and brought here for safekeeping so the world would not take advantage of or destroy them."

Lifting the torch up high, she quickened her pace, going to the other end of the ark to the ramp going down to the belly of the boat. Benaiah thought to himself, *What could be more important than the awesome stuff I've seen already?*

Quietly making their way through the ancient hallway and passing one of the lit-up bowl stands, the only sounds were footsteps and the flame from the torch flickering as it lit their path. Both young adult minds privately had gone into two silent directions. Benaiah's was running a hundred miles an hour as he started to comprehend the enormous size of the ark and its historical importance. Then an explosive question came to him that he hadn't gotten an answer to when they first stepped into the ark. He asked, breaking the silence, "How did Noah's Ark get into this mountain?"

She didn't respond.

He asked again a little louder. Still nothing. He finally clutched her arm, stopping them as he said, "Hold on, wait a second. Why aren't you answering me?"

It almost startled her as she had sadly drifted in thought of her family and friend's deaths. She was drenched with overwhelming grief as tears had been clouding her vision. Trying to conceal her emotional state, she slowly wiped her eyes within the shadows flickering in and out as the flames from the torch bounced around.

As she turned to him, he realized Mariah wasn't ignoring him but was in a different mental place. Forgetting his question for a moment, he asked, "What's wrong?"

"Nothing." She looked away, not wanting to show signs of weakness.

"Are you upset because I called you out back there?"

She shook her head.

Benaiah thought for a second, and then it came to him, *She lost her brother and Jahar at the same time.*

Unexpectedly to the both of them, he took the torch from her and put his arm around her, bringing her into his chest without saying a word. She simultaneously laid her head deep into him and began crying. The emotional roller coaster from their conversations were taking a turn downhill, with her getting mad at him and then pinballing back and forth, finally landing in the hole of grief.

Moments past as the two shared a reality that no one wants to experience—the loss of loved ones. Calming down, she recovered, wiping away the tears as her breathing awkwardly chattered.

He took a half step back, looking into her eyes as he asked, "Are you going to be all right?"

She slowly nodded and then turned, taking the torch. "We need to keep going."

As they began walking, the question from earlier came to mind, and he asked for the third time, "How in the world did this get inside the mountain? We came through a winding small narrow tunnel underwater. There's no way these giant wood beams came through there."

Benaiah was relieved when she stopped and slowly exposed her beautiful smile again, sensing she was better and had a great answer at the tip of her tongue. He asked, "Okay, what is it?"

"Again, cutting a long story short, before the ark was here, this was a large open cave set back in, similar to the size of the commons area high above, but with a wide opening to the outside. The stream making the waterfall that runs through the commons area flowed a completely different way out of the mountain.

"Shuriah and his army, along with King Hiram's men and the Queen of Sheba's men, reassembled Noah's Ark in here, putting everything thing back in each stall exactly as they first found it buried in the snow and ice. When it was done, they coated everything with the protective sap we still use today from the special trees in the forest. Then carefully, they filled in the cavern, surrounding the ark with dirt and rocks, burying it deep, cocooned from the outside world except for two hidden entrances.

"From the outside, in the forest, looking at the mountain, it appeared to be a normal rocky part of the mountain. Then to put the finishing touches of camouflage, they redirected the stream in the mountain to go through the commons area, digging a hole going outside on the other side, forming the waterfall in front of the freshly buried secret."

Benaiah followed her story as it was making sense, thinking to himself, *There is no way she could have come up with that story out of midair just now.* Then he asked, "You said two entrances?"

"Yes, the other is a long, wide spiral rock staircase that goes straight down hundreds of feet from Jahar's...or I should be saying your private living quarters next to the commons area, ending down here at the ceiling of the cavern.

"When closing in the ark, they did not put anything on the top deck, so there is a small space from the caverns ceiling. Permanent wooded stairs have been anchored at the bottom of the inner mountain staircase resting on the upper deck.

"That's pretty smart, I guess."

"We will be going out that way. It will keep us out of sight, and that is where your guardian wardrobe is waiting for you. We will get you cleaned up and dressed as I go over ceremonial instructions."

"You keep talking as if I will be the guardian. I haven't made up my mind."

"I have faith you will." She patted the middle of his chest, turned around walking, and said, "I believe you are about to have a life-changing experience. One which you have never had before."

When they got to the ramp turning down to the lower level, a deep groan suddenly escalating in volume echoed throughout the lifeless hollow ancient structure, jolting tingling fear into them. The flooring beneath them started to shake as they grasped onto each other for balance and security. Unable to say a word from the shock and intimidation of what was happening, all adventure and confidence was sucked out of the two, filling them with complete childlike helplessness.

The shaking of the floor slowly came to a halt as the agonizing moan that brought the ark and mountain to life faded away back into the darkness below.

As silent stillness appeared, a blast of air bellowed out from the lower level, jetting up the ramp and forcing their eyes to squint as dust and fossilized decaying smells wisped by them. The flame of the torch Mariah was holding fought frantically to stay lit as it leaned heavily in the direction the air was going.

When the exhale of wind calmed to a halt, Mariah was frozen like a statue as she heard in her head a familiar voice speaking Hebrew with extreme gentleness but with unquestionable power, *he must come to me alone.*

She was awestruck more than frightened, knowing what was hidden safely down there. Then images of old flashed before her of the life and power they once held. Hesitating and thinking it through, she finally decided to hand him the torch, saying, "You must go alone."

He looked at her as if she was crazy and replied, "Why? Are you scared? Underground trembling happens like this all the time." He said it in a way to hide his own fear and to come up with his scientific opinion of what happened.

"No, on the contrary. Fear of this world has no place when we are with God."

"Oh, so this is a God thing that just happened?" he sarcastically asked.

She slowly shook her head at him, being so naïve. Then she gave a friendly grin as he took the torch from her, knowing he was about to see and experience something that would bring anyone to their knees, changing their lives forever. She answered, "You could say that."

Continuing with boldness and shadowing his own fear, he tried to encourage her to go with him. "I've been on many excavations deep within the earth, only there were no wooden structures to go through just rock. A little earth shaking and spooky sounds are nothing to be afraid of."

"I agree, but there are some things down there you need to see by yourself. You will understand once you see them. Now go, I'll be waiting for you right here." She took off her backpack, getting out her headlamp, and sat down, leaning up against the wooden wall.

He watched her, a little taken aback that she was just going to sit there as a thought came to him and he asked jokingly, "This isn't a trap or something?"

"No, no trap, but it definitely is something!" He saw her big smile as the light from the flame glistened off her face. "Now hurry up. We do not have a lot of time left until the burial of Jahar this evening."

He hesitated but didn't want to look afraid, so he turned, looking down the ramp with the torch held way out to see as far as he could. Then he said to lighten the atmosphere more for him than her, "In the words of Arnold Schwarzenegger, 'I'll be back.'"

Benaiah walked down the ramp, and when he got to the lower level, he loudly asked, "Where am I going?"

"Keep walking straight down the hallway to about the middle of the boat. You will come to more of a room than a stall. It has two larger swingout doors, floor to ceiling. You cannot miss them."

"Got it." He looked down into the hollow tomb-like darkness, having second thoughts as he asked, "Are you sure you're going to be okay by yourself?"

"I will be fine." She knew he was stalling from fear but not wanting to show it. She gave him a verbal poke. "So will you, Benaiah, descendant of King David's mighty warriors!"

He received the words clearly from her tone whispered under his breath, taking a careful step forward, "Mighty warrior. Yeah, right..."

He made his way slowly, peering into every stall and hoping not to find something waiting for him. After a little ways, he started calming down and picking up his pace.

Soon, he came to the doors Mariah mentioned. Next to the doors on each side was a torch. He thought to himself, *This must have been a special area or maybe living quarters.* Then he thought again, *No, this couldn't be living quarters. That would have been on the upper level. Maybe it's a storage room.*

Hesitating for a moment, his mind began to work, trying to guess what was behind the doors that would be so important, and then, with less than a whisper, Benaiah thought he heard from the other side of the doors the words, *Come to me.*

Straightening his back up and widening his eyes, he quickly looked around, swiping the torch back and forth to see better and scare away whatever he just heard. Seeing the two torches again, he lit them up, brightening the hallway to expose what sent cold tingling sensations up and down his spine. Nothing was there. Calming down, he said to himself, "Let's get this over with."

He slowly reached out, grasping a wooden handle to one of the doors. It was soothingly warm, catching him off guard. Cocking his head at the feeling, he cautiously opened the door as it loudly creaked, piercing the silence. But instead of being spooky, for some reason, it sounded more like he was opening the lid of a treasure chest, making him anxious.

With the door fully open, he first held the torch in front, trying to see what was inside. Not seeing anything yet, peace swept through him as a calming warmth of air gently permeated out with an aroma of freshness and life, hypnotically drawing him in. He took several steps into the large room, looking forward at the back wall and seeing the normal hieroglyphic symbols on the upper deck.

Slowing scanning to the right side, his eyes caught a flash of light flickering and getting brighter the more he turned. Once Benaiah was fully faced to it with the torch held out in front of him, it took a second to completely absorb what was brightly reflecting the flame.

When it finally hit him, not only did it shattered all thought, but physically incapacitated him.

Dropping his mouth open, he was unable to say a word as if the life inside him was being strangled. Getting weaker by the moment, his knees buckled, dropping him to the floor and letting go of the torch. It bounced and rolled around, spilling some hot ash.

On the floor, Benaiah found himself kneeling face down with his arms stretched out in front, completely at the mercy of what was in the room. With emotions of awe and extreme inadequacy surging throughout his body, Benaiah fought, clearing his head to regain strength. Only moving his eyes parallel across the ancient floor to locate the torch, he reached out, grasping it and turning it upright. Finally able to get a full breath into his lungs, he slowly raised his head to peer up at what he considered impossible.

Very carefully, and with deep respect, he raised his upper body, sat on the back of his heels, and wobbly stretched the torch out as the fires reflection was almost blinding. Slowly recovering from the shock, he helplessly gazed up at an ancient decorative golden box forty-five inches long, twenty-seven inches wide, and twenty-seven inches high. It had two golden cherubim statues kneeling about twelve inches high, one at each end of the lid of the box facing one another. Their wings were stretched out in front of them, almost touching the others wings in a protective position. Two long golden poles were on each side of the box running through golden rings anchored to the box used as carrying poles.

With the powerful scene and the realization of what was in front of him, Benaiah's body began to tremble as choppy breaths came out of his mouth. He said aloud, "The Ark of the Covenant is real..."

Chapter 15

Mariah sat on the wooden floor, leaning up against the ships wall in the dark. She had turned her headlamp off to conserve the battery, not knowing exactly how long Benaiah was going to be. As time went by, her mind wandered to the silent mission she initiated, pushing the green button on her large armlet outside next to the waterfall. A mission her heart had been terrified about but knew, for some reason unknown to her, that it was the prompting of God, even though it completely went against every purpose of her being a descendant.

She looked at the time on her wrist, calculating the timing of the mission and the timeframe of the burial ceremony. Then she sent out a message confirming a few things and then shut the armlet off.

Leaning her head back on the wooden wall, she closed her eyes, saying out loud, "Lord of heaven's armies, why are you having me do this?" She stayed silent for a while, hoping to hear an answer from God. When nothing was replied, she said, "I do know, Father, I will never understand your ways or comprehend your thoughts. So I will have faith you are using me in a great way for your kingdom.

"Please speak to Benaiah in the bottom of this ancient structure. Help him transform his heart so he may become the next guardian. If he does not…I am not sure if I can follow through with his demise. I have truly fallen for him…" She hesitated as Jahar came to mind. "Which was Jahar's dream for so many years. I never thought I would, with him being unequally yoked. Let him hear your voice, for your words are warm, gentle, loving, and inspiring even to the hardest of people against you such as Saul was, who you renamed Paul when he transformed."

***

Still kneeling, Benaiah was wide-eyed, staring at something which, to this point in his life, was only nonsensical, fictional religious objects seen in pictures and described in the Bible. But here

245

it was, in all its glory and grandeur. Trying to wrap a plethora of scattered thoughts and emotions into one explainable package was almost impossible. Then everything he was thinking about began to dissolve as his insides felt like they were turned inside out, leading with his heart and soul, and completely exposing his innermost secrets.

He knew good and well throughout his adult life that he had turned away discarding God and all that surrounded the spiritual world. But in this moment, a somersault of transformation was happening. Everything he believed was the truth in his evolution mindset completely dissipated as his own words echoed in is head, *Dr. Benjamin Maschel, you're a complete fool and absolutely insignificant in the presence of God.*

It was silent except for the quiet flicker of the torch in the dark room as his heart pounded. He had no idea how long he had been staring and soaking in the details of the ancient powerful relic as his mummified soul was being unraveled. Emotions of regret, sorrow, and fear started showing their heads in anticipation for it to be completely exposed as, suddenly, words gently and confidently whispered, *"Benaiah, my child."*

Like waking from a daydream, he flinched and looked around. His heart knew who it was, but his mind didn't want to admit it, thinking if he just ignored the words, maybe he would go away and not have to confront him.

"Benaiah, my presence no longer is in the Ark of the Covenant. Stand and see."

The words were soothingly inviting, but when he began to stand, suddenly, he felt weighted down and unable to rise as a dark sarcastic voice rebuked, *"Doctor, you know better than this. This so-called God is always in a box or a book or somewhere hiding. Look at the facts."*

Benaiah was confused for a moment, not understanding what was happening, and then it came to him as he said out loud, "Mariah and Jahar both said I would have to choose faith or fact."

"That's right, and you better chose what's best for you, Doctor, because you only live once. You know what is truly real—only things you can see and what mathematically adds up."

Benaiah, still kneeling, looked down at the floor where he had laid himself out in complete submission moments ago and thought, *Why would that be my first reaction if I didn't believe in God?*

"You do, my child. Now stand and see me through my Son!" God's tone was loving but firm, giving Benaiah a surge of energy through his legs, almost making him jump up to his feet. As he stood, God's voice was heard again. *"Look beyond the Ark of the Covenant, and you will see me for who I Am and where my heart is for you."*

Benaiah didn't move his eyes as fear with its long bony black fingers, crept from behind to suffocate him. Its dark voice flickered its forked tongue in his ear, saying, *"There is nothing to see. Stop wasting your time and go out tonight, claiming Solomon's signature ring, and you will be as great as Jahar!"*

The voice was creepy, but moreover, the words instantly soured him, almost getting him mad as he replied out loud, "I don't want to be like Jahar, caged up and hiding in tunnels under a mountain while keeping history and important artifacts from the world!" Benaiah wasn't sure if that was a knee-jerk reaction and defending himself from the dark voice or if he was offensively telling God he selfishly didn't want the claustrophobic job in the Congo he was being called to.

Consuming the darkness, the bright loving whisper refocused Benaiah, saying, *"Look up, child. My Son has been patiently waiting."*

Peacefully redirected, Benaiah slowly raised his head, not sure what to expect. He did not see anything at first, but the dark sarcasm spoke again, *"See, Doctor? Nothing is there. You're being played as a fool."*

Mentally fighting off the prince of darkness, Benaiah said out loud, "What do you want me to see, God?"

"I am lifting the veil from your heart and eyes. Raise your torch and step forward between the carrying poles to the edge of the Ark of the Covenant. You will see what the Light of the world did for you, fully explaining who he was, who he is, and who he is to come."

Benaiah looked down at the long carrying poles sticking out, hearing the harsh dark voice exclaim, *"Don't do it. It's a trap!"*

"I have no need to trap my children. You are free to choose."

So I must choose... Benaiah thought with confirmation as his exposed heart was having a tug of war over what or who to trust but was gradually being pulled in a new direction of his life.

"Benaiah, either trust only what you can physically see, taste, touch, hear, and smell which only glorifies my creations. Or trust the senses of your heart and soul, where my Spirit can dwell that glorifies me, God, who created all things."

His mind halted external thoughts as the calming words of God breathed soothingly through him. *"Life is not meant to be understood or satisfied with your knowledge of it, but to freely live by faith, trusting in me through it. Only by living faithfully by the spirit will you see me for who I am, the great I Am!"* The last words were said with boldness.

Benaiah blinked several times, shaking his head as all the pieces were falling into place, and then he slowly looked back up. At first, the backdrop of the room behind the glowing golden Ark of the Covenant and cherubim was only a dark shadow. But as his eyes adjusted, it mystically came into view with the details revealing themselves.

Already overwhelmed, Benaiah stepped back as he grasped his mouth, with tears swelling full in his eyes as his heart gushed with emotion. His soul wrenched back and forth with sorrow and joy, pain and freedom all at the same time upon seeing the most powerful, passionate, and humblest construction known to man which tells the most incredible story without saying a word.

"Benaiah, my Son, your God, is not dead. But the cross he died on tells the story what he did for you."

Visions of Jesus being nailed to the tall aged worn-out cross was leaning against the back wall. It was the cause for Benaiah's spiritual meltdown.

"Jesus, your Lord, is alive with me. You know now what I ask of you, for the only way to me is through my Son."

Benaiah's eyes slowly moved up and down the cross, noticing items on it. Identifying each article, his body was becoming weaker with every breath. A crown of thrones was hanging to the side off the top vertical beam as an old roman whip was draped over one side of the horizontal beam and a pile of large metal spikes were stacked on the other side. The final item was an old roman spear leaning against the bottom vertical beam, completing everything that caused Jesus pain and to bleed as he gave his life for all mankind.

Again, his knees buckled as he knelt between the carrying poles draping forward using the Ark of the Covenant as an altar. The word *surrender* went around and around in his head as he was seeing clearly the Truth of the world fully for the first time in his life; Jesus's sacrifice was for the love and life of his children.

Benaiah wept, talking with Jesus, asking for forgiveness for having walked away from him, fully giving his life to the living God in a room with the Ark of the Covenant which held God's devotion to the nation of Israel which rested in front of the cross Jesus was crucified on, where he shed his blood for the world, all secured in the belly of Noah's Ark buried deep within a mountain somewhere hidden in the middle of the Congo in Africa.

After a short time, Benaiah leaned back on his heels, taking in and exhaling a deep breath. Refreshing new life had completely unraveled and cleansed his selfish, dirty, and mummified soul as it now had a sensation of glowing brightly. He lifted the torch up high to peer at the old rugged cross and again heard God's voice. *"Benaiah, descendant of King David's mighty warriors, you believe because you have seen these things, but I say blessed are the ones that have not seen but do believe in me.*

"Even so, I choose you, Benaiah, to be the guardian of guardians to show the world these wonders of old that Solomon wisely keep secret until my appointed time, and that time has come. The religions of godless science and evolution will be confronted head on as they are at their pinnacle of blasphemy as with all the other religions that do not proclaim my Son as the God of salvation. I will, again, as I have done countless times over millennia, show my greatness and love to my children by giving the world another chance to come to me before it is too late.

"Your past unbelief and experiences have given you knowledge which I will use to strengthen you to endure resistance as you greatly influence for my kingdom. Just as I chose Saul, changing his name to Paul, to be a powerful apostle, you will no longer be Benjamin Maschel but Benaiah, as Jahar explained."

Benaiah was taken aback at first, which quickly turned to excitement that God and he were on the same page about showing the world these great wonders. But then, it turned to worry. Instantly, he knew the people of Journey's End would highly reject him for wanting to do this. First, it would go against Solomon's orders, which was their whole life purpose for the past three thousand years. Then, even though he was in the bloodline of Jahar, he still grew up on the other side of the world, subsequently an outsider to everyone in the Congo. On top of that, he was in conflict since he got here with their spiritual beliefs as well as being frustrated with them not allowing the world to see and know the wonderful things they had.

He said to himself, "They will probably kill me and take the signature ring away and then fight over who should be the next guardian."

"All will be well, Benaiah. Through your time away from me, I have prepared you for this moment of change at Journey's End as well as another from here to do my will in assisting you in this mission. Now listen and store this knowledge I give you. It is of great importance, which Noah has scribed on the walls of the ark.

"Through Noah's three sons came all the people who populate the world and the different races of the world I created within their wives' wombs when I gave the world a fresh start. I did this to set apart one specific nation of many to come, which I would call my chosen people through Abraham, whom you know as the Israelites—the Jewish nation.

"It was through Noah's oldest son, Shem, whom Noah asked me to bless, that the original race which started with Adam and Eve was continued. Ham and Japheth, I began in them to multiply children with distinctly different skin colors and facial features but all equally having the same abilities that I blessed mankind with—emotions, personalities, and natural instincts to survive and prosper, and the gift of choosing who they will follow as their god as well as the innate knowledge, through my creations, that a supernatural Creator God exists.

"I also had one of the son's wives, who had Nephilim blood in her, continue, for a short time, the physical lineage to be used for my purpose, which were the same people of the land of milk and honey the Israelites feared because they were giants but then were conquered after Moses and

the Israel nation spent forty years in the desert. Many years later, the remaining few giants all died off shortly after boy David killed Goliath who was, again, used to glorify my kingdom.

"I did all this to present myself for the people of the world in a new way for man to easily identify and see me through my people and to be set apart from false gods through a specific nation to later carry on my laws of moral and spiritual living.

"But man once more quickly thought highly of himself as the different races stayed together and built a city with a tower reaching to the sky to symbolize man's great achievements, not mine. So again, I had to remind them who was God, so I confused them all by giving the many races different languages. This is when the great human migration of the world started separating the races. At the same time, I was still having land slowly separate itself into many pieces. They were free to be their own people, choosing and developing for themselves societies, cultures, and even creating their own gods. But through my chosen people, Israel, I delivered the one God, whom I am, and with what and when I created all things, along with the laws and boundaries for righteous and moral living which all men are free to choose to follow, then and now.

"As time went on and the world population grew, many nations covered the earth, continuing to freely follow their own futile ways of living. With perfect timing, I sent my Son Jesus to be the sacrifice to rescue all mankind, giving them salvation if they accepted him as their Lord and Savior. Again, I made it easy for all my children to know me, especially when the roads of life are difficult, no matter what race or nationality they are.

"Benaiah, direct descendant from King David's mighty men, you have been chosen to share with the world the ancient artifacts of old to help the spiritually blind to see my holy words of old are true and alive. For soon, the prince of this world, the prince of darkness and his crown, will be thrown into the fires of hell that it was made for, along with his demons and all who did not follow my laws in days of old, and who has not accepted the gift of my Son Jesus now."

Benaiah suddenly got giddy inside, rejoicing at what God just said and repeating it over and over in his head. *You have been chosen to share with the world the ancient artifacts of old...*

God's kind voice continued, *"I am a fair and loving God who will try again and again to help my lost children find their way to my open arms until their very last breath that I allow all to breathe. I instructed Jahar to let you choose to grow up in and learn the filth of this world and its feeble understanding of it for you to influence the world later with these majestic artifacts from one of their own who knows exactly how they think and believe.*

"What you need to know about the great I Am is my wisdom and knowledge of being is far beyond what you could image. That is why, before I created man, I created time, space, and matter for simplicity for your childlike understanding to be able to comprehend my glory and character, but not me, which will always be too much for you to fathom.

"As I had Moses write in the first book of the Bible, I separated space and matter, creating every detail within them so your senses of body and mind could be filled with glimpses and visions of my abilities and size. I orchestrated night and day and then seasons so time itself could be calculated, giving you an idea of what eternity is, in which I live. Remember what I had Isaiah write in his book, Isaiah 55:8–9, 'For my thoughts are not your thoughts, neither are your ways my ways,' declares the Lord. 'As the heavens are higher than the earth, so are my ways higher than your ways and my thoughts than your thoughts.'

"If you believe you understand me, you have been fooled by the dark prince, for you cannot even begin to understand my ways or thoughts. That is why you will never comprehend how I created the heavens and earth and everything in them in six days. Your godless science only proves you will only have more questions, not answers. Man's facts are foolish attempts to crown one's self as all knowing.

"All I ask, Benaiah, is for you to have faith in my holy words, the Bible. No more, no less. Beyond that, it is all but human foolishness and selfish attempts to be my equal."

The sweet whispers of wisdom from the Creator ceased as a female voice softly called out his name as though she was in a long tunnel. "Benaiah, are you all right?" Mariah's voice carried down the hallway outside the large room as she was getting closer, repeating herself several times.

He took a second to clear his mind and then wiped his eyes from being emotional, not wanting her to see him this way as he replied loudly, "I'm fine."

She got to the door as the light from her headlamp pierced the darkness behind him, and then she shot in his direction as she walked to his side. Turning off the headlamp, the glow from the torch reflecting off the gold artifact was bright enough. She could see on his face and tell from his posture that there was something different about him. Being wise about men's pride, she looked away to the Ark of the Covenant and the cross to distract from the emotions at hand as she asked, "Are they not magnificent?"

Clearing his throat and looking back up to them, he answered, "Yes, they are."

"It is amazing how the descendants of old knew how and when to secretly collect major historical items like these. Just imagine how many things we have here that people think never existed or was destroyed. Especially these great things here. Even all the descendants above do not know we have these, which are incredible fingerprints of God."

Benaiah thought to himself, embarrassed, that he was one of those mighty men himself.

Mariah said in awe, "The Ark of the Covenant, it is so inspiring. Just think, they hold the tablets of the Ten Commandments and where God's presence used to be for man."

"What did you say?" Benaiah exclaimed, quickly twisting back facing her.

"Where God's presence used to be."

"No, you said the Ten Commandments are still in there?"

She frowned as if he was mentally losing it. "Yes, where else would they be?"

He looked back to the ark and then back to her.

Seeing his excited interest, she asked, "Do you want to see them?"

His eyes widened and he dropped his mouth open, saying, "Yeah…" shaking his head as his shoulders and hands raised up to say, *Of course, are you crazy?*

Mariah looked down at her wrist. Touching the screen and seeing the time, she said with a little urgency, "Sorry, I talked too soon. As I said before, we will have plenty of time later to look at everything in detail. We need to go. That is why I came to get you." She turned and started walking out of the room. Not seeing the torch light following, she glanced back and saw Benaiah was looking behind the Ark of the Covenant into the darkness. She smiled, knowing what had his complete attention as she stated, "Unbelievable what Jesus did for us."

He turned to follow her with a solemn look and replied, "Until moments ago, I truly never realized it." Putting on a half-grin while clenching his lips and trying not to get emotional, he looked away to the wall opposite from where he had been facing this whole time. From the light of the torch, he saw what appeared to be old small wooden crates arranged in a ceremonial fashion.

"What are those?" Stepping up to them, he noticed what appeared to be Hebrew writing on the ends with decorative carvings all around each one.

Mariah came to his side, looking down and saying as she pointed to each one, "Those are ossuary boxes. Believe it or not, that one has the bones of Moses. That one has King David's, that one holds King Solomon's, and those are the disciples including Paul."

For a brief moment, they both stared quietly at the ancient wooden boxes. But Benaiah, as he has done many times during this trip, was mystified, putting together what he was looking at and what the explanation of what they were, and then he gradually replied, "Well… All righty then. I guess we include these items in that conversation for another day along with the hundreds of other things?"

"Yes, absolutely."

They both turned, walking out the door as Benaiah said, "Wow, I'm continuously blown away by Journey's End. Every time I turn around, there is something completely unexpected."

Proudly, she boasted as she extinguished the two torches in the hallway, "We have done a great job keeping everything secret and invisible. Could you imagine what the world would do if they knew about everything we have here?"

At first, he didn't respond at her comment. Then he said cautiously so as not to raise her suspicion about God's new direction for Journey's End, "Yeah, just imagine."

As they walked out of the belly of Noah's Ark, Mariah was quiet knowing that Benaiah was in a completely different place spiritually. Once on the middle level, she said, "We will retrace our steps as we go up to the outer deck above to exit. We need to extinguish all the fire pits and close the main side entrance that we came in."

Making their way through the levels of the ship, Mariah only spoke if he initiated it until they got to the bottom of the wooden staircase on the upper deck that led up into the long spiraling rock staircase ending up hundreds of feet in Jahar's private quarters.

"This is a very tough climb spiraling almost straight up. Are you going to be okay?"

He was slightly offended at the question. "Why wouldn't I?"

"Sorry, I did not mean to insult you or insinuate you were not capable of..."

He butted in with a smile. "It's okay... Just go, I'll follow." Having been holding the torch, he reached out to give it to her as it was getting close to being depleted.

She went to grasp it but accidentally wrapped her hand around his, sending electrifying tingles through them both. Looking into each other's eyes, the compassionate spark was definitely strong between them as Benaiah shared with confidence, "You are released and free to move forward to have this relationship with me."

Surprised at the unexpected statement, she replied, "I am?"

"Yes, so you may kiss me now."

Her eyes worked his as her heart began to rapidly beat. He slowly leaned forward, gently touching her lips with his and then straightened back up.

Staring for a moment at each other, she asked, acting naive, "So you did have an encounter with God?"

"Yes, at the cross."

Mariah's body language demonstrated a heavy burden was unloaded as a new explosion of excitement surged through her. Suddenly, she jumped up at him, wrapping her free arm around his neck and squeezing her soft lips tightly against his. They enjoyed an intimate moment, slowly swaying their heads and romantically adjusting their lips tighter into one another.

Locked together as one, they were captivated longer than expected. Separating, the dying flame from the torch finally had exhausted itself. Pitch black, they swiftly turned on their headlamps, lighting up the area seeing an extra glow shining from one another's face.

Mariah was full of questions and dreams as her romantic heart's door was swung wide open, becoming vulnerable like she had never been in her life. Benaiah, on the other hand, was completely motivated for conquering everything in his path. But right now, there were many paths to go down, causing him to wisely prioritize them as he said tenderly, "Mariah, may that kiss be the first of many to come…" He paused to think through what needed to be said. "And hold us until all is well in Journey's End after I become guardian. I must be at my best for what is to come, which means no distractions. The direction God has laid out for Journey's Beginning will be difficult for all."

For a split second, she was stumped, and then the logic of the big picture revealed itself, projecting that Benaiah was thinking and speaking like Jahar. Giving out a deep sigh, she smiled, lifting a hand and stroking his face as she said, "Whatever happened to you in the lower room was definitely from God, and I must respect it and be obedient."

Her fingers stopped at his lips, pressing softly, "You have instantly captured my heart, and I find myself being a slave to a man for the first time in my life." She paused and finished, "I will be at your side, and when you move to the left or right, I will do the same. When you slow down or speed up, the shadow you cast will be me." Her eyes gleamed as they squinted passionately as though saying, *I love you.*

He stood hearing and seeing clearly what she was saying and replied, "You have a way with words, Mariah, and I pray they are true. For what is about to happen, I will probably need an army of David's mighty men at my side."

Not having any idea of what he was truly talking about, she smiled, saying, "I am an army. God has been preparing me my whole life for war." She winked at him and then patted hard against his chest with the same hand that was gentle on his face. Turning, she readjusted her headlamp and started up the long staircase. He hesitated as concern swept through his mind that she was going to be involved with the consequences of the news he was bringing to the people of Journey's End.

A while later, finally at the top, Mariah stood on a wide landing, waiting for Benaiah to catch up. After a few moments, he was by her side, bent over, grasping his knees, and breathing heavy. She didn't say anything as he lifted his head, with sweat pouring down his face, to see her quietly smiling back. Noticing she was in a slightly victorious stance, with her hands at her waist and barely showing signs of being tired, he stated between gasping breaths, "I'm going to have to go up and down this all the time?"

She chuckled through her smile, replying, "You will get used to it or…" Mariah bent down, looking evenly into his eyes and putting her hands on her knees, changing her tone. "You can give it up for someone else to be the guardian who will watch over the thousands of historical artifacts while reading and writing in the book of time as they bask in the mountain of Solomon's gold and silver." She stood up straight, putting her hands back on her hips, ending with, "At that point, I would have to put you to death because you know the secrets of Journey's End."

For a split second, peering up at her stern expression, he couldn't tell if she was kidding as a horrid thought crossed his mind. *Was she pretending to like me? Subconsciously wanting me to give up so she could kill me and to hide my body deep under the mountain for no one to ever know what happened to me?*

Then like Jekyll and Hyde, she batted his shoulder with a giggle, saying in a fun tone, "Just kidding…" She turned to the flat rock door where the stairs ended, lifting her hand up to a small peephole cover. Stopping before she opened it to secretly look into the bedroom, she added staring, back at him, "Horasha will be the one to kill you. You are originally his responsibility."

Leaving Benaiah hanging, she slowly opened the small cover and peered into the bedroom, looking in all directions to make sure no one was in there. Satisfied, she closed it and then turned the large door handle hearing a significant click, as a faint sound of pressure releasing was felt and a cool breeze instantly blew toward them. She slowly pushed the door open just enough to slide their bodies in sideways.

Benaiah stood up, thankful for the fresh air as his breathing slowed. Watching Mariah slide into the room, he thought to himself, *If she thinks that's romantic conversation to encourage me to be the guardian, this is going to be a wild relationship.*

He followed her lead, slithering past the door. Once in the room, she firmly pressed it closed, hearing a suction sound sealing it airtight and then a click signaling it was locked again.

Standing back to see the large door from the interior room side, Benaiah realized it was disguised with a huge life-sized framed painting and no doorknob. It took a moment to understand the picture, and then suddenly, he popped his head back, saying, "Are you serious? But then again…why should I be surprised, right?" He stared at the large painting for another second, confirming who he was looking at as he stated, "Who besides Jahar would have a painting of Mother Theresa on his left and Billy Graham on his right."

Again, taking a moment to soak it in, he asked, "How could this happen? I thought Journey's End was a secret?"

She looked at him, raising an eyebrow and adorning a sarcastic smile as she said, "We never said you could not invite people here, but when they leave, they can never mention this place existed—or else." Ignoring her own threat, she looked to the painting and added, "Jahar wanted to have an in-depth private conversation with the two most influential religious leaders of his time. So a little over thirty years ago, he invited Mother Theresa and Billy Graham here to have that conversation. You know we have our ways to get someone here." She glanced at him with a smile as he rolled his eyes, embarrassed.

Landing back on the painting, he remarked, "That has got to be one of the coolest arrangements of people ever."

"Yes, it is," she stated, quickly turning around to walk across the room as the urgency refreshed itself to continue for the evening ceremony. His eyes followed her as the room came into full view. It was one great room with a rounded ceiling and walls like the other caverns in Journey's End, but much smaller, perfect for one person in charge of a small kingdom. The lighting and sounds were that of the large personnel living quarters, imitating the outdoors and changing from day and night.

Every area of the room smoothly flowed into the next. The sleeping quarters was one the imagination could only dream about for kings and queens of old. The extremely large bed was the center focus of the room. Everything else was hugging the curved walls. It had massive decorative pillars at each corner boldly rising from the ground and embedded in the high arched ceiling as though holding it up. A cloud-like skirting draped down, anchored to the ceiling centered between the pillars that encapsulated the whole bed at the bottom, giving it a semi-hidden and mystical appearance.

Mariah spoke up, grasping his attention and stepping up to the washing area against the wall. "We need to get you out of those guard clothes, showered, and dressed for the burial and your guardian ceremony." Benaiah walked up, looking at a small soothing waterfall coming out of a protruding rock outcropping pouring down about eight feet into an open area with a decorated flat rock floor.

Mariah continued, "The shower is natural mineral water coming out of the rocks. When you walk in, say out loud what temperature you want the water to be and it will automatically adjust. A mirror folds out from the rock wall to the side of the water so you can see yourself as you shave." She turned, pointing next to them. "Obviously, next to you are the drying towels waiting on the towel warmer for when you walk out."

"Where is the toilet?"

She raised her eyebrow at his word choice and answered maturely, "The lavatory...you cannot see until you walk around the showering area and behind the outcropping rock wall where the water comes out." She pointed to the area next to the shower. "It is secluded in case the housekeeper is cleaning the room when you are in here and need to use it."

"No door?" Benaiah questioned, starting to see a picture of no true privacy in the bedroom.

Acknowledging his concern, she replied, "Benaiah, this is now your private room, the most secured in Journey's End. As guardian, you will control how private you want your room to be or any room in Journey's End."

He wavered his head back and forth at the possible uncomfortable situations that could occur in this fancy cave being used as an extremely large bedroom, wide open for anyone's eyes to see all.

Looking at her wrist again, she said, "We are on the clock here. Get into the shower. We have stocked up on your shampoo, hair supplies, soaps, cologne, deodorant, toothbrush, and toothpaste you normally use. They are in the storage cabinet. I'll bring them to you.

"Then I will retrieve your new guardian clothes and sandals, setting them over there in the dressing circle with all the mirrors."

Proud of her good old friend, Mariah smiled, saying, "Jahar has had everything prepared and waiting for you for a long time. He could not wait to see you take his place." Her excited face turned downward as she realized she ran the conversation emotionally into the ground as visions of Jahar floated through her mind. A sad pause powerfully yanked on her heart.

Benaiah felt her pain as he lifted his hand to her chin, raising her head so their eyes met and stroking his thumb up and down the side of her cheek. "Mariah, in the brief moment of time with Jahar, he has made a lifelong impression on me. He was definitely a great man. I can tell you two were very close and spent a lot of time together. His essence comes out in you." He paused to make a warm ending statement as he openhandedly moved his hand down, gently pressing against her upper chest and finishing with, "He will always be in here for you."

Looking into one another's eyes, she pressed forward, wrapping her arms around him as he did the same with her while whispering into his ear, "Thank you."

Pulling apart, she repeated, "We have to get going. Go get into the shower. I will get everything out for you."

She walked away as he looked at the waterfall and then back to her. "So you're going to be in here while I get ready?"

She only turned her head back, saying bluntly while knowing his concern, "Yes, you do not have anything I have not seen before. We live in close quarters here in Journey's End. Now hurry up!"

After he finished showering, shaving, and fully using the facilities, Benaiah went to the dressing area with a large towel wrapped around his waist. Mariah had set out his clothes, identical to what Jahar wore. A thin, soft, white, loose-fitting upper covering and pants which were very breathable and comfortable for the weather in the Congo along the equator.

Mariah came out of the wardrobe room area fully dressed in colorful feminine attire accentuating her figure. She had cleaned up in another area of the guardian's private quarters and fixed her hair while Benaiah was showering.

When Benaiah saw her walking toward him as he was trying to figure out what to do with the long scarf-like thing draping it across his body, he became mesmerized at how beautiful she was. Her long black shiny hair flowed down past her shoulders as her tan, olive-colored skin seemed to glow, matching her smile. "Wow, you look incredible!" he exclaimed.

"You do not look bad yourself," she said as she grabbed the sash, properly securing it across his shoulders and then around his waist. They both peered into the mirrors, making final adjustments, and then they looked at one another's reflection, standing side by side. When their eyes met, for a brief moment, they knew exactly what each other was thinking. *It looks like we are getting married.* Then they both looked away embarrassed as Mariah said, "We need to get going." She walked away, crossing the room and passing by the extraordinary bed with Benaiah following behind.

Passing the grand centerpiece of the cavern, he peered up at the sheer netting decoratively hanging down and seeing something out of place not seen earlier. It was attached horizontally high between two of the large bed posts that were at the head of the bed going from the floor to the ceiling. At closer examination, Benaiah said, "What in the world is that doing there?"

She glanced back, seeing what caught his attention, and then she grinned as a great idea crossed her mind. "It was a nightly reminder that Jahar had for himself."

"A reminder of what? It looks like it's just a sword hanging in the air."

She knew he had no idea what he was truly looking at as she replied, "Just a sword?"

"Yeah, it's pretty big, but why would someone have a sword way up high where he couldn't reach it."

She stepped to one of the posts the sword was connected to and said, "Step back." As she reached low around the bedding area, she pushed a button. The sword suddenly dropped straight down horizontally like a guillotine, stopping firm at the lower frame where the mattress was.

Benaiah jumped back, surprised, and exclaimed, "Holy cow!"

"No, it's not Baal?"

"What?"

She shook her head, knowing from his comment he probably would never correlate the two. "Never mind, this sword has killed more people than you could count. Jahar has even killed one person that snuck in, passing security while he was sleeping many years ago and attempted to strangle him. But he was able to cut the man in half with it, saving his life."

"Why the sword? Why not set up a regular guillotine?"

"The sword is here for a reminder more than for protection."

"How do you mean?"

"Walk around and hold it."

He did just that, taking it off the attachments on both ends. Groaning a bit as he lifted the sword up, admiring it, he stated, "This thing is huge. Who in the world could ever use it? It's got to be for decoration?"

"A giant," she calmly said with a smirk on her face.

He looked at her expression, trying to figure out another mystery. Then she added, "It is Goliath's sword."

He stared at her like he was in a coma, and then he looked down at the heavy military artwork of metal in his hands and then back up. He couldn't find any words.

"Yes, Benaiah, you know the story about David and Goliath. You are holding boy David's prize."

Many thoughts ran through his mind, but the only vision he had was the sword cutting Goliath's head off by a skinny Shepherd boy after he had flung a stone at his forehead, knocking him to the ground.

"Jahar had the giant of all swords put up there so he would have a reminder every night. A reminder that any battle or problem in our lives can easily be conquered no matter how giant they appear. All he has to do is put on the simple armor of God and give our battles to him. Then boldly walk forward faithfully in the name of Jesus, not by the facts we see or situations we are in. Because nothing is too big, strong, or impossible to be overcome by God.

"Even a boy with faith the size of a mustard seed, giants can be taken down and have their heads cut off with their own swords."

Benaiah physically straightened up his back holding his head high as he remembered two statements God said in the ark, 'I instructed Jahar to let you choose to grow up closely in and learn the filth of this world and its feeble understanding of it. All for you to influence the world later with these majestic artifacts from one of their own who knows exactly how they think and believe.' And 'Your past unbelief and experiences I will use to strengthen you to endure resistance, as you greatly influence for my kingdom.'

Then he thought to himself, *I've got two giants ahead of me. The descendant of Journey's End to open Journey's Beginning to the world. Then for the world of atheism and evolution to surrender to creation and the Creator. The second sounds easier at the moment.*

His face was changing expressions, and Mariah could tell he was in thought. "What is going on in your head?"

"Oh nothing."

"It has to be something."

Benaiah started to put the sword back on it attachments to the bed posts when Mariah said, "No, do not put it back. We are going to take it with us."

"We are?"

"Yes, what a great entrance to the ceremony with you holding Goliath's sword."

He looked down at the impressionable weapon, heavy in his hands. Then he took it by the handle, muscling the blade in the air and said, "Are you sure they'll take me seriously?"

Giggling again, she said, "Maybe not you, but yes to the sword. They know it was very important to Jahar, having an item from one of the greatest stories known to man."

She looked down at her armlet again and said, "We need to go. The sun will be setting soon."

She turned and walked across the room to a small round cut-out section in the wall that was approximately eight feet across and appearing to be some type of empty closet. Benaiah stepped in with her, looking down at a metal floor very different than that of the polished mountain rock floor in the bedroom. Looking to Mariah, he asked, "What is this?"

She pointed up, and to his surprise, as he looked up, he saw a very long shaft rounded just like the floor.

Thinking he was being smart, he stated more than asked, "It's an elevator?"

Mariah gave him a silly smile, saying, "You can say that. But when we get to the top and are outside of the mountain, do not—as you say in America—freak out."

Chapter 16

A very somber feeling quietly echoed throughout the Congo forest. All the Africans in the area that secretly knew of Journey's End loved its guardian, Jahar. Also, the killing of the pygmy chief had spread rapidly and was extremely disturbing, and they were not sure how to react toward the descendants after his burial.

The tombs of the dead was a special place halfway up the large mountain facing west and down in a deep ravine. Two steep cliff walls came together up the hillside like an arrowhead, with the end of the downhill side wide open to the sky. The edge dropped straight down over a hundred feet and then flowed back into the forest. The only walking entrance into the isolated spot was a built-up stone stairway in the middle of the valley at the point of the arrowhead separating the two walls. At the top of the stairs, where it met the forest, there was a sizeable open flat landing.

Down inside the ravine of the outdoor tomb site, a large triangle-shaped open rock floor had been leveled flat and polished. Centered near the wide open-end cliffside of the floor was a raised rectangular rock slab called the ceremony stone. It was three feet high by three feet wide and seven feet long and used to lay the deceased body during the life-honoring ceremony.

The individual tombs for the final resting place of the bodies were dug out in the two cliff walls. One wall was for the guardians, the opposite wall for the pygmy chiefs. The tombs openings were three feet high by three feet wide and spaced apart every three feet. The distance was the same as they stacked up on top of each other six rows high. Looking up to the top of the ravine rim, there was enough room to stack another ten rows of tombs on top of each other, which was enough space to hold enough guardians and pygmy chiefs to last thousands of years if they all lived full lives. Each of the closed tombs were engraved with the name of the one inside and the year in which they passed away.

The gathering on the ceremony floor was filling with Africans wearing brightly colored forest jewelry as they came down the long stairs in single file. Journey's End armed security personnel were positioned throughout the forest, high above on the rim of the small valley in their normal invisible uniforms. The descendants mingled with the Africans down on the floor, waiting for the official funeral procession of the pygmy chief to come out of the forest and the body of Jahar to fly in on an Inverse Gravity Transporter (IGT).

These transportation devices are saucer shaped, with a handrail circling the outer edge four feet high as people stood or sat within the railing. The IGTs were operated by a hollow graphic control board like in the book of time. It used gravity against itself for elevation as they moved horizontally, utilizing the earth's magnetic force. This combination was extremely powerful and fast and hardly made a sound, with an endless fuel supply. This science-fiction-looking transportation device visually appeared to be open air, with just a platform to stand or with seats to sit on and a handrailing. But what was not visible was the domed clear shield that surrounded the whole IGT while it moved. Again, using gravity, the invisible shield kept wind and moisture out while controlling the temperature within the dome. The other ability these IGTs had was to camouflage or cloak. When electrostatic energy was added to the invisible shield, it functioned like the security uniforms reflecting what the IGT was surrounded by to blend in—blue sky, green trees, etc.

Journey's End, with its highly advanced technology, had many sizes of these transporters. From large cargo all the way down to small individual size. They were also used to travel not only in the Congo but all over the world. There was no range limit except in the outer atmosphere of earth. They also were extremely effective for security and warfare. The battle IGTs were fortified with a solid, bulletproof flooring and four-foot-high walls going around the edge in place of the open hand railing and then donned with multiple weapons.

Even though they were effective and efficient, the IGTs were rarely used. Only for long distance travel, bringing supplies from the outside world, emergencies, to get somewhere fast, or special occasions. They also wanted to blend in as much as possible with the forest and Africans as well as staying physically fit by walking, running, or climbing instead of riding them all the time.

The sun was getting low on the horizon, beaming straight in from the open side of the ravine which was the reason this spot was chosen for such important occasions and why the celebration stone was positioned were it was near the edge in that direction, giving everyone a spectacular view watching the sunset above the lush green canopy of the Congo below, and adding a peaceful ambience to putting the dead to rest as the person's soul moved on into the spiritual world.

Soothingly, an orchestra of music was gradually heard in the distance as soft voices sang. All at the tombs of the dead who knew the beautiful song that was sang at every funeral joined in singing softly as shadows from IGTs began to appear inside the enclosed ceremony arena. Everyone looked toward the sun, seeing dark figures hovering in toward them. As the images got closer, details were beginning to show of people standing tall on the personnel IGTs and holding on to the side railings as they hovered in single file. When each IGT got to the cliff edge, it slowly descended systematically onto the smooth floor on each side of the body platform.

Everyone's focus was awaiting the arrival of the larger cargo IGT carrying the body of Jahar. As the smaller ones with high-ranking personnel of Journey's End landed, finally, a larger, wide dark shadow appeared on the horizon. All the people knew who it was, and instantly, everyone went on their knees, bowing, Israelite descendants and Africans alike. The cargo IGT hovered onto the ceremony floor, resting next to the celebration stone. When they touched down, the music slowly stopped as six guards surrounding Jahar's body lifted the decorative wooden gurney, stepping off the IGT and gently placing him on the smooth celebration stone. The guards stayed in place in a protective ring around the body as the pilot of the IGT hovered up, swiftly flying away and disappearing into the setting sun.

Like clockwork, the beating of deep drums loudly started thumping high above in the forest toward the top of the staircase. Everyone turned in that direction, forming an isle from the top of the stairs all the way down to the celebration stone. All the Africans began a chant, rhythmically swaying back and forth and dancing for the pygmy chief to be brought to his resting place.

The African warriors held the chief high above their heads, grasping the handles of the bamboo gurney. After slowly making their way down the long staircase and crossing the ceremony floor to the flat rock, they halted, wondering where they were going to lay the body.

Suddenly, everyone realized they never had a funeral with two leaders at the same time, as the center raised rock was made for only one body, and it was already taken. One of the tribal officials standing close to the celebration stone had an idea and calmly said to the guards surrounding Jahar, "Take Master Jahar off his carrying bed, lay him directly on the rock, and move him to the side to make room for our chief."

It sounded like the right thing to do, so the guards began to follow the instructions, when suddenly, a loud shout in Hebrew was heard to stop. Horasha, along with many of his guards, had quietly hovered in from many directions as everyone's attention was on the pygmy chiefs procession.

Landing their IGTs, instantly, everyone was on edge as the handsome and distinguished Horasha boldly strutted in through the crowd with his guards following him. Once at Jahar's body, he knelt in respect and then stood proudly as though he had the most controlling power, looking around and taking a moment to choose his words, and then he stated loudly, "Jahar was guardian of all Journey's End. He ruled with great honor and has no equal and owed this grand respect. Your chief will not lay equally with Master Jahar. If you want the chief to lay on the ceremony stone for his ceremony, it must take place another day!"

Silence was heard throughout as the atmosphere instantly got extremely heavy. The Africans began to look at one another, whispering, and then, from high at the top of the rock staircase, an older weak female voice was heard speaking in her native language, "Horasha! You will have no say in what we do with our chief's body! You murdered him!"

Horasha was taken aback by someone who was bold enough to challenge him by saying such a thing, especially a female. He quickly responded in her language, "Woman, you are out of line and have no say here!"

The female was dressed brightly, with colorful feathers and flowers adorning her headdress and waist wrap for the funeral. Slowly and carefully making her way down the stairs to the floor with a younger pygmy helping her, she purposely did not respond to make a statement that she was not under his control.

It was Uba, the older pygmy woman. Walking through the ocean of people, she finally stepped up to Horasha, eye level to his chest. Looking up and raising a long, decorated walking stick and holding it in the middle while pointing it to his chest, she stated, "Our chief will share the celebration stone with Master Jahar. They were like brothers, equally protecting Journey's End with honor."

"How dare you, old woman! Jahar has no equal!"

She inched closer to him with a straight-up glare and said, "Careful, young man. You have been gone too long from the Congo watching over the next young guardian."

"What do I have to be careful of, and how do you know about the next guardian?"

"Like I said, Jahar was like a brother to our chief. Have you forgotten that we know everything you do and many things from before? And for more generations than I can count, we have protected Journey's End side by side with your people. We were the ones to show you the secret caves of the Congo to safely hide your precious treasures in our forest."

Horasha hesitated, being put in a very tight spot as he glanced around to everyone watching on. Slowly, he reached into his pant pocket, feeling for Solomon's signature ring. Moving it around between his fingers, he was hoping it would give him powerful wisdom like Solomon, but nothing was coming to mind. Taking his empty hand out of his pocket, he looked down at Uba still glaring up at him for an answer, and he finally said, to clear her accusations of murder, "I was only protecting the signature ring. We have always been trained to protect it with our lives no matter what. Seeing it in your chiefs hand was the first time I had never seen it on Jahar's finger. I only reacted from orders and my training."

"No matter. You took a life that was not yours to take. You know what the law of Journey's End is. We will put this charge against you to the side for now. The ceremonies will continue this day, and tomorrow, you will face your charges."

Horasha aggressively swatted Uba's walking stick to the side and then bent down into her face, raising his voice, "You are not in charge here, old woman!"

Uba's stick quickly rose up as though she was going to hit him on the side of his face, stopping short.

Everyone froze, looking at the end of her stick, including Horasha, as she blocked two long and thin poisonous darts from hitting him in the neck. They flew in from somewhere high above in the forest to stop and kill Horasha from attacking her.

"No more!" she yelled, holding up her hand toward the forest. "Horasha will control himself from now on." Uba stared into his surprised face with her sunken, black-pearl-colored eyes surrounded by her weathered, dark, wrinkly skin mentally willing him to agree.

He gave her a slight nod in agreement as he slowly straightened up. They stood staring for a moment, and then Horasha turned to the guards surrounding Jahar's body and said reluctantly, "Do as she says. We will honor both great leaders together."

Immediately, Jahar's body was moved close to the edge. Then the chief's body was lifted off his gurney and laid shoulder to shoulder with Jahar. They fit on the ceremony stone, but it was tight, even with both men being of smaller and slender stature.

Horasha looked around, trying to spot the two people they had been looking for, but they were nowhere to be seen. He turned his body sideways so Uba could not see what he was doing and then whispered in Hebrew toward where his communication earpiece was, "Everyone, call in."

"For a few moments, the earpiece was constantly full of many voices systematically responding from different areas in the forest and inside the mountain all saying, "Negative, no sign of them."

Under his breath, while gritting his teeth, he said, "I am going to kill her!"

"What did you say?" Uba asked.

"Oh, nothing," he said still looking away.

Uba attempted to move the ceremony forward under the tense but emotional time and asked, "So where is the new young guardian Jahar has been talking about? He needs to be here to accept the signature ring you took from our dead chief." Uba cocked her head, putting on a questioning grin and inquiring, "You still have it, do you not?"

Not able to submit calmly to her accusations any longer, Horasha's busted out, "Old woman, why question my honor?"

She did not move as they had a staredown again.

Feeling the pressure of everyone glaring at him, Horasha was the first to react. Moving his hand in and out of his pocket, he boldly held the ring up and out for everyone to see. Instantly, orders were firmly yelled out in Hebrew and the native Congo language from a lead guard standing next to Horasha for all to hear who could not see what he was holding up. "Everyone kneel! The ring of our king!"

Simultaneously, everyone down in the ceremony floor, even Uba and up high in the forest, knelt. The loud body movement sounded like an army adjusting position, and then complete silence took control.

Horasha was the only one standing, looking up at the ring in his hand held high as the remaining sun glistened off it. Everyone's head was bowed in complete respect of the power the ring held. The moment was beginning to consume him, with everyone bowing in his direction. He swiftly went through everything that would be at his fingertips if the ring was officially placed on his hand.

First, what came to his mind was the cavern holding by far the world's largest collection of gold, silver, jewels, and other riches. Second, the power of technology Journey's End held that could easily control most of the world instantly without involving military actions. Then his mind thought, *What would be the fun in not having any battles?*

Finally, his family would be the one to be served as the leaders of the most important place on earth, boldly upholding the command of King Solomon to protect Journey's End.

A dark voice intervened in the middle of his thoughts, saying, *'Horasha, your bloodline goes all the way back to the beginning of Journey's End. The time has come for a new bloodline of King David's mighty men. Jahar is gone, and Benaiah, the last of Shuriah's blood, is unworthy of the honor of the ring. You and your family must take it now to keep Journey's End safe. There is no time to waste.'*

As everyone knelt, Horasha loudly took control from Uba. "All blood family of mine, rise!"

Heads from all over looked up with questioning expressions at the statement of a sensitive topic that always put the descendants on edge. As though planned, men, women, and children dotted around all over as well as the guards at his side slowly but proudly stood up.

Looking around at his extended family surrounding him, his boldness continued as his hand holding the ring was still raised high, "Benaiah, the last of Jahar's bloodline, is nowhere to be found. It appears he has fled Journey's End like his cowardly parents!"

"How dare you, Horasha!" Uba yelled as she stood, putting her weight on the walking stick to help her stand. As she straightened up, her eyes caught a glimpse of the deadly darts still stuck in the end of the stick. She grasped the two long thin fangs, pulling them out and holding them at her side in a position as though she was going to use them.

Horasha's guards saw what was happening and swiftly pulled up their weapons. The one closest to her pointed his at her as the others surrounded Horasha, pointing their guns in all directions.

Horasha lowered his hand with the ring. Then with his other hand, he touched the guard next to him on the shoulder, saying with gentle authority, "Lower your weapons. This woman has no intentions of hurting me. She knows how strong our bloodline is and how long we have been waiting for this moment to lead Journey's End."

He looked down at Uba, not having to raise his voice too loud because the ceremony floor surrounded by the tall rock walls rebounded his voice perfectly for everyone to hear as he said, "Our forefathers, as well as all of us..." Horasha opened his arms wide to everyone, slowly turning around and showing the ring to all. "Descendants and Africans alike, have served Shuriah's bloodline from the beginning to Jahar, honorably and respectfully. More than we can count have died protecting the secrecy of Journey's End and Solomon's treasure that is hidden within it, even from our own people in Israel.

"I am not veering from King Solomon's orders but continuing to honorably carry them out, willing to take on the burden of guardian to protect and serve with my life and the lives of my family!

"Everyone..." He turned around again, this time raising his voice, stopping to face Uba and the long steep staircase behind her. "We all knew this time was coming, and it is with our generation, three thousand years later, that the changing of the bloodline has come to continue on for another three thousand years.

"The sacrifice Jahar's bloodline has endured..." He paused, appearing to be getting emotional as he compassionately looked down at Jahar's body and then knelt, kissing his cold forehead. Rising back to his feet, he continued, "Enduring the assaults and assassinations by the thousands over the years has finally taken its toll, leaving only one of Jahar's family members alive. His name is Benaiah, great nephew of Jahar. Benaiah's parents cowardly and selfishly ran away from Journey's End over twenty-seven years ago, not having any honor, courage, or respect to take over when Jahar passes.

"I have watched over and guarded Benaiah ever since he was born in the United States. I brought him here over a week ago by Jahar's request. He is not a person of our faith but worships man's knowledge. Jahar did his best from afar to influence Benaiah to know his heritage as an Israelite, but he rejected it at every avenue just like Benaiah's parents did to him when they left the Congo. And now he cannot be found here at Journey's End. So we assume he has runaway, disgracing his bloodline like his parents, or he has been killed."

Suddenly, there was a lot of murmuring. People whispered back and forth, acknowledging in agreement with Horasha. Then there were others bringing up the point of how someone from another place could suddenly disappear in or around Journey's End and the Congo without one person knowing. Their technology was too advanced for them not to know anything. One of the Africans close to the ceremony stone said aloud in Hebrew, "Impossible! No one can just disappear from here without someone knowing about it, especially an outsider."

Horasha knew the man had a very strong argument as everyone intently looked on. He was aware Mariah was with Benaiah, and if she wanted to escape Journey's End without anyone knowing it, she would be one of the few that could do it.

As though reading his mind, Uba acted innocent and looked around as she asked out loud, "Where's Mariah?"

She knew it was the last name Horasha wanted to hear. By saying it out loud, Uba wisely knew how much it would dramatically change the direction he had so gallantly and honorably orchestrated his speech to persuade everyone to go down the path he was taking them.

An uproar started as everyone knew she was loved by Jahar just like a daughter and assumed she was there amongst them at his side but was nowhere to be seen. Bringing her up was done with such precision that Horasha knew he had just lost major ground to be the next guardian. To make things worse, and setting him off again, someone from her bloodline spouted out, "Mariah and her bloodline should be the next guardian!"

Someone else added, "Mariah spent more time with Jahar than anyone. She knows things that no one else knows and is the most well-trained military person at Journey's End."

A sudden outburst from guards and all the different bloodlines erupted, half in agreement, the other half completely against the comment made.

Uba took a quiet step back away from Horasha as one of the much larger African tribesmen slipped in front of her to protect her upon seeing the rage coming across Horasha's face. As he did this, she happened to look out to the last sliver of the bright sun setting across the canopy of trees across the Congo forest, getting concerned for Mariah and Benaiah. Then she thought she saw something like a large bird in the distance gliding along the tops of the trees. Taking a second look through her aged eyes and squinting hard to better focus as it got closer, she realized what and who it was.

Uba tried hard not to get excited as she moved her eyes back to Horasha. A flood of fear swept through her of what he and his family would do to them when Mariah and Benaiah landed inside the tombs of the dead, experiencing what his clouded vision did today to her village and chief.

One of Horasha's guards looking in the direction of the IGT silently coming in stepped forward to Horasha's ear to let him know what was happening behind him.

Quickly twisting around, he saw two people flying in and whispered back to the guard giving him orders. The guard then talked into his earpiece, telling all the guards within the ceremony arena to go to the landing zone and surround the transporter when it lands.

Swiftly, they went into action, but once they formed the perimeter, they were taken off guard when the IGT maintained its elevation, continuing high over their heads and parallel to the upper rim. When it got to the landing at the top of the stairs, the Africans standing on it backed away into the forest as it softly touched ground.

Instantly, everyone understood Horasha's intent to control and overtake Mariah and the new person to Journey's End. Without saying a word, the Africans that had parted, making room for Uba walking down the stairs, militaristically closed in tightly so none of Horasha's men on the ceremony floor could run up the stairs to get through. All the other Africans, pygmies, and half of the descendants followed suit and surrounded the bottom of the stairs, forming a thick wall of human bodies.

This sudden chain of events psychologically created an absolute division between everyone at the ceremony. And for what seemed like minutes but was, in actuality, only seconds, silence echoed out in the forest down in the tombs of the dead. Eyes glanced back and forth, waiting for someone to make a move, but what held everyone at bay was that no one truly knew what to do. Were they to fight or separate, going away in different directions? It was a questionable moment where no one wanted to make the first move.

Without warning, a flash of light shot down and around every-one from the top of the stairs where the IGT landed. Many people ducked or moved out of the way, not sure if it was a silent weapon going off shooting at them. When nothing else happened, they real-ized it was an object reflecting the last glimpses of the strong sunlight as it slowly faded away. When the sun disappeared behind the forest canopy and the bright light was gone, Journey's End was held in suspense.

They saw the stranger doing his best to hold straight up an extremely large, shiny, double-edged sword as though to stab the sky. The blade was as long as his body, and the handle swallowed his hands. Another set of hands his size still wouldn't cover the whole handle. Grasping hard and doing everything he could to hold the mighty sword up over his head, Benaiah finally yelled out, "Journey's End!" He paused to make sure he had everyone's attention as his voice echoed down to the ceremony floor spewing out into the forest.

Boldly looking all around, up on the upper rim and down on the floor, Benaiah was making eye contact with as many people as he could. Then he proudly said, as Mariah interpreted everything, first in Hebrew and then in the African language, "I am Benaiah! Descendant of King David's mighty warriors! In the bloodline of Jahar..." he paused again as he tried to contain the fear boiling inside his chest from showing its face to everyone staring at him as he strug-gled to firmly hold the sword in place above his head. Taking a deep breath, he exclaimed, "I am next in line to continue as guardian of Journey's End!"

Silence deafened the ravine and forest again as every man, woman, and child soaked in the news. Reprieve from the direct heat of the day came since the sun disappeared, but the lingering humidity still presented discomfort on the side of the mountain that equaled the people's emotions with Benaiah's exclamation.

But one by one, the people that placed themselves as a defensive wall followed their natural instincts when the guardian was formally in their presence and began kneeling in his direction. Lowering the heavy sword, he stepped off the high-tech transporter a couple of yards away, getting closer to the top of the staircase. Benaiah watched with Mariah at his side in amazement at the reaction of his words.

His eyes started with the pygmies and Africans around him on top of the ravine and working their way down the staircase as he saw them go to the ground like dominos falling in a harmonious wave that quickly spread wide once it got to the ceremony floor and suddenly stopped at the celebration stone. The slow, comforting relief Benaiah was beginning to feel at seeing everyone bow to him instantly halted. Holding her ground and wearing her brightly colored mourning clothing, the short older pygmy woman had a huge smile on her face as she proudly peered up toward the soon-to-be new guardian.

Uba knew that probably everyone behind her on the ceremony floor and many above up on the rim and in the forest would stand their ground in defiance to the words the young stranger proclaimed. The bigger protective tribesman, now behind her since they all turned around to look up at the top of the staircase, had kneeled as well, leaving her as the only visible ally standing.

As inconspicuously as she could, Uba stepped back and to the side to get closer to Horasha and around the African as she loudly displayed a bow and then slowly kneeled with the help of her strong walking stick, putting much of her weight on it, grasping it with two hands.

Horasha stood his ground, with the eyes of his bloodline watching on. He was thinking of the best way to gain the respect and devotion from the ones that were bowing to the unworthy worldly man standing above as though he was deserving to wear the powerful ring in his hand. To him, being the only one in Journey's End that was physically by Benaiah's side his whole life, he truly knew what kind of person Benjamin Maschel was inside and out. His people and the Africans were naively going through the motions, knowing nothing about the stranger. Benjamin had nothing to offer or had any qualities of commitment to protect and lead Journey's End into the future.

Suddenly, excruciating pain came from both of his shins as his knees buckled and he hit the ceremony floor hard. His hand holding

Solomon's signature ring felt equal pain as he collapsed onto all fours. His hand shot open, releasing the ring, and it bounced in front of him next to the kneeling feet of the tall African that had protected Uba.

Uba snatched up the ring, putting it in the hand of the African and instructing him to quickly run it up to the new guardian. Everything happened so fast that Horasha, still on all fours and not realizing the ring was gone and nearly halfway up the stairs, was at a loss at what was going on.

When Uba knelt, she calculated her position from Horasha, and then, as swiftly as she could, she hit him hard with her solid wood walking stick at both shins as he was looking around. She knew if things went as they appeared, time was going to be wasted and a possible fight was going to break out. The authority of the ring and the guardian position would be the ones to ultimately suffer through this selfish conflict.

When Horasha realized the ring was gone, he looked up at the man running up the stairs, putting the puzzle together, and he yelled out for his guards to chase him because he stole Solomon's ring. Twisting his head sideways to Uba down at her level, he saw her defiant look and grasped the stick in her hand, breaking it over his knee as he stood.

A sudden surge of people quickly acted, pressing forward to the stairs, pushing everyone that was kneeling to the side and knocking them over to get through.

Uba, eyeballing Horasha, yelled out herself to protect the runner with the ring. Then she stood, looking up and around, lifting her arms and instructing everyone on the rim and in the forest to protect the new guardian, saying in broken Hebrew, "Benaiah, the descendant of King David's mighty warriors, in the bloodline of Jahar, is to be the next guardian. Jahar told this to my people who he said were the only ones that could be trusted with this knowledge because he did not know who to trust within the descendants."

All the people who had surged forward from Horasha's orders slowly stopped at the words spoken by the old woman. It was like air being let out of a balloon as the men comprehended the underlying meaning, especially with the last statement, "He did not know who to trust within the descendants."

Everyone, especially the descendants among the Africans and pygmies at the tombs of the dead, understood what the words meant. This was the silent curse Journey's End has endured over a thousand years. Battling for power between the bloodlines was the Achilles heel even though most of them were always faithful to the bloodline of Shuriah. The few that were not faithful would show up here and there, assassinating a member or starting a riot with Shuriah's lineage, hoping to deplete them in order that their own family would wear the ring and be the guardian family of Journey's End.

When these assassins or leaders of the anarchy were always overtaken, they were brutally tortured in front of everyone in a manner to disgrace the bloodline as well as to implement fear in those who were not faithful to Solomon's orders regarding the leadership process he put in play and acted as God themselves.

This knowledge of the horrible consequences for what they were about to do is why they were second-guessing their actions.

"Do not listen to the old woman. She is not an Israelite!" Horasha screamed out in anger.

They all looked at one another, frozen and not knowing what to do.

The African runner made it to the top of the stairs and then knelt, not at the feet of Benaiah but to Mariah. Holding the ring up toward her, Benaiah eyed the ring as he still clumsily held onto Goliath's sword.

Two older men from Mariah's bloodline had calmly moved their way through the crowd behind the IGT on the landing and then out to the sides of the two young adults during the ordeal between Uba and Horasha below.

Mariah caught movement out of the corner of her eyes and then smiled to her family members who had come to their side for support.

The man at Benaiah's side bowed and then said in English with a heavy accent, "Please allow me to hold the sword for you, Master Benaiah."

Having the sword was extremely cool, but Benaiah was relieved to hand it to him. The man bowed again, taking the sword and then backed away behind him, out of Benaiah's way. As this was happening, Mariah had gently taken Solomon's ring from the African. She suddenly had an image of it being on Jahar's hand, weakening her spirit as sadness washed over her.

The African slowly stood still in a bowing posture and raised his head to look at her as movement behind Benaiah captured his attention.

Without hesitation, he screamed out in his African tongue, wildly leaping between the two young adults and shoving them off to the sides, ending up where Benaiah was standing. For the next few seconds, everything seemed to go in slow motion as all the people in the forest and down on the ceremony floor watched in horror.

The courageous African man that had originally stepped between Horasha and Uba and who had now taken Benaiah's place just had his head cut off. His body dropped straight down, and his head bounced on the landing, rolling to the edge of the staircase and then bounded all the way down.

The relative of Mariah that had taken the sword from Benaiah had whorled the long sword around like a lasso after stepping behind him and then swung it out to cut Benaiah's head off. Once he realized he had not killed Benaiah, he yelled out in anger and began to whorl it again.

In complete disbelief, Benaiah looked down at his sheer white ceremony clothes that now had blood splattered all over it and across his face. Then he moved his eyes down to the body of the headless man, his blood and other body fluids seeped out onto the ground. Instantly, Benaiah bent over and began vomiting.

Mariah, on the other hand, had her own trader. When she was pushed off to the side, losing her balance because she was focusing on the death of Jahar, she bumped into the relative next to her. Simultaneously, he ripped the ring out from her fingers, shoving her to the ground to have an advantage. Glancing up at the man with the sword, she saw his next intention as he now lifted the sword high to cut Benaiah's head off as he was bent over and heaving.

Before she could react, the air was filled with sounds of things swishing bye. To her relief, the man's chest had six arrows deeply embedded in him as dozens of blow darts found their marks all over his body.

As the man stood and went into unconsciousness, wobbling around with Goliath's sword up in the air, she heard two hard thumps and then a man groaning out in agony off to her side. She turned to see the thief hitting the ground on his back, with two short spears vertically in the air as they were deeply pierced into his chest. Moving her eyes up, two pygmy men stood over his body as one bent down, taking the ring from his hand.

The pygmy stepped up to Mariah, holding his hand out and helping her to her feet. A foot above the pygmy's head, she looked down at him peering up with a bright big smile and giving her the gift of the ring.

Benaiah was finishing his episode of seeing a ghastly thing followed up with the explosive realization of how dangerous being the guardian was going to be, even though Jahar and others fully warned him ahead of time.

Mariah sorted through the heavy burden at hand which Jahar and the many other guardians had to carry. It wasn't the first time, and she knew it would not be the last, of seeing this continuous selfish human nature of her people, no matter what bloodline. Trust continued to fail among her people, but the ones who always showed signs of loyalty were the Africans and especially the pygmies.

She looked down at Uba still on the ceremony floor, appearing extra small next to the large overpowering Horasha. Thinking quickly of what to do, and knowing they were surrounded by uncertain faithful, she decided to order out to whoever would protect Benaiah to do so as she did her best to escape with him.

Before she could get a word out, an unexpected loud deep pinging gong evenly sounded out, echoing throughout the whole mountain and surrounding area of Journey's End. There was not a person that didn't hear it, and everyone universally knew exactly what it meant except Benaiah. All the attention went to the sky as everyone silently waited, looking in all directions and then looking at their wide wrists armlets.

Benaiah, not knowing what it was, looked around mystified at the earth-shaking sound. The descendants focused on their small flat screens as they saw information going across, saying over and over, "Intruders, distance eight kilometers from ground zero—latitude 0.0356 degrees north, longitude 19.212 degrees east. Twenty-five large drones, canopy level, are flying in with air-to-land missiles having photography, thermal, and infrared abilities. Speed, sixty-five kilometers per hour. Nationality unknown."

Benaiah saw the majority of the Israelites now looking at their wristbands as all the guards along the rim in shooting position were facing all directions in the air above.

"What's going on, Mariah?"

"We have intruders from the outside world," Mariah calmly stated as she looked down at Horasha and Uba.

To their surprise, Horasha yelled in Hebrew, "Mariah, take Benaiah to his new living quarters and stay with him! Uba, take your chief, and we will take Jahar, both returning tomorrow when the sun rises to put our great leaders to rest. Everyone else, to your homes or guard positions. These intruders will be eliminated from the face of this earth!"

Instantly, a night-and-day change in the atmosphere drenched everyone as an overwhelming militaristic shout echoed out with explosive exciting energy from everyone—descendants, Africans, and pygmies. Unifying, all were together in the protection, safety, and secrecy of Journey's End. Every generation for three thousand years shared this oath no matter how bad the differences were in the struggle for selfish power within.

Benaiah was completely baffled, understanding there was a sudden unification. If he hadn't seen it firsthand, he wouldn't have believed it, especially as three people were just brutally killed. He didn't have a clue what Horasha said until Mariah stepped over the dead bodies, grasping the heavy long sword and then got into the IGT, giving him the information.

"What are we going to do?" Benaiah innocently asked.

"I'm going to protect you as Horasha stated."

"What are they going to do?" he pointed out to everyone.

"Destroy the intruders, eliminating any evidence they existed. Locate where they originated and do what we need to do so they do not do this again."

She gave him a quick glance, raising an eyebrow and handing him the sword, not saying anything, and then she engaged the IGT, taking off in the opposite direction of the inbound intruders.

As the IGT lifted off, swiftly skirting through the tall trees and not going above the canopy, Benaiah asked, "Wonder if they are innocent?"

"It does not matter. You know by now that no one is to know anything about Journey's End even if they are innocent."

There was a pause as he was absorbing all that transpired in such a short time. Mariah asked, changing the subject for the both of them, "You have not seen the cavern of treasures. Would you like to take a stroll through more gold, silver, and jewels than you could imagine?"

Grateful for something that didn't include killing people, he replied, "Is this the place everyone thinks Journey's End is about?"

She only smiled while giving him a wink.

Chapter 17

Mariah gained elevation through the dense forest, staying hidden as they slowly rounded upward on the mountain. Benaiah sat down on the center bench, still in awe at how they were traveling as they flew silently on the metal saucer driven by touching a holographic screen. Breezing by the trees, he couldn't even feel the air going by as they maintained perfect balance no matter the angle or direction they turned.

He was beginning to feel lightheaded again, but this time, he believed it had nothing to do with what just happened on the side of the mountain. This was different as his heart seemed to start pounding and anxiety was washing through him. Lowering the sword on the floor of the IGT, he put his head into his hands.

Mariah saw his unnatural position and got concerned. "Are you all right? Are you hurt?"

He slowly moved his head sideways, saying no and explaining how he was feeling.

She thought for a second and then stated, "We have not eaten a full meal in a long time. Combine that with all you have been through in one day, I am surprised you have lasted this long."

Lifting his head up, he said, "How about you? There has been no difference between us."

"My mind and body have been conditioned for times like these. You are a big city man, remember…" she teased, trying to make light of the moment.

With sarcasm, Benaiah replied, "Thanks for reminding me I'm not only emotionally weak but physically as well. Tell me again why you want me to be the guardian?"

He dropped his head back down into his hands as she amended his comment. "Do not be hard on yourself, Benaiah. You have had a huge disadvantage. From experiencing Jahar dying to seeing Journey's Beginning while having a life-changing moment with God. Everything back there…"—she lifted her hand, pointing back with her thumb toward the tombs of the dead—"would take a toll on anyone, no matter who they were or where they were from outside of this most special of all places."

It was getting dark when they quietly snuck through the forest, heading toward an upper section of the mountain. Mariah pressed one of the transparent buttons and spoke in Hebrew, "Control, this is M081093O approaching commons eye. Requesting pass through and landing."

"M081093O, you are not on your assigned IGT. State your situation."

"Jahar's bloodline Benaiah is with me whom is to be the next guardian. We started in Jahar's private living quarters to get ready for his burial ceremony and Benaiah's guardian inauguration. We used Jahar's IGT from there."

"We have no record of you entering Jahar's quarters. State your situation correctly!" The controller was not willing to believe the answer given as he replied in a harsh tone.

Benaiah asked what the conversation was about. After translating, Mariah paused to think, and before she responded, Benaiah charged in in English, "That is no matter of anyone's at the moment. Horasha ordered Mariah to protect me. Will you comply or not to her request? Think carefully before you speak. The wrong decision will have punishable implications!"

There was silence for a moment as Mariah looked at him, surprised he spoke up in the manner he did.

The controller answered back, "M081093O, confirm Benaiah's identity number."

Now speaking in English, "B031393S."

"Identity number and Benaiah's body configuration match. You may continue. Shield will be lowered when you arrive, and landing is permitted."

"Thank you, Control." She smiled, pushing the com button off, and then she said to Benaiah, "I am impressed. Quick-witted and persuasive… You are in the making to be guardian."

He had dropped his head down again, still feeling bad, and then he looked up to answer her, "I'm hangry."

"You mean angry?"

"No, I'm hungry, which makes me angry…hangry."

"I see. We do need to take care of your situation sooner than later."

"That would be great. Also, I need something for my head. By the way, what were those letters and numbers you and the controller went back and forth on?"

"Identification numbers. Everyone one has one. The first letter is the first letter of your name. The numbers are your birth date, and the last letter is from what bloodline you originated from."

"Got it. Your own style of social security numbers."

Mariah nodded and then lifted her wrist screen, pushing a few buttons as she said in English, "Kitchen, this is Mariah. I need two meals with protein, vegetables, and drink immediately to the commons area lounge."

Listening, he crinkled his forehead, not knowing truly what food she was ordering in the middle of the Congo.

Seeing his face she smiled and replied, refreshing the order, "Correction, two hamburgers—one with cheese, ketchup, and pickles and with a root beer on ice. The other fully loaded with an unsweetened tea, no ice. Both meals with a side of French fries."

Seeing his bloodied shirt and the splatters on his face, she added, "Also, Benaiah needs a change of guardian attire when we land, body cleaning towels, and pain medicine for a headache."

He gave her a quick smile and a short forced laugh, saying, "So you know other meals that I like and what I want on them? I'm not surprised." Then he lowered his head back down.

They soared up the mountain a little while longer as the wide oval eye entrance of the commons area came into view. Before flying through the commons eye, Mariah paused the IGT for a moment, hovering over what appeared to Benaiah to be a wide flat platform. She looked at her armlet screen and began pushing buttons and sliding her fingers back and forth. For a split second, she closed her eyes, stopping her finger in a pointing down position. Taking a deep breath and mumbling to herself and then opening her eyes, she tapped the screen. Benaiah looked up to her and asked, "Is everything okay?"

She shook her head as though it was nothing and replied, wishing he had not seen her, "Everything is fine. Just formalities and instructions for Control." Then she flew the IGT forward, ignoring she ever did anything.

Hidden interior lighting softly came on throughout the big forested garden as they descended. Mariah landed the IGT next to the round marble floor lounge.

Several women were waiting where they landed. When Benaiah stepped off the IGT, one of the them approached him with a bow and then said in broken English, "Please hold out your arms." Surprised at the quick response and the straightforwardness, he let her do what appeared to be her normal job. She swiftly untied the long scarf wrapped around his body while taking the bloodstained top off at the same time. But when she bent down, dropping his pants to the floor, and asked him to step out of the legs, the full realization he was almost fully naked in front of who knows how many watching on hit him.

Another woman now approached as the one that undressed him took the clothes away. This servant had washing items with her and quickly cleaned off and sanitized his skin where the blood had soaked through. After drying him off, the last woman dressed him as fast as he was undressed.

Benaiah looked around once dressed to see everyone's reaction to what just happened, but there was nothing different—as though this happened all the time.

Once Benaiah was taken care of, Mariah picked up Goliath's sword and walked around the low table as Benaiah dropped one of the large pillows off the couch, sitting down where he was the day before, having a discussion with Jahar. Mariah stated, "No, the guardian spot is there." She pointed over to where Jahar had sat.

Not sure why it was so important, he shrugged his shoulders and moved over one couch. Setting the monstrous sword on the floor between the couches, she sat down on the floor with a pillow in his original spot. Several other servants approached the sitting area with trays of food and drink.

They stood at the edge of the marble floor, looking at Benaiah as Mariah interjected, "They are waiting for your permission to approach the table with our food."

Benaiah hadn't engaged his authority mindset yet because he wasn't wearing the signature ring or hadn't gone through the guardian inauguration and said, "But I'm not the guardian yet?"

"It does not matter. You are of the reigning bloodline."

He swayed his head because of all the continuous mindless formalities and replied, "All righty..." Then he waved them over.

Two servants set out the meal on the table as the third one approached Benaiah with a different serving platter. It had two pills on top of a sterile towel and a clear glass of water. The server bowed low, holding out the tray for Benaiah to take, saying, "For your headache, Master." As he took them from the tray and held them in his hand, the servant woman gave him a gentle smile, nodding her head. Mariah caught the inviting facial expression, which was not normal from this specific person who had been a servant for many years.

Benaiah watched as all the servers began to leave the lounge area, and then Mariah stated unexpectedly, "Do not leave. Maintain your positions here to serve Master Benaiah." Mariah's suspicions were heightened by the split-second glances of the servant bringing him the pills to the lead guard standing close by as she crossed the lounge.

Watching the activity of many people focused on him, what Jahar warned him about trust came full circle as his anxiety hit a new level. Wanting to take the pills to get rid of his pounding headache and finally eat, the uneasiness was beginning to control him, and he didn't know what else to do. Thinking about what Jahar did by using his guard, he looked out, not quite sure who was there guarding.

The one closest to him appeared to be in charge, so Benaiah asked for him to step forward as Mariah translated. She was surprised at his instant request but was relieved that he knew what he was doing.

The lead guard acknowledged her and then looked next to him, pulling rank, and he told the guard next to him to go to Benaiah. Without hesitating, the second guard stepped up to Benaiah. Benaiah didn't feel right with what just happened. It caught Mariah's attention as well, confirming something was not right.

Thinking for a moment, Benaiah asked Mariah to cut the hamburgers in half. She only reacted by pulling a knife hidden within her clothes without asking why. Then he told her to put one half of each hamburger onto one plate and then to call the lead guard forward.

When she called the lead guard to come to them, he unnaturally hesitated for a second and then stepped next to the guard he originally sent in his place.

Everyone now knew Benaiah's intentions as his eyes moved to the halves of the two hamburgers and then back to the lead guard without moving his head. The faintest of smiles came across the lead guard, and without being verbally told, he leaned forward to take the plate of food to taste test it. Before his hand got to the plate, Benaiah swiftly leaned over, holding his hand out above the food, exposing the pills and staring down the guard only inches from his face. The lead guard stopped and quickly retracted himself, standing next to the other guard. Benaiah never took his eyes off him as he stayed seated on the floor, telling Mariah, "Tell him to take these and drink the water."

Mariah slowly stood cat-like, staring at the lead guard.

The guard boldly responded in broken English, looking down at Benaiah, "Until you have officially become the guardian wearing our king's ring, you have no authority over us."

Many guards and the servant women gave out a shallow gasping sound of disbelief, taking slight steps back and knowing a confrontation was about to happen.

At that moment, Benaiah knew that no matter what, his next move must be made with precision as all eyes in the commons area, and probably throughout Journey's End, were watching and listening by camera or something else.

The large door to the tunnel of the medical facility opened as guards quickly flew in on an IGT with Dr. Mitanual yelling, "Master Benaiah, do not take the pills! Do not take the pills!"

Everyone turned to the commotion across the cavern except Mariah. She saw what Benaiah saw on the lead guard's face and was not going to take her eyes off him. When the large door opened, it gave her the split second advantage to overtake him without hesitation.

Just as everyone looked toward the door, she sprang like a tiger still with the knife in hand from cutting the hamburgers. Now she had it deep in the throat of the lead guard as she spun around him, jerking his shoulders backward with her knee in the center of his back and shoving him hard and straight down to the ground. As he was heading to the ground, she grasped his weapon from his chest and then stepped in front of Benaiah, pointing it outward to anyone reacting in an offensive manner.

Everyone froze at the sudden events as the doctor got to the marble platform. His guards surrounded him as everyone looked on at the guard taking his final gasps of life, and then his body went limp.

After a few moments, the doctor said, "I guess I did not need to come to tell you someone switched the medication for Master Benaiah."

Mariah, still wary of the doctor's actions yesterday, said proudly, "Benaiah was the one to first catch the guard in his wrongdoings." She bent down, slowly pulling the knife out of his throat and cleaning it off by swiping it back and forth on the dead man's chest. As she stood straight up, she quickly spun around, facing the servant women and threw the knife across the lounge, sticking it with precision between the feet of the woman who had handed Benaiah the pills.

Everyone looked at the woman, wondering what Mariah's intension were. Uniformly, it came to them as the servant went to her knees with her head slumped down and she began to cry. She knew she had been caught as one of the perpetrators. Everyone except Benaiah fully turned to her, knowing what her next move was, with Mariah presenting the knife to her.

The woman slowly pulled the knife out of the ground, grasping the handle with both hands tightly and with the blade facing her chest.

Benaiah stared on, not comprehending what was happening, and then suddenly it hit him as he yelled out, "No...!" But the woman had already shoved the knife deep into her chest. It went silent as everyone looked on, watching her slowly fall forward dead.

With his arms stretched out in denial and his mouth and eyes agape and astounded by the woman doing what she did, words babbled out of him. "Why? What did she do that for? Why did you throw the knife at her feet?"

Mariah sternly stated loudly for everyone to hear, in case there was someone else having ill intent toward the new guardian to be, "Either take her own life now or be tortured in front of everyone and then be killed."

"Why?"

"They were in on this together." She looked down at the man lying at their feet, "He probably quickly planned this while listening in on our conversation with control as we were coming in. Then he told his relative..."—she pointed to the dead woman—"to switch pills so the doctor would get blamed for giving you the wrong medicine, but she made several mistakes."

Benaiah's mind was blown away as he looked at the lifeless man and woman and then to the doctor, saying, "Can I have a word with you, Doctor?" Then he turned and walked several steps away from everyone and out into the garden.

With their backs to everyone, Benaiah leaned in and quietly asked, "I believe you would know better than anyone else at Journey's End..."

"What's that, Master Benaiah?"

"How many people...no, how many of *our* people at Journey's End continuously die because of the guardian position?"

The doctor saw the fearful question on his face, paused, and then as calmly and confidently as he could, answered, "Every time there is a change in the guardians, the book of time steadily tells us that is when the height of power struggles happen. So you are seeing it probably at its peak."

"Probably? So you're saying more will be killed, maybe even me?"

He wavered his head back and forth and then said, "Yes, but your chances of survival are good."

Benaiah popped his head up and then loudly said in his normal sarcastic tone, "Thanks for the inspiring talk, Doctor." Then he went back to look at the dead guard. New servants had come in and were already taking his body and the body of the woman in the grass away as others were cleaning the area of the blood that poured out all over the marble floor and grass.

Mariah pointed to the second guard who was innocently directed by the other to eat the food, and she stated to the younger man, "You will stay by Master Benaiah's side all the time unless I tell you otherwise."

He straightened up, expanding his chest slightly, understanding he was being trusted, and then he responded confidently, "Yes, Mariah."

"Everyone else clear the area." She stepped next to the doctor, gently grasping his arm before he left. "Thank you for protecting Jahar earlier today and Benaiah right now. Sorry I doubted you."

"Mariah, you know this is an unfortunate burden we carry. If I did not know and experience how much God loves us, I would be a very weak person in this world. Jesus has proven to me over the years that no matter what happens, he will make all things, even the bad, to work favorably for those who love him according to his purpose." He paused, putting his arms around her. "One day, we will not have this thorn in our side anymore."

He pulled back and then, with a hopeful expression, he said, "Maybe with Benaiah becoming guardian being one from the outside, Jahar's wisdom would prevail, and he would be the one to make a change, whatever that is, that we have unknowingly but wholeheartedly been waiting for for hundreds of years."

Benaiah was standing right beside them and looking away, giving them their privacy, but he heard every word. When the doctor made his last statement about him making a change, Benaiah swiftly turned to the doctor, who was looking at him with a smile over Mariah's shoulder, and he thought to himself, *Does he know what God told me to do?*

The doctor gave him a wink for confidence, letting Mariah go, and he started walking away, telling one of his guards to fly the IGT back because he wanted to walk back to the medical facility.

As the doctor walked over the small rock bridge of the stream, Benaiah, Mariah, and the young guard stood alone on the center platform. Benaiah looked around with everyone gone except for the camouflaged military guards he knew had to be all over the place, and he was amazed, thinking to himself again, *It's like nothing tragic happened. They all reacted as though this happens every day and it's no big deal.*

As his eyes looked up, scanning the beautiful night setting in the garden with evening sounds of crickets and frogs while music softly played in the background, then his stomach reminded him of why they were here in the first place. Peering down at the hamburgers on the low coffee table and feeling completely numb everywhere else, he asked, "Can we still eat?"

Pointing to the ground next to their meal, Mariah said, "Absolutely, and then look over to the guard."

Without hesitation, the guard bent over, taking a plate with two halves and saying to Benaiah, "Master, please allow me…"

Benaiah raised his eyebrows at the fact that they were still going through the formalities as the guard seemed to be enthusiastic about it. He replied, "Go ahead. Thank you."

The guard slowly took a bite of each sandwich and then sipped each of their drinks. Stepping off the round marble floor, he stood at attention only a couple of arm's lengths from Benaiah. Watching the guard, Benaiah's mind was thinking almost too deeply about the situation. He thought to himself, *This is sick. We're waiting to see if he is going to die. This can't be the rest of my life?*

In his heart, Benaiah heard an unexpected reply. *My child, the time is very near to let the descendants of Journey's End know what has been kept secret from them under the mountain for over three thousand years. The purpose of their life here has run its course and will end with a grand new mission for them to grow my glorious kingdom in the outside world. You will work everyone here with others I am bringing you to assist in moving the ark from its mausoleum, bringing it back to life by putting it on the Congo River.*

"When Noah's Ark is ready to sail, only take what is in it now and the translated transcripts Jahar has hidden from everyone. No more, no less, except for every descendant, young and old. Sail to Israel. My glory will give you safe travels.

The picture of what was said completely took him for a loop, and he had two thoughts, *The ark is over forty-five hundred years old. How will it ever float? And, what will happen to Journey's End and the plethora of important historical artifacts and King Solomon's treasures?*

Knowing Benaiah's thoughts, God continued, *I will destroy the mountain and everything in it for all the human efforts it holds—riches, technology, historical dictation, and artifacts manifested by man from the past to the present, which are not foundations to draw my children to me through my Son Jesus. What is in the ark presently has my fingerprints and shows my efforts and love for mankind.* The grand whisper of the Creator was overwhelming, putting him into a daze sitting there on a pillow next to the low table."

"Benaiah…Benaiah." Mariah reached over, touching his arm and looking at him as though something was wrong with him staring into midair.

The guard stepped to his side, looking all around his body for anything that could have been silently shot from somewhere without them knowing. He said, "I do not see anything foreign."

Benaiah spoke up as though he had fallen asleep with his eyes open. "What'd you say?" He looked back and forth at the two staring at him.

"Are you all right?" Mariah said with concern.

"Yeah, I'm fine," he reluctantly said.

Calculating that he was overwhelmed by the last hour of the multiple killings, she calmly said, "I know all this is shocking to you, having never seen people killed in front of you. But take comfort. As we have mentioned before, it is all for your protection, which will continue all your years as guardian."

Her words were disturbing, as though a person dying had no meaning, especially for a follower of Jesus Christ. He replied, "Do you hear yourself? People are dead—your people! And you act as if it's all justified and normal—part of life." He stood up, grabbed half a hamburger on his plate, took several bites and walked to the edge of the marble floor and looked out into the dimly lit garden.

Clearing his mouth, he added, "This is not normal. You all... I guess I should say we are all family and part of the family of God. God's original chosen ones, Israelites, are we not?"

"Yes, we are." She adorned a small light-hearted smile with his sudden use of historical biblical knowledge.

He turned, stepping close to her to keep the conversation confidential as he asked in an authoritative tone, "Do you not think that God is sad or angry with what is going on here? Family killing family over what...the exact same thing your almighty King Solomon tried to save his own children, the Israelite nation, and others nations from—loving money and power?"

Mariah was the one now silent with a glossy look on her face. His words mentally slapped her into a new realm of thought.

He stepped up, grabbing the other half of his meal with the guard's bite in it and asked sarcastically in a harsh whisper, "What? Is the realization of you and everyone here believing the lie they are above the rest of the world and the law of God?"

She glanced up and then stood, arguing in the same heavy whisper, "How dare you? We are obediently following ancient orders from the wisest king this earth has ever known."

"That's very admirable of you, but if I'm to be the guardian of this place, I will follow only the orders from the wisest King the universe has ever known, Jesus."

Mariah was floored. She could not make up her mind to hug or slap him. What he said was true. But it was disturbing that he had been completely sold out to the world and suddenly was speaking wisdom far beyond his experience as though he had walked with God his whole life.

Benaiah himself secretly mirrored her thoughts about himself, wondering how the words just flowed from his mouth without much thought.

She leaned over, taking half of her hamburger with everything on it and a few French fries, leaned back, and digested what he said. There was a silent truce between them for a short time as they finished eating side by side.

Her armlet started vibrating to get her attention as a live picture of Horasha appeared across the small screen. Mariah tapped a corner that lit up, and then she spoke in English so Benaiah could be part of the conversation. "Mariah here."

"The intruders have all been eradicated and are being disassembled and will be recycled. Is Benaiah safe?"

"Yes."

"Any problems?"

"Yes, we were going to have something to eat, and the lead guard attempted to poison Benaiah, but I slit your relative's throat." she sarcastically stated to make a point of whose family members were trying to still kill him.

Horasha became aggressive. "I told you to go to his private quarters. Why are you in the commons area? All eyes are watching you there."

"That is correct. All eyes are watching…my innocence, intelligence, and loyalty."

She had strong points and continued to outsmart him every step of the way while underhandedly insulting him at the same time.

She continued, "While you finish the cleanup, I will be taking him to the treasury. He has still not seen it."

"Do not do that! Until he is guardian, that is none of his concern."

"None of my concern?" Benaiah blurted out, and then he bumped shoulders with Mariah, looking down at Horasha in the screen.

"Yes, that is correct. No one from the outside world has ever seen the treasury. You will not be able to handle yourself when your eyes lay upon it. Your eyes have already witnessed its destruction with the ones who have been born with it. You will become very weak. I know this, for I have watched over you since you were born. Please, Mariah, do not do this."

There was something in Horasha's tone and sudden change of heart that was making her think twice. She paused and then said, "I will show him the treasury but will wait for you to go with us. Benaiah deserves to see all of Journey's End for a complete understanding of why we do what we have done for three thousand years. He must share the weight of the burden of temptation equally with his fellow descendants before he becomes the guardian." She gave Benaiah a wink, telling him their secret of Journey's Beginning was safe as she continued, "To fully engage the use of all his senses and the strength of the Lord of heaven's army to live by mentally, physically, and spiritually."

Horasha was the one to pause, and then he replied, "Even though I did not hear those directives from Jahar, you have a wise point. Stay at the lounging area. I will be there shortly."

They disconnected as Benaiah asked, "How does he know we are here on the marble platform?"

The innocent part of Benaiah showed up as Mariah warmly smiled, saying, "You will see. Let us finish eating and rest while we can. Nothing this far is progressing in their normal timeframes—Jahar's ceremony and yours. So I am not sure when everything will be rescheduled or what other unexpected things will happen." She oddly looked back to her armlet as though keeping an eye on the time.

Benaiah gulped down the food in his mouth and then blurted out, "That's for sure!" He turned his head away, not wanting to give away that he knew something she didn't. He knew she might not take it well if he was to tell everyone at Journey's End the secrets of secrets let alone informing everyone now that they were to move it and present it to the world from Israel.

After finishing their meal, the young adults laid back on each couch waiting for Horasha. Mariah went into her normal shallow sleeping posture, not going too deep that she was not conscious of hearing anything around her but just enough to rest her eyes, taking long deep breaths.

Benaiah, on the other hand, fell hard into a deep sleep and immediately started dreaming. His closed eyes went back and forth, working the visual movie going on in his mind. He had been asleep for about forty-five minutes when he felt his arm being touched. Not fully understanding if it was part of the dream or not, he suddenly felt it again, this time much harder, and at the same time, his name was clearly spoken, snapping him completely out of unconsciousness.

His eyes sprung open, and he momentarily didn't know where he was or who was looking down at him. He jerked back on the pillow without much success as a large olive-skinned man with a very prominent beard and black hair looked down at him with determined dark brown eyes.

As he blinked several times fully waking up, everything mentally came into focus, and he reluctantly said out loud, "Oh great... I'm still in a cave."

Horasha spoke up again. "Ben, are you all right?"

Horasha verbally slipped, saying Benaiah's old name by habit from over twenty-seven years of silently watching over him. It took everyone by surprise, even himself, and then Benaiah, hearing his name, stated, "I remember you now!"

He sat up as Horasha stepped back next to Mariah, who had been watching on, and he continued, "Several years ago, I was alone in my car and got into an accident at an intersection downtown. I was a little dazed with my head planted in an airbag. I remember someone calling my name over and over, saying, 'Ben, are you all right? Ben are you all right?'

"When I fully got my bearings, I was looking at you saying my name, and I kept asking myself how this guy knew me. I'd never seen him before."

Horasha put on a smile, knowing the story, and said, "You scared me. I had flashbacks of your parents being murdered in their car accident."

He looked away, slightly disturbed as Benaiah asked, "The people that hit me... Were they trying to kill me?"

Horasha glanced to Mariah, giving her a nod of his head for her to answer. Benaiah followed with his eyes as Mariah said, "Yes, and if we had not had your car reinforced for safety, they would have succeeded."

Horasha proudly added, "I killed both men involved very painfully the following day and fed the sharks in San Francisco Bay by throwing the many pieces of their bodies off the Golden Gate bridge that night."

In an off-colored tone, Benaiah asked, "And you're proud of that?"

"Absolutely. That was my job and still is, to protect Journey's End at all cost and its next guardian. That is my life's duty."

Benaiah stepped into guardian mode as he got up into his face, asking, "Then why were you trying to kill me at the tombs of the dead?"

"I was not doing such a thing!" Horasha's forehead wrinkled up as he closed the gap between them both and added, "First, the protection of Journey's End is top priority. You and Mariah disappeared…" He gave her a quick glance. "I had no idea what her true intension with you were, so I was attempting to put you back under my wing of protection, using force and words towards the people so they would willfully go along, handing you to me."

Turning his body to Mariah's direction, he stated, "And that is what I am assuming she was doing and thinking as well?"

"Of course." They intently stared into each other's eyes, waiting for the other to blink or give a facial expression of backing away in defeat, but it wasn't happening.

"Great, now that we are once again one big happy family, I want to see this treasure of King Solomon's that's supposed to be so spectacular."

Horasha and Mariah couldn't help but react to Benaiah's small-minded ignorance. They quickly changed their demeanor and started smirking until they both laughed out loud.

"What's so funny?"

Horasha gave out a big sigh at him and said, "We can only show you. No words can explain the treasury. When your eyes lay upon it, you will understand how naive you really are about Journey's End."

Only moving his eyes, Benaiah gave Mariah a sudden glance upon seeing what she was thinking. She ever so slowly shook her head and then squinted her eyes for a second, mentally telling him,

"You better not say a word about Journey's Beginning or you are a dead man."

He gave her a nod to show he wasn't going to say anything. He looked back to Horasha, patting his shoulder as though they were buddies now said, "Lead the way bodyguard."

"Have a seat." Horasha pointed to what now seemed to be the head seat of all the couches as he slumped his shoulder for Benaiah to release his hand from it. Benaiah sat back down in Jahar's spot. "Now lay your hand on the arm of the lounging sofa and spread out your fingers."

He followed the instructions as Horasha pressed a button on the underside of the open arm of the couch beneath Benaiah's hand.

The synthetic arm of the couch surprisingly lit up under Benaiah's hand as a red beam flowed back and forth, scanning his fingerprints, blood type, and ultimately determining his DNA. The scanning red beam stopped as the synthetic armrest glowed green.

Horasha and Mariah looked at each other and then back to Benaiah with big excited smiles. "What's this all about?" Benaiah asked.

Mariah answered, "It has cleared you as a match with your DNA as a blood descendant of the reigning guardian bloodline, unlocking the first protection system of the treasury. There is a microphone in the arm of the couch as well. Now say clearly out loud, 'Benaiah, bloodline of Shuriah,' three times." She then pressed the button from underneath the armrest twice as the armrest itself began glowing the colors of the rainbow floating around in it like clouds.

He went along with her, saying, "Benaiah, bloodline of Shuriah. Benaiah, bloodline of Shuriah. Benaiah, bloodline of Shuriah." The colors bounced around in multiple directions with every word. When he finished, the colors organized themselves in a distinctive pattern and saved uniquely only to his tone, accent, and volume levels per letter.

"Good, the system has your voice tones and patterns documented and saved, which is the second key to unlocking the treasury." She unzipped a small hidden pocket inside her top where she safely kept the signature ring. After retrieving it, she paused, looking at it closely as many things went through her mind of its history and the ones who had worn it.

"It will be all right. Hand it to him, Mariah," Horasha gently said, understanding what she might be thinking about reflecting on his own reaction down at the tombs of the dead.

She glanced to him, appreciating his unusual soft encouraging words, and then at Benaiah, handing him the ring and saying, "You must wear this temporarily for the third and final key to unlock the door to the treasury. With it on your finger, only then can the door be unlocked and combined with your DNA and voice recognition— all three at the same time."

Memories from when she was a child of sitting on Jahar's lap on the same couch as he explained the three keys of the security system to the treasury and then correlating them Biblically came to her. She smiled, thinking it was something good to share, and she said, "Similar to our God who is three persons in one. Do you remember in Genesis chapter one, when God was creating everything, and on the sixth day, he said, 'Let us make man in our image to be like us?'"

Benaiah, not remembering each specific word, shrugged his shoulders and went along with her, "I think I do."

"When God said the word, *us*, he was talking about himself as being a whole and complete God and Creator of the universe— three persons in one. If it was only him, God the Father alone, our relationship would not be much of one. It would be more of a non-relational dictatorship. But being three persons, God the Father, our DNA physical makeup, second, God the Son, Jesus Christ, who represents the signature ring giving us true eternal identity, passage, and power. Finally, God the Holy Spirit, miraculously, is the presence and voice of God living within us here on earth, whispering guidance and demonstrating affection. All three together make a complete God of the three working as one for mankind for a fulfilling, complete, and understanding relationship, easily separating the only one true God from any other created by man."

Horasha, hearing the explanation, shook his head, grunting out sounds of agreement and backing Mariah, hoping Benaiah would finally open himself up to God. Still unknown to him, Benaiah had the heart transformation with God already.

Benaiah understood what she was saying, but he wasn't raising his hand to take the ring from her but only stared at it.

Not sure why he hesitated, she lifted it closer to him and said, "You need to put this on to open the treasury."

He backed his head up as her hand got closer, saying, "The last time I touched that, it was on Jahar's hand, and I was almost killed."

"You are fine now. Then, you were..." She tried to find good words. "You were ignorant and stupid." Horasha smirked, surprised at her choice of words as she continued, "Now you know better and understand the circumstances. Put it on so we may show you the secret of Journey's End for your knowledge." She gave him a friendly wink that was out of Horasha's sight.

Benaiah slowly raised his hand, grasping the large golden ring. After examining its details, he gradually slid it to the end of his ring finger. Holding it out for all to see, he said, "Wow, a perfect fit!"

The young guard next to him loudly announced in Hebrew upon seeing the ring on his finger, "Bow! King Solomon's ring is on our master's hand!"

A shallow echo of many, mostly camouflaged security guards going to their knees throughout the grand cavern could be heard as the announcing guard proudly hit the floor with Mariah and Horasha.

Chapter 18

"No, no, don't do that. I'm not the guardian yet," Benaiah spoke out, surprised at everyone kneeling to him.

Mariah stood back up with Horasha saying without thinking, "You will be...you know God has called you, accept it." Suddenly she regretted saying that out loud not sure of Horasha's reaction.

Surprisingly, Horasha spoke up as though supporting Mariah's comment to help Benaiah not knowing where she was coming from, verbally reached out as though it was Benaiah's last chance. He knew, as everyone else, that if Benaiah did not come full circle and become a complete Jewish Christian, he would be put to death, for he knew too much of Journey's End. "You have been called by your bloodline and God since you were born, Benaiah. Soon, you can be the guardian. Let go of your worldly thinking and allow the Creator God you knew as a child to speak to you. Fully embrace his son Jesus Christ as your Lord and Savior. If you do not..." He scanned over to everyone listening and giving out an unfortunate expression. "You cannot be the next guardian, and you will be...put to death."

Benaiah momentarily looked away into the garden, away from everyone staring at him and feeling the unwarranted pressure. Taking a deep breath, he stood, stepping up to Horasha with complete confidence and a gentle smile. Horasha mentally lifted a shield, unsure of what was coming his way from the heathen.

Quietly making his words semi-private, he raised his hands, grasping both of Horasha's shoulders, and said, "I am no longer the man you've been watching over all these years. In my absence from you the past night and day, I saw and experienced God in a very special way, in a very special place, clearly understanding what Jesus did for me. I went to my knees, doing exactly what you asked of me just now." Benaiah nodded to confirm what he said and then patted one of Horasha's shoulders, dropping his hands to his side.

Horasha, not sure if he was being mocked, looked to Mariah next to him.

She gave him a confident smile and a slow nod of her head just as Benaiah did.

Horasha paused. The large stout man was beginning to crumble inside, realizing his prayers over the past twenty seven years instantly were answered, making his spirit soar. Then the heavy mental pressure continually building from the exhausting hard work protecting the godless Benjamin Maschel following Jahar's instructions evaporated in a blink of an eye. He had convinced himself that his life's work was worthless, haunting him for years, though he would never give up as his heart remained true and committed to protecting Journey's End and following Jahar's and King Solomon's orders until his last breath.

Mariah stepped into the conversation seeing Horasha was having a difficult time responding. With pride knowing Benaiah had already jumped over his highest hurdle to becoming the next guardian said, "With the ring on your finger it will unlock the final key to the largest collection of worldly riches ever known to man."

Mariah lifted her wristband, pushing a button on the screen and then speaking into it, "Control, this is M0810930. Is the outside perimeter secure?"

"M0810930, all is secure. No foreign activity within a hundred square kilometers."

"Thank you. Please lock down the commons area. Is the security profile programed for B031393S?"

"Copy, B031393S. Profile is secure and programmed. Initiating lockdown."

Secondary locking systems were echoing throughout the cavern from every door going down the hallways as well as high above at the large eye opening, as a solid door was being lowered from within the ceiling. The commons area was always double secured from the outside world when the guardian opened the passages to the treasury.

Benaiah moved his head around, trying to peer through the garden where each of the locking sounds were coming from. But what caught his attention the most was watching the opening above slowly close like an eyelid.

Horasha said, "Sit back down, Benaiah. We are going for a ride."

When he said that, Mariah glanced at the young guard standing by in the grass. She moved her head and eyes for him to step onto the round marble platform, and he quickly and quietly did so.

A guard of Horasha that came in with him, standing on the other side of the platform, saw what happened behind Horasha's back and copied the other guard's movement.

Horasha reached out gently, grasping Benaiah's hand, twisting the ring around his finger to his palm side, and then spreading out Benaiah's fingers, placing his hand and the signature part of the ring on the armrest. He stated, "You and you alone, Benaiah, are in control from here on." The armrest automatically began to scan his hand once the signature ring touched the synthetic arm.

Horasha told him to give instructions. "Say out loud, 'The treasury.'"

Benaiah did so, and the platform faintly jerked as it unlocked itself and then slowly gained speed, lowering down into the ground. Benaiah gripped the arm of the couch, not sure what was happening.

He looked up at the new round opening with the ceiling of the cavern getting farther away and disappear as a false floor slid sideways at the surface concealing the round hole. From above in the garden, it appeared to be a continuation of grass of the garden so no one would know there was ever something different in that spot.

Soft lighting reflected off the marble floor as miniature lights had automatically came on from under the couches and coffee table. Before Benaiah knew it, the round lounge came to a stop and Mariah said, "By voice recognition, you now instruct the security system to expose the final entrance, the treasury door."

He looked at her for more instructions to come, but he was being stared at by her, with Horasha and the two guards silently standing behind them.

"Okay… What am I to say?"

"Keeping your hand on the arm of the couch with the ring down, say, 'The treasury door.'"

He shrugged his shoulders and said, "The treasury door."

Horasha and Mariah stepped to the side as Benaiah watched, astonished, as the coffee table raised up out of the floor about ten feet exposing a glass elevator door. He peered at the others, definitely amazed with the continuing hidden passages to the treasury.

Mariah added, "Now, walk in front of the glass door, and it will scan your body like your hand was scanned on the sofa armrest. Once it opens, we will step inside and the door will close. When you turn around, you will see on the wall to the right next to the glass doors is a round key hole that is waist high. Place the signature of the ring straight in, matching the patterns like a puzzle. After it locks in, twist it to the right a quarter turn. After it is unlocked, it will release the ring and the elevator will go down a short ways into the treasury."

Everyone was waiting for Benaiah to move, but the only thing that did was his eyes going to the glass elevator doors and then to Mariah and Horasha. Without warning, the excitement of the moment churned in Benaiah's stomach, taking a nosedive into worry and fear. He wasn't sure of the sudden change, but an echoing voice bounced back and forth in his head from Jahar, warning him, *Do not trust anyone but God, me, and yourself.*

Dropping his eyes to the ground at his feet and thinking, Goliath's sword between the couches caught his attention. For some reason, it gave him peace, reflecting back to what Mariah told him why Jahar had it attached to his bed. Giving him comfort and being reminded every night that God slays our giants. He bent down, picking it up with both hands. Putting on a firm face and working his hands and eyes up and down the shining massive weapon, he slowly said, "I was told by Jahar not to trust anyone. Why am I to trust any of you to go with me?"

Catching everyone completely off guard with his unexpected statement, it was quiet for a few seconds. Then the young guard behind Horasha that had tested the food for Benaiah and Mariah said, "Have we not already proven we can be trusted?"

The guard's voice surprised Horasha, him not knowing he was there. He twisted around, pulling a knife from his waist, ready to defend or attack. In the moment, his sudden reaction caused both of the guards to pull their weapons up, swaying back and forth to everyone, unsure what was happening.

Horasha straightened up after seeing the two young guards and slid his knife back into its concealed sheath, saying, "What are you men doing here?"

The guard that had spoken up replied, lowering his weapon, "Mariah told me to come along."

The other guard said, "I saw what they were doing behind your back, so I stepped on the marble floor to cover you."

Horasha twisted his head to Mariah, raising his eyebrows. She responded by shrugging her shoulders and leaning her head to the side, answering out loud to his mental question, "You never know?"

He grinned, giving a smile to everyone, saying in a slightly sinister tone, "Smart. You are right. We never know, do we?"

"Enough!" Benaiah raised his voice. "Enough of this foolish and childish behavior! I am tired of this deadly cat-and-mouse game. For such intelligent people with the greatest technology and supposedly having the largest treasure chest in the world who started out as God's chosen people, this place is a nightmare. I see why God included the Gentiles to be chosen as well. Historically and now, we're a bunch of goats trying to always stand at some superior point, devouring anything we can get our teeth sunk into, even if it is garbage! God is calling us to be sheep. Do you remember what is said in the scriptures? Some people will be goats and others sheep, and we all will be brought before the Lord to be judged."

Taken aback by his grand boldness and sudden theological question, the four were silent.

Quickly, he added, "The goats will be ordered to follow Satan and his demons into the lake of fire that was prepared for them in the first place because they aimlessly wandered around through life following their own shadows of self-glory and preservation. The sheep will be welcome into his Kingdom for eternity with loving open arms because they trusted and selflessly followed, serving God."

Still grasping the sword, he pushed his way past Horasha and Mariah to the glass elevator door, saying, "Guards, you are with me! Horasha and Mariah, you will stay behind and do whatever you need to do to each other. Kill each other and get this game over with for all I care."

The scanner went up and down his body several times, and then the door opened. He stepped in and turned around. The four were frozen, unsure what they should do with Benaiah's unexpected instructions. He looked at the guards with a stern face and growled out, turning the sword upside down and stabbing the floor, "Guards! By my side, now!" The sword was so long that the handle was shoulder high as he held it firm.

They looked to Horasha and Mariah for instructions, but Benaiah spoke out first, "Now! Or you will be punished and replaced!"

Both the guards didn't hesitate and almost jumped into the elevator. The glass doors closed as Mariah and Horasha stared at them, almost petrified at what Benaiah was doing without them. Then Horasha yelled out, "Benaiah, do not do this without us. We must be with you for the protection of your life!"

Benaiah spotted the round key hole, following Mariah's instructions. The elevator began lowering as Mariah and Horasha leaped to the glass door, pounding on it and pleading, "Take us with you. There is more you need to know. Your life is in danger!" But Benaiah paid them no mind as both of the younger guards stood on each side of him, wide eyed with confusion.

The elevator went down about thirty feet, stopped, and the glass doors slid opened. The only light was from the elevator glowing out. As they took one step out into the darkness, Benaiah held the sword in a protective posture. He felt a cooler temperature change and an odd odor filling his scenes. It was different from the fresh garden high above and the historical wooden smells way down below at Journey's Beginning. Soundless noise eerily penetrated through him as he slowly spun around, attempting to see anything in the black air.

"Perhaps you need to tell the lights to come on, Master Benaiah," one of the guards suggested.

"You guys don't know?"

"We have never been here and know very little details about it. It is off limits to lower-ranking guards."

Benaiah now realized what the concern Mariah and Horasha might have had as the three of them stood staring into the unknown. He decided to go for it, saying loudly, "Treasury lights on!"

His words echoed outward a far distance as lights from the ceiling came on circling the elevator and then turning on systematically following the echo of his voice, spiderwebbing outward.

The young men stood speechless as their brains were having difficulty interpreting the impossible sight that their eyes were showing them.

After a few moments, one of the guards said, "When the treasury is silently spoken of, I always envisioned what you see in the movies, a grand reinforced vault with a large thick metal door with a high-tech security system, and when you opened it, there are rows of safety deposit boxes along the side walls filled with jewels as stacks of gold and silver bars in organized rows filling the middle section."

The other guard replied, "This definitely is not what I expected either."

Benaiah at first didn't say anything, looking at the details of what voraciously was on display and admiring the view. He felt there was no need to hold onto Goliath's sword anymore, so he leaned it up in a corner of the elevator and then very slowly strolled around the circular platform going around the elevator. The platform was made of large stepping stones decoratively patterned with different markings inscribed on top of each stone.

A quarter of the way around, the guards heard Benaiah expressing himself. At first, it was a whisper of disbelief. "No way…" Then he got louder and louder every time it appeared he saw something completely different as he continued around, examining everything from a distance. "No way…. No way! It can't be!"

The physical sensation inside the cavern was peculiar as it appeared that they were actually closer to the ceiling than the cavern floor looking downward, as though they were standing at the peak of a mountain centered inside it.

The guard Mariah instructed to come along on the lounge floor took a few steps to the edge of the platform, looked downward, and said, "Steps circle all the way around with the platform going down into the…the massive ocean of treasure or whatever you want to call all this."

Benaiah made the complete circle, stepping to the guards side and bewildered as the other guard stepped to the other side of Benaiah, asking, "How far down or deep do you think the stairs go?"

They were looking at eight steps exposed, angling down and away from them until it reached the overwhelming plethora of gold, silver, and artifact items randomly heaped up—coins, statues, gold bars, silver bars, jewelry, furniture, portraits, exotic weapons, armor, etc. pocketed with other items such as red rubies, green emeralds, diamonds, and many other precious stones sparkling lively throughout.

Benaiah speculated, "Well, to the far end of the upper part of the round cavern wall from here, which appears to be the center of this cave, I would guess it's a half a football field in front of us and the other half of a football field length behind us."

"Are you talking American football or the normal football that you call soccer?"

There was a pause, and then the three guys looked at each other, suddenly breaking out in laughter, knowing it made no difference in the monstrosity of what was in their presence.

Calming down, Benaiah attempted to answer his own question. "It looks like each of those steps are about two feet long by one foot high. So doing the math, I would guess if the steps went down all the way back to the far lower wall, we're looking at about a hundred and fifty to a hundred and seventy-five feet deep at the cavern wall way down below. Then if we average out the slope from where we're standing, all in all, we are looking at approximately seventy-five feet deep and a hundred yards long of all…this, all the way around the cave from the center point here." He swayed his arms out wide to everything in the whole place.

One guard responded, "We could fill probably at least four Noah's Arks with all this."

Benaiah glanced quickly to him, asking, "Why did you say Noah's Ark?"

The guard shrugged his shoulders, answering, "I remember the measurements of it from the Bible." He looked around the whole area and continued, "So I did my own math. Do you not agree?"

Benaiah mentally stepped back, not wanting to expose what he knew as he said, looking around, "Sure, I'll take your word for it."

The guard added, "King Solomon definitely had much, much more than I had ever imagined."

"This wasn't originally all his!" Benaiah corrected with excitement.

"What do you mean?"

"Here in front of us, taking up more than a third of the cavern definitely, is probably his wealth dumped in the giant pile. There was so much, and it probably kept coming and coming that they couldn't keep it all neatly organized. But look over here." They walked less than a quarter the way around the platform, pointing out, "All this is Egyptian, probably from the time of the pharaohs."

Stepping over a little more, he stated, "This section is holding the prosperity of the great Roman and Greek empires."

Taking a few steps further, he said, "All this is from east Asia. More than likely from the Ming dynasty time frame, including Attila the Hun and the monarchs of India."

Again, walking over a little bit, he pointed out, trying to control his excitement, "If I'm right, this is from the Inca civilization. Maybe some things are from the Mayans, even the Aztecs as well, but mostly from the Incans."

A guard spoke up. "It looks like small gold structures or buildings within all the other gold things and objects out there."

"Sure is, from a very old city in Peru called Paititi, also known as the Lost City of Gold. The Spanish in the fifteen hundreds first tried to find it and, still today, we're looking for it. But…"—he threw his hands in the air—"it's here, hidden from the world." Benaiah suddenly got disgusted with what he was seeing as he shook his head, clenching his teeth. Then he continued attempting to stay focused and composed. "And this over here…"—moving over before making the full circle back to Solomon's large section of the cavern—"is more than likely a conglomeration of things from historical Europe and northwestern Asia such as Spanish, French, English, German, and Russian from the height of the czars' rule."

"So we pretty much have the world's greatest fortunes and artifacts from all different places and times," the other guard stated.

Benaiah quietly shook his head again, reveling in the revolting demonstration of paranoia, selfishness, and thievery. Not only from this exhausting plunder whose worth would be impossible to guess, but all the other things he'd seen and what they'd said they had from day one hidden within the mountain in the middle of Africa. He fought quickly to understand why Solomon and God would approve and instruct something of this magnitude to transpire.

Then he heard a familiar voice instantly putting him at ease. *"Benaiah, only look forward, trusting me that all things will work for the good, no matter how distorted things appear. You have been chosen for this moment when I need you to serve me, transforming the journey of the descendants.*

"The riches of Solomon and from others the descendants had gathered over time and from around the world being here is only a simple distraction for a moment in time in order for you to tell the world right now about me through Journey's Beginning. Through your adult life and the modern times of today, you see clearly of the wrong man has done in their attempts to erase me from their lives as you have repented of doing the same. I will do everything, arranging all situations from any moment in time to come together so I may be glorified, the God and only God who loves his creations and whose only desire is for them to spend eternity with us. That is why I sent my Son, Jesus.

"Expose the true secret, sailing it to the Holy Land. Ten years will be given to you for this task. Tenth the amount of time I gave Noah to construct and prepare for the first destruction of most everything, for the next and final destruction of all things is near. But I will do everything for my children to be able to see and hear their Father calling them to himself before it is too late."

"Master Benaiah, are you all right?" a guard asked.

Benaiah blinked several times, coming out of deep thought. He replied, "Yes, I'm fine." He walked over to where they first started, saying, "Let's take a closer look at what King Solomon's stash looks like."

"Sorry, Master. Stash… We are not familiar with that term."

Benaiah chuckled under his breath, thinking how restricted these people were from the real world and looking through the lens of the illusion of illusions created by man and said, "His hidden treasure."

Both the guards nodded in understanding.

As Benaiah stepped down the stairs to the first stepping stone, it felt as though it faintly compressed down. When he lifted his foot off to go to the next lower tier, he thought he heard something click but didn't think anything about it. At the final eighth step, he bent down, looking at the flow of gold items as though they were seamlessly wedged together as a body of water calmly settled against a dam. Reaching down and picking up what appeared to be coinage of old, Benaiah's body instantly jolted back in terror as pain exploded in his arm, and he clenched his fist tight with the gold coin in it.

Shadowed within the gold mass, a deadly cobra sprung out, stabbing its fangs deeply in Benaiah's forearm.

He screamed out in pain, lying out backward on the stairs. The guards reacted with lightning speed, leaping down to his aid. Mariah's guard landed on the bottom step between the danger and Benaiah, standing tall as a shield and shooting the deadly snake in half. When he lowered the weapon, he slowly turned to his master. The other guard was kneeling next to Benaiah, taking his pack off and getting out a tourniquet to restrict blood flow.

"Sorry, Master," The guard standing in front of him said, turning around to them as he began gasping for air. "I will not be able to…protect you anymore."

Benaiah and the guard attempting to put on the tourniquet looked up at him as horror continued to sweep through their veins. His body wavered back and forth and then collapsed dead, falling into the ocean of riches. The front of his body was riddled with poisonous darts.

The first step down going all the way around the circular platform had a camouflaged security system. When Benaiah's foot lifted off the first step, it triggered the protective system, which searches for its invading targets by sensing movement, sound, and heat. From Benaiah's quick movement of jumping back and screaming out, the darts zeroed in on him, but the defensive guard's body got in the way during flight.

The other guard frantically searched around in the air for more incoming killers as he laid his body out on top of Benaiah. Not seeing any he shouted out, "To the elevator Master!"

They exploded up the steps as the guard pressed up against Benaiah, feeling frightening sensations littering his back. At the platform, he began to stumble behind and yelled out, "Dive to the floor out of the way!"

Benaiah was hearing soft swishing sounds coming from the ceiling before the guard gave instruction. Reacting to his words, he crashed to the elevator floor as his body skidded to the back wall, coming to an instant halt. Squirming fast to get out of sight, he crawled next to the side of the doors where the circular key hole was. He put his hand up to insert the ring and yelled, "Where are you? Get in here!"

Not getting a response or hearing anything, Benaiah cautiously peeked around the corner, trying to control his panic-stricken breathing, and he saw him lying on the ground several feet from the doors. His head was struggling to look up, reaching out with his hand, and then he suddenly dropped his head as his hand went limp, dead.

Benaiah stared at the scattering of poisonous darts sticking up from all over his backside and thought to himself, *They never had a chance…It's my fault. I didn't let Mariah or Horasha come along to protect me or them. Jahar was right on the walk in at the first encounter with a cobra, anything and anyone appears to always want to kill you. We can never let our guard down.*

His arm was singing with pain and reminding him that he would be dead himself shortly if he didn't get help.

As he kneeled back over to the key hole, working the ring into place, Benaiah began to sense the effects of the venom.

The elevator doors closed as he sat down, leaning his back against the corner hidden from the glass doors while holding his arm. Shortly, he was back up to the marble floor. As the doors opened, he didn't move, unsure of what he would find after leaving Mariah and Horasha, hoping one or both weren't dead from killing the other. Or they might be very angry at him for what he did and were going to punish him when he got back.

It wasn't more than a couple of breaths after the doors opened when he heard Mariah say, "Horasha, they did not return… He was killed! We failed!"

Both Mariah and Horasha were getting to the point they were convinced that Benaiah and the two guards were dead. Without the naïve ones knowing how to get around or turn off the deadly security systems below, they knew it was practically impossible to come back alive. But when the elevator came back up, they were shocked, and a glimpse of hope sparked their spirits.

Mariah had been nervously sitting and trying her best not to cry as Horasha angrily paced back and forth, mad at himself that he lost Benaiah in Journey's End, especially in the treasury after all these years. When the elevator came up and they couldn't see anyone immediately through the glass doors, Mariah began to emotionally break down.

Benaiah found himself having a hard time speaking out after hearing her words but he still pushed out, almost in a whisper, "Help."

Silence penetrated the elevator for a second, and then Horasha loudly leaped in to see where the whisper came from. He stared at Benaiah, surprised to see him alive and crunched up in the corner behind the small wall next to the key hole. His demeanor switched like lightning as he cocked his head to the side, putting on a serious face and drawing his knife. Benaiah's eyes widened as Horasha boldly stepped up with the knife pointed at him, reaching back to stab forward and said, "You must die!"

"No… I love him!" Mariah screamed out as she stepped in the elevator behind him.

Horasha's knife went forward, stabbing deep through his target as the tip of the blade made a tinging sound, hitting the metal side wall.

With Horasha's body blocking Mariah's view, she couldn't believe what he just did and then dropped to the floor in anguish.

Proud of his accomplishment, he stepped back from Benaiah as he held up a large black scorpion impaled at the end of his knife and said, "If this would have stung you in the neck, you would have been dead very soon." He smiled and then turned to Mariah to make fun of her. "I did not know you loved this scorpion, Mariah?"

She looked up defeated but sprang to her feet, understanding what he truly did upon seeing what was squirming at the end of his knife. The scorpion had come into the elevator from the gap between the elevator and the elevator shaft wall when the doors were open in the treasury. It quietly creeped up to Benaiah's shoulder and appeared to angle his wicked tail at Benaiah's neck without him knowing.

She jumped to Horasha, giving him a hug and saying, "Thank you." Then she looked down to Benaiah, changing her tone and wiping the tears from her eyes and angrily stated, "You scared me! Do not ever do that again!" Looking around in the elevator and only seeing Goliath's sword leaning in another corner, she asked, "Where are the guards?"

In a humble tone and speaking slowly, not quite slurring his words yet, he said, "Dead. They're both dead…from saving my life."

Mariah and Horasha knew there was something wrong from the way he was acting. Then Benaiah moved his hand with blood on it, exposing the two needle holes. Mariah did not hesitate and screamed out, "Horasha, pick up Benaiah! He has been bitten by a snake!"

Horasha picked him up quickly, taking him to his couch. Grabbing his hand, he turned the ring around, spreading his fingers out as he pressed it on the arm rest. When it lit up, Horasha told him, "Say out loud, 'the commons area.'"

Benaiah was starting to have problems moving his muscles as he awkwardly worked his lips. "I…ca…n't…taaalk."

Horasha grabbed Benaiah's face, staring deep into his eyes, and yelled, "Do it now! Say it! You have to or you are dead! We cannot move without your voice recognition!"

Horasha let go as Benaiah tried hard to work his mouth, pushing out with all he had, "The…commons area."

The security system recognized Benaiah's voice as it was reading the pattern of the ring and his DNA at the same time. The elevator lowered as the coffee table on its roof stabilized into its correct position on the marble floor and the circular lounge began to rise.

Mariah sat down on Benaiah's couch, and quickly fastened a tourniquet around his arm using Benaiah's sash that was draped around his shoulder and waist. Then using her razor-sharp knife, she cut slits where the snake penetrated his skin and began sucking out blood, hoping it contained some of the deadly venom.

When the ceiling cover slid sideways, opening up to the grand cavern, it also opened up the communication to the outside world for them.

Horasha touched a couple of buttons and then talked into his armlet device, "Medical facility! Urgent! This is Horasha. Master Benaiah has been bit by a snake and is quickly losing muscle control! We are returning to the commons area from the treasury. Send an IGT stretcher immediately and notify the doctor. Our next guardian must live!"

Chapter 19

B enaiah was peacefully lying unconscious in the same room and on the same bed he was in almost a week ago when he was knocked out from being hit in the head with a rock thrown from a sling. Dr. Mitanual kept him in this comatose state purposely for over a day so his body would stay relaxed and assisting in dissipating the poison from his body. Also, Benaiah was in great need of rest and was dehydrated.

While sedated, the high council of the descendants decided it best to have Jahar's burial ceremony without Benaiah. With Benaiah not present under the circumstances, they would be able to finish both burials of the pygmy chief and Jahar without disgraceful interruptions.

The nursing staff had fully undressed, bathed, and rubbed healing oils all over Benaiah's skin and then reclothed him with normal guardian attire. Mariah and Horasha were standing at the foot of his bed calmly speaking to the doctor and discussing his conditions; physically, mentally, spiritually, and socially within Journey's End, finally having wise cordial discussions. Ones they would have with Jahar, calmly talking to each another with respect and honesty, thoroughly thinking through and considering what the other person had to say.

Horasha and Mariah had dropped their guard, coming together as Jahar would have them, forgiving one another for killing each other's brothers. They understood that one was done in self-defense as the other was from the illusion that Benaiah needed to be protected under the circumstances. They also erased any ill will toward each other to move forward in combined strength for Benaiah and his future. They concluded that they both were fully in support of Benaiah being guardian, especially with the new and very surprising evidences coming to light in the medical room about him.

Mariah informed the doctor and Horasha of Benaiah's mental transformation of Jesus which miraculously changed his heart, astonishingly giving him sudden wisdom, and revealing things from memory when he was a child and teenager raised in the church. She did not say where this happened, keeping Journey's Beginning oblivious to everyone, but she said God spoke to him after Jahar died in a way that raised the veil from his eyes similar to when Saul was renamed Paul in the New Testament.

Then, as the nurses were preparing Benaiah to be bathed, the new surprising find was publicly exposed which Mariah had to explain as well. In all the excitement of the past days, she had forgotten what took place while she was taking care of him during the three-day elephant ride in the forest at the beginning of his venture.

Horasha now understood why Jahar firmly instructed this type of old-style travel instead of using an IGT, feeding Benaiah distracting stories of old and why and how they travel in and out of the Congo.

On the bottom of Benaiah's feet, Mariah had tattooed the design of King Solomon's symbol of a roaring lion with the all-seeing eye in its mouth, exactly matching the signature ring. Half of the picture on each foot, and when the feet were together, the big symbol was very prevalent.

Jahar instructed Mariah to do so when Benaiah was unconscious in the privacy of the enclosed travel hut on the elephant. No one was to know of its existence, especially Benaiah, except for her, Dr. Mitanual, and himself. Jahar said it was for Benaiah's protection and to safely secure the guardian position in case he himself passed away before Benaiah came full circle spiritually.

This would tell the descendants that Benaiah was not a mistake and had the full blessings of Jahar and God, giving him instant social and psychological power that he was the chosen one through his bloodline. This was why, in the pygmy hut, Uba and the other leaders of the pygmy tribe bowed to him when he was kneeling and upon seeing the bottom of his feet together and exposed while he was conversing with Mariah.

"What are you all talking about?" Benaiah groggily asked, blinking and trying to clearly focus.

"Benaiah, you are awake!" Mariah turned giddily as she quickly went to his side, putting a hand on his shoulder.

Everyone turned to her, surprised from her unnatural reaction and tone.

Feeling the expressions shouting her way from everyone in the room, she blushed with embarrassment, trying to hide by slightly tilting her head toward the floor.

Benaiah slowly answered a bit embarrassed himself but also flattered, "Yes…I am. How long have I been out?"

A nurse spoke up in broken English as she looked down at her armlet screen, "Thirty-three hours and seventeen minutes."

He rolled his head on the pillow toward her to thank her. But as his eyes landed on hers, she realized she was very insubordinate spouting out as she did. Dropping to the floor on both knees and bowing so low her face was almost touching the ground, she said, "Forgive me, Master, I will never do that again." Suddenly, everyone except Mariah went to the ground copying the nurse except they knelt on one knee.

Benaiah looked around, trying to sit up and attempting to understand what was going on. Mariah adjusted the bed in the upright position as he asked, looking into her eyes, "What did I miss?"

She hesitated and then whispered in his ear to save face for him, "We will explain momentarily. Right now, accept her apology and tell everyone to rise, dismissing everyone except us three." She pointed to Horasha and the doctor.

Awkward formalities again, he thought and then he followed her guidance. "I accept your apology. Now, everyone rise and leave the room except for Mariah, Horasha, and the doctor."

With precision from years of experience, everyone stood at once uniformly and then bowed and left quietly. Benaiah watched as he could obviously tell there was something different than the ordinary guest respect and guardian-to-be mode he had been receiving.

"What gives, you guys?"

The three looked at each other, and then Horasha stepped to the other side of the bed, bowed, cleared his throat, and explained, "Master Benaiah, guardian of Journey's End. We found out while you were asleep that Jahar had already proclaimed you guardian before you arrived here."

Benaiah frowned, definitely confused, and shook his head as though to clear his foggy mind. He asked, "I don't understand?"

Horasha looked across the bed at Mariah, nodding for her to take the conversation from here.

Benaiah followed his eyes, staring at Mariah as she stuttered at first and then finally got her words out, "Well, Jahar…um…I… All right, Benaiah, you need to have an open mind."

"About what? Am I dying?" Benaiah suddenly got serious from her abnormal behavior, completely ignorant to where she was going.

"No, no, you are not dying. You are fine. The reason why they are honoring you that way and Horasha said what he did…is that you have been marked as guardian by Jahar's orders."

"Marked?"

"Yes, permanently…tattooed," she cringed out.

"Tattooed? What are you talking about? I don't have any tattoos!"

She took a deep breath and then delivered the news. "When you were asleep in the traveling hut on the elephant, I…I tattooed the sacred and secret sign of King Solomon to the bottom of your feet."

Coming completely out of nowhere, Benaiah paused, trying to put another puzzle together. Crinkling his forehead, he asked, perplexed, "You did what?" Then his face flushed as his eyes opened wide, suddenly remembering situations from the elephant ride to when he was last laying in the same bed in the medical facility. The pieces were coming together.

Mariah had continually taken care of his feet as they hiked, applying an oil she said was to keep his feet healthy in the humid forest. Then, when he and Jahar got to the tent up on the side of the mountain, it was one of the first things Mariah did, giving him a cleansing foot massage with the same oil. Finally, he remembered when Jahar stated someone would come to him to explain his foot imprint image.

He bent his knee, pulling his foot upward and looking at the bottom and doing the same with the other. Not saying anything for a moment as he straightened out his legs upon seeing the proof, he asked, "How come I never felt any pain?"

Amazed that he was not angry and almost relieved, the doctor answered, "I infused a very potent painkiller in the healing oil they continually applied, numbing the bottom of your feet for most of each day. When you were brought in for your head wound, which is, by the way, healing nicely—I cleaned up the skin adhesive Horasha put on and pulled the staples out this morning." He glanced, pointing up to Benaiah's head and then continued, "I applied a final coat of a different ointment on your feet that would last for days. Obviously, it worked. You never knew anything was different with your feet."

Mariah added, "I did worry slightly when you were showering in Jahar's living quarters that you might look at the bottom of your feet. But you did not."

"And you know that why?" Benaiah asked, putting her in a corner and giving her a very questioning frown.

"Well...you apparently had no idea it was there."

"Wonder if I'm playing you, and I knew it was there waiting for someone to confess what they did to me?"

Horasha jumped into the conversation with his bold tone, "We do not play!"

Horasha's response didn't surprise Benaiah as he replied with a smile, "Oh, that is very obvious, my friend!"

The doctor laughed, chuckling out, "He has you there, Horasha."

Horasha kept his mouth shut, folding his arms and giving his reply as a grunt. "Uhm." Then he turned his head away, but his eyes glanced back with appreciation at Benaiah calling him his friend.

Turning back to Mariah, Benaiah stated, "You watched me shower in that exotic indoor waterfall Jahar has."

Mariah blushed as she defended herself. "Do not flatter yourself. I had to keep an eye on...I mean...I can never let you out of my sight for your protection."

Benaiah only hummed out, "Uh-huh." Then he looked down at his feet again to see her work.

"Let me get you a mirror, Master, so you can see the whole signature at once," the doctor said as he walked to the door and then called out for one to be brought to them. A nurse handed him a round framed one and then stood at Benaiah's feet, adjusting the angle as Benaiah saw what would be with him for the rest of his life.

For some reason, this didn't bother him, but it powerfully confirmed the direction of his life's work, giving him peace even though he thought it was a weird thing to do. He turned his hand up, looking at the design of the big gold ring and then back to the mirror image on his feet.

A sudden cold wispy, raspy voice breathed worry internally. *They will kill you when they find out what you're going to do with their home.*

A frightful twinge came across his face as his eyes quickly scanned the three admiring faces watching him.

He looked down at the mirror again. This time, he thought, *It is a curse!* When he said that in his mind, his dad's voice from his childhood jumped in, blocking the dark spiritual attack as Benaiah remembered him saying many times, *With Jesus in your life, there are no curses, only bumpy dirt roads in our lives being worked on, making way for smooth highways of experience which leads to wisdom.*

With that thought, his parents visually came to mind. *Mom and Dad?* The parental comforting security of them protecting, guiding, and loving him without failure extinguished the flash of fiery fear and worry of moving forward as the guardian. For all they had done and who they were, he knew he could trust them more than anyone on the planet.

Without thinking, Benaiah blurted out, "I want my parents brought here!"

Completely out of sight and mind, it took a second for a response, and then Horasha replied, "They are of no importance of yours anymore, Benaiah. They were only used as….as foster people so you would grow up in the outside world, as order of Jahar's. They have no need to come here to be with pureblood descendants."

An explosion of rare rage not seen erupted as Benaiah boldly fought to get out of bed, grasping the IV tube and pulling it with him until he was standing up nose to nose to Horasha. The Biblical knowledge Mariah mentioned he had suddenly spewed angrily from his mouth as Horasha took a step back. "How dare you! Most of King David's mighty warriors were not pureblood Israelites. They were men in distress, debt, and discontented from different nations and ethnic backgrounds. God blessed and used them because of their obedience to the one that was to be the king of Israel, honoring the Lord of heaven's armies as they experienced the loving greatness of God accepting him in their lives!

"Many of the great growths for the kingdom of God came from… from foster people that weren't Israelites, Horasha! Balaam, Rahab the prostitute, Pharaoh's, one with Joseph, and the other with Moses. How about the Queen of Sheba, Nebuchadnezzar, several Roman guards, the good Samaritan, Luke, the gentile physician who wrote the books of Luke and Acts and so many other people…!" Benaiah was now yelling at him as saliva splattered out with his face turning red.

After he finished his rebuttal, he took a breath, then his face went flush as his body was losing balance with his eyes rolling to the back of his head. The doctor reached out, saying, "He is passing out."

Horasha instinctively grasped Benaiah as Mariah helped him put their unconscious master back in bed as the doctor called out for the nurses to assist. He was still very weak from the powerful snake bite, and lingering sedative that was influencing his body.

Mariah batted the side of Horasha's shoulder, saying in Hebrew, "You need to start thinking before you open your big mouth. Now, go, have your guards that are on site with his parents bring them here now. They should understand and come without argument. Jahar told them this day would come."

Keeping to his harsh personality, he replied, offended that she was telling him what to do, "I was there when he talked with them, remember? Oh no, you do not! You were an infant yourself."

She gave him a fun grin, knowing she rubbed him wrong and said, "It is not the time to be a smart mouth, old man. Just go. I will not leave Benaiah's side."

"I will say this again. This is not a good idea."

"Are you serious? Did you not hear the wisdom coming out of him? He now has the power to have you killed with the snap of his fingers. The ring has been passed on even without a ceremony, and we are slaves to his words." She looked down to Benaiah and gently stroked his face.

Horasha already knew this but was having a hard time as his mind was only seeing the old Benjamin Maschel before he had been reborn. He took a deep breath and then asked the doctor, "When will Master be healthy enough for the ceremony of guardianship for all the descendants to witness?"

"I would give him two more days for full recovery."

Horasha looked at Mariah. "I will have my guards have his parents here by then, unless…"—Horasha put on a joking frown and added—"you think his parents need to be brought in the way Jahar had us bring Master Benaiah?"

"No, normal transport with an IGT will be fine." She smiled back at his change of attitude.

***

For the next day, Benaiah lay in and out of unconscious in the medical facility as his mind went into nightmares of dark delusional chaos. Cold sweats and the twitching of his extremities continued as his eyes rapidly went back and forth, watching frightening visions underneath his eyelids. The doctor was concerned for his medical welfare but had an idea it wasn't an ailment but Benaiah undergoing spiritual warfare within his mind and spirit.

He called in all the elders and rabbis of Journey's End to lay hands on their master and to go into spiritual battle through prayer, petition, and meditation by his bed side until his body was back to normal.

The tattoo on Benaiah's feet competed for attention as the descendant leaders had never seen the sacred mark anywhere else except briefly on the highly protected signature ring. It was forbidden to repeat the mark—punishable by death. But for Jahar to give the orders for it to be done under the circumstances, everyone concurred to the wisdom.

Finally, the following day, it appeared to the crowd watching on that their master was being relieved from the grasps of spiritual darkness. His body relaxed, and his breathing calmly leveled out. The nurses washed away the toxic sweat from his body and changed the drenched sheets on his bed.

The doctor had everyone leave except Mariah, who was asleep in the back of the room on another bed and getting some well needed rest, and the on-duty guardian guards. Mariah was receiving her own attack from the evil one breathing atrocious thoughts her direction and trying to negatively influence the fruits of the spirit she had in her life. The doctor woke her up so she would be by his side when Benaiah did.

Drowsily, he was stirring, so Mariah leaned over, gently encouraging him that he was going to be all right. Hearing her, Benaiah slowly reached out for her hand, feeling her stroking his shoulder. She softly took a hold of it as he drew her in close. Still with his eyes closed, he took several deep breaths and whispered, "You said you loved me…in the treasury elevator. Did you mean it?"

Mariah didn't move, stunned that he heard her and remembered it. Moreover, Benaiah was bringing it up now at this awkward moment. Not letting it simmer, she gingerly replied, "Yes. Yes, I did."

Keeping his eyes closed, he gave her a grateful facial expression and then adjusted his body. Before drifting back to sleep, he groggily stated, as though talking in his sleep, "I hope you still do…when I carry out God's instructions. Love…you…" He fell asleep before he finished his sentence.

The doctor, listening on, asked her, "What did he mean by that?"

Mariah shrugged her shoulders. "I have no idea."

***

Later in the day, Benaiah fully woke up alert. Mariah had fresh clothes brought to her as she showered and cleaned up in the medical facility. She was not going to be more than a shout away from him. The atmosphere in Journey's End had transformed as the news of Benaiah truly being the new guardian swept through like a lightning bolt. Even though he had not gone through an official ceremony, with the ring on his finger and the shocking tattoo of King Solomon's signature permanently on his body, the selfish fight for a new bloodline to take over the guardian position evaporated like morning dew on a hot summer day.

The atmosphere was fresh, exciting, and mysterious all in one. The news of the heathen archeologist raised in the United States becoming aware of his roots as a descendant of King David's mighty men and accepting Jesus Christ as his Lord and Savior was great news. Then for him to become a permanent part of Journey's End, especially the guardian, was a first. How he would rule and what new changes Master Benaiah would make created a sweet aroma for dreamy conversations.

Uba and the other elders of the pygmies spread the news, as well, throughout the forest as they clearly understood firsthand Jahar's intent and relationship with Benaiah before anyone else in the Congo. Because Jahar had already had private conversations about this with his close friend, their chief, as well as Uba and the elders.

This was confirmed when they saw the evidence of this upon seeing Benaiah's tattooed feet when Jahar died in their hut.

**

The official guardian ceremony was being pressed to happen sooner than later as the excitement to see and hear from their new master grew. The arrangements were made for the following day with Dr. Mitanual's permission, as Benaiah stated he wanted as many of the leaders, descendants, pygmies, and other Africans to be present along with as many of their people that could fit into the commons area for the ceremony.

Benaiah and Mariah had gone back into his new living quarters the normal way—through the secured door connected to the commons area—to put Goliath's sword back where Jahar had it attached high between the bed posts as well as to regroup with the new reality of Journey's End and to start thinking how he would want his new giant bedroom to be redesigned.

They ended up spending more time looking closer at all of Jahar's personal items as a servant took notes of what needed to be taken away or replaced. As they opened drawers and cabinets while sorting through things, Benaiah felt as though they were looking for something more than rearranging or getting rid of Jahar's personal effects, but he had no idea what it was.

Slowly making their way around the room, they stopped at the large portrait of Jahar sitting between Billy Graham and Mother Theresa standing on each side of him. Still in awe of the three together, Benaiah admired the details and spotted something they both hadn't noticed before.

Kneeling to get a closer look, something round and smooth was being held up pinched between Jahar's forefinger and thumb, about two inches in diameter, as his hand rested naturally on his lap. Mariah asked, kneeling next to him, "I never noticed that. What is it? It looks like a smooth stone with Hebrew writing."

"You're right. What does it say?"

"It say's…" She squinted at the small writing. "1 Samuel 17:45."

Benaiah glanced around the room, trying to think if they saw a Bible anywhere and asked, "Do you know what the verse says?"

Mariah lifted her arm up, pressing on the armlet screen, and then asked into it, "What does 1 Samuel 17:45 say?"

Words came across the screen as she stated out loud, "David replied to the Philistine, 'You come to me with sword, spear, and javelin, but I come to you in the name of the Lord of heaven's armies—the God of the armies of Israel whom you have defied.'"

Both of them paused and then, in amazement from understanding what they were looking at, blurted out together, "The stone that killed Goliath!"

The resounding great power of the scripture written on the ordinary small stone echoed in Benaiah's mind as he began to warmly shiver with comfort, seeing a clear picture of God dissipating the vision of the impossible giant in his own path. The enemy of God had been ruthlessly challenging him that it was futile to carry out and fight the frightening battle before him. The anticipation was heavy of how the descendants would react or even kill him when he informed them of something that was hidden from them by all the guardians before him. Then telling them they have to leave their home, identity, and purpose behind after three thousand years of faithful service.

With him being an outsider, a new believer, hardly knowing anyone or anything about their home; who was he? Even if he was a direct bloodline descendant and granted the guardian position by Jahar, what gave him the right to erase King Solomon's orders and force them to do such outrageous things with the secrets of this special place of all places?

Out of the corner of his eye, Benaiah slightly glanced to Mariah, thinking, *What is she going to do when I inform the rest of Journey's End's inhabitants that Jahar and her have been keeping the ultimate secret from everyone and that their purpose of hiding Solomon's riches was only a smoke screen?*

Wanting to be done with taking inventory and going over remodeling ideas, Mariah turned to the servant, dismissing her. When she was out of the great bedroom, Mariah asked inquisitively as she turned around, glancing around Jahar's old room, "I never knew he had the stone that killed Goliath. I wonder where it is?"

Benaiah followed her lead, looking around himself. He asked, "Do you think he would have kept it in here somewhere?"

"Things with deep meaning keeping him focused, he held very close. So yes, it probably is."

As they thought where to look, already having gone through most of his private things, the comforting soft sound of the small cascading waterfall shower constantly perfumed the living quarter's air. Benaiah watched the water splash onto the flat and polished rock floor as the backdrop of a multistonewall behind the free-falling water kept its natural texture.

Benaiah engaged the paleontologist in him, thinking through how to find fossils hidden underneath the surface of the earth, blending in and camouflaged with dirt and rocks.

"Camouflaged within the rocks..." he whispered out.

"What did you say?"

"I have a hunch where it might be." Benaiah looked back at the portrait, confirming the backdrop behind the three wise people posing. Focusing on Mother Theresa, he saw her hand gently grasping Jahar's shoulder. But at second glance, he noticed her index finger on his shoulder was somewhat lifted as though pointing to something behind them. Looking over to Billy Graham, his hand was on Jahar's other shoulder, with a finger slightly pointing behind them as well.

Benaiah whispered, "I got your messages." Then he quickly turned, walking to the natural shower, and asked, "Can we turn the water off?"

Mariah reacted without a word and stepped to the side near the entrance to the lavatory. She reached up to a small box on the rock wall. She flipped the box open and pushed a button. Within seconds, the waterfall was only straggling droplets and then completely dried up.

"Is that what you are wanting?"

"Yes, thanks," he said as he stepped into the shower, reaching around and fondling the rock wall. He got to a spot that was directly behind where the water fell approximately head high. A specific rock, grapefruit-sized, stuck out a little more than the other surrounding rocks. Looking closer, he saw it had a small etching in Hebrew.

Pointing to it, he asked, "What does this one say?"

She stepped up, looking at it quickly and stated, "Isaiah 26:4." Both of them did not respond, unsure of what the verse was. Mariah pushed on her wrist screen again and then spoke into it. "What does Isaiah 26:4 say?"

Letters lit up the screen as she read out loud, "'Trust in the Lord forever, for the Lord himself is the Rock eternal.'"

Pausing for a moment to think, he started to believe it was a key to something more and said, "This has got to be the place." Probing around the rock, Benaiah found a hole on the side big enough for his finger to slide into.

Sensing it might mysteriously lead somewhere, he pushed his finger in, hearing a click as though pressing a button.

Instantaneously, the sound of pressure releasing was heard as the outline of a door suddenly appeared amongst the cracks in the rock wall, spewing a mist of water outward.

Benaiah wiped the dew-like moisture splattered on his face, stepping back as a door slowly swung open. Mariah was the first to speak up. "I never knew this existed. Why would he keep it from me?"

Benaiah stepped to the opening, and she grabbed his shoulder. "Stop! Remember the last time you went into something without me."

He ignored her warning, pulling himself from her grasp and said, "If you didn't know this was here, he is the only one that did. He wouldn't have it booby trapped because no one would know how to get past it without being killed. Besides, I believe this was a place only for him and probably the guardians before him to be alone to call his own—like a sanctuary."

"His sanctuary was the commons area," Mariah stated more than implied.

He looked back, giving her an irrational expression. "You call that a sanctuary? It's a bullseye for death, in my opinion!"

Boldly stepping forward, lights automatically came on. Instantly, his prediction was confirmed upon seeing items and things arranged in a very casual and comfortable way. A desk straight across the small room was against the wall. It had a stack of papers and an open Bible with reading glasses lying on top of it. A couch similar to the one in the book of time was off to the side against the wall, with a box of tissue sitting in the middle of it. Laying on the floor in front of the couch was a thick cushioned mat. Peering closer, he saw two round compressions, side by side and centered on the mat. He thought for a moment, and then it came to him, *This is where he did his private praying and devotions.*

Mariah stepped forward, and Benaiah twisted around, putting his hand out to stop her from going any farther. "You are not allowed in here."

"What are you talking about?" She went to push his hand to the side, and he stepped right up to her face.

"This is a place for guardians only. There are some things and moments when one needs complete privacy to call their own. And I believe this is that place."

She almost couldn't control herself, attempting to move to the side, but he kept in step with her so she couldn't see inside.

He gently placed a hand on her shoulder saying, "Mariah, Jahar loved and trusted you more than anyone else. You alone he told all the secrets you needed to know about Journey's End. But he had the right and the need, as anyone else, especially being a man in leadership, to have a secluded place for himself only. A spot hidden from the world that is for God's eyes and ears only. I anticipate this is that special place where he would be able to be Jahar, only a simple man. Leaving Jahar the guardian and Jahar, the bloodline descendant of the great Shuriah mighty warrior, behind. A place to expose his brokenness, to share with God his fears and worries. To let his hair down, per se, where he didn't have to wear a mask. Completely exposing his soul, out of sight of everyone so they wouldn't see one speck of weakness in being the powerful leader of the most powerful place on the planet." He reached back, pointing into the private room and finished, "This was Jahar's...sanctuary. It will be mine now. You, and only you, will be the only descendant that knows of its existence." Bringing his arm back, he lowered his head slightly, looking up with his eyes directly into hers as though looking over a pair of glasses as Jahar always did. He mentally was shooting an exclamation point into her vision.

Mariah's emotions were rattled as tears came to her eyes.

Not expecting this reaction, he asked, "What's wrong? Why are you crying?"

She wiped one of her eyes and then answered, "Oh nothing."

"Nothing? Mariah, the...deadly weapon of Journey's End is crying. It has to be something."

She sniffled herself dry, gently shaking her head. "My heart...my heart is leaping for joy but very sad at the same time. A transformation far beyond what I imagined has truly taken place. One Horasha and I told Jahar would probably be impossible. And Jahar's remorseful response was, 'I am so disappointed that in all my life attempting to reflect God, I failed you. I failed that the descendants do not understand our clear relationship with God, faithfully accepting and surrendering to his greatness which we cannot fathom. Having God expectations, trusting he will conquer and make possible what we perceive as impossible.'

"Speaking for myself, I did not understand the depth of what he was saying until now. You, Master Benaiah..." She bowed in respect. "Truly, you are a miracle proving you have been touched by God to be a wise leader. I could never visualize you being where you are at now. In literally days, you have begun to think, perform, and believe with understanding and wisdom at a level with Jahar. How did Jahar know and have so much confident faith you would come full circle in your life to take his place?"

Benaiah looked back into the private room, glancing at the well-used padded kneeling rug on the floor and tattered Bible on the desk and then back to her and said, "He imitated Jesus."

His three-word answer wasn't very impressive as she waited for some added deep theological explanation.

Seeing anticipation on her face, he continued, "Our relationship is a simple one with God—spend time with him. Jesus always was alone with his Father in secluded spots in the wilderness or private places, his sanctuaries. You know that. It appears Jahar was doing what his Savior did, spending a lot of time with the Lord of heaven's armies alone, where eyes and ears of others are excluded, even from you, Mariah."

As he talked, he had a change of heart and decided to strengthen her own relationship with God by showing her where Jahar's strength came from as well as to extinguish her curiosity and future temptations of finding out what was behind him. He stepped to the side, saying with a smile, "It's probably best for you to see what I'm talking about this one time to help rid you of temptations to sneak in here when I'm not around."

She hesitated and then mimicked his smile, grateful he changed his mind and took a careful step into the quaint room that was permeating peace with a comfortable and casual atmosphere.

Staring at the details of Jahar's personal effects and how they were arranged, she knew they had to hold important private meaning to him. Now, Mariah understood why Benaiah acted and concluded the way he did.

Recognizing an object on the desk on top of papers, she stepped over and picked it up. "Hmm." She said, "So…he is using the stone that killed Goliath as a paperweight."

Benaiah, now at her side, reached up, taking it from her hand and saw the writing on it matched what was on the portrait. He replied, tossing it up and down and checking out its weight, "Wow, this is super cool." Raising it to his forehead, he added, "Could you imagine this slamming into your head?"

She shook her head at his boyish mindset and then replied, "Not mine. But yours, I could…" Then she laughed at him.

It took a moment, and then he got it, reaching over to where the doctor removed the staples on the side of his head. "Oh yeah, how quickly we forget. It could have been me with a stone sticking out of my skull if they wanted to kill me." Then he laughed at himself.

Looking back down on the desk, handwritten papers appearing to be biblical study notes were arranged in a specific order as the well-used Bible lay open next to them. At the head of the desk, against the wall and above everything, were three different oddly shaped sizable containers appearing to be very old and expensive. One, Jahar had filled with tissue paper. Another was filled with pens, pencils, a letter opener, and other like items. The third was halfway filled with wrapped candy as several used wrappers lay crunched up next to it.

Picking up the aged, octagon-shaped, so-called candy jar with the lid sitting next to it, Benaiah admired the fancy and colorful designs on the outside and then noticed unfamiliar writing was decoratively engraved on it.

"Do you know what that says?" Benaiah pointed out.

Mariah thought for a moment, taking it from him, and answered, "It is an old dialect from the far eastern regions of the Arabic world, maybe Persian time frame. If I was to guess…I would say it says, 'From a king of a country…to the King of the world, the King of the Jews.'"

Setting it down and then picking up a triangular-shaped extravagant pencil holder next to it, she twisted it around, staring at the strange patterns. It looked like a body of a female with a small ruby in the center of her forehead with many arms and hands reaching around the jewels and precious metals integrated within the material of the container balancing it all together. Benaiah spoke up, "That looks like it's from India?"

"I concur." She removed the items in it, looked inside and searched for any inscription not seen on the outside. At the flat bottom inside, she found her answer. "It is definitely Hindu, it says, 'The world was created by one God, not many. For there is only one Light that shines on this world, the King of the Jews.'"

Benaiah quickly grabbed the last container, having an idea what these were as Mariah sat the second one down and said from glancing at it, "This has to be from China. Look at the design of dragons wrapped all around it."

Taking it from him and seeing the ancient writings along the side of the beasts bodies, it took her a second to translate. "I think this says… 'Before time, during time, and after time, only one King reigns—the King of the Jews.'"

Instantly, the two looked at each other, stating with excitement, "The three wise men from eastern lands!"

Mariah laid it down gently, adding with enthusiasm, "These were filled with the gifts given to baby Jesus, Mary, and Joseph when he was born—gold, frankincense, and myrrh. I have never seen these until now."

Benaiah added, "And Jahar is using them as ordinary containers for his desk? Don't you think that's like sacrilegious or something?"

They both stared back down, thinking for a second, and then Mariah said, "It is not like they are holy."

"Yeah, but…" He thought for a second and then continued, "You're right, but how and where do you people get things like these? This is crazy!"

She proudly stated, "We have told you, we are everywhere around the world, present all the time since King Solomon, secretly watching and gathering information and things from all parts of the world."

"You've got that right! But you're not just collecting information, Mariah. It's unbelievable the riches in the treasury and artifacts like these all over this place." He picked up boy David's stone, tossing it in the air and catching it again, and then he pointed to the three containers.

She innocently shrugged her shoulders, replying, "We were only told not to interfere in current worldly events with governments, politics, wars, relationship, etc. Our king did not say anything about collecting or retaining things in the aftermath of changes, collapses of societies, deaths, defeats, destruction, ships sinking, etc."

"So basically the descendants have been pirating the world of its gold and highlighted historical items without killing anyone in the process?"

Mariah wobbled her head back and forth, agreeing but not wanting to admit he was basically right. Waiting for an answer, he looked beside her on the floor and against the wall next to the desk. A fairly large, old-style wooden trunk with an arched lid was blending in with the natural-looking rock wall. The wood slats were striped with tattered leather straps holding it together. The lid was closed as the rustic metal latch in the front was unlocked. Benaiah bent down next to it, looking around for any identification. Below the latch, he saw, carved into the wood, large capitalized letters in a classic old-style font written in English. "G.W."

"Who do you think those initials belong to?" Mariah asked.

"Not sure. Let's see what's inside," he said anxiously as though he was expecting to find it filled with more treasures. Slowly lifting the aged lid, it quietly opened as the hinges were tattered leather straps. Peering inside, to his surprise, it wasn't what he was expecting. To one side, carefully placed, were what appeared to be very, very old scrolls, tarnished and yellowing and almost filling the trunk, stacked on top of each other. On the other side were six large old and very thick books approximately twenty inches high by twenty inches wide by five inches thick. They were definitely aged, but not as the scrolls were.

Mariah carefully pulled one of the large books out from the middle of the batch lined up. They were thick pages pressed together and bound with a thick leather string snaking itself at the back end of the pages. Thick leather flaps were used for the front and back covers. On the front flap imprinted in Hebrew, Mariah read the title to herself, *Journey's Beginning.* Below the title read, *"Kenan Generation Four through Mahalalel Generation Five."*

"Here they are!" she excitedly exclaimed, slowly and carefully opening the pages.

"What are they?"

"These are the translated manuscripts from Noah's Ark—Noah's diary!" She closed it, slid the large book back into place, and then gently pulled the first one in order out while looking at the front.

"What does it say?"

With a joyful smile answered, *"Journey's Beginning, The Garden of Eden through Adam and Eve, Generation One."*

Benaiah looked down at the scrolls, picking one up and then gently unrolled a portion of it on Jahar's desk. He examined the paper-like material and the writing saying, "This is definitely very old. It appears it has your clear sap coating on it or something like it."

Mariah reached over, softly stroking it, and replied, "It does have a preservative layer on it of some kind." She looked at the writing on the scroll material, interpreting a few lines and said, "These scrolls were probably the first translations of Noah's writings on the ark's walls. Then one of the guardians of old copied them into these bound-up pages, putting them into book form."

She opened the book in hand, examining the old fine print and how it was organized and said, "I am repeating myself again, but I have never seen these before either. Jahar only talked about them."

Benaiah gently rolled the scroll up, putting it back and saying, "I guess this is the best place to hide such information if the guardians needed to keep Journey's Beginning a secret."

They were interrupted as Mariah's wrist bracelet vibrated. She put the book back and then looked down, pushing on the glass screen with Horasha's face appearing as she answered, "Mariah here."

"Benaiah's…" Horasha paused, changing his tone to make sure he did not offend him if he was listening and kindly finished. "Step-parents have arrived. Where does he want them taken to?"

Mariah looked at Benaiah as he quickly replied, "In the commons area."

"We will meet you there shortly," Horasha stated.

She tapped the screen, ending the conversation and then said, "I hope you know what you are doing having them here. They are now in danger."

He bent over to close the lid of the trunk, saying, "Maybe, but having them here…" Benaiah stopped talking, lifting the lid back up fully so the light would brighten the inner side of it. Leaning closer and squinting his eyes to focus, he grunted out, "Uh."

"What is it?" Mariah asked.

"There's an inscription on the inside of the lid that says, 'Congratulations, George, on your accomplishment. You will do wonderful things for the colonies now being united. We love you. Signed, Augustine and Mary Ball Washington.'"

Mariah responded, "GW is for…George Washington?"

"Sounds like it. This must have been a gift to him when he became the first president of the United States."

Chapter 20

"What are you going to do with your parents?" Mariah asked.

Benaiah thought for a moment and then answered, "I want to do the Jahar thing. Talk with them in the commons area for a while. Then we'll have my ceremony so they are witnesses to the next chapter of my life."

There was silence for a moment as they both scanned the room, making sure they hadn't missed anything in the small hidden sanctuary for the guardians. Their thoughts about everything seemed to be colliding and happening fast. She gently touched his shoulder and asked with concern, changing her attitude about his parents being here. "What are you going to say?"

"I'm not sure yet. But I will be telling them the truth about everything here. No secrets. No more of that!" he stated firmly.

She popped her head back with a frown, about to reply, but he cut her off, saying, "This is all new to me as it is to you. The one thing I do know is I can fully trust my parents with advice and my life better then what almost everyone here has proven to me so far." He paused and then added, leaning forward to make their conversation somewhat private, "All I ask is that you first... walk by faith with God, trusting everything he has told me to do as the new guardian when he spoke to me." Benaiah pointed a finger downward as she understood he was pointing to Journey's Beginning at the bottom of the mountain. Turning to the door, he kindly gestured, "Now, I need to follow in the steps of Jahar and spend time alone with God."

She stood there, at first insulted and bewildered that he suddenly was taking on his role with more and more authority, making her somewhat uncomfortable. But as her thoughts flowed through the wise words of what the room was for, her heart powerfully and obediently guided her back out into the bedroom. Without another word, she pondered in the back of her mind, *What did God tell Benaiah to do that would be so different than the other guardians?*

***

Benaiah's parents had entered Journey's End under heavy guard on an IGT through the hidden formal entrance made for rare visitors on the middle of the mountain. They were escorted straight down one of the tunnels into the commons area and seated in the center lounge.

The sun was at the perfect angle, brightly shining through the upper opening and exposing the grandeur of the garden. Birds and butterflies fluttered here and there, with the stream doing what came naturally, softly babbling as sweet fragrances of exotic floral permeated in the giant cavern.

The older couple had many questions unanswered throughout the unexpected, quick, and bizarre trip even though they were foretold mysterious things like this would come to pass at the beginning, when they started this journey twenty-seven years ago as extreme life instructions and gifts came from a stranger when they brought their new baby home.

The stranger was a handsome older man with long graying hair, tannish, olive-colored skin, and he was shorter and slender in stature. His heart was soft as clouds, and his wisdom flowed deeper than the Grand Canyon. Speaking with confidence that was strong as steel, he told them his visit was one-of-a-kind and was to be confidential, never to be spoken or discussed with another person, especially Benjamin. Jahar was never seen again by them.

In their conversation, Jahar informed them they were specifically chosen for who they were in their hearts and physical features, being of Mediterranean descent, and their foremost duty for their new baby son was to train him in the way of the Lord, for his future would be one of great mystery of old. Then one day, he would be called upon to serve, for his true ancestry demanded it. They weren't sure if he was talking about serving God or serving something else. Jahar never divulged anything further—even who he was or where he was from.

The parents were sure the stranger had something to do with the miracle adoption, for they were told it would take at least a couple of years waiting for their number to come up in the system, but then they received him within weeks.

Their prepaid gift for following his instructions was a lifetime of modest financial freedom, physical protection, and continuous prayerful blessings for God to work in their lives.

Before leaving, Jahar performed a ceremony with baby Benaiah, explaining he was of Jewish descent and then added a special baptism signifying Jesus Christ was his Lord and Savior.

They never understood clearly the purpose and whole spectrum of the visit and what it all completely meant, but they did their best to stay true to the instructions of the generous and God-fearing stranger for everything he asked of them which was their hearts intentions already.

The atmosphere of the commons area helped sooth the anxious parents who were waiting to see their son. They were completely oblivious of where they were in the world through the whole trip, even on location in the giant cave confused the situation further. They were not drugged like their son, because they had a moment-in-time experience with Jahar, faithfully following his words all these years, and knowing they could be trusted. But also, Jahar needed Benaiah tattooed without his permission and knowledge.

Benaiah's mom attempted to control herself, sitting patiently and sipping on a drink the servants brought to them. His dad, on the other hand, was more impatient as he paced around the round lounge, wanting to step off the marble floor. But when instructed to take their shoes off, they were also instructed to stay on the hard surface.

A large, solid door could be heard opening and closing across the garden as his parents came together, holding each other in antici-pation and looking in that direction, only seeing the beautiful forest. What came next surprised them as a man powerfully shouted an announcement in a foreign language from that direction. Mirroring the language, a reply of what sounded like hundreds of men shouting back surrounding them and from up high followed by movement as though people were kneeling.

From the explosion of voices, fear flared up as the anticipation escalated to a new level as Benaiah's mom held her husband tight and started to tremble. She asked, "What is going on? Where are all these people shouting? Do you see them?"

"I don't know..." His eyes caught movement on the other side of the rock bridge. "Wait, here comes some people. Maybe they'll tell us what's going on."

When the small group approached the lounge, Benaiah's parents were speechless. In front of them was their son dressed in what was now his normal soft snow white guardian attire with a long, wide purple sash draped across his chest and tied around his waist with one end dangling down toward his knees. His feet were adorned by light-fitting sandals perfectly matching his attire.

A beautiful woman, well dressed, with long black hair and having the same olive tan skin as his was on his right. On the other side of him stood the older man closer to their age, tall, with a strong beard and a distinguished appearance who had met them when they first arrived. Surrounding them and coming into view were a half-dozen or so men dressed in illusive military attire that made them almost disappear when they stood still.

At first, they both thought something was very wrong, but as they stared at their son, now looking more of a grown man than ever, peace swallowed their emotions. His eyes spoke loudly as he seemed to be able to peer into them with warm affection and wisdom, bringing joy to a mom and dad without saying a word.

"Benjamin!" his mom shouted out, overwhelmed to finally see him, dropped her grip on her husband and jolted to her son.

In a blink of an eye, three guards walled themselves in front of him as she bumped up against one of their chests. Mariah, already anticipating what the guards' actions would be, gave orders in Hebrew before Benaiah could respond. "Stand down. Our master's parents are of no harm to him."

Instantly, the guards gave her a bow, and the one she ran into speaking broken English said, "Our apologies. Our duty is to protect our master at all times."

Seeing the puzzlement in his parents' eyes, Benaiah stepped forward, opening his arms and giving his mother a long warm hug. Embracing him, she felt a fresh new person in her arms, not the critical hardened person he had become who had distanced himself from the family. Stepping away, he looked over to his dad and said, "Father, it's good to have you here."

His dad smiled and then looked around the garden wondering where here was replied, "You too, we were beginning to think something happened to you."

Looking back to his son, he stepped out on the grass without shoes and shared a rare embrace, patting each other heartily on the back. Separating, Benaiah removed his sandals and walked them back on the marble floor.

"How was your trip?"

His mom answered, "It was...different, to say the least. Where are we?"

Benaiah looked to Horasha, questioning how they traveled. He instantly knew what Benaiah was thinking and said, "To London, as you arrived. Then from the secluded small airfield on a private jet with shades pulled down on the windows, they flew to a secure hidden airfield outside of the forest with the last trek on a luxurious IGT to here."

"What, no elephants?" he joked with a slight smirk and winked.

"No, no elephants, Master Benaiah." Horasha faintly bowed his head, reflecting back a small rare smile.

His mother slanted her head at him and asked, "Why do they keep calling you master, and what is a beenia?"

"It's pronounced Benaiah. That is my bloodline name handed down from a very long time ago."

"I don't understand, son. What's going on here?" His dad's tone was serious.

Mariah leaned into Benaiah, inconspicuously touching his hand as he sensed she was asking permission to answer the questions. Giving her the okay by slightly bumping her hand back, she answered, "Mr. and Mrs. Maschel, I am Mariah..." She respectfully bowed and then continued, "Myself and Horasha..." She gestured to him. "We are Benaiah's personal caretakers. Horasha has been with Benaiah before he became your son who was renamed Benjamin to disguise his true identity before you adopted him. Horasha watched

D.L. CRAGER

over him and you both almost every moment of everyday and night in the United States up until he was called home back here.

"You had a brief visit with…" She hesitated, looking to Benaiah for permission to say his name as he granted it and continued, "Horasha and Master Jahar at the beginning when he gave you very secret detailed instructions. To which you have followed with precision, and he was very grateful to you for doing so. Master Jahar recently knew he was passing away, and Benaiah…" She pointed to him using the name they knew. "Benjamin…was next in line to be guardian of where we are now, which was the reason for the cautious and secret steps taken at the beginning of you raising him."

His dad still mildly but impatient prodded, "So where is here for the second time, young lady?"

She glanced to Benaiah and then to Horasha as he gently shook his head. Benaiah knew the two were doing their best to avoid giving out vital information. He took back control, saying, "Let's sit down, and I will quickly explain what I can in the short time we have."

Mariah pointed to where they were to sit as Benaiah took his spot. Benaiah was presented a chilled drink on the low table when he sat down. He looked over to the new lead guard standing closest to him. Without hesitating, the guard stepped forward, taking a small drink and then wiped the rim where he touched with his lips with the napkin it was sitting on and got back into security position.

Horasha stood directly behind Benaiah, keeping an eye on everything as Mariah sat on the same couch next to him. His parents watched the odd motions of their son and the others, perplexed.

Benaiah watched the guard for a moment and then grasped his mom and dad's attention, answering their questions. "We are in a special place in Africa which we will discuss later. They are calling me master because Master Jahar has passed away and I have taken his place. My official inauguration ceremony will be held shortly. That is why I'm wearing this and invited you here." He pointed to his attire and then swayed his arms, looking around out into the garden. "As Mariah mentioned, I am taking Jahar's place because I am in the direct bloodline of our relatives from many, many years ago."

342

He looked to Mariah, giving her a quick wink and a twinge of a smile. Then he glanced back to the guard, making sure he was still alive and not looking sickly. Mariah saw who he looked at, knowing what he wanted, saw the guard herself was doing fine, and gave Benaiah the okay to drink.

After taking a couple of swallows, he went to continue, but his dad stood up aggressively, getting more and more upset, and loudly stated, pointing his finger to the ground, "Stop this masquerade right now, son!"

Guards naturally reacted by swarming in. Their action frightened his mom as she jumped to her husband, holding her hands up in defense and saying, "Benjamin, what's happening? This place is scaring me."

He swiftly held his hand up, stopping the men in their tracks. Then he waved them back into position. Benaiah stood, stepping to his parents and raising his own hands, gently grasping their arms to calm them down and saying, "There is so much I want to tell you, most of which is complicated, to say the least. You knew there was something different about me when Jahar approached you years ago and gave you direct instructions."

Benaiah paused to think as both his parents caved in, nodding their heads, confirming that they were informed by the stranger as he continued, "We know things happen for a higher purpose and work for the good of those who love the Lord, right?"

"Are you quoting scripture, Ben?" his dad asked, stunned and changing his tune.

He smiled. "Yes, yes, I am."

The parents looked at each other and then back to their son as his mother asked, "When did you... Why are you...?"

Helping her out with her questions, he said, "It says, in the book of James in the first chapter, 'Believe our prayers will be answered or they will be tossed around like a rogue wave in the ocean here and there.' You raised me in the way of the Lord, planting many seeds along the way. And your faith is strong in him, believing your prayers will be answered, and God has responded. He opened my eyes to his greatness, and my salvation in him is secure."

The parents slowly looked again at each other, mystified, this time, as deer in headlights. His father glanced around the area and then looked at Mariah and then to Horasha, trying absorb the plethora of ingredients of the emotional stew simmering in his head. A blurred picture instantly flashed in his memory while staring at Horasha, and then he stepped around the couch, stopping face to face and pausing for a moment, and then he asked, "Haven't I seen you somewhere before? And I'm not talking about twenty-seven years ago when we were closer to Benjamin's age."

Horasha loosen his stiff stance and answered, leaning forward to privately say in Dad's ear, "A year ago, your wife was in the hospital having her special female surgery…"

Dad flinched back that this stranger knew about that, then he leaned forward to hear more.

"Master Benaiah was visiting by her bedside, and outside the room in the hallway, someone had collapsed…"

"I remember that!" Dad whispered excitedly.

"I killed that man by bumping into him so the security cameras would not catch me injecting a lethal poison into his kidney."

Dad quickly stepped back, asking loudly, "What? Why would you do such a thing?"

Horasha put on his power smile of intimidation and answered, "He was going to kill Benaiah, you, and your wife."

Stunned by the conversation, his mind put everything together and replied with excitement while pointing at him, "You were the doctor leaning over the guy and calling out for a nurse in the hallway! That's where I saw you."

Horasha smiled proudly. His job was well done, and he said, giving him a slight bow, "Only pretending to be a doctor, Mr. Maschel."

Benaiah smirked out a slight laugh and then controlled himself.

His mother gently slapped his arm, saying, "Why would you laugh at someone being killed?"

Benaiah and Horasha looked at one another, and both poorly held in a moment of laughter, attempting to contain themselves as guards nearby chuckled as well, and then Benaiah answered, "Sorry, Mom, its' not funny. It's just…you need to get to know Horasha."

Mariah looked down at her wrist screen and then quickly stood, seeing the time, and whispered over to Benaiah, "Benaiah, your ceremony."

His mother watched on as her mind ran around many different things, and she asked out of the blue, "Ben, what does this have to do with archeology and dinosaurs, and you getting the invitation for research? Did you get the job?"

The question was so out there and completely out of place that even the guards near them looked at one another at the bizarre inquiry.

Benaiah raised his eyebrows at his mom's innocence as his heart knew she was either slightly traumatized from the outrageous turn of events or wasn't completely connecting the dots of the reality going on.

"Teresa..." Dad replied slightly embarrassed at the question. "This is the invitation. He didn't know himself what he was being invited to...or did you?" he asked Benaiah, angling his head to him.

Benaiah shook his head with a confident grin, saying no as everyone looked at him.

"Uh...mmm." Mariah cleared her throat to get his attention, pointing to her watch.

He stated in a tone that showed he was tired of her pushing him because of time, "Okay, Mariah..." Then he asked her, "Our pygmy friend, the older lady we met at her village...what was her name? Uba?"

"Yes, Uba?"

"Have her meet me up there on that platform very soon." He pointed up to the open entrance high above.

With a questioning look, she started to ask why, but he again cut her off, responding first, "I need to have a private conversation with her before the ceremony. Also, I do not want the ceremony in here after I've thought about it. I want it to be moved outside next to the small lake at the base of the waterfall."

Horasha remained silent but narrowed his eyebrows, wondering how Benaiah knew of Uba and when he was ever at the base of the waterfall. Mariah, on the other hand, could hardly control herself and stepped into Benaiah's face, stating firmly under her breath, "No, you cannot move it there! And at this late hour!" Completely out of character and at a request totally unworthy of her forceful response, it went silent in the lounge area. Understanding her outbreak was out of line, she took a step back, looking away.

Benaiah inhaled deeply, doing his best to keep calm and not to let the cat out of the bag regarding his intentions for the new location so as not to expose his own secret. Maintaining his virgin authority of Journey's End, he decided to ask, "Why not there?"

Catching herself off guard with the question and not wanting to answer with the truth, she quickly manufactured a response. "Well… we have already moved the ceremony day and time around because the incident at the tombs of the dead and with the delay of your recovery in the medical facility."

Seeming to be weak and an odd answer with no true depth, Benaiah looked to Horasha and then back to her and asked, "I don't recall anything here at Journey's End being on a time clock, is there?"

Horasha enjoying Mariah being put on the hot seat and quickly answered, "No, Master. Every day here presents its own agenda. Only the sun rising and setting is on a schedule."

Mariah glared at him, wanting to debate the topic, but she knew it was futile. Attempting to control herself and not to appear distressed, she said calmly, "But we have already rearranged the location to in here for your benefit. Moving the location means changing the time…"

Benaiah turned directly to her as her unusual demeanor was getting irritating and stopped her again, holding his hand up. Then, with a stern expression, he turned, looking at all the descendants he could see, including Horasha, and asked loudly, "Is there any reason…why we cannot be flexible with my inauguration on where and when I want it held?"

Looking back and forth at the descendants around him, all shook their heads, with Mariah being the last one to answer, reluctantly agreeing. Benaiah tilted his head to her to carry out his request with Uba as he glanced up to the opening in the ceiling.

Mariah bowed, acknowledging her obedience in front of everyone and then said, "Yes, Master."

Adjusting his clothes a little, he took a moment to regroup and then reached out, waving his hand toward himself and said, "Dad, come back around here please." He wrapped his arm around his mother and then gave instructions to everyone else. "I want a moment of privacy with my parents, so if everyone would please wait at the bridge…" He nudged his chin up in that direction. Seeing hesitation in Mariah and Horasha as everyone else moved away, he tilted his head with a demanding glare, waiting for them to move. Reluctantly, they joined the guards and servants.

Once alone, and still standing, he brought them in close, speaking as Jahar did so no one could read his lips. He told them, "Mom, Dad, I know you have a storm of questions, but I don't have time to answer them at the moment. I'm going to tell you to do something, and I need you to just do it without questioning me. Do you understand?"

"Son, that was always our line."

His dad pointed to his chest, smiling, as his mom added, "Of course we understand, Ben."

Thinking to himself, *Wow, that is ironic. They did tell me that all the time when I was a kid.*

Putting his head back down, he said, "This won't make any sense now, but it will later. This ceremony we're talking about is a big deal, and many different people will be there—descendants and the local African tribes."

"Descendants?" Dad asked.

Benaiah didn't answer but kept going in a quiet whisper, "There will be an older pygmy African woman…" He held his hand up to the middle of his chest. "She's the one I'm meeting up there. I am giving her instructions to slip you two quietly away right as the ceremony starts for your protection."

"Pygmy woman?" This time, his mom questioned, slightly raising her voice.

Keeping his voice low, he said, "Come on, you two, just go with me here. This is very important. Believe it or not, I'm the most protected man on the planet, protected by the deadliest people on the planet. God has given me a secret mission here as their new guardian. And they're not going to like or possibly believe the mission given to me by God. So I need you two out of the way and safe just in case it gets crazy."

His dad looked around in the garden, ending up at the group of people, staring them down at the bridge, and he asked, "So there's more to this place than flying saucers and an incredible underground forest?"

Benaiah puffed out a quiet laugh, knowing how naïve they were, only recently being in their shoes, and he answered, "Oh, you have no…

idea, Dad. And I can't wait to show you things that will blow your mind. But for now… Please, without hesitation, do as I say when the time comes by following and obeying Uba after you meet her. Understand?"

His mom commented, lifting her hand to his cheek, softly patting it proudly, and answered, "We understand, Ben. You're so grown up, taking charge like this in a strange place. You are going to make a good manager like your father at his office."

"Mom…" He took her hand down, embarrassed, holding it low, and shaking his head that she wasn't getting the importance of what he was saying. Then he looked over to his father with a serious expression. "Dad, I am not mocking or making fun of you like I used to. I'm a completely changed man, believe it or not. Right now, I need one of your powerful prayers. I trust you and Mom without hesitation more than anyone on earth, and I know your hearts are completely for Jesus. This is one of the main reasons I sent for you."

He pulled them closer, almost touching each other's heads, whispering softer, "Also, I want you by my side where the authority, power, and blessings of God must be revealed for what he is telling me to do as guardian of Journey's End. Only by miracles will they happen." Thinking to himself not to alarm them, he thought, *And not kill me in the process.*

Taking Benaiah by both shoulders, his dad said slowly, "Ben, there is nothing too big or difficult for God to physically do in this world—he made it. The one thing that is a true miracle is the invisible changing of a man's heart of faith, since that is one gift God will always leave for man to open on his own."

He paused to emphasize his next statement as his wife put her hand on his shoulder, signifying she was agreeing and supporting where he was going. "You…are one of those miracles."

His mom took her hand off her husband's shoulder, putting it up against her chest and, with a motherly happy and emotional frown, sighed out, "Oh, my baby boy."

Benaiah rolled his eyes as his dad dropped his hands from his shoulders and asked, "So what is it God is telling you to do at the end of this journey you're on that you're supposed to be guarding?"

Benaiah's thought to himself, *You've got to be kidding me. They aren't listening to a word I'm saying. What was I thinking bringing them here?* Then it struck him how the words rearranged gave it new meaning as Journey's Beginning came to mind.

A faint whisper from the Holy Spirit flowed through his body. *The descendants hearts have been invisibly yearning for a new beginning. Unknown to them, they have been desiring to be guided for a change, like Moses and the Israelites enslaved by Egypt. The descendants are enslaved, and I am using you, but in a new time and place for a different purpose.*

The parents were trying hard to put the puzzle together and make sense of everything going on and what he was talking about. His mom asked innocently again, taking Benaiah on another quick boomerang ride. "Are you guiding them on a special dinosaur expedition somewhere here? It looks like a good place to do your work. Is that why they hired you?"

Completely ignoring his mother's questions and fighting frustration, he couldn't tell them more at the moment. He took one of each of their hands, saying, "As you pray, Dad, keep your hands on me as I kneel. And pray big, bigger than you ever have for me."

His dad stared into his son's eyes as they heard Mom's breath briefly being taken away. Finally, after all these years, words he'd yearned for were delivered to him inside the beautiful garden hidden underground somewhere in Africa as a bunch of strange people with very strange customs stared at them.

His father, not seeing a clear picture of what was going on or what was going to happen, did fully understand the depth of the request and the urgency in the moment they were in.

Benaiah knelt before his parents as they both put their hands on him. Before Dad could get a word out, a command was shouted out in Hebrew by Horasha, who was closely watching every movement his master was making. The sound of everyone going through the motion of kneeling, heard earlier, imitated their master throughout the garden and high above. The parents looked around at the ones they could see, blown away at the respect everyone was giving, but they weren't sure if it was honoring their son or God, but it did give them a glimpse of the unique faithfulness to whomever they were giving it to in this odd place.

An idea came to Benaiah as he looked up, saying softly, "Dad… pray loudly so everyone can hear you. You know, like you do at the men's retreats and…in the name of the Lord, as the prophets did in the Old Testament." His dad put on a stern smile, understanding what he was asking and remembering back in the earlier years when Ben used to go with him before college.

The moment melted his heart, but he fought to compose himself. Then he took a deep breath and proudly prayed for all to hear, praying in a way to acknowledge God's supreme position as the Creator on the throne of the universe and giving thanks for his many blessing and finally asking for his protection, guidance, and love for his family and the ones here in Africa and in the cave while spending a large amount of time on Benaiah. He pleaded for God to bless him with his love as their Lord Jesus loves all his children and to bless him with the obedience of Abraham, the courage and endurance of Moses, the heart of David, and the wisdom of Solomon…

When he said the name Solomon, the kneeling descendants with their heads bowed and listening murmured in a very respectful tone in English so the one praying understood their favor. They repeated, as they always do when their king was formally spoken of, "Our king, whom we faithfully serve!"

Benaiah's heart was shocked as though he was touched by a defibrillator flashing clarity to his brain and realizing whom they were truly worshipping. They were not actually living for God and following instructions through King Solomon, but the complete opposite. They were living for the dead king in the name of God.

Having been blinded over time, they had lost clarity of the difference as they focused so hard on their worldly duty. Their identity of being descendants from bloodlines of the mighty warriors of old and Jews accepting Jesus doing a duty in the name of God, but not for God, were the qualifying features. They were clearly in the wrong natural order and heart of how their Creator intended the relationship with him to be—to worship him first above anyone or anything.

Dad had to pause for a second as he was taken off guard as well, hearing such an extreme awkward honor given to someone from nearly three thousand years ago. He shook it off and then continued, "The strength of Samson, the boldness of Paul…"

After saying other things, his ending words were "I pray all this..." He paused again to grasp their attention, knowing Benaiah wanted them to hear, and he said boldly, "In the name of the Lord of heaven's armies...Amen!"

"In the name of the Lord of heaven's armies, amen!" was shouted out so loud and uniformly as a battle cry that the three on the marble floor thought the cavern would cave in. It echoed back and forth off the rounded walls until it slowly became silent, leaving only the sound of the babbling stream. It finalized the prayer in a way that Benaiah saw a mental picture of God's joyful love and purpose for his children continuously flowing in the mists of the chaos and brokenness of humanity.

The three opened their eyes in awe of the moment, feeling as one with the descendants and God. Even though Benaiah understood the unconscious flaw of their priorities being out of order. Then, with the stream softly singing in the background, he understood why Jahar loved his people and this place. A sudden change of heart about Journey's End was happening; it no longer felt as an underground prison with cold dark tunnels running all over the place but a beautiful home with a giant family.

***

Mariah had the lead guard that tested Benaiah's drink send for Uba to bring her back on an IGT meeting them at the wide opening at the top of the commons cavern just outside. Uba and her tribe leaders, with many of the other African inhabitant leaders, were already making their way to the hidden guest entrance more than halfway up the mountain for the special ceremony of the new guardian.

Control gave Uba's location to the guard retrieving her. He informed her of Benaiah's request to meet with her, which she gladly accepted. Everyone else was given the new instructions of Benaiah's new location for his ceremony by other guards and servants.

Benaiah was waiting alone highly against everyone's warnings on the platform at the mouth of the grand opening. He did let them keep the invisible shield active and the upper guards within thirty yards from him, but not Mariah and Horasha. He had them wait with his parents at the lounging area below, making them both very uneasy, especially irritating Horasha. He brewed over Benaiah being reckless. While keeping to himself, he still had reservations about Benaiah being a fully qualified descendant to take Jahar's place—even if he did say he had given his heart to God.

Mariah was acting extremely uneasy as well when Benaiah went to the upper platform but played it off like she needed to relieve herself in the lavatory outside the commons area. Once she was in the privacy of the stall in the ladies room, she turned around, facing the locked door but never sat down. Instead of relieving herself, she stayed fully clothed and quickly started tapping on the communication screen on her wrist, almost in a frantic fashion. As she typed out a message, Mariah began to sweat from anxiety as her heart beat abnormally fast. A fumbling of words quietly flowed out of her mouth. "Why? Why did he change the location, especially to the small lake? I should have never done this! What have I done?"

She stopped working her fingers on the screen, holding her breath and waiting for a reply. When the reply came back, she stared with disbelief as her whole body language and inner spirit slumped in complete despair. With the toilet lid closed, she flopped down on the seat, sitting with her head buried in her hands as she whispered out, "I followed your orders. You are supposed to know what you are doing. Why this? I trusted you, God…"

High up, Benaiah looked out onto the impressive forest rooftop, seeing Uba arrive and dressed again in her colorful ceremony attire. The IGT hesitated before the approach to the platform as the transparent shield was disengaged and then reengaged after it passed through.

Benaiah held out his hand to politely assist her off the IGT, but she only stared at him. Taken back by her expression, he soon understood he was out of line in his superior role as the guard driving the IGT assisted her off.

Uba bowed once she was on the ground and then stood face to face in an awkward moment as they both were in wonder of the other. One was peering down into old wise eyes yellowed with age and patient with a lifetime of experience and knowledge. The other looked up into bright white eyes of youth filled with energy and ambition yet glimmering with worry and fear.

Uba broke the silence, asking what he called her there for. Unfortunately, Benaiah completely forgot there was a language barrier, not understanding a word she said. With a natural response, he looked at the guard for translation, instantly realizing he had another problem of confidentiality.

Understanding the look to translate for the new guardian, the guard stated, in broken English, Uba's question as Benaiah stared at him, wondering if he could be trusted. Then Benaiah turned, taking a step up to him as the guards eyes widened, wondering what he did wrong.

Pausing as his mind rumbled around how to find out if he could further trust the guard even though he didn't hesitate to test his drink, Benaiah started going through different movies scenes for the answer. Not immediately coming up with one, he asked, "What is your name?"

"Jashen, Master."

"Jashen, who's bloodline are you in?"

Not what he expected, the guard answered plainly, "Abiezer."

Benaiah pointed down into the cavern at the lounging area. "Is that in the bloodline of Mariah or Horasha?"

Staying on the platform, the guard innocently looked out into the open over the edge at the people below looking up at them and then shook his head, saying, "No, Master."

"Who would I know is in your bloodline?"

The guard worked his eyes back and forth and then answered with excitement, "Dr. Mitanual. You were under his care a couple of times. He is my uncle."

His answer wasn't bad, but Benaiah grimaced with frustration over trust and how come this special of all places, which originally was to be a place ordained by the God of truth, oozed thick of deceit. The guard was beginning to show signs of nervousness that he was making the guardian uneasy and asked, "What is it that you need from me, Master?"

Benaiah blurted out in a slightly frustrated manner, "Trust… How do I know I can trust you?"

The guard relaxed his shoulders as he openly said with honesty, "I would do anything for you. You wear…the ring." The guard knelt and then gently grasped Benaiah's hand with the ring, leaned forward, and kissed it.

His words and actions were impressive, but these formalities of king and queen rituals were beginning to appear only as show. Jokingly, Benaiah took the guard for his word and responded by pointing with his other hand to the large wide open commons area. "Prove it. Step off this ledge."

The guard looked up at the odd request and then stood without hesitation and said, "As you wish." Giving Benaiah a quick bow, he then stepped to the edge, past the platform, and onto the wide garden area where the floral vines that flowed over, hanging low into the cavern, were strongly rooted, and he looked down. Turning to face his master, he spread his arms out looking like a human cross as he shouted out in broken English, "For our Master Benaiah, our king, and the Lord of heaven's armies!" Then he leaned back into open air.

When the guard boldly turned to him and spread his arms out, Benaiah instantly knew the man had an unselfish, innocent heart and was completely trustworthy. But when the words he stated soaked into his brain, and he began to lean back, Benaiah's stomach sank in horror. The man was following through with his stupid and outrageous order, not believing for a second that he would actually do it.

Without hesitating, Benaiah jumped out to the man, diving prone to the garden area and was able to grasp a booted ankle with both hands. The dead weight was so much that he was dragged himself to the ledge with his arms straining down and holding onto the guard as his own body slowly inched over.

Flailing around and looking up to see why he wasn't falling, he saw his master holding onto him and yelled up, "No, Master! Let go of me! You will fall yourself and die!"

Chapter 21

B enaiah strained to hold on for all he was worth, growling out with teeth gritted as his face turned bright red. Wide eyed in fear and looking straight down approximately three hundred feet, he was slowly going over the edge himself.

Screaming from the lounging area was heard as his parents witnessed the horrifying scene. Horasha stayed professionally calm and sprinted out through the garden, dodging trees and bushes to get underneath the ledge as though he was going to catch his master. Mariah, completely composed to her normal self, was just getting back to the marble floor from the lavatory when she saw the event unfolding and swiftly shouted out orders to guards in the cavern as organized chaos exploded.

IGTs swiftly came into view, darting across the open air from the two side staircases. Men could be heard yelling to one another from the high opening, who were held a distance away by Benaiah during the private meeting.

"I'm losing my grip!" Benaiah yelled out as the guards boot was slipping from his hands. He added, "Help me, guards!"

Everyone hearing the plea from their master echoing out gave a surge of energy that no one could deny. Then, when they heard their master's final scream, "Save him, Jesus…!" The commons area erupted with a power never felt before as everything seemed to suddenly move in slow motion to everyone. It happened in such a manner that every eye watching saw in perfect harmony as the guard slipped from Benaiah's hands, dropping only a couple feet onto an IGT that had rushed in under him. Benaiah's body had slid over far enough that it was following suit with nothing for his hands to grab onto except for fragile dangling floral vines. His toes were dragging the ground as the last resort before the lower part of his body went over the edge as well.

A sudden jerk was felt as his body halted all movement. Two guards had grabbed an ankle each. Benaiah, at first, had his eyes closed, convinced he was falling to his death. But now, as he was dangling in midair as though he was floating, he slowly opened his eyes.

In less than a heartbeat, it went silent in the grand cavern. A moment passed, and then an eruption of another kind exploded. A cheer from all deafened every ear as if a victory had been won.

Through the loud roar from being saved from the grip of death, Benaiah clearly heard, internally, a voice vividly say, *"My child, I am the one to make nothing something, nowhere somewhere. I see what is not there and everything hidden behind that. I wonderfully use wrong doings, mishaps, and bad to work for the good. Ultimately, your impossible is my possible. Trust in me alone, Benaiah...In all, for all, with all, and I will bless you in ways beyond your heart's desires and in your comprehension of me and with everything I created. Let go of your understanding and allow me to fully reign, and you will see and experience me, your loving God."*

Benaiah was pulled safely back to the middle of the platform as the guards that helped him inquired if he was hurt.

As the roar quieted down, footsteps of many approaching the platform and murmuring was heard from everyone, discussing the confusing event of why the guardian risked his life for a guard. Mariah, Horasha, and his parents soon stepped off an IGT coming to his side as other IGTs with leadership and governing personnel flew in or ran up the side staircases with great concern. It was quickly getting crowded as cloaked guards swarmed in from the forest outside the opening and inside the commons area, forming a human wall around Benaiah. He was in the open, and even though the invisible shield stopped any airborne transports or objects, their master was still in a vulnerable spot, especially with the chaotic commotion.

Horasha was the first to question him, teetering between relief and anger. "What were you thinking, Benaiah? I warned you not to go without us! Again!"

Everyone else joined in with Horasha's campaign as Benaiah stood silent, not listening to anyone or feeling anything. He pondered the powerful words from God which answered questions he was struggling with—who and how do I trust?

"Do you not have anything to say for yourself? You are the guardian. Never take chances like that!" Mariah stated, looking at him as though he was crazy.

Then his mom reached in, giving him a hug and saying, "Oh, son, we're so glad you're safe. Why did you do that? You almost died."

Verbally and physically not responding to anyone, her last words captured his attention. He stepped back and then raised his hand to stop the inquisitions and disorder of everyone seemingly blasting at him. Instantly, it went silent except for his parents, who weren't use to such commands. Looking around, they asked what was going on, not paying attention to their son's hand raised. Mariah put her finger up to her mouth in front of them and then gently pointed for them to face their son.

He relaxed, dropping his hand, and then he looked down at his clothes which were again stained but with green and brown, not red blood. He brushed himself off and straightened up his clothes. Retightening the purple sash, he took a deep breath and then looked up at everyone as he stepped away from the group, strolling around the people, stopping near the ledge where the guards had pulled him up. Gently pushing one guard of many who walled the ledge for safety out of his way, Benaiah looked down and then out and around the grand cavern. Hundreds of descendants had appeared out of nowhere, filling the garden below. Many were diverted here as they were making their way to the base of the waterfall, hearing the lighting quick news of what happened. Descendants were still coming out of the living quarters, even the medical staff, as Dr. Mitanual swiftly made his way with some staff members to the upper landing on the emergency medical IGT.

Landing next to one of the other IGTs, the doctor urgently weaved his way through the crowd to Benaiah, extremely concerned and asking, "Are you all right, Master? Are you hurt anywhere?"

Benaiah raised his hand, stopping him in his tracks as he approached, saying, "I'm fine, Doctor. Check on the guard, your nephew Jashen." He pointed to him as he was quietly but harshly being interrogated by Mariah and Horasha of why he put the guardian in such danger and not having any empathy for him that he almost lost his life.

The guardian peered around to everyone up at the caverns light source, most of whom appeared to be leaders and governing figureheads. Then with all the people filling the garden floor that haven't traveled or returned from the waterfall because of his stupid episode, he instantly changed his mind again. Change the location of the ceremony to where they were at, at the moment and to do it right now to get it over with. So he could finally explain God's plan for Journey's End and show all the leaders present on the platform, Journey's Beginning, through the hidden staircase in his new living quarters.

He looked over to his parents standing back and watching the commotion and drama surrounding him. He thought, *I should have listened to Horasha and not have brought them here. At least until all the formalities were over.* He realized he was using them for more of a crutch than to include them for celebration purposes.

Spotting Uba in her ceremony headdress sticking up within the crowd, he spoke up, "Horasha, please bring Uba to me." Then he told Mariah to bring the guard forward after the doctor looked him over.

Surrounded close by Horasha, Mariah, Jashen, Uba, and his parents somewhat secluding themselves, the crowd of people respectfully backed away a short distance with the help of guards doing minor crowd control. Jashen the guard was very uneasy, especially after he was just harshly grilled by Horasha and Mariah. Seeing he was in low spirits Benaiah put the guard's mind at ease, saying in a normal volume while catching each other's eyes, "I apologies, Jashen, for my ignorant behavior and loose tongue almost getting you killed. Your obedience to follow such thoughtless babble from me has escalated you to a height of admiration and trust I have for very few people."

Jashen bowed, saying, "Thank you, Master, though it would have been an honor to die for you."

Benaiah glared bewildered, thinking to himself, *These crazy people... How is one able to ever understand them?* Shaking it off, he lowered his voice for privacy and told him, "Jashen, tell Uba I want her to take my parents right now and hide them. Hide them so they cannot be found by Control."

"What?" Mariah questioned the puzzling request.

Benaiah ignored her. "I need her people to protect them until I...I call for them." Benaiah was pointing to his chest. "And I want you..."—pointing to the guard's chest—"You to stay by their side to translate and provide extra security. I will make it known when I want them brought back to me when it's safe. Will you do that for me?"

The guard bowed, swelling with pride and understanding he was trusted with a great mission from the new guardian. He responded boldly, "Yes, I will not fail you, Master."

Patting him on his secure emergency backpack, he said, "Thank you, Jashen." Looking to Horasha, Benaiah told him, pointing to the guard, "Remove his tracking device in his uniform."

Horasha was stunned that he knew anything about such devices as Benaiah turned to Jashen. "Remove your wristband and anything else which the Controllers can track you by."

Everyone was bewildered why Benaiah was taking illogical and drastic measures as he asked, "How else can my parents and Jashen be tracked besides your different sensing security systems?" He looked around to everyone listening as they looked back and forth to one another.

"With your silence, there is. What is it?"

Horasha stepped to his parents, reaching up to each collar of their shirts and removed a tiny tracking device.

"What else?"

"The IGTs are tracked," the guard said encouragingly.

"Okay, use an IGT for the four of you to fly to the base of the mountain of Uba's choice, and then leave it behind. What else?"

Mariah asked, "Why are you requesting this?" Then out of place, she checked her wrist device, watching the time.

Horasha eyes caught her movement, faintly wrinkling his forehead. He had been noticing she had been checking her armlet frequently, which was an out-of-place mannerism. Journey's End personnel rarely checked for time because it was of no consequence unless there was a specific military mission planned or major event happening that needed pinpointed monitoring from somewhere around the world. But beside that, they were their own people, separate from the world that spent most of their time underground.

Peering to the six watching on, Benaiah replied with a comical expression, hoping they would see at least a speck of humor in what he was going to say. "I've change my mind. We are going to have my inauguration right here, right now, after my parents…are safely hidden away." He glanced to Horasha, giving him a side mouth grin and letting him know he was somewhat correct when he jumped down his throat in the medical facility from his comment about his parents being here.

Horasha did respond with a proud inhale, slightly standing a bit taller as he folded his arms across his chest and nodding his head in agreement.

"That is great!" Mariah quickly exclaimed with relief more than excitement as it was obvious to Horasha and Benaiah there was a huge change in her tone and behavior.

Being stared at for her sudden response, Mariah quickly contained herself with a swift intelligent reply. "Everyone is already here." She looked around, pointing at the people at the eye of the cave and down in the commons area, adding, "Plus, the evening dinner festivities are being held inside here. It is going to all work out." She smiled as she placed her hand on Benaiah's shoulder, patting it and then grinning brightly to Horasha and the others. With her hand still on Benaiah's shoulder and bringing her eyes full circle back to him, she slightly twisted her wrist just enough to glance with lightning speed at the time on her wrist screen without everyone noticing. But someone did.

"I have had enough, Mariah, daughter of Shamar." Horasha leaned over and, as fast as a snake striking, grabbed her arm and looked at her wrist to see what was so important for her to continually look at it.

The senior rabbi in charge of official ceremonies was one of the many that had shown up hearing the young new guardian had hero-ically saved the life of a guard and almost dying himself. Pressing his way back to the center of everyone who gave the small group their privacy had overheard Benaiah's new plans. Also saw there was possi-bly a confrontation erupting with Horasha and Mariah.

Seeing his opportunity and duty to make the quick ceremony arrangements and distract the crowd's eyes and ears, he clapped loudly to the descendants. Getting their attention on him, he shouted out in Hebrew, "Praise to the Lord of heaven's armies! Our new guardian was protected!"

A shout of joy was heard from everyone. "Praise to the Lord of heaven's armies!"

As it quieted down, he gave instructions, changing to English. "The timing of this wonderful ceremony for Master Benaiah needs adjusting. The new location has brilliantly been changed to assist in accommodat-ing the majority of our people who are here right now." He look through the crowd to Benaiah smiling and granting him the credit. Hoping he himself was doing the right thing, he continued, "And what a spectacular place to officially crown Master Benaiah the new guardian of Journey's End right here, with the grand Congo forest as a backdrop as the great commons area does what it does best—bring tranquility into the eyes, ears, and spirit of God's chosen children. Now go, descendants." He lifted his arms, flapping out his hands as though shooing them away. "Gather with your families in the garden we cherish so much."

Turning to several of his assistants, he said, "Tell the tribesmen of the new location and for them to position themselves in the backdrop forest side of this platform over there." He pointed to the open area on the side of the mountain outside of the wide opening. "We will allow plenty of time for them to make it up here. If their elders need assistance, use our IGTs." The men stepped up to an IGT, spoke to Control to disengage the invisible security shield, and then took off.

Mariah stated slowly, but with attitude, piercing Horasha with narrowed eyes. "Let go of my arm!"

They had a staredown for a moment as he tightened his grip.

"What are you two doing?" Benaiah asked, being in the middle of this quickly brewing skirmish next to his head, stepping to the side and drooping his shoulder for their hands to drop off. Horasha let go as they resumed their lifelong family feud face-off.

Mariah answered, "Horasha is being extra cautious to the point he is paranoid."

"Paranoid about what?" Benaiah asked.

"I am never paranoid! I am protective. This woman is not acting herself."

Mariah wouldn't let her eyes off Horasha's as she did not want to verbally engage to escalate the accusation. Benaiah looked at both of them in their normal state of headbutting posture, and seeing their peaceful truce was over, he asked calmly, "Is there something going on that I should know about you two?" He said it in a way not to show favoritism to Mariah, who his heart began falling for days ago.

Horasha knew he needed more evidence to pursue his suspicion that she was up to something, but not knowing what this something was, he was the first to decline, not in a defeated manner, but one where he was giving space for Mariah to make a mistake. "No, Master. There is nothing wrong at the moment. Just observing detailed signs of others."

Benaiah asked, "Detailed signs?"

Mariah answered, diverting any attention to her still staring at Horasha, "If Horasha would concentrate on the detailed signs of caring for his life duty, maybe our master would not have been put in danger—three times now—since you arrived at Journey's End."

Horasha's nostrils began to flare as his face got red, wanting to with all his heart, soul, and mind put an end to this tick of a woman who had been burying herself deep under his skin ever since he and Benaiah arrived.

Uba, quietly standing and watching the eruption play out, stepped between the two as her tall and wide headdress wisped in their faces, causing them to step back. Raising her decorative walking stick, she broke the heated but frozen atmosphere by tapping Mariah's forehead and then Horasha's, almost startling them. She said in Hebrew as they looked down at her, "This anger must end between you two. Jahar would be very disappointed at how you are acting at his great nephew's guardian ceremony."

The senior rabbi who had quietly stepped back up to the group heard Uba's guidance and decided to assist her to move forward with the activities at hand. He bowed to Benaiah and then said in English, "Master Benaiah, I am Rabbi Talamar. I will be the master of ceremonies for your induction to officially be the guardian. May Elder Uba, this guard, and your parents…"—he pointed to them, watching on from the dispersing crowd—"leave now from your directives?"

Benaiah looked at Horasha and then to Mariah, in a way almost wanting permission, then he answered, "Yes, let's make this happen. Thank you, Rabbi." He warmly showed his appreciation of how he had softly taken control of the situations relieving him of the pressure. Benaiah gave this new lead figurehead a smile and a faint head bow, wanting to shake his hand, but he knew this was something the descendants didn't do.

Jashen assisted Benaiah's parents and then Uba onto a larger IGT. His parents were not happy that they were leaving their son since they had just got here. Then were confused by what was going on and why there was such hostility between the ones that were caretakers of Benjamin. But went along with his instructions, knowing he had something very heavy on his mind and something important to do, but what made it easier to leave was that their hearts were filled with joy. After all these years, he finally included them in his life as an adult—a Jesus-following adult. And then to have his father pray for him the way he had was almost overwhelming.

"Will we see you soon, Ben?" his mother asked as she sat down.

"I pray we will. Uba will take very good care of you in the meantime."

The guard called Control for the shield to be disengaged again and then took off once cleared.

Shortly the platform was vacated except for Horasha, Mariah, Benaiah, the rabbi, and a handful of guards standing at a distance and doing what they do best—staying in a defensive ready position to protect or attack, invisible to the untrained eye.

The rabbi reviewed what was to happen as he read to them the guidelines from an ancient book he had brought with him. It was a first for all of them, not being alive or old enough to remember when Jahar was given King Solomon's signature ring and granted the guardian position. Reading, he discussed how this ceremony was to be conducted and what was to be said.

Also, the lineage was reviewed of the guardians before him—names, dates of birth, and dates of service of the men in Benaiah's bloodline who were all registered in this book. Pointing to the lines under Jahar's information, he said, "As soon as you are officially ordained guardian, I will put your name here below Jahar's."

Benaiah looked at the long list of men written in Hebrew and remembered seeing their portraits in the tunnel to the book of time. Taking a deep breath, in a sighing manner, he thought to himself, *I definitely don't want to be put on that doomed death list. Jahar needs to be the last guardian of Journey's End.* Pausing to change his attitude, he prayed to himself, *Thank you, God, for giving me this mission of excavating Noah's Ark and bringing all its knowledge to the world. I never could have dreamed, as an archeologist, that I would be digging up something so amazing and different than anything else the earth is hiding under its surface. I'm going to do my best to trust you that they won't kill me over it. But at the same time, please don't let my life be anything like these guardians of old. Put an end to the guardian responsibility...* Suddenly an idea struck Benaiah as he finished praying. *May this event change the world to the point only you, Jesus, will be the only guardian the descendants, Israel, and rest of the world puts their faith into as you have preserved the ancient artifacts that have a direct connection to you and you alone, demonstrating what your fingerprints look like for all mankind to see and experience.*

The rabbi had continued to talk, and during the discussion, Mariah was becoming more and more nervous as her body couldn't stay still. It was easy for Horasha, the rabbi, and the guards a distance away closely observing to see this very unusual behavior from her. All her young life, she was a rock being by Jahar's side. Then, when she went undercover, joining the Israeli Defense Force and making sporadic visits back to the inner Congo, she wasn't afraid of anything or anyone except Jahar. This renowned character gave her a reputation escalating respect almost to the point it was a fear from everyone.

The forest outside the large breathing hole of the grand commons cavern was becoming alive with pygmies and other African tribes that had received the message of the new location. Inside, the garden was filling with descendants patiently and excitedly waiting for the celebration to start for their new guardian. The atmosphere was getting louder and brighter as they beamed with pride, having a fresh new perspective of this outsider taking Jahar's place to rule over them. He had demonstrated in front of everyone; opening his true heart, he valued their lives and was willing to sacrifice his for them. Then for him to cry out to Jesus as his final words before he was to die—it washed away all hesitation and fear the Journey's End inhabitants had of him becoming the guardian.

For some reason, instantly every living thing—man, animal, and bird—went silent. Scanning the air as though a sixth sense or intuition was whispering to listen, they waited for something unknown to happen. Seconds went by, and then the loud deep *ping* was heard echoing throughout the broad leaf forest and inside the mountain caverns and tunnels. The descendant looked at their wrist screens for information of the emergency, and then the gonging *ping* sounded out in three bursts, signaling an immediate emergency was in progress.

Horasha tapped on his armlet screen, attempting to talk to Control, but there was no response. Slight panic began to permeate as everyone was becoming aware that their normal communication devices were not working. Higher-ranking security began giving out orders to their teams to position themselves at key locations to protect Journey's End. The unknown emergency automatically was treated as though they were being attacked at the mountain itself.

Horasha instructed a guard to test the invisible shield protecting the wide opening to the commons area. The guard slowly moved his transport to where the shield was and then slowly passed through as though nothing was there. Horasha then shouted out, "The shield is down! The shield is down!" Within seconds, dozens of combat IGTs flew from within the cavern and from outside, forming a defensive wall for anything that might be coming their way.

"Run! Run everyone! Run to the living quarters!" Mariah screamed out over and over as she had quickly stepped to the ledge, looking down and out to all who could hear. Then she turned, running out toward the forest and speaking in an African tongue, "Run away! Run away to the other side of the mountain! Away from the waterfall!"

Horasha, believing she had something to do with what was happening, since she gave such precise directions, sprinted to her, grabbing her shoulders tightly and asking with a scowl, "Mariah, what is happening?"

Her face went white as snow as tears came to her eyes as she weakly tried to get away from his grip without fighting and frantically shouted, "We need to get everyone far away from the base of the waterfall and this side of the mountain now!"

"What is going on! Tell me! Tell me now!"

Trying her best not to say anything, she could not hold back anymore and fumbled out, "A-a missile is coming!"

Knowing she would not make such a thing up in her distraught behavior, Horasha turned to Benaiah, grabbed his arm and swiftly pushed him up on an IGT near them, yelling out and waving to the other two, "Get in! A missile is coming!" Then he turned toward any guards in earshot and said, "Protect yourselves, descendants!"

No sooner did Mariah, Horasha, Benaiah, and the rabbi elevate off the ground on the IGT than they heard, in a split second, the swishing of a rocket flying in from an unknown location. In the blink of an eye it went silent, then a volcanic-like explosion erupted. The mountain inside and out trembled with such a powerful vibration that anyone standing could easily fall over. The trees in the commons area swayed back and forth, imitating the forest vegetation outside.

Pieces of the ceiling broke apart, sending huge chunks of boulders crashing down, adding to the chaos as a few people were crushed to death. Different and much smaller explosions began to be heard throughout the mountain as internal energy grids, computer systems, and many other electrical and natural gas units were compromised in a grand way, causing leaks, overloads, and outages.

Screaming injured people could be heard as mothers and fathers ran around shouting for their children, which added to the volume of noise saturating the senses of every living thing. Before everyone knew it, the violence of the earth came to a halt as people moaned hurt and parents were reunited with their children. Some pipes and wires that had been hidden were now exposed and softly hissed throughout tunnels and caverns as their insides escaped with varieties of different liquids, vapor, or electrical sparks.

The stream in the garden had disappeared. Its bed was pooled up with water left behind from one end to the other.

Horasha had flown the group away, staying within the forest, weaving in and out of the vegetation while staying out of sight below the canopy of the trees. He was heading to the other side of the mountain as Mariah instructed the Africans. They were all quiet as each attempted to understand what was going on except for Mariah. She had loaded up on the IGT behind everyone. The farther they traveled away from the explosion area, the heavier her heart became. Soon, she found herself slumped on the floor, hiding her face with her hands and softly said as tears streamed down, "What have I done? What have I done?"

Flying fast and far enough, they quickly reached the edge of the tombs of the dead. Horasha cautiously peered out and around, hidden in the thick vegetation before exposing them to the open. Not seeing anything, he gritted his teeth upon noticing Mariah's guilty condition and smartly asked, "Are we in danger here, Mariah?"

She shook her head and then answered, "No."

"How can we believe you?"

In her turmoil, she blurted out, "No! I said we are safe here. There will be no more attacks."

The rabbi and Benaiah looked down at her, surprised that she was obviously a part of what just happened.

Horasha floated them down into the small valley landing between the towering walls at the base of the long staircase. When the transport touched down, Horasha quickly turned, pushing the two others out of the way and grabbed Mariah by the hair as she sat submissively on the floor. Without her resisting, and in a completely weakened, broken-down mode, he dragged her off the IGT onto the smooth rock floor backward.

She reached up only to fight the pain. Letting go, he swiftly turned around, backhanding her across the mouth and sent her sprawled out flat on her stomach as blood began to drip from her lip.

"What have you done!" he shouted.

She rolled over to face him, giving him a clear opening to kick her in the stomach. She gasped out, trying to inhale, but her lungs needed a moment to relax to be refilled.

"Stop it! Stop it, Horasha!" Benaiah spouted as he bent down to her and then he saw him reaching at his waist and slowly drawing out a knife.

"Put that away!" Benaiah stated as he stood, boldly facing him as the guardian as well as to protect the woman he had fallen in love with.

With no expression, Horasha said, "Step aside, Master. She has now become something worse than our enemy. She fully understands our laws and the consequences if they are broken."

"We don't know thoroughly what she has done."

"Do not be naïve. She planned to kill you and everyone else down at the lake during your ceremony. She had this all timed and planned out. That is why she has been watching her armlet." He paused for a second and then said, "Come to think of it, she probably was the one that tried to kill us with that invasion of drones when we were all together here for Jahar's burial."

"That was only a diversion…" Mariah said softly, pausing as she sat up and wiping blood running down her chin. Then she added, "I did not conspire to kill anyone. That is why I was glad Benaiah changed his mind on where to have his ceremony the last time."

"What do you mean a diversion?" Benaiah asked.

She wiped her mouth again with her hand, taking a moment to collect herself, then she said, "Control resets our computer system with new security codes for our satellites, shields, radar, and heat-tracking systems after any military engagement with the outside world—such as that diversion. During the reset process, there is a short window of time to implement a virus for ones that know our computer system. Our system is now infected with the Mirror virus."

Benaiah was stumped as his blank face expressed his thoughts. *She has been lying to me this whole time. But why? Why would she do that to Journey's End? And to...Jahar?* He reflected back to her expressing deep childhood love for her mentor, friend and father figure.

"What does this Mirror virus do?" Horasha asked, tilting his head, slightly surprised she was divulging the information so freely.

"When it is timely activated, it reverses the directive of every security systems program internally, but the system visually reads on the monitors that everything is working normally."

"I do not understand?" Horasha asked.

She answered, wanting this conversation to go away, "When you close something, you are actually opening it. On would be off, in would be out, and so on."

"And why...?" Horasha asked in a sinister tone, kneeling down to look in her eyes.

She looked past him up to Benaiah and began to breathe heavily, clenching her lips closed and trying hard not to say anything. Knowing it was no use, she said, "So our distant relatives, our people from the Holy Land, could have a chance to share in what truly is theirs as much as it is the descendants."

Horasha looked up at the other two men as they moved their eyes to one another, trying to understand.

The rabbi asked, "But, Mariah, King Solomon's law is to protect all of mankind until God says otherwise. You have put them in great danger of the powers Journey's End holds."

"I know, Rabbi, but they are God's chosen people as much as we are. We are them and they are us. All this time I have spent with them since I was old enough to join the IDF, my heart has wanted to reach out in honesty for them. Everything we have belongs to them as it does us. The world is closing in, and the prophecies for the end times are coming true everywhere. Everything happening in the world is pointing to Armageddon. With everything hidden in the treasury, our advanced technology and the knowledge hidden away in the book of time, all of Israel would be as wealthy, strong, and wise as they were in the time of our king, giving every chance to be victorious over any painful situation or adversity. Would that not be what God had King Solomon hide his treasures for? For the most terrible days of the end times to bless his children?"

Horasha was getting a crazy look in his eyes. He was about to explode with the knife in his hand as he said, gritting his teeth, "Mariah, are out of your mind! Who are you to play God? You disobeyed our king's orders and disgraced all the guardians in that book he is holding…"—pointing to what the rabbi was carrying—"who gave their lives protecting this place for three thousand years faithfully for what you threw away in an instant!" He paused slowly, inhaling deep as his body appeared to inflate with strength. He said, "I am going to make your death a painful one for what you have disgracefully done. I knew you could never be trusted. Poor Master Jahar…" Still kneeling, Horasha looked out and up toward a specific place on the guardian side cliff wall where Jahar's tomb was. "He put all that time, care, and faith in you only for you to throw it away as soon as he was dead."

Mariah's attitude was beginning to change. Upon hearing the false accusations, she slowly stood. Horasha mirrored her movement, standing with her and growing in anger. Benaiah saw his body language and calmly stepped between them as they eyed one another. He reached up, softly touching Horasha's strong barrel chest, and gently spoke, "Horasha, Jahar wisely knew something different was coming after his reign as God guided him. Maybe that's why he believed it was in my best interest for my future and the future of Journey's End to be raised in the outside world. Living it firsthand gives me wise experience for whatever God has in plan for me to do. Since our time now is drastically different, especially with technology, than any other point in time since the creation."

Ignoring Benaiah and considering what he said as excuses, Horasha pressed forward to get to Mariah. But Benaiah held his ground. Now pressing him back, he said, "I'm proof that there's something completely different in store for Journey's End." Lifting up his other hand for Horasha to see, he said, "You know good and well I wouldn't be here wearing this ring, and with King Solomon's signature tattooed to the bottom of my feet, if there wasn't."

"Step aside. This has nothing to do with you. She is admitting she..." Horasha hesitated and looked to his side, thinking. Then he backed away as Benaiah's hands fell to his side as Horasha still held the knife low in his.

Narrowing his eyebrows, Horasha slowly lifted up the knife, pointing it in Benaiah's face and said accusingly, "You are in this with her. I knew there was no way you would have had a transformed mind to change your heart about God for no reason in such a short time." He put a puzzle together verbally. "You two disappeared for a long time after Benaiah left me for dead in the book of time. No one could find either of you. We looked everywhere. Where did you two lovebirds go to do your sinful planning against your home and family?"

"He did nothing! Put the knife down now!" Mariah ordered, grasping his attention, and fully regaining her emotional strength, she stepped forward to Benaiah's side in defense.

Horasha looked at the two younger ones. Shaking his head, he said, "Unworthy, selfish spawns of Satan. We obediently obeyed the law, allowing you to take the most powerful position in the world against most everyone's instincts."

"Horasha, watch your tongue!" the rabbi blurted out as he looked back and forth from Horasha and the guardian. "Master Benaiah is still the guardian of Journey's End chosen by Jahar and, for all we know, God himself. It does not matter what we feel about him or what he does with the power they trust him with."

Eyeing Benaiah intently, Horasha stated, "I have known this pagan all his life. He might have the blood of Jahar, but he does not have the same heart. He is a wolf in sheep's clothing only pretending to have a changed heart. He knows just enough Bible from his childhood to fool many, but not me. I see right through you, boy. You live by the ways of this world. Your god is not our God!"

Benaiah slightly cleared his throat to affirm every ear listening, as Jahar would do he when was going to talk, and then he said with confident gentleness, "Horasha, only God can see through me. You have no idea what my heart beats with, even when I am wearing it on the outside of my chest. For you are mentally deaf, running your life by your rollercoaster of spastic, angered emotions while being spiritually blinded over time by a twisted condition that has evolved with the descendants following Solomon's orders.

"This king of yours that has been dead for almost three thousand years has become Journey's End's god. And it appears all of you can't see it except perhaps Jahar and Mariah, seeing clearly the twisted minds of their own people…" He lifted his hand, putting it against his own chest, and added, "Even though…your hearts are in the right place."

He paused, beginning to see that God definitely had a plan already in play to assist him in exposing what was hidden for so long deep in the Congo. He gave Mariah a smile, hoping she would continue being on his side, and said to Horasha, "During the time of our absence that you speak of, Mariah showed me an invisible secret per se from everyone in Journey's End, which only the guardians know about. Jahar trusted Mariah with this incredible…thing, in case he suddenly died before the new guardian was put into play. The secrets Journey's End holds are not what everyone thinks they are. This secret I speak of is called…"

He glanced again to Mariah, seeing her eyes widen and rapidly shaking her head, she burst out, shoving her way between the two men, and now, with the knife in her face and safely away from Benaiah, she boldly said, "No, Benaiah! I will be the sacrificial lamb." Looking intently into Horasha's flaming eyes, she said, "As I said, Horasha, Israel deserves everything in Journey's End. But it was God that told me to expose it in a grand way by crippling the mountain to draw everyone's attention. And the lake is what I came up with to be the safest place possible.

"My actions were not selfish ones but orders from God speaking to me for a year to deliver what I said I was feeling so strongly about with Israel." She reluctantly looked back to Benaiah, to the rabbi, and then back to Horasha as she said, "The secret Benaiah is talking about is called Journey's Beginning."

Not blinking an eye, Horasha held firm as he and the rabbi adorned inquisitive expressions. Horasha peered past her to Benaiah. When their eyes met, Benaiah said, gently pushing Mariah to the side, "If you remember, I have already mentioned that name to you, but I didn't know what I was asking about, and you didn't, either. Jahar mentioned Journey's Beginning privately with me, but he hadn't explained it or showed it to me yet. Only after his natural death in the invisible ones' elder hut did Mariah show me. That's where we disappeared all the time you were looking for us."

Not comprehending what they were talking about, Horasha was convinced they were playing him as a fool and growled out, "There is no such thing as a…Journey's Beginning. You are making this whole thing up using the Lord of heaven's armies as an excuse for your blasphemous actions. How dare you!

"You two are in this together, attacking your own people. More than likely to steal what you can from the treasury. But neither of you will get an ounce of gold for the descendants and Journey's End has been resilient, with much greater odds against it than this. This is no different of a battle than the many hundreds over the past three thousand years. We will rid it of this selfish poison you have created! We will be victorious again!"

With unpredictable confidence, he stared at the tip of the knife that Horasha was holding up and pointing at him. Benaiah slowly reached up to Horasha's wrist. Without force, as Horasha loosened his arm, Benaiah pressed it down so the knife was pointing at the ground and said, "I will believe what Mariah said that God spoke to her. For I know he has spoken to me several times about this as well." Tilting his head slightly, and with a light-hearted tone, he added, looking to his side at Mariah, "But not to the dramatic proportions as hers."

Looking back to Horasha he said, "I have been scared from the moment I was told to tell the descendants about Journey's Beginning. But what has petrified me the most is telling them, the mighty warriors of King David, that we are to share Journey's Beginnings and what is inside of it with Israel. From there, we are to show the rest of the world the greatest secrets and fingerprints of God known to man.

"You see, men…" Benaiah turned his head to grasp the eyes of the senior rabbi, making sure he had his full attention. Then finished, he looked back. "Journey's End is filled with mind-blowing proportions of human fingerprints. Things valued and things done by man for the progress and prosperity of mankind. Such as what fills the treasury and the tangible artifacts everywhere in the mountain. This would include the recorded human activities, accomplishments, and heroic historical deeds in the book of time.

"Journey's End has been filling itself with things to be stolen, destroyed, or to decay, rust, wither away, or eaten by moths over time no matter what security it has or how much special tree sap you apply as well as historical events to be forgotten that are of no matter and are worthless in the end of times. For all these things have no spiritual heart or eternal value.

"King Solomon followed God's guidance and, using the wisdom he was blessed with, had the descendants believe Journey's End was their purpose." Again, Benaiah paused, looking to the rabbi and then back into Horasha's hardened eyes. "But it was truly only a smokescreen—a decoy per se. To hide from all man the most powerful fingerprints of God that man has ever known until his appointed time in the future, which is obviously now…" He peered to Mariah, wanting her surprise teamwork to be acknowledged between them, but she didn't reciprocate his intention as she was hyper focused on Horasha with the knife still in his hand. He looked back into Horasha's cold staredown. "To be displayed for the world to see and graciously remind mankind once more before it is too late that the Son of God, Jesus, is the treasure and plan of the world."

The rabbi cleared his throat, wanting a moment in this confusing conversation and still not understanding what he was talking about. He asked, "Master Benaiah, forgive me for being ignorant, but I am not comprehending what you are talking about. You have said wise words, but nothing is coming together. You are talking as if this…Journey's Beginning is a thing, not a place as with Journey's End. You said 'it' and 'inside it.' What does this mean?"

Benaiah smiled as a fluttering sensation of joy sprouted within him. He was finally going to share the deep secrets he had been petrified to share with the descendants. Looking back to the unmoving Horasha, Benaiah didn't care; what he was about to say would completely change the whole atmosphere and everyone's attitude. He answered, "Rabbi and Horasha, what I'm about to tell you will blow your minds. It will sound completely impossible. But I ask you two men to believe more than you ever have that anything is possible with God. I can say this because when I walked in it and saw what was inside…" He stepped closer to Horasha, placing a hand on his shoulder to make a personal connection. "I didn't have a close relationship with him as you two have. But when I came out of Journey's Beginning, I was a completely changed man." He dropped his hand from Horasha's shoulder, spreading his arms out wide to show the new person he had become.

He tried again to get a glance from Mariah, but it was like she was in a trance staring at Horasha. Stepping back a half step and expecting an astonished physical and verbal reaction, he said, smiling, "Journey's Beginning is…Noah's Ark!"

There was silence. No reaction, not even a blink of an eye. Just breathless silence. Benaiah's eyes worked the three statues. After a few seconds, he couldn't take it anymore and excitedly stated, "Did you hear what I said? Noah's Ark!"

Still nothing from the other two men.

"Journey's Beginning is Noah's Ark. It has been hidden this whole time under the mountain." He looked at Horasha and the rabbi, astonished they weren't doing anything as he poured out a plethora of information. "Noah's Ark was why King Solomon had the descendants create Journey's End here in the middle of nowhere. It's filled with incredible God moments in time, all the way back to Adam and Eve.

Still no reaction, he said, "Come on are you hearing me? It also has the Ark of the Covenant in it, and the cross Jesus was crucified on!"

Putting his hands up to the side of his head befuddled, he asked, "Are you kidding me? You have nothing to say?" Then he added with more excitement, "Here are things that really blew me away. It's filled with dinosaur bones and…"—he paused to make a splash to get them excited—"dragon eggs or leviathan eggs is the Biblical name for them. Well, empty broken dragon eggshells. Isn't that exciting?"

Benaiah couldn't believe there was no reaction of any kind, and he stared at them, silently shaking his head.

"I do not think so," Horasha said, opening his lips just enough to coldly get words out. "I am tired of these lies. We finish this charade right now. You two have done enough damage with your disobedience!" His knife, tightly gripped in his hand down at his side, swiftly thrust straight up to Benaiah's throat. Benaiah, completely oblivious that anything was going to happen and believing he spoke the truth wisely, had no time to move.

The next thing Benaiah saw was the back of Mariah's hand spread open wide, with the knife stabbed through her palm sticking out from the backside of her hand, the tip less than an inch from his throat. Mariah never let her guard down ever since he had pulled the knife out. Like a flash of lightning, she stopped the killing blow, sacrificing her hand.

With the knife painfully secured, she slammed the side of Horasha's face with the speed of a viper with her other hand as a stunning distraction. Recoiling her arm back, she opened her hand in a spearhead fashion, with the fingers straight out and tightly together. Horasha, dazed for a split second, gave her enough time to assault him again, but this time deeply penetrating with her fingertips, stinging the muscles and nerves in his strong forearm that was holding the knife. Automatically, his hand sprung open, letting go of the knife and freeing her impelled hand.

Simultaneously, she powerfully kneed the side of his thigh, hitting the sciatic nerve and collapsing the leg. Horasha cried out in pain, hitting the hard rock floor of the tombs of the dead with his knees. She spun to his back like a tornado, grappling his body with her legs around his abdomen and locking her feet together as her arm wrapped around his neck, falling backward with her body weight and squeezing with all her might. His feet got tucked behind him under the weight of his own body, rendering him immobile. He was being strangled as though a giant anaconda was cutting off his circulation and the ability to breathe. The added difference was she had the tip of the knife still stabbed through her hand slightly pressed to the side of his neck, a flinch away from severing his carotid artery. Her good arm was wrapped around his throat, as the hand clenching the handle of the knife in the wounded hand was ready to press inward to end Horasha's life.

It happened so fast that Benaiah and the rabbi stared in disbelief until Mariah looked up to Benaiah, calmly asking with a sinister smile, "May I kill him now?"

Chapter 22

Seeing Horasha less than a whisper from death, Benaiah instantly saw the picture of a stranger putting his hand out, saving him from death in the ocean when he was a boy, only to recently find out it was Horasha. Knowing he needed to save his life right now, he shot his own hand out toward the danger to rescue and began to yell, but the older rabbi blurted it out first. "Stop, Mariah! Do not kill your father!"

It was as if lightning had struck them all at the same time. But instead of starting them on fire, it instantly froze everyone to the bone, zapping their breath away.

After a few moments, Benaiah slowly unthawed, lowering his hand in the moments of shock and crisis. He changed his demeanor as a powerful peace swept through him from the stunning news, changing his thinking about this relationship the other two never knew existed and said calmly, nodding his head in agreement, "Don't kill him, Mariah."

Acting as though he had old guardian wisdom, Benaiah bent down and, angel-like, touched her good hand holding the handle of the knife that stuck through her other hand, saying softly, "Let go of him."

Fighting within herself for what to do, she maintained her position, not believing what the rabbi said. But for some crazy reason, deep inside, it made sense. Gritting her teeth as she strained to hold the powerful man, she smartly broke out, "But he tried to..."

Cutting her short and overriding the direction of where she was going, Benaiah stood looking down at them and said, "Horasha was protecting Journey's End, and you're protecting me. Both of you are very good and dedicated to your callings as descendants. Actually, good isn't honorable enough. Extraordinary—yes, that's the word to explain you two. Extraordinary."

Benaiah looked to the rabbi as his words connected more dots from hearing they were related and gave the rabbi an expression that he might be right.

Mariah, holding the knife to the side of Horasha's neck, was still squeezing the life out of him. Benaiah strangely seemed suddenly unconcerned anymore as he rambled on in the intense moment. "I thank you both for your dedication to Journey's End and this position I'm in as guardian."

Horasha's face began to turn pale as his breathing was reduced to only gargling sounds. He started to rapidly tap out for Mariah to let go because the painful reality of no oxygen getting into his lungs started to panic him.

Benaiah continued the conversation as though he forgot Horasha's state. "This killing has got to stop. Do you not see what the descendants have become? Carnivores! Carnivores! Do you see that picture inside here?" He pointed to his own head. "There's no need for this anymore. God is releasing the descendants of the burden and responsibility, freeing us so his..." Benaiah now pointed in the air, mimicking Jahar's mannerisms. "His fingerprints can be exposed to the world. Do you all understand? It's like when Jesus died on the cross to free us of our sins once and for all. To never have the burden of the law of old but to have full freedom in what Christ did for us! Not what we do for him!" He gazed into the eyes of each one, ending at the rabbi with an optimistic grin.

The rabbi heard what he said, doing his best to agree as his eyes went back and forth, concerned about Horasha's dying situation as well as what was going to happen to himself for divulging his own secret that only Jahar, Dr. Mitanual, and himself knew. He answered quickly, "I do, Master!"

Benaiah looked to Mariah with an expression, waiting for her to answer, seeing blood still on her chin. As the blood dripped down from her hand onto Horasha's shoulder, he grimaced as though feeling her pain, asked in a somewhat lighthearted tone, trying not to get sick, "That's got to hurt? We need to get you to the doctor. But first, do you understand what I said, Mariah?"

Mariah stared Benaiah down, working her eyes back and forth with his, then jerked herself away from Horasha hovering over the defeated and prideful man. Looking down at him gulping for air, feeling around his throat with no expression asked herself as his normal skin color was coming back, *There is no way he could be my father? Is there?*

When his eyes slowly looked up to hers his thinking was similar as he thought, *They told me the baby died as did my wife giving birth. Why would they lie to me about that?*

Without any reaction to pain, Horasha watched Mariah slowly pull the knife out of her hand, demonstrating she was as tough as he was with a very high tolerance for pain and answered Benaiah's question in a short tone, "I do, Master."

Benaiah, seeing and hearing her gruesomely pull the knife out, unexpectedly bent over and started to gag. Then he said, "I...think I'm going to...throw up."

Even with this possible new truth of being related, the two battling warriors continued to play this teeter-tottering emotional chess again with each other as Mariah, showing courage, handed the bloody knife to Horasha disrespectfully blade first with her blood on it. As he took it from her, they both looked at Benaiah, slowly swaying their heads faintly and changing their expressions as their mighty guardian demonstrated the narrow boundaries of his manliness, spitting out saliva onto the rock floor and trying his best not to vomit.

While this was going on, the rabbi retrieved an emergency backpack from the IGT, pulling out the first-aid kit and then applied a blood-clotting bandage, wrapping it around Mariah's hand. When finished, he presented Benaiah with a bottle of water, asking, "Do you need this, or are you going to be all right, Master Benaiah?"

"I'll be fine." Raising his hand so as to shoo him away, he embarrassingly rose back up knowing they were disappointed with him having a weak stomach.

Horasha slowly stood with a limp, favoring his sore thigh, and put his knife away. Straightening up his torso with a few more deep breaths of recovery, Benaiah stepped up face to face to him, pausing as their eyes locked and then said, "Do you understand what I said as well and where the direction...God is obviously leading Journey's End, not us?" He pointed to Mariah next to him.

Looking down and thinking what else to say, Benaiah remembered hearing God's words when he was in the bottom of the ark. *You believe because you have seen. But I say, blessed are those who believe and have not seen.*

He peered back up, stating to Horasha, "When I understood I was actually in Noah's Ark and then saw all those things in it, they influenced me to give my life fully to God. Then he told me, 'You believe because you have seen. But I say, blessed are those who believe and have not seen.'" Pausing again as they eyed each other, he then added, "Believe before you see what we are telling you so that you may be blessed in a special God way."

Benaiah lifted his hand, touching the center of Horasha's chest, meaning to touch his heart and then took a step back and stated firmly, making sure his tone was received as fact, "Because when we show you Journey's Beginning, your spirit and your perspective, and probably your purpose of life, will completely change, growing you beyond your imagination once you fully understand and experience what I did."

A hesitation came out of Horasha, glancing to Mariah and seeing she was not budging and sensing she was standing firm fully behind this outrageous theory of a Journey's Beginning. Moving his eyes to the senior rabbi, the rabbi gave him a slight tilt of his head as he raised his shoulders to nonverbally say, *What do we have to lose.*

Always short for words, he finally replied as the others did. "I do, Master."

"Good," Benaiah said, a little excited that it was appearing to be working out, then he turned his back to Horasha in faith and said, looking directly to Mariah, "I understand how you feel about sharing Journey's End with Israel and how difficult it was for you to carry out God's instruction to expose King Solomon's secrets. Believe me! But how it was done... What were you thinking? Having the Israel military secretly send a missile in to blow a hole at the bottom of the mountain?" Lifting his hands in the air, he added, "Wonder if you have damaged the ark and its contents?" Lowering his hands and changing his tone said, "I've been holding back from you that God told me in the ark that we were to take it to the Congo River and sail it to Israel with all the descendants and only the priceless items within it."

Horasha took a limping step to Benaiah's side to be involved in this mounting absurd conversation and put his hand on Benaiah's shoulder for temporary support. With his movement, Mariah swiftly and smoothly stepped in his face, drawing her own knife and holding the blade to his throat and sternly said between her teeth, "You ever try to kill him again..." She barely pressed the razor-sharp blade to his skin, which drew a drip of blood. "I will not ask for permission to kill you, I will just do it!" She paused, looking for any truth in his eyes per the rabbi's statement and then added, "Even if the rabbi is telling the truth that you are my father."

"Are you two seriously going to continue this?" Benaiah was taken aback. She quickly forgot what he just told them.

She adorned a smile while piercing Horasha's eyes with hers to convey two different messages. One for Horasha, mentally telling him she was serious and would take pleasure killing him. The other was for Benaiah, telling him she was wholeheartedly with him, answered out loud, "Only to protect you from now on, my love. Journey's Beginning and End, as far as I understand it, are in God's hands, not yours."

At that moment, the wrist screens of Horasha, Mariah, and the rabbi sounded off as a hologram of a person illuminated up from their screens about five inches. Benaiah had never seen this function before and stared in awe as the person said equally on their screens, "Descendants, systems are back online and have regained control over a virus that manipulated our security systems. All available non-security personnel, concentrate efforts on assisting with the wounded and lost."

Control disengaged communication with everyone else, deleting the holographic image. Then reaching out verbally, they called on Horasha and Mariah's armlets only with their ID codes. "H112167R and M0810930, what is your status and location?"

Mariah answered, "Control, this is M0810930, H112167R and…" She looked to the senior rabbi needing his ID as he stated aloud to be heard through her screen.

"J032949N."

Control paused and then stated, "You have confirmed the IDs we are sensing from your wrist comms. But we are seeing four of you at the tombs of the dead."

"Correct, Control. We have—"

Horasha cut her short, grabbing her arm and covering the wrist device, and then he barely whispered, "Confirm they are who they say they are." Then nodding towards Benaiah added, "Keep him out of sight and protected."

It was an awkward moment for all of them, even Horasha himself. He wasn't sure if it was a knee-jerk reaction from always protecting Benaiah for all those years or if it was for the guardian position he was in. Even Benaiah gave him a crazed look since, moments ago, he attempted to kill him.

Mariah took his advice. "Control, four visitors were brought to Journey's End yesterday. Where are they?"

It was silent for a moment before they responded, "M0810930, your number of visitors and day are invalid. Who is Master Jahar's mother?"

Both parties knew they were being tested as Mariah answered, "Master Jahar's mother is Jerusha. She passed away when I was two."

Control replied, "Correction, she passed when you were five."

"Identity confirmed," Mariah answered.

"Agreed. Identity confirmed."

Mariah answered their original question. "Our fourth person will not be named but the signature of our king, he stands on."

The three men listening to this code-breaking conversation all grinned with surprise at her quick-wittedness.

Control replied, "His identity confirmed. Is security or medical emergency in need?"

"Negative, Control. What is the status of Journey's End?"

"The explosion from the missile left a large crater where the lake was at the base of the waterfall. Behind the waterfall, a large portion of the mountain collapsed, avalanching boulders partially filling in the new crater."

Benaiah and Mariah both made noises of surprise as they stared at each other wide eyed.

"The vibration from the explosion also has done something with the stream flowing through the commons area. It is not flowing in there anymore, which means the waterfall does not exist. We have yet to find where the natural spring was rerouted inside the mountain."

Horasha chimed in, "What is the status of the assailants?"

"We are not sensing anything of significance within the inner perimeter. But our outer perimeter satellites and contacts on the thousand kilometer barrier show potential movement coming in from three different locations with possible military personnel and air support. Nothing we cannot easily neutralize."

Benaiah took his turn. "Control, this is B031393S, what is the status with the injured?" Just then, he instantly remember his parents and burst out, "Do you have any news of my mom and dad?"

"Negative, the virus we eradicated in our system was engaged timely just after their IGT passed through the shield at the upper platform. None of our systems are able to locate them, but we are now bringing the inner perimeter satellite back on line as we speak." Changing his tone, the controller lowered his voice and said, "We have another situation, B030393S. Master, are we able to speak privately?"

Benaiah looked at Mariah's armlet, surprised at the request and thought for a second as he peered at the three, with them just as surprised as he was. Concluding there possibly couldn't be anything he would need to keep from the ones he was with, he stated, "Control, openly discuss with all four of us what this situation is."

"Yes, Master. The timely engagement for this unique virus was implanted within our inner perimeter. It had to be a descendant, but we cannot precisely identify who it was."

The three men slowly moved their gaze to Mariah as he replied, "Thank you, Control. I'm confident with the ones I'm with can be trusted. Please contact us as soon as you have information about my parents."

"Yes, Master."

The three, still looking at Mariah, didn't say anything as she somewhat looked away, slightly embarrassed.

Benaiah looked to Horasha and then back to Mariah, saying smartly, "Satellites? Did you forget to mention something?"

Getting back with them much sooner than expected, they heard, "B031393S, we located the IGT they were on." The controller paused and then added, "It is near the explosion site and completely non-functional. The majority of it...is crushed with large debris."

Benaiah turned white as his legs got weak. Going to his knees, he cried out, "No... I killed my parents!"

Everyone was silent as Benaiah began to break down, putting his head in his hands.

Mariah froze as his words echoed in her head. Then she changed the blame, thinking to herself, *No... I killed his parents.*

For the first time in a long time, she wanted to be sick, mumbling out, "What did I do, what did I do?"

The rabbi knelt down, wrapping an arm around Benaiah appropriately and consoling him. "Son, let us first seek the truth before we dive into despair. They might have left the IGT and the area before the incident."

As Mariah overheard the rabbi, hope leaped into her heart, especially since Benaiah gave the direct but strange orders to Uba and Jashen the guard. She bent down on the other side of Benaiah, wrapping an arm around him as well, leaned her head on him and whispered, "It is my fault if something happened to them. I gave the IDF the location to send the missile thinking the lake was the safest spot to have a nonharmful explosion."

Horasha stood watching the three as his mind went to Benaiah's step-parents, seeing them over and over from the past twenty-seven years. He thought, *They were good people, even if they were not Israelites. They obeyed Jahar's instructions to the very end.*

"M0810930 and H112167R, this is Control" was heard from Mariah and Horasha's armlets as their wrists vibrated.

Horasha answered for them, letting Mariah continue to console Benaiah. "Go ahead, Control."

"We have onsite intel at the IGT as security has arrived and analyzed the situation."

The three on the floor overheard and reacted by looking up.

Horasha stepped away as he pointed for all of them to stay so he could confidentially hear the news. Once away, he responded, "Go ahead, Control."

Control gave him the information but continued the conversation longer than the three thought it should have lasted. Horasha replied several times with questions and then finished the conversation by tapping the screen of his communication device to hang up. He kept his back turned as he crossed his arms for a few seconds thinking and then slowly turned with a surprised expression.

The rabbi stood, as did Mariah, with her speaking up, "What is it, Horasha?"

He raised his eyebrows, fighting hard to hold back the information as he attempted to figure out his own interpretation of the news from Control.

Benaiah slowly stood, stepping up to him. Clearing up his distraught emotions, he reluctantly asked, "Go ahead, Horasha. Give it to me. What did they find?"

"Not what you think and definitely not what I believed."

Benaiah looked to Mariah with a questioning expression and then back to his lifelong bodyguard, raising his hands out non-verbally as though asking, *So what did they say?*

Completely out of character, Horasha lightheartedly said, "There is no one at the crash site. They are nowhere to be found."

A huge sigh of relief came out of Mariah and the rabbi as they both reached out, joyfully hugging Benaiah's shoulders. He dropped his head, closing his eyes and whispering several times over, "Thank you."

"What is the other thing you did not believe they would find?" The rabbi asked.

Horasha began shaking his head in bewilderment. He wasn't sure if he wanted to believe what he was told or was excited of the news. Then finally he said, peering to the three patiently waiting for him, "Control said we needed to get over to the blast sight. The guards have found something."

There was silence, and then Mariah asked, "What is it?"

Pausing, he then replied, "I guess I need to ask you that question, because it sounds like you two have the answer. The explosion caused a portion of the base of the mountain to collapse behind the waterfall, exposing what appears to the guards onsite an entrance of what was a giant exterior cave at one time. And from the edge of the exposed outer arched ceiling, it is possibly bigger than the commons area high above it."

He stopped talking even though it was very apparent he had more to say. The rabbi, sensing the obvious from him, pressed him, "Horasha, there is more to the story. What is it?"

Slightly putting his hands in the air and shrugging his shoulders, he finished with what was told to him. "There is a small pitch black hole at the top of the rubble of boulders that had cascaded down like an avalanche. With curiosity, a guard peered into this opening, illuminating what was inside."

Mariah and Benaiah both put smiles on their faces as she was getting giddy, grasping his arm tightly.

Horasha was having a hard time controlling unusual emotions himself upon seeing the looks on their faces and continued, "The guard stated to Control that there is an extremely large structure hidden behind the enormous wall of boulders and"—he shook his head again in disbelief—"it appears to be made of wood."

The rabbi stepped to Horasha, putting a hand on his shoulder and said, "Are you toying with us?"

Horasha looked to Benaiah with a grin as Benaiah knew his reply and answered for him, "Horasha doesn't play games. He's telling the truth."

***

One of the largest unexpected gatherings of descendants from all over the world, and of course the pygmies and local Africans, were at ground zero where the small lake use to be. Water no longer poured out from high up on the mountain that had smoothly flowed through the commons area. The crashing water use to be heard from far distances as when Benaiah first heard it when he arrived at Journey's End with Jahar, who told him, "This whole place is awe-inspiring—where the power of God is seen through his fingerprints."

It used to be a beautiful scene of cascading water splashing into a refreshing clear blue lake with lush green vegetation hugging it tight like a jewel as the abundance of wildlife—birds, monkeys, etc.—called out to one another as though they were the background instruments of the beautiful roaring symphony.

Now, the grand exterior center piece of Journey's End looked like a large scab amongst the green broad-leafed forest as the only sounds heard at the moment were the resounding voices of humans. The missile explosion had formed an unexpected amphitheater-like atmosphere with a somewhat round flattened floor. Large grayish brown boulders had collapsed, avalanching down perfectly, stair-stepping themselves upward to the small dark opening into a mysterious new world behind it.

Over a week had passed since the major earth-shaking experience. Mariah explained to the leadership at hand that the decoy drones and missile attack to the Israelites was conceived as a highly secret training exercise teaching dense forest tactics and procedures, as the IDF still had no idea of Journey's End's existence. As Israeli-owned satellites saw implanted images of the explosion site by Control sending pictures of the natural forest and the remanences of the explosion but leaving out humans and the flying saucers.

Confirmation of her imaginary invasion story was recognized and cleared by Control as the outpost sentinels and satellites invisibly penetrated IDF's communication system and training plans, though the IDF was bewildered to what happened to their drone fleet that had vanished into thin air with no trace they ever existed.

The computer virus manipulation was completely of her creation and implementation. It was instantly added to their tools of offensive weapons as Mariah was congratulated for her clever abilities.

Repairs to the facilities power lines, plumbing, etc. throughout the mountain had swiftly been taken care of, impressing Benaiah of the continuous efficiency of his people. Same with the attention to the structural damages in the large caverns and tunnels being repaired and reinforced as well. Pretty much everything was back to normal except for the underground stream that flowed through the commons area.

The intense vibration of the mountain reopened its very old channel that was closed up thousands of years ago by the descendants to redirect the water through the commons area to create the Garden of Eden effect, ultimately camouflaging the secret of secrets behind it. The stream was reunited with its original passage, draining out into the forest in a different location. Uniquely, this underground tunnel is the last half of the emergency exit tunnel that leads out of the living quarters cavern that Mariah had escaped through.

The mysterious dark opening at the top of the avalanche was put on heavy guard and was restricted to everyone by the new guardian. His parents were still nowhere to be found, but to his comforting surprise, minuscule hints of their healthy welfare were left in places for him to find that he alone, out of sight of Horasha, would be able to recognize was of his mom and dad.

Two major conversations happened between Mariah, Horasha, Benaiah, the senior rabbi, and Dr. Mitanual. The first one was with Dr. Mitanual and the senior rabbi verbally rewriting Horasha's and Mariah's family story that they never knew existed, explaining that when Horasha urgently left for his new mission around the world twenty seven years ago, his wife did truly pass away while having their child. But his new baby, Mariah, had survived and not died during delivery as they told him.

The doctor explained that Jahar always intended to tell Horasha about his daughter, but the responsibility of preserving and protecting the life of the guardian-to-be was much more important for Journey's End long term. Jahar knew Horasha was and has always been the most qualified person for the job and understood Horasha could not afford any distractions that would take his focus off Benaiah and his step parents.

Mariah, on the other hand, was always told her parents had security positions in Israel as undercover intel officers playing their role as a married couple. They were honestly killed accidently in a cafe during a freak bombing by the Palestinians. Using the same story but in reverse, the descendants were told this undercover couple that were killed in a bombing in Israel had a baby there while on a three-year mission and survived the bombing.

Subsequently, the doctor went to Israel, pretending to bring back this baby with the bodies of the deceased parents, whom all of Journey's End took turns raising along with her bloodline family. Jahar always gave her extra attention loving Mariah as his own, knowing she would grow up living through what had to happen for the best interest of King Solomon's orders.

Through this long and very emotional conversation, it was brought to light why Horasha always had a harsh attitude, especially toward his responsibility, Benaiah. He subconsciously always blamed Benaiah for taking him away from his family when they needed him and who he never got to say goodbye to.

It also exposed why Mariah had such a passion for Israel her whole life. Believing her parents died there, mentally, she felt closer to them than in isolation under a mountain far south in Africa.

The two struggled with Jahar and the others lying to them because of the depth in living out this lie for years. But they understood, through the lens of following the orders of their king, that protecting Journey's End at all costs made it somewhat bearable as they were also used to and numb to the continuous deceptions that had plagued their home for hundreds of years.

The second more difficult conversation after the private tour down into Journey's Beginning was what was going to happen with it next. Benaiah fully explained in detail what God told him right after his heart transformation and for the next few days. But he stated he wasn't disappointed to oblige carrying out this new mission and that he was extremely excited because it made complete sense of his life, why he was in the field he was, and why Jahar was wise to have him raised where he was with looser boundaries outside of Journey's End to experience the world in order to have a much clearer understanding of God's fingerprints and how they will influence our lives.

Adding fuel to the flame of convincing the others of everything going on and what was to happen was God breathed. Benaiah again used Jahar's original scripture in Isaiah to explain that we may never know how life is going to work out until it has happened, for man only has accurate twenty-twenty hindsight. God is the only one that has precise twenty-twenty foresight.

Explaining, God demonstrated this by working through Mariah, pressing her no matter how uncomfortable it was, even when she could not comprehend why she was to do what she did, and then he told the group that she was the most faithful of them all as the Holy Spirit asked her to walk on water of faith. Everyone concluded that the Son of God knew what he was doing.

There was fresh enthusiasm within the grand crowd of people that had gathered at this birth site of something new. The partially shaped colosseum perfectly rebounded everyone's voices significantly magnifying them, creating its own natural speaker system. The roar of hundreds of conversations going on was becoming so loud it was difficult to hear the person standing next to one other.

The revelation of something possibly astronomically large and mysteriously hidden behind the waterfall in a very creative manner was shocking. Everyone was aware; they were completely oblivious that something like this ever existed right under their noses, especially the elderly with more years of wisdom and experience, being born and bred to be masters of camouflage themselves for thousands of years. They could not comprehend how such a grand event could have happened, never hearing one rumor or a possible story verbally or written down in the book of time leading to something of this magnitude. Though they did understand that for such a strict undisclosed secret to be kept, possibly thousands had to have been put to death for complete silence and cover up over time as they had no clue this was the first of all the thousands of things hidden deeply in the Congo from the world.

No one had yet been told or allowed to see what the explosion had exposed except for Horasha, the senior rabbi, and Dr. Mitanual as Mariah and Benaiah gave them a very private tour. They entered from the hidden entrance in Jahar's old quarters, very grateful it hadn't been damaged. The lone secret staircase going way down began the mind-blowing experience for the three men seeing Noah's Ark for the first time.

Benaiah didn't want anyone else knowing they knew what was hidden until he was able to present it in a fashion to create a huge build up for a celebration, with every ear equally hearing the news of what was inside. As he simultaneously and boldly delivered the new direction that God had given him for Journey's Beginning and the descendants.

This would also help explain how one of their own, their beloved Mariah, could have done such an outrageous thing to her people and their home, purposely disobeying King Solomon's orders in reaching out beyond her understanding by faith to obediently following the direction of the King of the universe.

Flying in on a medium-sized IGT from near the top of the mountain, Horasha, Mariah, Dr. Mitanual, the senior rabbi, a guard carrying two large duffle bags, and Benaiah arrived at the top of the rockslide. They stepped off the hovering IGT onto a wide, flat, and somewhat stable bolder with the human-sized black hole behind them. The guards surrounding the protected entrance backed away, allowing their new guardian room. To everyone's surprise, he was dressed drastically different than he had been since Jahar's death. He was actually wearing his rugged outdoor archeology dig site attire that he brought and also wearing his work boots.

The massive amount of people waiting suddenly stopped talking as they stood and peered up at their new master with great expectation. At first, it was an odd sensation as the roaring crowd went deafeningly silent. It took a moment to clear everyone's ears, and then little by little, the natural sounds of the Congo forest started coming back to life, giving everyone a soothing peace that everything was going to be okay.

The guard driving the IGT moved it to the side to be out of the way for everyone to get a direct view of the passengers it left behind but not too far just in case the six he just dropped off needed a quick and secure getaway. Benaiah looked out to the several thousands of people staring up at them. Hesitating to speak, the rabbi slowly stepped up behind him, putting a hand on his shoulder. Leaning up to his ear, he whispered, "Benaiah, as you have heard us tell you, we are fully behind what God has pressed on your heart. I believe the descendants and Africans alike of present time are subconsciously ready and have been in the waiting for the Lord of heaven's armies to release them of this duty of old. They see you as their master. They will follow you."

As the rabbi stepped back, Benaiah looked to Horasha at his left and said, "Horasha, I have never thanked you for watching over me and my parents all these years. Your sacrifice has been great and your honorable commitment greater."

Looking to his right at Mariah while still talking to Horasha, he continued, "And thank you for having such an incredible and beautiful daughter that you never knew you had until now."

He turned and smiled at Mariah. Now talking to her, he said, "I have tried to wake up from this dream ever since I first saw you on the elephant. But now, I pray I never wake up."

She smiled back, replying, "I have been patiently waiting for my life to begin. Jahar always told me to never give up and that when I least expect it, God will show up in only the way he does—with extraordinary peace fulling my hearts desires I never knew I had."

"Uhm..." Horasha grunted, getting their attention as he angrily narrowed his eyebrows. Pausing for a moment, he then slowly put on a smile, letting them know he was pretending and said, "That is enough, you two lovebirds. We have an impossible task at hand. Let us see how the Lord of heaven's armies makes this possible as he did for me, bringing my baby girl back from the dead."

Mariah gave him a faint girly smile but held back so as not to send too much of a loving daughter message quite yet.

Benaiah let the moment sink in and then stepped out with Mariah at his side and lifted his arms. The crowd quickly bowed as they went to their knees and then stood. He then loudly said in English, "Descendants…family Africans. Today…is the day that has been in the waiting…for 3,000 years…!" Mariah interpreted for him in Hebrew.

Benaiah gave his speech in a gentle manner but with authority, mirroring the last guardian the people loved so much. He informed them of the massive fingerprint of God, Noah's Ark, behind them, telling the incredible unknown story and secret heroic events of Shuriah the first guardian. Everyone was wide eyed and at the edge of their seat at this unbelievable moment. You could hardly hear a human sound except for the two speaking at the top of the rocky amphitheater until he began divulging the information of the God-breathed items that changed his life in the bottom of the ark. With this information, heads began turning to the side as murmuring between the people started a slow eruption of conversations. It got so loud at one point that Horasha stepped forward, shouting out in Hebrew, "Silence!" Then he grabbed Benaiah's hand with the ring and lifted it up for all to see.

Instantly, the bewildered conversations and excited building energy ceased as everyone again went to their knees in complete submission to the authority of King Solomon.

Benaiah continued after they stood back up, moving the topic to Noah's history book, written out on the ship walls, and the first ten generations living on earth before God destroyed everything. Then he brought up his favorite things, holding the best for last in his mind—dinosaurs, dragons, and the Nephilim—and trying his best not to get giddy and appear childlike as he informed them of what he has seen inside and what information Noah left behind over 4,000 years ago about these exciting things.

Once he covered enough information without getting too detailed, he switched the subject but not without glancing at the others around him as they encouragingly nodded approval to continue.

He took a moment to think his thoughts through and then readdressed everyone. "Family of the Lord of heaven's armies. What has been entombed here for 3,000 years...must come out, for it and all the descendants have a new mission of epic proportions only mighty warriors can do!" He shouted out to build new excitement.

After Mariah translated, a roar echoed up and throughout the forest as the descendants and Africans released the hemorrhaging excitement.

Allowing their enthusiasm to play out its course, he then held up his ring. Still to his amazement of their respect and honor, within seconds, a pebble could be heard dropping off one of the large boulders as they went silent, kneeling, and then he dropped his hand.

When they stood, he continued, "First, I must address a heavy concern to redirect the descendants as a family. What I have to say will not make sense as it will falsely appear to go against the law of the king whom you follow." He paused as heads again turned to one another, but no one dared to say a word.

"I am going to raise my hand back up into the air, and when I do... You...will...not...kneel."

It was like a sonic boom exploded out of his mouth as the shock wave hit the thousands staring at him after Mariah translated. He turned to the five up around him as they again nodded with approval but not without hesitation, knowing this could be a moment that could destroy the unity of Journey's End, causing a civil war.

Slowly raising his hand so as not to surprise them, the crowd successfully fought within themselves not to kneel. Then he stated as the crowd intensely listened, "I...Benaiah, was born in the bloodline of Jahar, a direct descendant of Shuriah, who was a warrior student under Uriah, one of King David's mighty thirty-seven warriors. Shuriah later becoming the personal bodyguard of King Solomon and general of the Israelite army."

Pausing as he looked out, attempting to make eye contact with every person, he slowly said, "I...will...not...be the next guardian.

Jahar…will go down in history as the last guardian of Journey's End. For the end…of its journey has arrived!"

Everyone looked to one another with concerning questions, trying to understand if they heard Mariah clearly after she translated.

He continued, "I will not be addressed…as master anymore." He swayed both hands out to the sides.

Whispers were heard rising up all over the place as the crowd seemed to be getting uneasy.

Raising his voice, he asked a general question in a way not meant to be answered by them. "Who is this Lord of heaven's armies we mention all the time?"

After Mariah interpreted, he quickly answered so they didn't have time to think, "Jesus Christ the Son of God! He is the only Master…of our lives and of this world! There is…no other!"

He watched on as heads turned, whispering in ears throughout the base of the mountain. Then he continued, "I bow to him, and him alone! I will *not*…" He raised his voice at the last word, "…bow to a lowly human, even to a wise dead king who was only flesh and blood and died returning to the earth as dust in which God created him from.

"Bow only…to the supernatural that created man, the Creator of the universe! The Lord of heaven's armies!" he yelled out as he shot both his hands high in the air, expecting a sudden roar of support.

But it was stone cold quiet. No one knew what to do; they were frozen. These words were so foreign—almost blasphemous. But on the other hand, they knew it in their hearts to be completely true.

After Mariah translated, the six stared back down at the thousands that were in a state of confusion. They could see in their eyes that their hearts wanted to agree, but the deeply inbred nature in their minds passed down for over a hundred generations was fighting hard to keep control.

The moment felt like hours waiting for the descendants to respond as it wasn't feeling too good. Then a surprise shout in English was heard at the back of the huge crowd where the end of the old lake and forest came together. Hovering about twenty-five feet off the ground on an IGT, Benaiah's parents, Uba and Jashen the guard had slithered their way in without detection. They had been listening, hearing this news of what was behind the dark hole.

It was Benaiah's father that got everyone's attention, understanding the moment decided to come to the aid of his son, boldly yelled out with Jashen translating, "Benaiah is telling the truth!" It was very unexpected in the moment of another voice to sound off, especially from behind them as everyone surprisingly looked back. "I am his father and this is his mother." He stepped to the side pointing to her then continued, "Jahar told us twenty seven years ago, our new son we adopted was very special and would have a great impact for the Kingdom of God.

"Benaiah has been searching for the truth his whole life. God allowed him as he does everyone to experience false teachings and manmade gods. So later in life, which is now, Benaiah would know the difference between what is right and what is wrong. And he…" Benaiah's father sharply pointed up to his son, "…he has chosen wisely what is right! The Lord of heaven's armies; heart and soul, not flesh and blood. Join him and see what magnificent blessings God has had in the waiting for each and every one of you!"

Uba spoke out in her African language as Jashen translated for her. "Jahar knew the world was changing around us. Something different was on the way even though he did not know what it was.

"But by faith in the living God, whom he prayed and listened closely to, he obediently trusted him, knowing Benaiah was the key for what was to happen next with Journey's End. He spoke of this in private many times in our elder hut with our chief, his closest and most trusted friend.

"There is nothing to be afraid of! For there is nothing to lose but all to gain when we trust in the Lord of heaven's armies and in him alone! For he is the King that is not dead!"

Seeing his parents and hearing the surprise valuable support, Benaiah sensed it was the moment to spill the whole story God gave him. Taking the invisible microphone back, he stated as everyone turned their heads back up to him, "Descendants and African families, we have a new mission. A mission that has been in play by God through King Solomon and is the true reason Journey's End ever existed. God, again, is giving the world another chance to see his fingerprints clearly to greatly encourage all of mankind to come to him once and for all before it's too late!"

Chapter 23

T he rabbi stepped up to Benaiah's side opposite Mariah. Believing his influence would help, he stated, "For too long, we have endured what has become a never-ending task. Never ending, until our Lord returns riding in the clouds on a white horse with his cape flowing behind him drenched in blood. Relieving us from this…" He searched for the right words and then blurted out, "This lifeless burden that is only an illusion to the rest of the world. We inhale but we do not actually breathe life's breath. We chew but we do not swallow and digest life's food. It all has become a hollow repetitive life without complete mental and spiritual satisfaction. We all have known this for more generations than we can remember.

"God has called upon Benaiah to help us breathe and eat so we may finally live again after 3,000 years for Holy fulfilment, which is the climax reason for living! So we"—he pounded his chest, getting very excited—"the descendants of King David's mighty warriors, can come along the side of heaven's armies to fight the darkness of this world, slaying the evil works of Satan and his demons, bringing God's Light to the world in a new and fresh way, taking Noah's Ark to the world. So the kingdom of God may grow and for him to be honored and glorified by all his creations!"

He looked to Benaiah and then held out his hand. Knowing what the rabbi wanted, he reached into his shirt pocket and handed over the stone that killed Goliath. The rabbi looked back to Horasha, nodding to step to the side of Mariah. Horasha understood his part in this display and did so as he reached over his shoulder to something sticking up behind his head, hidden from all to see. Slowly, he drew out the long, heavy, brilliant sword of Goliath.

For the final touch of their presentation, the doctor stepped to the side of the rabbi. Raising his arm and looking down at his armlet, Dr. Mitanual began touching the screen. With a final tap, he extended his arm out, pointing the armlet into the sky over the descendants.

In a remarkable manner, a larger-than-life, full color, 3D hologram of Jahar appeared above them. Everyone watching on gasped out from the shock of who they were seeing. Jahar smiled, looking around as though he was actually there in flesh and blood and then gently began speaking in Hebrew. "My family… If you are seeing this prerecorded hologram of me, it means I have gone to be with our Lord of heaven's armies. I have entrusted this conversation to my friends, Dr. Mitanual and the chief of the dedicated ones of 3,000 years, the Invisibles.

"I have a clear and wise understanding the world is changing faster than ever. And in such a global dark manner, the return of Jesus Christ is near and the destruction of mankind is inevitable.

"I cannot foresee what exactly God has in store for my great nephew Benaiah, but I know it will be something that no guardian has ever done before. This I can see."

Jahar paused, turning around as though truly looking at everyone and then added, "We have served and served well! I applaud each and every one of you. Now, I am asking you to continue to serve without fear, no matter how big or different the giants are when the Lord of heaven's armies call you to war!

"Remember the boy David and what he said to the giant confronting Israel. 'You come to me with sword, spear, and javelin, but I come to you in the name of the Lord of heaven's armies—the God of the armies of Israel, whom you have defied.'

"Descendants, there is no giant too big for our Lord to work through or defeat that cannot be conquered. Trust in whom God has placed before Journey's End for its next battle. For the battle has already been won when Christ Jesus died on the cross for all his children.

"May the Lord of heaven's armies be with you and bless you all."

The hologram projection lasted a few more seconds, with Jahar smiling at everyone, and then automatically shut off.

Everyone, even the group standing in front of the dark hole, rapidly blinked, taking in deep breaths as though waking up from a trance, watching and listening to their deceased guardian, digesting what he said.

To their surprise, as Jahar was giving his last speech, hundreds of military IGTs had stealthily flown in from around Journey's End and other parts of the Congo surrounding the mass gathering. They hovered above the hundreds of ground security personnel carrying their weapons who had slithered through the forest to join their airborne comrades at arms. They all exposed themselves from their camouflage by dropping their face coverings as the cloaking shields on the IGTs were disengaged.

The crowded thousands hesitated in a scared state, not understanding their intentions and began to believe that what was being told to them was destructive, blasphemous, and punishable even by death. They all started to squirm around, speaking to one another, and then Benaiah boasted out, "People of Journey's End, Jahar has spoken the truth!"

He pointed to Horasha as Horasha powerfully stabbed the grand sword into the sky.

Then Benaiah elbowed the rabbi as he raised his hand with something small and round pinched between his finger and thumb.

Benaiah looked out to everyone confidently and said, pointing to the raised sword, "You know Jahar valued this prize the boy David earned that was made by man's hands. But what you don't know is that Jahar kept this a secret from everyone." He pointed up to what was in the rabbi's hand, proudly stating, "A stone—a simple rock from a stream that was created by God's hands that killed Goliath.

"But it wasn't the stone that truly killed the giant. It was the fearless obedience of a simple young shepherd confidently believing God will show up to fight his battles for him. All he had to do was faithfully move forward in the name of the Lord of heaven's armies!"

Benaiah stepped forward to the edge of the big boulder, away from the others raising his arms, again asking, "Are you with me to fight the real giants of destruction moving forward with the Lord of heaven's armies…Jesus Christ!"

His last statement echoed out, fading into the forest as every eye and ear anxiously waited, almost waiting in a cowardly manner for someone else to respond as the eyes started to turn around, watching the reactions of the intimidating security force that had arrived moments earlier. Through the silent seconds, a short commanding signal was heard over the guards' armlets in Hebrew.

One by one, the ground guards began to put their weapons in rest position against their chest as the IGT guards pushed buttons powering down their weapons. When they were all back up at attention, a lone shout from the head commanding guard was heard.

No more than two seconds passed and all the guards who fearlessly surrounded their own people and the African tribes unanimously roared out shouts of approval, piercing deep down into every soul that could hear as they raised their arms-bearing fists.

The roar stunned the massive crowd at first. Then, as though God perfectly planned the moment for a change and cleansing, it began to rain on them at the base of the mountain. The cool soothing drops of water felt extremely refreshing as they were gathered closely on the rock piles in the hot and humid forest.

The roaring guards continued as the thousands they encircled joined in on the celebration for a change of a new day and a new battle for Journey's End.

The six at the top of the rocky avalanche looked on in awe, listening to the extraordinary emotional moment. The IGT at the back of the crowd with Benaiah's parents, Uba and Jashen the guard, made its way over the mass of people through the rain. When it got to the black hole at top, they unloaded as Benaiah's parents grasped their son, proud of this accomplishment at hand.

Uba and Jashen had spent the week in hiding, revealing the whole story of Journey's End and it inhabitants to the parents. Then Uba, understanding there was obviously something going on with the secrets of secrets, informed Journey's Beginning to Jashen and Benaiah's stepmother and father.

After a long hug, Mariah gently grasped Benaiah's hand, getting his attention away for his parents, and said, "I love you, and I am ready to go to war with you."

Facing her, he smiled, reaching up with his other hand, moving some of her wet hair out of her face, and replied, "I love you too. But before we go to war..." He looked behind him at the guard who had been patiently waiting this whole time carrying the two large duffle bags heavy with the translated books rewritten from the old scrolls they found in Jahar's sanctuary. "...we need to go inside the ark and follow the drawing as you and the rabbi read through all of the thick history books from Noah. I can't wait to hear the stories of dragons protecting Adam and Eve and the next nine generations from the plethora of dinosaurs and the larger-than-life Nephilim."

He let go of Mariah's hand, pointing into the dark hole behind everyone, and said, "It's kind of ironic at this moment. We are getting out of the rain into the protection of Noah's Ark." He smiled, looking to his father. "I think we'll be missing the men's retreat this year, don't you?"

About the Author

Born and raised in the Rocky Mountains, adventure has always been part of D.L. Crager's life. Living in this majestic landscape and having strong mentors greatly influenced and motivated him at a young age to always live in great expectation. With determination and hard work and the endless support from his wife, he has owned several successful businesses, served in church leadership, experienced a lifetime of extraordinary things in the wilderness, and has journeyed around the world.

Married for over thirty years, Darran and his wife Shelly have enjoyed the blessings of their children and grandchildren. He credits his success to an amazing patient and loving God who has guided his footsteps on extraordinary paths, leading him to new heights he never imagined.

Readers from all walks of life will thoroughly enjoy and be inspired by Darran's high-impact, adventurous stories filled with mystery, conflicts, challenges, and relationships, leaving the reader thirsting for more.

CPSIA information can be obtained
at www.ICGtesting.com
Printed in the USA
BVHW082239130920
588318BV00002B/2